Tom Holt was born in London in 1961. At Oxford he studied bar billiards, ancient Greek agriculture and the care and feeding of small, temperamental Japanese motorcycle engines; interests which led him, perhaps inevitably, to qualify as a solicitor and emigrate to Somerset, where he specialised in death and taxes for seven years before going straight in 1995. Now a full-time writer, he lives in Chard, Somerset, with his wife, one daughter and the unmistakable scent of blood, wafting in on the breeze from the local meat-packing plant.

Find out more about Tom Holt and other Orbit authors by registering for the free monthly newsletter at www.orbitbooks.co.uk

D0499314

TOM HOLT

Little People

orbit

www.orbitbooks.co.uk

An *Orbit* Book

First published in Great Britain by Orbit 2002
This edition published 2003
Reprinted 2004

Copyright © Tom Holt 2002

The moral right of the author has been asserted.

*All characters and events in this publication are fictitious and any
resemblance to real persons, living or dead, is purely coincidental.*

All rights reserved.
No part of this publication may be reproduced,
stored in a retrieval system, or transmitted, in any form
or by any means, without the prior permission in writing of the
publisher, nor be otherwise circulated in any form of binding
or cover other than that in which it is published and
without a similar condition including this condition,
being imposed on the subsequent purchaser.

A CIP catalogue record for this book
is available from the British Library.

ISBN 1 84149 185 3

Typeset in Plantin by M Rules
Printed in Great Britain by
Clays Ltd, St Ives plc

Orbit
An imprint of
Time Warner Book Group UK
Brettenham House
Lancaster Place
London WC2E 7EN

For Melody, Paul, Beetle, Matthew
and everyone in the village.
Be seeing you.

CHAPTER ONE

I was eight years old when I saw my first elf.

It was a Monday evening in July or August: school holidays, I'd just been watching *Star Trek* on the box, and Mummy let me out in the garden to play. I was being Captain Kirk in the secluded patch between the spuds and the compost heap, and I'd just phasered next door's cat into oblivion through a gap in the fence when I looked round and there, quite suddenly, he was.

If I close my eyes, I can see him yet. He was at least a foot high, maybe thirteen or fourteen inches, with sharply upswept pointed ears, short black hair and a slight but noticeable greenish tinge to his skin. As I recall, he was leaning against a nascent iceberg lettuce (God only knows why my stepfather grew the loathsome things; none of us liked them, him included) and he was rolling a tiny cigarette in a wrapper of withered spinach leaf. Stuck into the dirt directly in front of him were a miniature pickaxe, crowbar and shovel, like something you might expect to find among the accoutrements of a pre-Glasnost Soviet doll's house – Heroine of Agriculture Barbie, or My Little Comrade. He was wearing a cute little yellow top, black tights and big clumpy boots, and when he'd finished rolling his fag, he gave his nose a quick ream-through with a tiny black-edged fingernail before lighting up.

I crouched there, staring, for at least fifteen seconds, which is a very long time indeed to hold perfectly still, especially when you're eight. Quite possibly I could've stuck it out even longer if a wasp hadn't materialised out of thin air a few inches from my nose, triggering an instinctive flinch-hop-skip-swipe procedure. By the time I'd landed and looked round, the elf wasn't there any more, understandably enough; but that was OK. I'd seen him, which was all that really mattered.

'Mummy, Mummy,' I yelled out as I ran back into the house. 'Guess what! There are Vulcans at the bottom of our garden!'

Mummy and Daddy George (my stepfather) were sitting out on the patio, glugging some kind of amber booze from small glasses. It was what they usually did in the evenings.

'What the hell are you talking about?' Mummy said.

'Vulcans,' I replied, too preoccupied to point out that she'd just used a Bad Word. 'I just saw one, down by the compost heap. He was only little, about this big, so there must've been a transporter malfunction, probably a mis-aligned EM coupling in the plasma conduit, and he was wearing a yellow shirt, so he was probably bridge crew, though I didn't see his rank insignia—'

'Hang on,' Daddy George interrupted. 'Where did you say this was?'

'Down the garden,' I replied impatiently – I'd already covered that point in my initial report, why was it that grown-ups never *listened*? 'He had pointy ears and everything, just like Mister Spock. But then a wasp came and when I looked round again he'd gone, so he must've beamed back to his ship . . .'

'Michael,' said Daddy George, in his extra-quiet-meaning-real-trouble voice, 'go to your room.'

Well, you didn't argue with him when he used that voice; not if you had even a faint residual trace of a survival instinct. So I did as I was told: no arguments, no protests, no it's-not-fairs, just a slump of the shoulders and a slow trudge up the little wooden hill to HM Prison Bedfordshire.

(Show me an eight-year-old kid who wants to go to bed at seven o'clock on a summer evening, and I'll show you a clear case of demonic possession, alien abduction or both.)

As I went, I could hear them talking; Daddy George was saying something like, I thought I told you never to let him something I didn't catch; Mummy was coming back at him with the old don't-you-talk-to-my-baby-like-that-you-pig line, but I could tell it was very much a rearguard action and her heart wasn't in it. For my part, I couldn't see what all the fuss was about; but ten minutes or so later I got a Class One Official Warning from Daddy George, all flared nostrils and eyebrows meeting in the middle. A quarter of a century has slipped by since so I can't give you the exact words, but the general idea was that smart cookies don't go around seeing small green-faced people in gardens; and even if they do, they keep very quiet about it for fear of being classified as dangerous loons and taken away to places with high walls and handles on one side of the door only. He added a few choice remarks about wicked children who made up silly stories just to get attention, coupled with a reminder that that part of the garden was (a) out of bounds and (b) infested with poisonous snakes, spiders and scorpions (and if that wasn't making up silly stories, I remember thinking, I'd love to know what was) and left, slamming the door behind him. After he'd gone I climbed into bed and studied the ceiling thoughtfully for a while; there was a little wisp of cobweb in one corner that'd been there ever since I could remember, and focusing on it helped me drift into a state of deep and insightful meditation. Just before I fell asleep, I distinctly remember thinking about something he'd said: small green-faced people in gardens. Small, yes; I'd said small, also pointy-eared and yellow-shirt wearing. Not green-faced, though. I hadn't mentioned that aspect at all.

About Daddy George, my stepfather. From the above you may have got the impression that he was a grumpy, miserable little man who shouted a lot and was no fun. This isn't entirely accurate. He wasn't little. Quite the opposite: at the time I formed the impression that he was at least twelve feet high and about the same across the shoulders, with a shout they could probably hear in New Mexico, wherever New Mexico was. In reality he was no more than six foot five, six six at the very most, and it wasn't the shouting you needed to worry about; it was when he turned quiet and looked at you for two or three seconds without saying anything at all. That was definitely a cue to leave the area, change your name and if possible your species, because Daddy George had a temper you could use to generate electricity.

He'd come on the scene when I was about four, four-and-a-half. My other daddy had slung his hook for some unspecified reason and I wasn't to talk about him any more. About the same time we moved house, from a town or city I can barely remember to a big, way-cool house in the pseudo-country, a few miles on the quieter side of the M25. That was extremely good; likewise the fact that Daddy George ran a big, successful shoe factory, which made lots and lots of money and (better still) occupied most of Daddy George's time. As I got older, it became easier for me to be out of the house when he was in it, an arrangement that seemed to suit all of us pretty well; and just before my fourteenth birthday I was sent away to boarding school. This took a certain amount of arranging, since (as Daddy George made a point of informing me) I was far too thick to get into this school by the conventional route of passing the entrance exam, and Daddy George had to build them a new science block before they'd take me off his hands.

Boarding school wasn't perfect, by any manner of means – looking back, I get the impression that the bunch of misfits who ran it had drawn on ancient Sparta, Rugby in the reign of Victoria and Wormwood Scrubs as their main sources of inspiration in figuring out their operating philosophy – but it did have the overwhelming advantage of not being Home. True, this was a quality it shared with a whole lot of other, warmer places, but nobody was going to let me go to any of them, so at a fairly early stage I resolved to keep my face shut, my head down and my nose clean, and make the best of it. And it wasn't so bad, at that; it was far enough away that the risk of my parents dropping in while they were in the neighbourhood was reassuringly negligible, and I did manage to learn some useful stuff, most of which concerned keeping warm and staying hidden. One piece of advice I brought from home that did stand me in very good stead was Daddy George's warning about the danger of having seen elves. I quickly realised that in the basically carnivorous culture of a boys' school, any kind of aberration or difference from the norm quickly marks you out as being on the wrong side of the predator/prey divide. Admitting that you'd once seen an elf would've been blood in the water for sure, and in consequence I gave the topic of elves, fairies, brownies, pixies, goblins and little people in general a very wide berth whenever it came up in conversation. Nonetheless: the more I didn't talk about what I'd seen that evening and tried to forget all about it, the more it became part of me, something unspoken and therefore fundamental, like the British constitution. So I'd seen an elf when I was a kid. So what? Big deal.

Thus my first elf encounter stayed dark and buried in my heart like a tiny plastic aeroplane at the bottom of a skyscraper-sized cereal packet until the day after my six-teenth birthday, when I happened to be doing something very unusual, very out of character and, as far as I was concerned, very scary indeed. I was talking to a Girl.

We had them at our school, in the sixth form; about two dozen of them, as against two hundred and fifty adolescent males. This was supposed to be a good thing; and all I can say is that whoever dreamed up that idea was either fundamentally misguided or else had origi-nated on the planet of the Plant People, where sex is a typo for a number between five and seven. What it was like for the girls I can't really begin to imagine, though

I've always tended to assume it must've resembled those primitive cultures where the king is treated as a god for 364 days of the year and gets ritually eaten on the 365th. For the boys – Oh, go on. Guess.

Consequently, from the age when I first started to be uncomfortably aware of them, girls to me were exotic, almost mythical creatures; more outlandish than Klingons and Romulans, *way* more outlandish than elves. And yet; on 10 September (day after my birthday; first day of term), there was I, alone with and actually talking to one. Bizarre? Yes.

Her name – well, that was part of it, I guess. Many parents name their children after fictional heroes and heroines, and little tangible harm results. Some parents call their kids after their favourite Disney characters, and still get away with it. It's amazing how resilient young people can be. Once in a while, however, you get a truly appalling act of nomenclature whose repercussions last a lifetime.

'Sorry,' I repeated. 'Your name, I didn't quite catch it.'

'That's because I didn't tell you,' she replied, scowling. She had a face that looked like it was built around a scowl, to the point where two hundred and forty-nine teenage boys had taken one look and headed in another direction. 'Where's the science block?'

'This way,' I replied. 'I'll take you there if you like.'

'Don't bother.'

'It's no bother,' I replied, quick as lightning. 'I was going that way anyhow.'

Which was, of course, as barefaced a lie as you'll ever find in the wild outside the Houses of Parliament; and she knew it, and so did I. But, for some reason, she didn't tell me to push off, with or without extreme prejudice.

Instead, she simply grunted, 'Yeah, all right,' like a shy, freckled warthog, and allowed me to lead the way.

'I'm Mike, by the way,' I said. 'Mike Higgins. So, this is your first day, is it?'

'Mm.'

'It's not so bad,' I went on, 'once you get used to it. Like Stilton cheese,' I added.

'What?'

'Not so bad, once you get used to it.'

'What's cheese got to do with anything?'

'Nearly there. Actually, my dad built it.'

'Built what?'

I tried to sound nonchalant. 'The science block. That's why it's called the Higgins Science Centre, actually.'

'Oh.'

I never met a human being who could invest the word *oh* with such a wide range of eloquent meaning. On this occasion, *oh* clearly meant, 'Even if I believed you, why the hell would I care?', a definition that for some unaccountable reason is missing from most popular dictionaries. In short, I was striking out; and it says quite a lot about the aura of pure unsullied miserableness that she radiated that, at that precise moment, I didn't really mind. If this was a Girl, I said to myself, you can have 'em. Give me plastic model aircraft every time.

'Cru,' she said suddenly.

'Sorry?'

'Cru,' she repeated. 'My name.'

'Ah.'

'Aren't you going to ask me what it's short for?' The way she said the words was equivalent to a slap round the face with a glove from a professional duellist; soon,

it told me, we're going to fight, and you're going to die.
'Well, aren't you?' she added.

'It's short for something, is it?'

'Yes.'

'Oh.'

Well, indeed. I may be stupid, but I'm not thick, and
when someone says, 'Come over here so I can bash you',
just occasionally I have the common sense to stay put.
Besides, once in a while I like to do the unexpected.

'Aren't you going to ask, then?' she said, a tad louder
this time.

'Let me guess,' I replied. 'Crudence?'

'No.'

'Cruese?'

'Cruella,' she said, 'after Cruella de Vil.'

I frowned. Genuine bafflement. 'Who?'

'Cruella de Vil. You know, in *101 Dalmatians*.'

I shrugged. 'Never seen it. Here we are, it's the big
grey building on the left, the one that looks like a giant
shoebox standing on end. Probably deliberate,' I added.
'My dad's in shoes, you see.'

'I couldn't care less if he was in black leather and
frogmen's flippers,' she replied, but it was obvious she
wasn't putting her weight behind it; just a token left-arm
prod, for appearance's sake.

'You've never seen *101 Dalmatians*?'

I shook my head. 'Or *Bambi*,' I said, 'or *Jungle Book* or
any stuff like that. We didn't go to the pictures when I
was a kid.'

'Right.' She stopped, and I stopped too. We were outside the science block, and there was no call for me to go
any further, or for her to stay. 'Well,' she went on, 'here
we are.'

'Yes.'

'You said you were on your way here.'

'I lied. Have a nice day.'

She twitched her nose, like a rabbit. Not many people can do that. I can. 'Be seeing you,' she said.

Suddenly I grinned. '*The Prisoner*?' I asked.

'The what?'

'Doesn't matter.' Didn't, either. It was still love at third sight, even if she hadn't been quoting from my favourite TV show. 'Be seeing you,' I repeated, and I did the little gesture, just in case. She didn't remark on it, and I went back to the main building, where I was now seriously late for double history.

And what, you may very well be asking, the hell had that got to do with elves? Well, I guess it depends on how you like your relevance: immediate, tangential or with lemon. I'm taking the line that it's because of that initial encounter that Cruella Watson and I gradually slid in love – a long-drawn-out process that started with a grudged and wary non-aggression pact and slithered sideways into an unspoken acknowledgement that, when the teams of Life were picked, we'd always be the ones left over at the end, and therefore some kind of alliance was grimly inevitable. She was sullen, razor-tongued and miserable as sin, having a father who lived behind a desk in a solicitors' office and a mother who despised her because her hair didn't go with the curtains. I saw elves. Who in God's name else would want either one of us?

Ah, you're saying, how sweet, and probably you're right. Sweet, though, wasn't a term you'd ever use to describe Cru, except together with the words *she isn't at all* or *not the slightest bit*. She crunched a path through life like a small, steady ice-breaker. As regards the chicken/egg issue, opinions differ; I take the view that she'd have been pretty much the same if she'd been christened Jane or Fiona, while she maintained that her parents' act of thoughtless whimsy had wrecked her entire life and therefore she wasn't to blame and could do what she liked. It was, according to her hypothesis, the defining incident of her life, and there at least I could see where she was coming from. Her Cruella was my elf.

That being the case, it was only a matter of time; indeed, it was as if I was under some kind of obligation in that regard. She'd told me her name. Honour demanded that I tell her about my elf. So, one wet and wretched Friday afternoon between last lesson and compulsory optional swimming, I did.

'You did what?' she said.

'I saw an elf,' I repeated. 'Years ago, when I was just a kid. It was leaning against a lettuce in our garden, smoking.'

She was silent for five, maybe six seconds. From my point of view, very long seconds indeed.

'That's bad,' she said eventually.

Didn't like the sound of that. 'What's bad?' I said. 'I really did see one, you know.'

'I didn't mean that,' she said. 'But I thought everybody knew: smoking can damage your elf.'

Completely deadpan, too, which made it worse. 'I knew I shouldn't have told you,' I grumped. 'It's just—'

'Oh, I believe you all right,' she interrupted. 'Let's see: about so high, with pointed ears, sort of yellowy-greeny skin, a bit knobbly round the knees and elbows.'

She was right. I'd forgotten the knobbliness, or rather it had always been there in my mind's eye but I'd never noticed it. 'That's right,' I said, 'how did you—'

'There was a picture of one,' she said, 'in my *Little Blue Fairy Book*; and even though I was only six, I remember thinking, God, what an ugly little runt, they must be real because nobody would make up something as ugly as that. Did yours have a pointy nose, like someone'd been at it with a pencil-sharpener?'

I nodded. 'Come to think of it,' I said, 'it did. Are you really telling me you believe—?'

She shrugged. 'Depends,' she replied. 'In the Peter Pan sense, probably not. In the sense of not actively not believing just because everybody's always told me not to, quite possibly. Did I ever mention that my mum and dad had the fireplace bricked in when I was seven, just to prove conclusively there was no Father Christmas?'

I frowned. 'Proving nothing,' I replied. 'He could just as easily get in through a window.'

'Not in our house. Not unless he's got an oxyacetylene torch and a jackhammer, not to mention Dobermann-proof trousers.' She smiled bitterly. 'But that's why I never needed to believe or not believe, you see. If there really had been fairies at the bottom of our garden, Dad would just have got a court order and had them slung out.'

'I see,' I replied. 'What you're saying is, there may be elves and there may not, you just aren't particularly interested either way.'

'I suppose so. I mean, it's no harder believing in little men with sharp ears than it is believing in God, or relativity, or film stars; they're all weird, and nothing to do with me. If you feel you want to believe in them, go ahead. If they're ever relevant to anything, be sure and let me know.'

I took a deep breath and let it out slowly. It had all

gone rather better than I'd expected, and now it was out of the way and we'd never have to go there again. A great weight off my mind, let me tell you.

Hah. As if. But there, I'm getting ahead of myself, like a derailing train. At the moment I'm talking about, everything for once seemed to be working out. I'd told her about It, the great big enormous issue in my life that made me screwed-up and defective, and she didn't seem to mind. I was sorely tempted to ask her to marry me, but fortunately I did no such thing; even someone with a name like Cruella can only stand so much weirdness in the course of one day.

After that momentous dialogue, however, things did seem to move a bit more easily, as the WD40 of openness and trust seeped its way into the rusted-up threads of insecurity and self-loathing. To put it another way: I stopped creeping round like I had some unspeakable secret disease, which probably made me slightly more fun to be with. Given that Cruella's choice of people to hang out with was limited to those who were prepared to put up with her moods and snippy fits – all one of me – the burgeoning of our relationship was probably not nearly as remarkable as I thought it was at the time.

Excuse me if I'm getting philosophical; it's a fault of mine, I know. Basically, I've always tended towards the view that life is just a bowl of cherries told by an idiot, as the sparks fly upwards; I accept the hand life has dealt me with passive, sullen resentment and get on with it. Back then, of course, it wasn't all unalloyed hatefulness. People were mostly a pain, but things were pretty cool; whatever else Daddy George may have been, he wasn't tight with his money, and when you're a kid you tend to look no further than the next cool thing, whether it's a skateboard or a Walkman or a better skateboard or a computer or an even better skateboard with carbon-fibre dampeners. As far as things were concerned, it was always pretty much a case of ask and ye shall receive the cash equivalent, plus the bus fare so ye can go and buy it yourself – Mummy and Daddy George believed very firmly in the time-is-money equation, and invariably opted to let me have the money and keep the time for themselves.

Wonderful, as far as your average kid is concerned; except that, when you're that age, at least half the fun of having some really cool thing is being able to wave it under the noses of your friends and bask in their jealousy and resentment. In my case, nobody ever seemed to care. If I had the latest model BMX bike straight from the factory gate or a pair of trainers so overwhelming in their coolness that I lost at least one toe to frostbite every time I put them on, nobody ever seemed to give a damn; I could even leave them lying about and nobody would deign to steal them. Accordingly, round about the time I first cut myself shaving, I stopped caring terribly much about mere artefacts and the kind of stuff I could have if I wanted it. Unfortunately this left a hole in my life about the same height, width and depth as me, and I was pretty well at a loss to know what to plug it with. True, that was about the time Cru came along; but I didn't make the mistake of turning her into my new hobby. Like I said, I may be stupid, but I'm not thick.

Even so . . . thanks largely to Cru and the opportunity she'd afforded me for the first full confession I'd ever made of my elf-seeing tendency, I was gradually working my way back out of the pit I'd managed to tumble into eight years previously. It was as though I'd finally found the courage to go and see a doctor and find out that the symptoms I'd been fretting about for so long were just a slight cold, and not terminal cancer after all. If it didn't matter about elves, I could start again; and gradually, day by day, that inner elf of mine started to fade. He was still there, but I didn't have to go there any more. Instead, I tried to find something to like; and since Cru had made up her mind, on evidence as slender as the finest surgical suture, that she was naturally artistic and destined to create wonderful things out of bits of old junk, I reckoned I might as well be artistic too. This was, of course, a load of what mushrooms grow in, but fairly harmless as misapprehensions go, and if I'd carried it through and made it my life's calling, I'd probably have turned out no worse than the average screw-up. As it was, I never got the chance.

Enter the second elf.

That particular end of term was hard for me. As if going home wasn't bad enough in itself, being parted from Cru for the whole of rotten Christmas and wretched New Year was going to be torture (and if it wasn't, every agonising, angst-crammed second of it, I'd want to know the reason why).

Our parting was such sweet sorrow –

('Well,' I said, as my train pulled in to the platform, 'bye, then. See you next term.'

'Yup,' she replied.)

– but not so sweet or so ostentatiously sorrowful as all that. To look at us, you'd think our relationship was something quite other – pedestrian and lollipop lady, for example, or stockbroker and not particularly affluent client. Then, at the very last moment, for the very first time, she grabbed at where my hand would've been if I hadn't moved it to scratch my nose. I reciprocated by putting my arms around her neck and carrying out a manoeuvre that would probably have ended with her head popping off her shoulders like a champagne cork if she hadn't snapped, 'Stop it, you're pulling my hair,' in a tone of voice you could've shaved with. Personally, even after all these years, I don't think you could get more romantic than that without a general anaesthetic.

'You'd better get on your train,' she said. 'You'll look bloody silly if it goes without you.'

'All right,' I said. 'Bye, then.'

'Bye.'

The train pulled away. I leaned out of the window and waved for as long as I could. She didn't exactly wave back, but she didn't exactly not wave either. I guess you had to have been there.

By the time the train reached my home station it was as dark as a bag and just coming on to rain, which suited my mood so perfectly that I decided I'd walk the mile and a half back to our house rather than take a taxi. After all, I wanted to arrive feeling weary, footsore, bedraggled and desolate, as a way of striking a theme note for the coming holiday. I put down my case, which was suitably heavy and cumbersome, wrapped my hand-kerchief around the handle, and set off at a deliberate slow trudge.

Half a mile into the mile and a half, I was beginning to feel that maybe gestures weren't everything. A fold in my sock had rubbed a patch on my right heel that was as raw as Parma ham, and in spite of the improvised padding the handle of the case was cutting into my hand like a cheese-wire. My trudge wasn't quite so deliberate any more, and it was also quite a bit slower. In addition, I was also going to be late for dinner, which would lead to a certain amount of ritual umbrage-taking and Force Two melodrama. *Sod*, I thought, and tried to pick up the pace a little.

Well, at least there's no better cure for a broken heart than a blistered heel and the prospect of a family row. I hadn't thought about Cru even once since the folded sock started to make its presence felt, and that was surely a good thing, considered objectively. All I was thinking about at that precise moment was how much more of this ill-advised and rotten hike remained, and how very much nicer and more sensible it would have been to get a taxi.

The very, very last thing on my mind right then was elves.

It happened suddenly to say the least. One moment I was slouching along, thinking unhappy thoughts; the next I was nose down in a muddy puddle, feeling a sharp pain in my right knee and the palm of my left hand.

'Aaaaaa,' said a voice.

It was a curious sound – loud, but small, if you know what I mean, like the frantic buzzing of a wet bumble-bee – and it seemed to be coming from my navel. At first I assumed I'd fallen on my Walkman and somehow simultaneously ejected the tape and switched it on, the *Aaaaaa* sound being the resultant white noise. I revised that opinion when something wriggled under me and jabbed me hard in the solar plexus.

Two theories; either I was pregnant and the baby was kicking, or I was lying on something small.

Call me unscientific, but I rejected the first hypothesis out of hand without even reviewing the evidence.

The obvious thing to do was to get up and stop squashing whatever it was into the mud-coated tarmac, but that proved to be easier thought than done. For one thing, the mud I'd landed in was extra slithery plus, now with 20 per cent added slither. For another, my right leg seemed to be out of order.

'AasaaaaaaAAAA!' said the voice, pointedly.

As it so happened, I was pretty well used to that tone of voice, since it was one of Cru's favourites, and I had a fairly shrewd idea of what it meant. 'Hold *on*,' I snapped back. (Silly, of course, to talk to a rabbit or a duck or a baby deer or whatever it was, but that was just instinct, you know?)

'Aaaaaa*offme*!' shrieked the voice; and it was like when you're twiddling with a radio dial and the signal suddenly becomes clear enough to understand. Who/whatever it was, it was talking to me in English. With a slight Welsh accent.

'Eek,' I replied, and rolled over onto my back. From my point of view, this wasn't a good idea, since it meant I was now soaked to the skin and covered in runny mud the consistency of thin Bisto both front and back. But it shut up the little shrieking voice, so it was worth it.

And that was the moment when I thought, *Elves*. Or, to be precise, *Elves, shit, not again*.

'Hello?' I said. 'Who's there?'

'*Arsehole*.' The same voice again, this time with the gain turned up or the tweeter tweeted or whatever you call it when the signal's cleaned up and made easier to understand. '*You fell on me, you bastard.*'

Swift and fleeting as a half-glimpsed Perseid, the thought crossed my mind that this probably wasn't the

same elf that was featured in Cru's *Blue Fairy Book*.
Well, maybe in the director's cut, but not the version
that made it out on general release. 'Hello?' I repeated.

'Hello to you too,' the voice snapped back. It was
much louder now, and perfectly in tune. 'Now fuck off
and die, and leave me alone.'

'Are you all right?' I asked.

'Am I all right?' the voice repeated. 'Oh sure, couldn't
be better. Apart from the broken leg and the broken
arm and the three broken ribs, that is. Oh, and I think
you've trodden on my hat, too.'

I sat up and looked round, trying to figure out where
in all that wet dark the voice was coming from. 'Are you
serious,' I said, 'about the broken bones and stuff?
Where are you?'

'Serious?' jeered the voice. 'Me? Nah. That's not our
way, being serious. Smashed bones? Ho, ho, ho. Of
course I'm serious, you tall git.'

Something in the way he said it suggested that *tall*
was the worst possible epithet in his vocabulary. 'If
you're hurt, we've got to get you to hospital, quick –
Why are you laughing?'

More than that, though of course I didn't mention it;
every time he laughed, I could distinctly hear air
whistling, like a plastic bag with a tiny hole in it. Not just
broken ribs but a punctured lung as well. 'Where *are*
you?' I yelled.

'Where you can't find me, traitor.' The sudden bitter-
ness in the voice made me shrink back as if I'd just been
slapped across the face. 'So this is as far as I get, after all
that work; it's still out. Death is freedom too, tall bastard.'

'What the hell are you going on about?' I shouted.

'And will you bloody well stop playing about and tell me where you are? Please?'

More laughter, getting steadily more ragged and frightening. 'You'd love that, wouldn't you? Wanted, dead or alive – isn't that what you people say?' I'd found a bit of old stick and I was poking about at random, trying to locate the owner of the voice by touch. Well, you do some pretty dumb things when you're all rattled to hell. 'You won't find me, tall person. Oh, don't worry, I know who you are, I know you're able to see me; but I'm outside the limits, remember, I'm actually me again, even if it's only for as long as it takes to—'

Funny, I thought, *why's he stopped talking in mid-sentence like that?* Then I felt something soft and sort of padded under the point of my stick, and looked down. Odd that I hadn't seen it before, when I'd been looking at that exact spot just a second ago, or so I'd thought.

An elf. A palpable elf. Dead, but palpable.

Now that was a moment of great weirdness, let me tell you. I'd never seen a dead person before, but I'd seen plenty of roadkill, muddy corpses of foxes and rabbits and badgers. But what it – he – reminded me of most strongly was a doll or a teddy bear, pitched out in the mud and trodden on; more upsetting, in a way, than any dead life form.

Zippy, I thought, *absolutely bloody fantastic. Seen two; killed one.* And what in God's name was I supposed to do with a dead elf?

(*Hey*, said a nasty little voice inside me, *wouldn't that make a great one of those little Christmas joke books, a hundred and one uses for—*)

Real-life instinct cut in, and I spun round, staring into the gloom in case anybody'd seen me. As far as I could tell, I was on my own, unobserved. The sensible course of action, needless to say, was to run away as fast as possible.

One of these days, I may actually do the sensible thing, though most likely only by accident and coincidence. One of these days.

As I stood there, like a life-size statue of an idiot, several distinct trains of thought were chuffing chaotically through my fuzzed-up little brain. *Elves aren't human,* one of them whispered seductively, *so therefore killing one can't be murder, because surely it's only murder when you kill* people. *Nothing to be afraid of,* proclaimed another, *because after all, it was an accident, you didn't do anything wrong, you're innocent; and if you're innocent, well, what have you got to be scared about?* A third one was saying, *Don't listen to them, you've got to hide the body* right now *before anybody comes past, sees you and calls out all the coppers in Surrey. Furthermore* (continued the third tempter) *it's such a wee tiddly little body, surely it's not going to take all that much cleverness and ingenuity to find an equally wee and tiddly little coffin-shaped hole to stuff it into?* The fourth voice, which was just plain dead miserable, was warning me in a dull mumble against getting so much as a single elf hair or flake of elven dandruff on myself, because all modern forensic science needed to nail my bum to the floor was just a quarter of a molecule of misplaced DNA. There were fifth, sixth and seventh voices too, but even I wasn't gullible enough to take any stock of what they said; my guess was that in their spare time they wrote the leader columns for the newspapers with the small pages, they were that implausible.

While I was busy listening to all these bloody stupid voices, I guess I got so distracted I didn't realise what I was doing; because the next thing I knew, I was dragging the snuffed elf by its little ankles off the road and onto the verge. I've never had what you'd call outstandingly good night vision, but by a weird chance I did actually know precisely where I was; namely, five yards or so short of a field gate, on the other side of which was an old cracked cattle trough that ought to have been, according to my best guesstimate, just about long and wide enough to stow an elf in. I knew this spot so well because I'd fallen off my bike there about three years earlier and the surrounding area had well and truly impressed itself onto my mind, as well as other parts of my anatomy.

Of course, I was navigating entirely by dead reckoning and touch, and I'm still amazed and really quite proud of the fact that I found that damned trough, and it was more or less where it ought to have been. It was more of a job than I'd anticipated, hefting a dead elf over a gate and then trundling it over sticky mud and up into the trough; I've never been your barrel-chested village-blacksmith type, and I have an idea that elf-meat is heavier, cubic centimetre for cubic centimetre, than the ordinary human kind. Also, slipping over backwards and sitting down in the mud two or three times didn't help matters. Eventually, though, the moment came when I let go and the slimy green trough-water went 'glop' over the pathetic little body, the side of the trough and the front of my trousers, in that order, and I straightened my aching back and breathed a ragged sigh of relief. *Job done*, I thought. *So that's all right.*

I'd retrieved my case and was a mile closer to home when the flaw in my logic hit me like a wrecking ball. HORROR OF MIDGET DROWNED IN TROUGH, shouted my mind's eye's tabloid headlines: *police are searching for the crazed killer whose ruthless hands thrust itinerant circus artiste Thomas Thumb, 46, down into his watery grave. 'This unspeakable crime,' said Inspector Fang of Surrey CID . . .*

Yes. Well. Hysterical melodrama aside, it wasn't exactly the smartest thing I could have done under the circumstances. A dead elf lying by the side of the road is one thing; the same, face down in a watering-trough, is an entirely different kettle of piranhas.

I stopped dead in my tracks and tried very hard to figure out what I should do next. Go back, fish the little bugger out, put him back? Yes, but that'd be begging Providence on bended knee to line me up with one or more eyewitnesses; and even if, by some miracle, I got away without being seen, even the dimmest of coroners was going to wonder how a body found in the road came to be all covered with green trough-sludge. Besides, for all I knew the horrible thing could already have been discovered and the whole place crawling with fuzz; and what was that statistic I'd heard about the vast proportion of malefactors nabbed and incarcerated because of their lemming-like urge to return to the scene of the crime?

Short of finding a tree with a conveniently placed overhanging branch and hanging myself with my school tie, I couldn't see any way out of it at all. On balance, however, going back would be marginally more suicidal than pressing on home. Groaning aloud, I squelched the last mile and was welcomed home with the most eloquent and forceful telling-off I've ever had the bad luck to get in the way of. Water off a duck's back, of course: when you're facing the prospect of thirty years in jail for murder, even a level six tongue-lashing from your

Mum dwindles instantly into perspective. I kicked off my shoes, muttered something like, 'Yes, you're absolutely right,' and pottled sadly away to have my last-ever bath with the door shut.

But the night passed, and the following morning, and still the SWAT teams hadn't come for me. I sat and watched my formerly green-slimed trousers whirling round and round in the tumble-dryer, each evolution purging my sin a little more; I cleaned and polished my shoes to the point where light fairly ricocheted off them; and while I was at it, the radio news and the TV news didn't say a word about little men drowned in watering troughs. Eventually, on the third day (can you say unconscious symbolism?) I dredged up enough nerve to go and take a look.

When I got there, the trough was completely empty. Not a trace of elf to be seen. A Happy Easter 2.0 to all our readers.

As I stood in the mud staring into a tank of elfless green goo, I can honestly say I was more freaked out than ever before. A silly little voice in the back of my mind was saying, *Maybe it was foxes, or badgers*, but I didn't dignify it by taking any notice. As far as I could make out, there were only three possible explanations, and that was destruct-testing the tensile strength of the word 'possible'.

– either the little bugger had risen from the dead and climbed out; or

– he hadn't been dead, only stunned; or

– someone had come along, fished him out and disposed of him tidily in the manner advocated on the sides of beer cans without seeing fit to mention a word of it to anybody.

Yeah, I thought, *right; and will passengers waiting to board the 12.41 British Airways flying pig to New York please have their travel documents ready for inspection?* There was, of course, a fourth possibility, namely that there had been no accident, no elf and no death, nothing more to it than me slithering one notch closer to total insanity. For sure, that'd have to be where the smart money would go, because for starters there're no such things as elves –

Of course not. Everybody knew that.

Everybody, that was, except me.

I went home and sat looking out through the French windows at the garden, at the spot where the rose bushes obscured the view of the place where I'd once seen a little man with pointed ears smoking a roll-up. The garden was looking particularly neat and crisp that day, which I took for a nice bit of irony; the lawn tidily trimmed and edged, the flower beds as straight and precise as Pythagoras's Greatest Hits. Then again, I reflected, when hadn't it been thus? In winter, the bare earth was always impeccably groomed and levelled, in summer the grass was invariably immaculate, the flowers colour-coded, the vegetables smartly lined up on parade and presenting leaves—

Which was odd.

Which was bloody odd, since I'd never known Daddy George to get his hands dirty, Mummy was allergic to outdoors and we'd never had a gardener.

CHAPTER TWO

That was a long, hard holiday, believe me.

It has to be said that my view of Christmas is quite like those of the unregenerate Scrooge and fifty billion turkeys. It's not so much about the crass materialism that I object to (fact is, the crass materialism is the best thing about Christmas, and don't let anybody tell you otherwise) as the depressing convention that, at a season of the year when it rains non-stop throughout the severely truncated hours of daylight, it's somehow desirable for families to gather like condors around a dying llama and pretend to like each other. This notion would be daffy enough in midsummer, when you could at least escape outdoors and hide in the shrubbery until they've all gone home. In the deep mid-winter, of course, there's nowhere to run to. You have no choice but to turn and face them, like a bear baited by a hundred poodles, and do your best to endure.

That year, though, my mind was elsewhere most of

the time. Instead of cowering in nooks and trying not to scream every time some aunt falsely accused me of having grown, I blundered through the festive season shrouded in a cloaking device of preoccupation that in the event earned me far more privacy and freedom from intrusion than I had any right to expect. Unfortunately I was too wrapped up in my long, strange thoughts to notice, let alone enjoy.

Stuck in my mind like a haddock-rib in an unwary throat were some of the things the elf had said, just before he died. Something about death being freedom; also about knowing who I was and why I could see him, and something else about it not counting because he was outside the limits, whatever that was supposed to mean. And hadn't he called me a traitor at some point? I wasn't sure; after all, I'd been in a state of mild shock at the time and I certainly hadn't taken notes. But: the point I'm trying to make is that if none of it had made any sense I could've ignored it, filed it under 'miscellaneous' in the shoebox of memory and moved on. Unfortunately, there were one or two minuscule twinkles of sense winking up at me, like the eyes of Dutch paintings following you round the room.

Freedom, the poor little bugger had said, and outside the limits, and knowing who I was; and there was a garden out there, somewhere under all the rain, in which nobody ever worked but which nevertheless boasted a flower every 3.75 inches and lawn edges you could do trigonometry by. A garden where I'd seen an elf and then been firmly told not to.

Maybe there're people in this life who can bring themselves to ignore world-altering facts and events when they tread in them or trip over them. Maybe back in the twelfth century a man sat under an apple tree, looking up at the branches and rubbing the top of his head resentfully, and suddenly out of a clear blue sky the truth about gravity swooped down on him and gate-crashed his mind. But he looked the other way and hummed a tune loudly to drown out the voice in his head, knowing that it'd be far better for all concerned if he didn't get involved. After all, discovering and inventing isn't compulsory. You have the choice to look the other way when the coastline of the undiscovered country suddenly looms at you out of the mist; when you spill your bathwater, you can turn a blind eye to the physics and just mop the floor with a towel until all the evidence has gone.

Could you, really? It'd depend on the circumstances, such as whether the Inquisition was likely to drag you out of your kip at three in the morning and set fire to you, or whether there was good money to be made. But nobody was going to barbecue me for discovering elves, and nobody was going to pay me for it either, because there wasn't a lawyer's chance in Hell that anybody, with one possible but largely irrelevant exception, would ever take me seriously. So it stood to reason that if elves couldn't be true, neither could the disturbing little theory that was starting to coagulate in the back of my mind, since there was nothing for it to be true *with*.

So there I was on Christmas Day: Columbus with his hands folded behind his back, whistling perhaps a tad too nonchalantly and saying, 'New World? Nah, sorry didn't see anything like that, squire.' No wonder even my cousin Eileen and my cousin Derek left me alone and went and hassled someone else. By mid-afternoon, in fact, I'd reached the point where the effort of not reaching the only logical conclusion of my discoveries was starting to give me cramp in my spine, and I knew that if I didn't find someone I could explain my theory to and who'd tell me, *That's the stupidest thing I ever heard, go and sleep it off somewhere*, I was either going to burst or have no choice but to face up to that conclusion and have the whole world change shape all around me.

A day or so before the end of term, I'd asked her: *Cru, would it be all right if I phoned you a few times during the holidays?* And she'd looked at me and said, *Well*, for just long enough to make the rest of the reply unnecessary. This, however, was an emergency. I slipped away from the mob scenes in the drawing room, crept upstairs to Daddy George's study, where there was a telephone and a good thick door, and tapped in her number.

Needless to say, I'd never spoken to her parents or heard their voices before. From her descriptions of them, I was expecting either incoherent drunken giggling or something that'd have been perfectly at home announcing that it could smell the blood of an Englishman. When her dad answered and turned out to sound – well, *normal* – my immediate assumption was that I'd got the wrong number.

'Yes, of course,' the voice answered pleasantly when I chirped my is-Cru-there-please routine. 'Who's calling?'

'Um,' I said. No fooling, I had actually forgotten. Fear'll do that to you. 'Um, it's Mike.'

'Just a tick,' replied the very nice man at the other end of the line; and a very long thirty seconds later, Cru's voice jabbed into my ear. 'Mike? Is that you?'

She sounded annoyed. 'Yes, it's me. Look, I'm really sorry to dist—'

'So you bloody well should be, you pig. I've been waiting by the phone for *days* and you couldn't be bothered to spare me five minutes.'

Really sorry to disturb you like this, when you made it clear you'd rather I didn't call, was what I'd been about to say. Just as well this wonderful language of ours is so delightfully flexible.

'I'm really sorry,' I repeated.

'It's fine you saying that,' she snarled at me. 'Only goes to show, though. Just one lousy call would've done, just so I'd have known you were still alive and not dead in some ditch somewhere.'

I managed to choke back the ironic laugh before it escaped from my throat. Sure was funny, though: *me* being dead in a ditch would've been a slice of luck and a piece of cake compared with what I seemed to be up against. 'Well, anyway,' I said, 'I just wanted to, um, wish you Happy Christmas, and all that stuff. If it's OK, I mean.'

'Yes, all right,' she said, as if grudgingly conceding a point in a particularly fraught session of peace talks. 'Happy Christmas to you too, with brass knobs on. Well, is that it?'

At that point I realised that I wasn't going to be able to tell her about the dead elf and our beautiful garden after all. 'Pretty much,' I replied.

'Oh. Oh well, then, I won't take up any more of your valuable time.'

'That's OK, really,' I said quickly as I could get the words out. 'I mean, I wasn't doing anything else at all.'

'That's such a weight off my mind,' Cru growled ominously. 'It'd really wreck my day, probably the rest of my life too, if I thought that maybe you'd had to sacrifice ninety seconds of your day just to phone silly old me. I could have got ulcers worrying about it, you know?'

There's an old Australian proverb: the left foot of a man with a hangover makes an infallible mine detector, even if only once. In the same vein, I guess I could write an etiquette book listing all the things you must never ever say on the phone to the girl you love. All I'd have to do is tape my own phone calls and transcribe the result. 'I didn't mean it like that,' I said, and I think I just managed to get the word *that* out in time before she slammed the phone down on me.

I sighed. Yes, I could call her back; and she'd tell her dad she didn't want to talk to me ever again, and he'd have the embarrassment of relaying the message, and I'd have the embarrassment of saying, *Well, thanks anyway.* (Because you've got to be polite, haven't you?) That'd be bad, and not calling her back would probably be even worse. I was toying with the idea of writing her a letter ('Dear Cru, You'll never guess what happened, I was just about to ring you back when an asteroid landed in the lane outside and smashed the telegraph pole into matchwood . . .') when the door flew open, and there was Daddy George, looking like Grendel after a hard day at the office.

'What the bloody hell are you doing in my study?' he said.

It was one of those questions you wish people wouldn't insist on asking, since it's obvious to all parties that anything you say is going to make matter worse, even if it's only 'Um . . .' Which was precisely what I did say, as it happens.

'I thought I told you,' he went on, giving me a look you could've carried out surgery with, 'never to come in here without my permission. Well?'

'Yes,' I said, feeling I couldn't really go wrong if I stuck to the plain facts. 'Yes, you did say that.'

'So what in God's name do you think you're doing in here?'

Facts. Tell the truth and shame the devil. 'Using the phone,' I replied. 'Only, I couldn't use the one in the living room because everyone's in there, and I can't hear . . .'

He'd quickly gone from angry to intrigued. 'Who're you phoning, then? You never use the phone.'

Which was mainly true. 'Oh, just a friend,' I replied.

'Bullshit. You haven't got any friends.'

Also mainly true, except for one, assuming she was still talking to me, which was by no means certain. 'Someone from school,' I said.

'Really? Someone from school.' His monstrous swathe of eyebrows swept together; on a still day you could probably have heard the rustling in the next room. 'And this call to this someone from school's so bloody important that on Christmas Day you've got to sneak away from our guests and break into my study—'

'Um, yes,' I interrupted. 'It's my girlfriend, you see, and—'

He blinked five times, very rapidly. 'You've got a *girl-friend*?' he said, making it sound as if I'd just claimed I'd found the holy grail at the bottom of a cornflakes packet. 'Since when?'

'Since the start of last term, actually,' I replied. 'Her na—' I caught myself just in time. "I promised I'd ring her today, just to, you know, say Happy Christmas. But

I didn't want to call from downstairs, with everybody listening . . .'

He scowled thoughtfully at me for two seconds, then shrugged. 'Well, fuck me,' he said. 'Wonders will never cease. So what's she like, then, this bird of yours?'

He was letting me scramble past him onto the moral high ground, of course, but I don't suppose he cared. 'She's not my bird,' I said huffily. 'And that's a rather derogatory expression, if you don't mind me saying so.'

He grinned. 'Get stuffed,' he said. 'Go on, I'm interested. What's wrong with her, then? Fat? Spots? Embarrassing body odours?'

No, but she's got a really *freaky name.* 'Nothing's wrong with her,' I snapped back, trying to sound bitterly offended and upset. Which I was, of course, but I was also profoundly grateful to have seen the back of what-are-you-doing-in-my-study, and it's hard to work up a fine lather of righteous fury when what you really want to do is breathe a long sigh of relief and bust out grinning. 'Why must you assume—'

He laughed. If offensive laughter was a martial art, he'd have been the little wizened Grand Master with the bottle glasses who can beat up all the heavies without breaking into a sweat. 'Whatever,' he said. 'Now get your useless arse out of my study. Your mother'll be wondering where you've got to.'

So that was that; I'd escaped, but I hadn't found anybody to share the burden with, or to absolve me of it, so it looked like I was stuck with it. I spent the rest of the day hiding in the lee of the Christmas tree (we always had something that looked like an undercover giant redwood. Conspicuous consumption? Us? Nah . . .) with a box of someone else's Ferrero Rochers and a notebook, trying to figure out a properly scientific approach to the next phase of my research – it was research already, you'll have noticed. Well, when you're that age and for the first time in your life you happen to trip over something that actually engages your attention, there's a slight tendency to obsess.

Boxing Day was good, because the entire household could be relied on not to stir out of their pits until the nausea died away and the light stopped hurting their eyes, which gave me till noon at the very least, probably longer. I'd set my alarm for 7 a.m. – before you start revising your opinion of me I'd just like to point out that I'm not normally a morning person, but extreme circumstances justify extreme measures – and it turned out to be one of those bright, cold, brittle late-December days when it's deceptively easy to forget what a screw-up your life is, because everything looks so calm and relaxed and *meant*, if you see what I mean. I made myself a coffee, mummified myself in long scarves under a thick coat and let myself out into the garden.

I'll be honest with you, I don't know how all the Attenboroughs and the nature-documentary people hack it, unless the whole thing's a set-up and they're using stop-animation and stuffed animals. Ten minutes huddled motionless in a bush and I'd already checked my watch twenty-seven times, on several occasions shaking it vehemently to see if it'd stopped. Not a trace of any elves, of course. I drew the logical conclusion – that I was simply in the wrong place and that just the other side of the loganberry entanglements was a seething mass of elves – crawled out, stretched my apparently permanently mutilated spine and relocated. Ten minutes later, though, the new spot was just as elf-free. The only conclusion to be drawn was that my fieldcraft was at fault: I was making too much noise, or they could see me, or I was either upwind or downwind or at-right-angles-wind of them and they were scuttling back into their lairs with hankies pressed over their noses muttering, 'Coo, what a pong!' in Elvish.

I thought hard, trying to remember something I'd heard or read years ago about some bloke who hunted tigers by sitting up in a tree; tigers don't tend to look up much, apparently, so they don't see you so easily if you're twelve feet off the ground. There was, of course, absolutely no logical reason why a tactic that held good against huge stripy psychotic moggies should work with elves; I guess it was just one of those intuitive things, a sudden reprise of a million-year-old predatory instinct, linking me for one brief telepathic moment with my hunter-gatherer ancestors.

Didn't bloody work, though. Oh, the tree was no problem; there was a whacking great apple tree with thoughtfully arranged branches that even a sworn acro-phobe like me could get into without screaming, and from the naturally formed armchair about halfway up you had a wonderful view over the whole garden; you could sit perfectly still, screened by a swathe of branches and small twigs, and nobody'd ever know you were there unless you dropped your chewing gum on their heads. It was even fairly comfortable, as trees go. Just no elves showed up, was all.

I gave it a whole half-hour, which is a long time to sit dead still and pay attention to absolutely nothing what-soever going on around you. By this time, I was beginning to wonder if I really did care so passionately about the elf question, or whether there might not be a slim chance that I could carry on and live a normal life, indoors and not freezing to death, without knowing the truth about small pointy-eared people. It was at this juncture that I discovered that both of my legs had done what I should've stayed doing when the alarm went off, and gone to sleep.

Even our old apple tree wasn't so amenable that you could get down out of it with two numb legs, so it quickly became obvious that I was going to be stuck there a little longer. By now I'd come to the conclusion that for whatever reason there weren't any elves to be seen, and I might as well rest my eyes for a while by closing them.

Bizarre thing, the process of falling asleep. It seemed to me that I stayed where I was, and so did the tree, but that the landscape underneath it changed: a bit like a revolving stage in a theatre. Under the tree there was – well, a garden, but a different garden; bigger, more open, scruffier. Lots more room between the flowers, if you see what I mean.

The strangest thing about it was how normal it seemed; as if this was somewhere I'd been before, loads of times, no big deal at all. Certainly I wasn't the least bit nervous when I hopped down out of the tree and strolled towards where the house would have been if there'd been an equivalent to our house in this scenario, which there wasn't. Of course, I knew that, having been here so many times before . . .

Then, quite suddenly, I was on my hands and knees in a very soft flower bed that smelled overpoweringly of freshly turned earth and vintage horseshit. I swore, got up again and looked round to see what had tripped me. It turned out to be a miniature cliff face in the soil, part of an inverted plateau, something like eight inches below the rest of the bed and compressed flat, as if by a heavy weight that had descended from overhead. It was a big plateau, though much more long than wide, with an outward curve on the right hand side and a corresponding inward curve on the left. In fact, but for the excessive size of it, you'd have sworn it was a giant footprint.

Who left that there, then? I asked, under my breath and rhetorically. *Bloody lunatics, why can't they ever look where they're putting their feet?*

It was, of course, a giant footprint. Furthermore, it was *my* giant footprint – not mine in the sense of I-saw-it-first-so-get-lost. Mine in the sense of having been created by my left foot; which was ludicrous, of course, because for one thing my foot wasn't that big, and for another it was attached to the end of my leg, and I knew perfectly well where it had been. Still, I looked round and sure enough, there it was; the manufacturer's name, which was embossed into the sole of the trainers I was standing up in, but here standing proud of the dirt in mirror-written relief.

Well now, I mused with disgust; *maybe a trifle lacking in subtlety as regards the symbolism?* Just to make sure I was interpreting it correctly, I felt the top of my right ear. Sure enough, there it was; a sharp upsweep to the curve, finishing in a distinct point. *Still there*, I told myself. *So that's all right.*

At that moment my eyes snapped open. I looked down. Below me was our garden – the small, crowded version – and just beyond that, the house. The reason I'd woken up so abruptly was apparent from the angle at which this view presented itself. In other words, I'd slipped sideways while I was sleeping, and any second now I was going to fall out of the damned tree.

I managed to wiggle myself upright just in time, after which I carefully climbed back down again. My watch read 9.45. Now, though I was fairly confident that the rest of the house party would be fully occupied with wallowing in their hangovers till at least 10.30, I decided I'd better clear out and not take any silly risks. I still had one last job to do.

Fortunately I'd remembered to bring the makings with me as I'd left the house earlier on: half a pint of milk, four saucers and four slices of stale white bread. I poured the milk carefully, held the bread in it till it was soggy, and gently put each saucer down in the strategically ideal spot I'd selected for it earlier on. For the final touch I got the watering can and used it to turn a swathe of earth surrounding each saucer into a circle of sticky mud. Anything approaching the saucer couldn't help but tread in my mudbath and leave a tell-tale footprint. Neat idea, or what?

Just before going back into the house, I stopped and checked my reflection in the glass of the French windows. Yup, just how they should be, gracefully rounded without even the faintest suggestion of a point on the top.

Needless to say, nobody was up and about yet except me, and there I was in the front room, standing right next to the telephone. By now it was gone ten, a perfectly respectable time to ring someone, if I happened to have someone I wanted to ring. I thought about it for a long time before walking on past.

Nothing to do now except wait and see, two activities I've never been particularly good at. For want of anything else to do, I found a book and lay down on the sofa (*For pity's sake*, I heard my mother's voice in my mind's ear, *you aren't sitting reading again, are you? Haven't you got anything better to do?*) where, thanks to the unscintillating nature of the book I'd chosen, I was soon fast asleep once more. This time, my dream was different. The giant footprint was there once more, but this time it was even bigger, and right in the middle of the living-room carpet, and I was trying to explain to Mum why it wasn't really my fault.

When I came round again it was 10.45 and I could hear voices bumbling away in the kitchen. This reminded me that I was hungry and hadn't had any breakfast yet, unless you counted a very small corner of the dry bread, which I'd absent-mindedly nibbled at while I was setting my traps. A dilemma: on the one hand, in order to get food I'd have to go out and be polite and sociable to my relatives, while on the other hand if I stayed put or hid somewhere, I'd have to carry on starving. Sadly, it was no contest. I made for the kitchen.

After that, the day declined and slithered away into a regulation Boxing Day, tedious and endless. Illogically enough, I found myself hanging around within arm's reach of the phone for as much of the time as I could manage, just in case it rang and Cru was on the other end of the line. But it didn't and she wasn't; no surprises there whatsoever. Once or twice I did catch sight of Daddy George looking thoughtfully at me out of the corner of his eye, but that could just as easily have been general distaste rather than anything specific.

The afternoon gradually edged along like a slow day on the M25, and thickened into evening and then night.

After all those catnaps during the day, I found it annoyingly impossible to get to sleep; instead I lay on my back, staring up at the ceiling, trying to remember what the garden in my first dream had looked like. But it had faded away long since, leaving only a vague shape, like crop circles in standing corn.

It's always the way when you know you want to get up early in the morning but can't seem to drift off to sleep. Eventually you do nod off around a quarter to five and then you sleep like a log from the petrified forest, right through the alarm, and wake up to find it's three hours later than you wanted it to be and you've snored away the time you needed for the job in hand that needed the early start – in this case, inspecting my traps without being seen. I finally rolled out of bed around 10.30 to find the house infested with family and the way through the French windows barred by guardian cousins and aunts, as effective an obstacle as any triple-headed giant hound or fire-breathing dragon. I swore under my breath and settled down to grind my way through another slice of unmitigated family Christmas.

My luck was in, though, just for once; at three o'clock in the afternoon they all buggered off to watch some God-awful musical on the television giving me a glorious window of opportunity for a little supernatural nature study. As soon as the coast was clear, I slipped out through the French windows to inspect my saucers.

The first one, a complete blank. No sign that anything had been near it, no foot- or paw-prints in the mud, no decrease in the carefully noted milk level or evidence of nibbling on the soggy sludge the bread had become. A similar lack of anything to report from saucers two and three. *How depressing*, I thought. As I went to check the fourth saucer I'd more or less given up hope of finding anything, which meant that I very nearly missed it: a little speck that at first sight I took to be a small shred of fallen leaf, or something equally useless. Just as well I looked again, though, just to be sure, because it wasn't a leaf after all.

It was the butt of a tiny roll-up.

CHAPTER THREE

I fished the tiny, sodden fag end out of the milk with my fingertip and stood staring at it for quite some time, all security considerations temporarily forgotten. *Yuck*, I thought.

But it was evidence, something tangible (squelchy, but tangible). Couldn't modern forensic science scan fag ends for saliva traces and extrapolate the smoker's DNA, age, sex, race, religious beliefs, favourite Humphrey Bogart film? Sure, it was very small indeed and the milk probably hadn't helped any, but if they could put people in jail for life on the basis of a single strand of polyester from a snagged cardigan, a genuine cigarette end ought to be enough for a complete reconstruction of the elven genome.

Get real, I told myself. *What were you planning to do, anyhow? Barge your way into the science labs at Cambridge University, yelling, 'This tiny blob of disgusting white mush will prove that elves exist?'* I took in a deep breath and let it out as a sigh. I had enough proof to convince one person – myself. The rest of the world was going to need something a bit more substantial.

At this point, it occurred to me that I'd been standing in full view in the middle of a restricted area for several minutes; not smart at all, since the only thing standing between me and probable discovery were the singing and dancing skills of a cast of veteran Hollywood troupers. I closed the forefinger and thumb tightly on the fag end, threw myself on the ground and rolled sideways into the cover of a dense patch of bolted spinach.

I stayed put for as long as I could bear to, but quite apart from the cramp and the small inquisitive insects crawling up my trouser leg there was the issue of how long it'd take for my absence to be noted and remarked on. A curious thing, that: none of my family ever seemed to have much use for my company, but the absence of it seemed to give tremendous offence. Slowly and carefully I crawled out of the spinach jungle, checked for obvious signs of observation, and scuttled back indoors as fast as I could go.

Luck was with me for once, and I made it to my room without being intercepted. First order of priority was finding a safe home for my evidence; luckily I had one of those empty plastic film canisters handy, and I scraped it off my finger into that, sellotaped round the lid and cached the canister on the top of my wardrobe, among the dust and spiders' webs. That made a quick visit to the bathroom something of a necessity – the dust dissolved in the milk to form a fine, creamy-textured taupe mud, which I decided I'd probably be better off without. Once again my luck held and I was able to sneak back into my bedroom, shut the door and get down to a brief but intensive figuring-out session before rejoining the family downstairs.

It didn't take me long to resolve on a plan of campaign; it was basically just a minor tweak on what I'd already done, only with a degree more thought and insight behind it. Of course, I had to wait till early the next morning before I could do anything about it. Luckily, this time I managed to wake up when the alarm went off at 6 a.m. (horrible time of day, and don't let anyone tell you otherwise). I crawled out of bed, pulled a shirt and trousers on over my pyjamas, and snuck down as quietly as I could to the kitchen.

Preconceptions can be a real pain in the bum, can't they? For some reason I'd got it into my head that elves must be vegetarians – probably because of their alleged fondness for bread and milk, though the fact that they'd used my previous offering of same as an ashtray seemed to suggest they weren't all that keen on the stuff after all – so I couldn't bring myself to plunder the turkey carcass, just in case I mortally offended their principles, or whatever. So I burgled the biscuit jar instead, and dug about in the back of the kitchen cupboard for a bar of cooking chocolate I'd remembered having seen a while back – not parsimony, let me hasten to add; it was simply that after three days' infestation by my blood kin, it was the only unscoffed chocolate left in the house.

Fortunately, the booze wasn't a problem. True, they'd swigged a hell of a lot of it over the past few days, but Daddy George was far too canny to underprovide in that department; not that it mattered, since I was able to fill my saucers from the dregs of last night's unwashed-up glasses.

Tiptoeing down a gravel path in the dark while

carrying a tray of saucers three parts full of stale beer calls for precision footwork, excellent night vision and a certain degree of luck. It's not something I'd recommend to anybody who's inclined to be timid or slapdash in their approach to fine work – such as, on both counts, me. Still, I made it. The hardest part was locating the saucer-drop sites by dead reckoning alone, since I couldn't see what I was doing. It's amazing, though, what a clear mental image of a place you can drag into your mind's eye when you absolutely have to. As soon as the last saucer was in place I snatched up the tray and legged it back indoors, pausing only to hop up and down a few times and scream noiselessly when my unshod big toe found the large stone urn on the corner of the patio.

Mercifully, about half of the house guests pushed off that day, which eased the tension around the house to a certain small degree. We were still lumbered with Cousin Valerie, Auntie Chris, Uncle Pat and Psycho Jack, Mum's unlovely half-brother; it was nevertheless a blessing, like seeing off the boils and the locusts and only having the plague of frogs to contend with. By the time we were through with the waving-goodbye ceremonies for the ones we were managing to get shot of it was lunchtime. I was able to hide in my room until 4 p.m. on the pretext of having work to do for next term, and at 9.30 I synthesised a headache that got me out of the front room and back to safe territory. I got undressed, set the alarm again and dropped off to sleep as quickly and painlessly as if I'd been reading a Martin Amis novel.

The results, when I came to examine them the next morning by the feeble light of the little pen-sized torch that had fortuitously tumbled out of a cracker the day before, weren't nearly as encouraging as I'd hoped. One saucer of stale beer had become a sort of Agincourt for snails, and there was no indication that the biscuit and chocolate had been touched. As I approached the next saucer a very fat-looking pigeon tried to do an emergency lift-off, stalled about a foot from the ground and just about pulled off a forced landing in the leek patch. I don't know if pigeons can be prosecuted for drunk flying; if so, I hope it had the sense to hunker down and sleep it off, though I doubt it. If it was bright enough to do that, it wouldn't be a pigeon. My guess is that a badger got at the third saucer; that, or it was the victim of a very small-scale drive-by Greek wedding. In any event, the saucer was too badly smashed and the shards too widely distributed to give me any useful data about whether and by what its contents had been molested. That just left one more saucer, in the same part of the garden where I'd seen Elf One all those years ago, and sure enough all the beer had gone, along with nearly all the chocolate and two-thirds of the biscuit; also, there was a small puddle of yellowy-brown stuff that didn't smell nice at all and could conceivably have been elven vomit – but I couldn't confirm that, of course, since I had no samples of definitely genuine elf-puke to compare it with. What there weren't were any tracks, footprints, discarded artefacts or other clear evidence. A definite maybe, in other words.

Never mind. I gathered up the three surviving saucers, replaced them with the next instalment, and got back inside before sunrise had a chance to grass me up to the household. The day dragged by in the same tiresome pattern of obligation and evasion, and once again I set the alarm before going to sleep. By the end of the week, I didn't need it; I'd mutated, God help me, into an early-to-bed early riser, which only goes to show the sacrifices we scientists are prepared to make for the sake of our research.

But a pattern was starting to emerge. The only saucer to get any sort of result was Number Four in the lettuce zone. No more alleged elf-puke, and still no tracks or other visible signs, but something was scoffing the bickies and glugging the beer in a highly thorough, not to mention dedicated fashion; certainly enough to justify proceeding to Phase Three.

Assuming I was prepared to take the risk, of course. Putting down saucers of flat beer could just about be explained away as a science project or a sudden burst of compassion for asylum-seeking hedgehogs or something of the sort, though I suspect that if I'd been called upon to explain myself to Daddy George an explanation along those lines would've come across as unconvincing bordering on the Clintonesque. A camera, on the other hand, cunningly rigged with tripwires to set itself off as soon as anything jostled the saucer, was in another league altogether. Besides, quite apart from the security aspect, I couldn't make up my mind whether I was prepared to change the nature of my relationship with the putative elf –

I know, that does sound nauseatingly flaky. But look at it this way. Up to that point, all I'd done was give away free beer and calories, out of (for all the elf knew) the kindness of my heart. If the little buggers were capable of goodwill, I was due for some; likewise trust and all that stuff. If I was then to start loosing off flashguns under their noses like some ruthless paparazzo, we'd be straight back to square one, possibly even worse.

Furthermore, it wasn't just a matter of cold policy: I was starting to feel attached to the little tyke.

God only knew how or why; looked at logically, on the evidence I had gathered, my elf was the kind of person who drinks the equivalent of ten pints of beer and guzzles three packets of chocolate digestives and a half-dozen Mars bars every day. A mental image inevitably begins to condense around statistics like that, and in my mind's ear I was already imagining him burping a lot and talking with an Australian accent. Even so: the idea of trapping him with a hidden camera felt like betrayal. It might be the next logical step in my research, but I didn't want to do it. Simple as that.

When in doubt, prevaricate; as mottoes go it's neither use nor ornament, but it's what I tend to do, and it's my life. I put the decision off for another two days and carried on with the biscuit-and-beer drops, hoping that something would happen that would make the stealth photo call unnecessary. Maybe the elf was getting as curious about me as I was about him, and one morning I'd show up with the day's saucer and he'd be there waiting for me, poised to carry out first-contact protocols in a properly dignified and serious manner. Or maybe he'd get careless and leave something behind. There was a fair chance that with all the booze and chocolate he'd been getting through, I'd come down one morning and find him stone dead of heart or liver failure. Now that really would be evidence: a dead elf – *another* dead elf. But you can take nearly everything too far, and that includes scientific research. In fact, thinking it over, that was all the more reason to wrap up Phase Two and stop putting down the saucers, if I didn't want another death on my conscience.

Valid point, dammit.

So: next morning I didn't take a fresh saucer with me. No big deal, I told myself. After all, I'd proved the existence of elves to my own satisfaction, which meant I wasn't crazy, or at least not as regards elf-seeing. Surely that was all that mattered; besides, even if I completed my 'research' and came up with dead certain conclusive proof, who the hell was I going to show it to? Any scientist worth his lab coat with the row of pens in the top pocket would tell me to get lost as soon as he saw the word 'elf' in the title of my field notes. Nope; time to call it a day, pack it in, get a life . . .

I froze. Out of the corner of my eye I'd noticed something. Something strange – well, that wouldn't have been so bad. This was worse than strange, it was familiar.

It was an elf, sure enough. I could just make out the shape of his head through a screen of verdant weeds. Because of the angles and the height differential, I was fairly sure he hadn't seen me yet. Very slowly and carefully I turned my head until I could see him properly.

An elf: same size as the other two, same general appearance. This one was squatting on an upturned acorn cup with his tiny moleskin trousers round his ankles, smoking a miniature ciggy and reading a very small tabloid newspaper. *Bloody hell*, I thought.

I guess that if you're a trained naturalist, you don't get embarrassed. Must be so, since those guys spend all their time spying on God's creatures, with a somewhat dubious level of concentration on their reproductive activities. But this was the first time I'd done anything like this; and besides, the little fellow looked so much like a human that the natural social instincts cut in before I could stop them. And the first instinct was, of course, to apologise.

'I'm sorry . . .' I stammered.

The elf looked up and scowled at me. 'What the fuck do you think you're staring at, tall-arse?'

If it wasn't for the extreme mortification that was flooding all my systems at that moment, I'd have taken conscious note of the fact that, although the first couple of words seemed very faint and far away, as you'd expect of the product of a one-sixteenth scale larynx, something inside my head managed to turn the volume up, so that by the time he'd finished the sentence it was like listening to someone my own size. There you go, you see. A born scientist would've noticed that straight away, rather than having it dawn on him several hours later.

'I'm sorry,' I repeated, 'I didn't mean – I mean, I didn't expect—'

The elf snorted. 'What d'you mean, you didn't expect? Stands to reason, I'd have thought. Whole saucer of beer every night, on top of all that chocolate and biscuits, any bloody fool ought to see what that's going to lead to. The runs,' he added accusingly. 'Something chronic.'

'Actually—' *No*, I told myself, *don't try and explain further*. 'I'm sorry,' I said for the third time. 'Besides, if it didn't agree with you, why did you—'

'What, turn down a free drink?' The elf laughed harshly and flicked away his dog-end. 'Now, would you mind terribly much pissing off while I wipe my bum? If it's all the same to you, that is.'

I turned away so quickly that I nearly lost my balance and fell over. While I was still wobbling precariously on one foot, I realised that I was practically face to face with Daddy George, in a green-and-red-checked dressing gown and non-matching slippers.

'Who were you talking to?' he asked quietly.

'What? Oh, nobody,' I replied as best I could, though it wasn't easy; it felt as though my tongue was suddenly several sizes too big for my mouth. 'I was just—'

He waited a while second before prompting; 'You were just what?'

'Just, um, rehearsing.' *Christ,* said a voice inside my head, *couldn't you have done better than that?* 'For a play.'

He looked at me as if he'd just found half of me in an apple. 'What play?'

'School,' I said. 'Next term.'

'You didn't say anything about any play.'

'Didn't I? Oh well. It's only a small part, you see, and—'

His nose twitched once. 'Doesn't matter,' he replied. 'Like they say, size isn't everything. Tell you what – after dinner tonight, your mother and I can help you learn your lines. How'd that be?'

Was I really so transparent, I wondered. If so, I had a wonderful career ahead of me as a plate-glass window. 'That's really kind of you,' I said, 'but I've only got three lines, so it isn't—'

'Ah.' He nodded. 'I see. You sure about that?'

I gulped. 'What?'

'I made it four,' Daddy George explained. 'First you said sorry, then you didn't expect, then if it didn't agree with you, and finally—' He shrugged. 'You're right, it was just three. My mistake. Must be a funny old play, though, if that's all you've got to say. Pinter?'

'What?'

'Harold Pinter? Samuel Beckett? The playwright,' he added, 'not the time traveller.'

'Um,' I replied. I guess I've just got a knack for repartee. 'No, not them. Someone else.'

'Ah. Who?'

'I – it's on the tip of my tongue. Begins with an S.'

'Shakespeare?'

I shook my head. 'Sorry,' I said, 'it's just sort of gone, for now. It'll come back to me in a moment, I'm sure.'

He nodded slowly. 'I hope so,' he said. 'After all, it's fairly essential when you're acting to know what play you're in, otherwise you might wander into the wrong theatre by mistake and screw everything up for everybody. Well-known theatrical adage, that is. You ask Ken Branagh or anybody like that, they'll tell you exactly the same thing.'

'Thanks,' I muttered. 'I'll remember that.'

'Well, do your best,' he said. 'But don't strain yourself. I'd start with easy stuff, if I were you, like your name and address; then you can work your way up to remembering tricky things like playwright's names and bits of useless advice. Well,' he added, sniffing, 'I think I'll go in now. You coming, or are you going to rehearse some more?'

As I followed him into the house, not daring to look round at where the elf had been, I did a quick mental tally of the score so far. Clearly Daddy George knew that I knew something, but the fact that he hadn't said anything openly about it and had confined himself to menacing hints and similar melodrama implied that he didn't know for sure what I'd found out. On balance, then, a solid six out of ten was probably on the generous side of fair.

By dropping said hints, on the other hand, he'd tacitly admitted that there was something going on and that he was involved in it, and also that it was something at least vaguely disreputable (or else why hadn't he come straight out with it and yelled at me?) Once you'd taken out all the performance art and general presentation, even though I was the one who'd been careless enough to let himself be crept up on, when the whistle went for full time I'd learned rather more new and interesting stuff than he had. Seven out of ten for me, then, and there was a case to be made for upping that to seven point five or eight. That, of course, would depend on what action Daddy George now felt obliged to take. If the result was that he panicked and had me killed to stop me telling his secret to the world, my executors would probably feel they had no choice but to scale down that seven into a six, maybe even to a five-five.

Not that he'd go that far, of course.

Would he?

For some unaccountable reason I was as jumpy as a rat in a blender for the rest of the holiday. I was right off my food, didn't sleep much, stayed well away from mechanical or electrical apparatus; on the other hand, I was noticeably less antisocial, to the point where I was never alone from dawn to bedtime if I could possibly avoid it, which wasn't like me at all. When the holiday finally ground to a halt, I turned down an uncharacteristically considerate offer of a lift back to school from Daddy George, and made a point of not sitting in the seat on the train that he subsequently reserved for me. In fact, it was only once I was back in my study at school and I'd had a thorough snoop round for loose electrical connections, stray cobras and tarantulas and freshly loosened floorboards that I stopped twitching and managed to relax.

Next day, after close of business, I went looking for Cru. I felt I probably owed her an apology for something or other, and if I didn't she could book it in on account for the next time I screwed up. I found her down by the tennis courts, throwing bits of gravel at small, gullible birds who assumed they were biscuit crumbs.

'Hello,' I said.

'Bastard,' she replied.

Well, in a way it was nice to have my intuition confirmed. 'So,' I said, 'how was your Christmas, then?'

'Utterly horrible,' she replied. 'Go away and get eaten by rats.'

I assumed a stationary orbit, so to speak, and waited while she scored one direct hit and four near misses. Her hand/eye co-ordination always was excellent. 'Sorry you had a rotten holiday,' I ventured. 'Me too, actually.'

'Good. Serves you right.'

I sensed that something wasn't quite right between us. 'Is something the matter?' I asked.

'Yes. You. But nothing that couldn't be solved by you sharing a bath with an electric fire. Goodbye.'

I took a moderately deep breath. 'Have I done something wrong?' I said.

This time she turned round and looked at me. 'Yes,' she said. 'And if your IQ was greater than your inside leg measurement, you'd know that. I'm so glad I'm not as stupid as you are – it must be so infinitely depressing.'

'Oh well, then,' I said. 'See you around.'

She frowned. 'In the distance, preferably. Now, would you mind going and contaminating somewhere else? After all, what harm has this tennis court ever done you?'

I'm not totally insensitive; I can take a hint. So, with a glum sort of smile and a slight shoulder-shrug to convey bewildered regret, I pushed off and left her to her target practice.

It was easy enough to come to terms with the idea that my girlfriend – my only friend, if we're going to be grittily honest about it – had decided she never wanted to see me ever again in this or any parallel universe. After all, I'd never really been able to get my head around the idea that she'd ever liked me, let alone – well, there you go. There was a certain feeling of dreary inevitability about the while thing that made it easier to accept, though no less hard to bear. At least it removed a complication from my life; and one less thing to lose is one less thing to have to worry about.

(Did I ever mention that when I was nine my school nickname was Eeyore? Even the teachers called me that sometimes, when they weren't thinking.)

If there was a positive side to this development, it was that I could now give my full time and attention to the matter of elves. The drawback to that was that, in all honesty, I no longer cared. After all, what the hell was the point of gathering evidence for the existence of small, pointy-eared people? I already believed, and I'd long since reached the conclusion that I'd never be able to convince anybody else, not if I dragged out a live, kicking example and shoved it up their nose. What good would it do, in any event? The human race had managed to shuffle along quite happily for centuries not believing in elves. Finding out the truth would probably just get them mad at me.

Still, I'd come this far – which is just a sort-of-upbeat way of saying force of habit, but there are worse reasons for doing things. The first step, it occurred to me, was to make a start on some actual tangible written notes. Quite by chance, one of my Christmas presents had been a diary. To be precise, a give-away freebie promotional diary, the kind that businesses have done up with their name in gilt on the spine, so that every time you go to write down an appointment or whatever, you catch sight of the name and are reminded of their extreme generosity and general overall excellence. In case you think I'm just being paranoid, by the way, how else would you explain the fact that this particular diary, which came from my uncle Trevor the probate lawyer, was richly gold-embossed with the legend *T. J. Bardshaw & Sons Family Funeral Directors est. 1958*?

Not that that mattered a damn, since I wasn't even figuring on using it as a diary, just a useful notebook to write stuff down in. Besides, it wasn't as if anybody was ever likely to read it except me, so what difference did it make?

So: all I needed now was a quiet place to work and some privacy. Unfortunately, both commodities tend to be rare verging on non-existent in the context of boarding-school life. Short of locking myself in the lavatory, I couldn't rely on an undisturbed hour from wake-up bell to lights out. It's also an awkward fact of human nature that if you look like you're doing something you don't want other people to see, you broadcast some sort of psychic wave that attracts all the busybodies and amateur comedians within a two-mile radius. If you want to be left alone to get on with something, your best bet is to sit in the open in the busiest part of the premises; and if you keep stopping people and asking them for help with some aspect of what you're doing, suddenly you'll find you're the next best thing to invisible and inaudible.

(Of course, I'd learned this particular survival maxim back when I was seven and desperately trying to find an uninterrupted fifteen minutes to finish reading my *Secret*

Seven adventure. In our house, for some reason, sitting in a chair reading a book is and always has been interpreted as a cry for help, an expression of loneliness and depression one step removed from the empty aspirin bottle or the teetering walk along the window ledge. Just open a book at random – doesn't even matter if it's the right way up or not – and before you can say 'Jack Robinson', or even 'Piss off, I'm trying to read', you're surrounded by bouncy, cheerful people asking you how your day's been, and would it help to talk about it?)

So I parked myself on a bench on the westerly side of the dining hall, with my notebook open on my knee, some book picked out at random on the other side of me, and a pencil stuck behind my ear, as if I was locked in some particularly arduous and potentially contagious piece of homework. It should've worked; but I hadn't been there more than a minute when a shadow fell across my page, and I heard a voice above me saying, 'What're you reading, then?'

As a precaution, I'd made a point of noting the title of the book selected at random. '*Moby Dick*,' I told him. 'Got to get it done by tomorrow, or I'm history. And geography and possibly physics too.'

'Oh. Right.' The shadow (which belonged to an exceptionally annoying youth called Ben Thaxton) stayed where it was, right across my page. 'Funny word, that,' the voice went on.

I tried not to be too obvious about taking a deep, calming breath. 'What word, Ben?'

'Moby,' he replied. 'Looked it up once, couldn't find it. Not in the dictionary.'

'It's short for Möbius,' I replied, not looking up. 'I know,' I went on, 'Möbius Dick, it does conjure up a profoundly disturbing mental image. Still, that's writers for you. Perverts, the lot of 'em. Now, since you're here, perhaps you could help me out with this bit. It says here—'

Thaxton shrugged, gave me a funny look and moved on. I counted up to ten under my breath, just in case he decided to come back, and then opened the diary.

To start with, I'd decided, I'd draw up a grid with 'sightings' all down the left-hand side of the page, and—

I stopped, and blinked. On the first blank page in the diary, dead centre of the sheet of paper – useful addresses of some such – there was some writing. It said –

HELP

– in teeny-weeny little letters, traced in some kind of brownish ink.

Odd, I thought. I held the book a few inches from my nose, just in case I'd misinterpreted it or missed something else that might explain it, but there was nothing more that I could see. I had no idea human beings could write that small.

Looking at it was putting me off, spoiling my concentration, so I turned the page, found myself looking at a list of decimal conversions (you know – how many scruples to the kilo and how much is one metre in perches) and flicked on through in search of blank stuff I could write on. There was a nice white patch like a croquet lawn in 'Personal Details'. I picked up my pencil to begin writing, and—

HELP

– exactly the same as on the addresses page; even the same distinctive and rather unappealing shade of rusty-brown ink.

I studied it at nose's length, just to be sure, making a point of looking out for stray hairs, spots and discolorations. Nothing – not even a wispy fine spray of brown where the nib had dragged on something. What on earth could it mean? Had my uncle Trevor, or possibly even T. J. Bardshaw & Sons Family Funeral Directors est. 1958, been drinking, or just bought a new ultra-fine Rotring mapping pen? Maybe it was one of these new performance-art things, like the one where there's this guy all covered in white paint, standing on a plinth pretending he's a statue.

I sighed. Darwin probably never had all this trouble; nor David Attenborough. I flicked on a couple more pages until I hit more empty white. Only it wasn't as empty as it had looked at first sight, and this time, right there in the middle of the page, same handwriting, same ink, was –

PLEASE

Once the penny had dropped, it hurtled down like a bomb from a Stuka. Small, neat, florid handwriting. Small, neat, florid, *elfin* handwriting. The sort of handwriting you'd be likely to have if you were only six inches tall. As for the brown ink, it almost certainly wasn't ink. *Ouch*, I thought.

I lifted my head and looked round, to see if anybody was watching me; the very last thing I needed right then was some other idiot interrupting me. Then I started turning pages and examining them, one by one, starting with 1 January.

But the days dwindled down to a precious few: November, December, and no more little brown words, not even smiley faces or Kilroy's nose poking out over the top of the Ready Reckoner. Plenty of possible explanations for that, needless to say. The writer was interrupted, or he got bored, or his pen broke, or the cut he'd made in his arm stopped bleeding, depriving him of his ink supply. Could be anything like that – and chances were I'd never find out which.

Like it mattered, I thought. Even if this was elf handwriting, what did it mean and what was I supposed to do about it? No use at all just saying 'Help!' It would be as bad as shouting 'Look out!' when someone was driving fast on a motorway, without making it clear what they were supposed to be looking out for. (Whereupon the driver jumps on his brakes, the car skids and slews round sideways, right into the path of an oncoming lorry carrying concrete bridge sections—)

I resolved on one last check. It was just as well that I did, because I had missed something, tucked away in the coils of the Underground map like a goat being squeezed to death by a python. This time it was a whole sentence. It said –

PS: ELVYND SAYS THANKS FOR THE BEER BUT HE PREFERS GUINNESS

– which surely put the whole business beyond doubt. Didn't it?

One of the benefits of paranoia is the tremendous boost it gives to the imagination. Quite apart from the semi-rational, almost plausible alternative explanation (Daddy George with a bottle of brown Indian ink and a magnifying glass, playing games with my head) I was able to concoct at least three others, each one scarier and more bizarre than the last, though I can't remember offhand what they were, only that they were all further-fetched than British goods in Australia. Wonderful stuff, all of it. Catch a non-paranoid coming up with anything half so creative? I don't think so.

I closed the diary slowly, tucked it away in my inside pocket, dumped *Moby Dick* on the bench and went for a walk round the back of the football pitch. By now I was so thoroughly freaked out that I was fully expecting to see hordes of little green men with pointed ears gam-bolling about on the grass and pulling faces at me. Most of all, though, what I really wanted was someone I could tell about it all without the certainty of an incredulous stare followed by prolonged and uncharitable mirth. Someone like—

'Oh,' said Cru, hopping out from behind a tree, 'it's you again. Are you following me around, or something?'

'What? Oh, no. Sorry.' That was me all over. Captain Coherent to the rescue. 'I mean, no, I'm not. I didn't even realise you were—'

'Whatever. Goodbye.' She said the words, but stayed exactly where she was, directly in my path like essential carriageway maintenance on a busy summer motorway. For someone who didn't want me around, she was making it pretty hard to get away.

'Listen,' I said. 'Would it help if I was to say I'm sorry?'

She frowned. 'But you say it so often,' she sighed. 'All the bloody time, it's like Pavlov's dogs. I don't suppose you even know you're doing it, it's so instinctive. Have you the faintest idea how annoying that gets, after a while?'

I nodded. 'It must be,' I said, wondering what the

hell she was going on about. 'I don't mean anything by it, if that's any consolation.'

Another sigh. 'No, probably you don't,' she said. 'You know what your problem is?'

Well, talk about your no-brainers. Seeing elves, obviously. 'Um,' I replied.

'Your problem is,' Cru went on, 'you just don't stop and think about other people. Ever. As far as you're concerned, the world consists of you right there in the middle, and a lot of little flat cut-outs spinning round you, like one of those mobile things we had when we were kids. You—'

'You had one of them as well, did you?'

'What?' She blinked at me, as if she hadn't been expecting any input from my direction at that particular juncture. 'Look, do you mind not interrupting when I'm telling you something really important? Thank you. Oh hell, where'd I got to?'

'Mobiles,' I replied. 'I had one hanging off my ceiling, with Father Christmas and his reindeer. We made it at play school out of cardboard and silver paper.'

'Will you shut up about stupid bloody mobiles? Thank you,' she continued, breathing out through her nose. 'Where we'd actually got to, before you started drivelling about cardboard silver reindeer, was chronic egocentricity and total lack of regard for other people. Would you like to talk about that for a minute or so?'

Not particularly; but it had to be better than not talking at all. Besides, buried deep in the male survival kit of instinctive abilities there's an amazingly useful little function that allows you to look attentively serious, nod your head and grunt 'Mphm' in all the right places whenever the significant female in your life launches into a monologue prefaced by 'We really have got to talk this through', leaving the conscious mind at liberty to drift off and amuse itself with imaginary football matches, car-engine fault diagnosis, quadric equations and other more congenial stuff. I put the facility on standby, relaxed the muscles of my back and shoulders, and replied, 'All right.'

She sighed. 'What'd be the point?' she said. 'You wouldn't understand, it'd just be a waste of time and breath.'

I managed to keep myself from saying, *Oh good, that's all right, then*, and restricted myself to a contrite stare at my toecaps. False modesty apart, I'm good at that particular stare, probably because I've had so much practice. One of the few benefits of having spent so much time in the wrong I could claim it as my domicile for tax purposes.

'Anyway,' she said. 'We won't discuss that any more. I forgive you, even if you are a shallow, self-centred insensitive bastard.'

'Thank you,' I replied.

'Don't mention it.'

'So.' Cru fidgeted with her hands, like Lady Macbeth with a hangnail. 'You have a good Christmas, then?'

'No, not really.'

'Neither did I.' Her lower lip quivered – a warning to sensible men to remember appointments in distant cities. 'I had a thoroughly rotten Christmas, if you must know. Shall I tell you why?'

Though I'd spent most of my English grammar lessons drawing Klingon battlecruisers on the inside of my pencil-case lid, even I can spot a rhetorical question. I kept my face shut accordingly.

'I'll tell you why,' she said. 'Because I spent the whole lousy holiday waiting by the phone, just in case someone might deign to.spare the time out of his incredibly busy schedule to find a window to give me a call. Finally, on Christmas Day, the phone does ring, and what do I get? Yuletide greetings. The compliments of the season. Damn it, I got a more passionate Christmas message from the Damart catalogue.'

'Sorry,' I said;' then, as she was winding herself up for a really good explosion, I added, 'But there's a reason.'

Cru stopped her countdown with one second to go, just like in the James Bond films. 'Really?' she said.

'Really.'

She frowned. 'This had better be either wholly true or stunningly imaginative,' she said. 'For choice, both.'

I grinned feebly. 'Funny you should say that,' I said. 'Because it is. Quite.'

'Oh God.' She pulled a face. 'This isn't going to be about elves, is it?'

'Funny you should say that, too.'

CHAPTER FOUR

'Go on,' Cru said wearily. 'I'm listening.'

So I told her. The dead elf. (I sort of left out the bit about falling on the poor wee bugger and crushing him to death. Must've slipped my mind or something.) The experiments. The microscopic fag end. The eventual close encounter. Daddy George's suspicious manner and cryptic remarks. The whole incredible tale, right up to the diary and the tiny messages. When I was through, I looked up at her. Not promising.

'You don't believe me,' I muttered.

'Oh, sure I believe you,' she said, with a slight snort. 'That's not the point.'

'What?'

'You heard me. What's all this stuff about elves got to do with you not phoning me?'

It took a moment to remind myself that I was the selfish egocentric one in this relationship. 'Well,' I said, 'I guess I was preoccupied. And,' I went on, as wisps of green fire started flickering out of her nostrils, 'with my stepfather being so bloody suspicious all over the place, there was no way I could get to a phone. You see, there's a phone in his study and another in the living room, and that's it. And I couldn't use the one downstairs because the whole place was crawling with nosy filthy-minded relatives.'

Long pause, as if she was calling for a manual recount before making up her mind. 'Well, all right, then,' she said. 'I suppose if you couldn't get to a phone . . . Though you could've used a call box.'

I shook my head. 'The nearest one's five miles away, and usually it's not working.'

She frowned again. 'Five miles isn't that far.'

'Yes, but if I was gone that long, someone'd have noticed and I'd have been interrogated about where I'd been.'

'I suppose,' she said. 'So, why the hell didn't you tell me? What do you think I am, a telepath?'

She lobbed that one at me so gently, it was practically a fond embrace. 'I didn't think,' I replied. 'And, like I said, I was preoccupied. Which was very wrong of me,' I added quickly, 'but you know what it's like when something starts niggling away at your mind. It gets so that nothing else seems to matter after a while.'

'If you say so,' she said. 'Right,' she went on, in a much brisker tone of voice. 'Let's see this famous diary of yours, then.'

Much more like it. I fished it out, opened it and pointed. At least, I pointed to where the writing had been. Note the past tense.

'I can't see anything,' Cru said. 'You sure you've got the right page?'

I snatched the diary back and flicked through. 'It's gone,' I said. 'Vanished.'

'Away with the fairies, you mean.' She clicked her tongue. 'Or are you going to tell me it's lemon juice or special elven invisible ink?'

'I thought you said you believed me.'

'I did. That was before you showed me a page with no writing on it.' Her eyebrows started to close in, like hungry wolves round a wounded deer. 'When I said I wanted an imaginative excuse, I didn't mean something so wildly bizarre that it insults my intelligence.'

'But it was there,' I protested. 'Right there where I was pointing. I saw it.'

She looked at me sideways. 'This seeing-things-that-aren't-there aspect of your character's a new one on me,' she said slowly. 'I'm not sure I'm all that happy about it.'

'But—' I stopped dead. Have you ever put your foot in some really deep mud, so that it keeps going on down and down without meeting anything solid? The trick is, under such circumstances, not to thrash about and make sudden violent movements, or you really will get stuck. Same goes, in my limited experience, for protesting your innocence to a sceptical female. Keep still, say nothing, wait for someone to pull you out. Which, to her credit, she immediately proceeded to do.

'Maybe,' she said, in a vaguely conciliatory tone of voice, 'you thought you'd seen it because you've been so preoccupied lately. And,' she went on, 'just because you imagined some elf stuff once, it doesn't necessarily follow that all the elf stuff's imaginary.'

'True,' I mumbled.

'Besides,' she went on, falling in beside me and starting to walk back towards the main building, 'it doesn't actually fit in with the rest of what you've been telling me about these elves of yours. Like, what you were saying seemed to suggest that they're somehow being – well, held against their will. Forced to work as gardeners, or whatever. Anyway, they're localised to your dad's house, and maybe the immediate vicinity. That's a hundred miles away.'

I frowned. 'How'd you make all that out?' I asked.

'Isn't that what you told me? About the elf that died saying death is a sort of freedom, and it was finally outside the limits? Sounds to me like it'd escaped from – well, from somewhere. And then you said about your stepfather's garden being so perfect but nobody ever did any work there that you could see. And then you find there're elves there, with little spades and things; and your stepfather gets so incredibly hostile when he catches you hanging around the garden. Doesn't it stand to reason that . . .'

'Jesus.'

Well, maybe I had thought of it, at least on a subconscious level; but I certainly hadn't consciously fitted together those particulars pieces. Or hadn't allowed myself to, more like. Cru, on the other hand, was under no such disability and now she'd actually said it out loud, it wasn't ever going to go away.

Pity, that. I'd wanted understanding and moral support, not to have my nose rubbed in an uncomfortable, possibly life-altering hypothesis. A bit like running to Mummy to have a bumped knee kissed better, to find Mummy waiting for you with a chainsaw and saying she's going to have to amputate.

Cru just seemed annoyed that I'd interrupted her. 'Well, doesn't it?' she demanded. 'As far as I'm concerned, it's as obvious as an elephant sandwich. To be honest with you, I can't really see how you could've failed to—'

Gee, I thought; *if she's the sensitive, tactful one, I must be really crass.* 'Right,' I said. 'Well, you've given me something to think about, and no mistake.'

'Oh, there's more,' she assured me. 'For a start—'

'Yes,' I interrupted. 'Thank you. But if it's all the same to you, I'll try and get my head round this lot first. Shouldn't take more than the rest of my life.'

'I thought you'd be pleased that someone else believed you,' she said, sounding all hurt and spurned. 'Damn it, I was only taking an interest.'

. . . As the dragon said to the oil refinery. 'I know,' I said quickly, 'and I'm really grateful, truly I am. You've no idea how much it means to me. But I'd like to think about this on my own for a bit, if that's OK with you. No offence.'

'Please yourself, then,' she replied, sniffing fiercely. 'Let me know when you're through moping.'

I assured her that I'd do just that, and she flounced off towards the main building. I know modern women aren't supposed to flounce, but she must've been born with the knack; besides I think it's nice that somebody's keeping these ancient skills and crafts alive for future generations.

Well, it was one of those instances where the more you think about it, the more bewildering it gets. On the one hand, if she was right, it'd explain a whole raft of funny little things going right back to when I was just a little kid. On the other hand, if she was right, I was living under the same roof as a man who enslaved elves to dig his vegetable garden. Rather a lot of trouble to go to for a few scrawny little carrots and a meagre picking of Kevlar-reinforced runner beans. Besides, Daddy George didn't even like vegetables.

Since it was the only explanation I'd considered so far, it was simultaneously the most convincing and the daffiest. I tried to think of an alternative. I failed.

When you can't solve the whole problem, my aunt Sheila once told me, nibble off the simplest bit of it and try solving that; it probably won't get you anywhere much, but at least you won't feel such a total dead loss. So I thought about the diary and the disappearing writing, and had a shot at making sense of that. It was getting chilly outside, so I trudged back indoors and found a relatively secluded corner of the study area that I shared with a bunch of other guys. Then I pulled out the diary and ruffled through the pages.

It was back.

Damn it to hell, there it was again: four letters, tiny but unmistakably there. I scrabbled my way through the rest of the diary and, sure enough, all the other messages were there too, just where I'd seen them before.

Not funny, I thought.

Oh, there were rational explanations available, if I'd wanted them; some kind of chemical that was only visible under artificial light, or a compound that stayed inert unless gently warmed through by my body heat, permeating off my leg into my trouser pocket. There was also self-hypnosis, shared delusion, or the slender chance that some humorist had spiced the lunchtime roly-poly pudding with a generous dose of bad LSD. Those, however, weren't the sort of explanations I was looking for, thanks all the same. I was more concerned with *Why me?* and *What did I do to deserve that?* and sundry related issues.

You see, I'd already guessed the real reason. The message had been for my eyes only. Trying to share it with anybody – anybody at all – just wasn't allowed.

If so, that was going to be something of a hardship. What I wanted most of all, of course, was for the whole wretched business to go away; failing that, my second choice was for someone else to come along and take it off me, while I tiptoed away and snuffled round the trashcans looking for a life. The burden being mine and mine alone was something I could really do without, what with one thing and another. After all, I wasn't particularly interested in zoology or folklore, or even gardening. I could only conclude that it was a cat thing – you know, like that amazing ability cats have of choosing the one person in the room who doesn't like them, and then jumping on his or her lap with all claws locked outwards, curling up and going to sleep.

Still, what did my feelings matter? It was only me, after all, not anybody important . . .

While I was thinking all this stuff, I was on automatic pilot: putting books away, clipping the day's notes into ring-binders, general admin and clutter control. By the time I reached the industrial-grade self-pity stage, I was getting ready to make a start on the rather daunting raft of maths problems I was due to hand in before noon the next day. I guess you could say maths was my best subject, though only in the sense that his attention to grooming and personal hygiene was Darth Vader's most attractive quality. Maths was what I was least hopeless at, on a good day. But the impenetrable briar-patch of wiggly brackets and equals signs confronting me was so far over my head I could've wished on it; another reason, perhaps, why I wasn't in the most cheerful of moods.

Nevertheless, the sooner I made a start, the sooner I could legitimately give up in despair. I opened the stapled-up wodge of photocopied sheets, and looked at the first page.

At first I assumed it was simply a hardware problem, my eyes playing tricks on me or my stressed-out little brain overheating. So I looked away, eyes tight shut, counted slowly to twenty plus two for luck, and looked again. It was still there: a neat but minuscule paragraph of mathematical calculations carefully inscribed in the margin, apparently answering the question. *Oh please*, I whined inwardly, *not now, can't you see I'm busy?* I picked up the booklet and went through it page by page; next to each problem, an elegantly elfwritten answer, no letter or number more than two millimetres high but nevertheless surprisingly legible. There wasn't a pen made that wrote that small.

After I'd been sitting there for an indeterminate length of time, it occurred to me that it might just be helpful to run through one of these answers and see if it made sense; so I did. It did, too. Furthermore, the answer was so well presented and set out that, for the very first time, I got just the faintest sliver of a clue as to what all this guff was supposed to be about.

What to do?

Well. There's an old folk tale about a man who was walking down a country lane and came to a long single-storey shed, out of the front of which protruded an unmistakable dragon's head, while a similarly unmistakable dragon's tail stuck out the back window. Next to the shed was a magnificent crop of brussels sprouts, being weeded by a little old man in a bobble-hat.

'Excuse me,' the passer-by said to the old man, 'but is that a dragon in your barn?'

The old man looked at him for a while, then shrugged. 'Ain't no such thing as dragons,' the old man said, 'but their dung's mighty good for brassicas.'

Well, anyway, you get the general idea. Maybe the existence or non-existence of elves was making my life a metaphysical nightmare; but if they were prepared to do my maths homework for me, I wasn't going to complain. True, squinting at that tiny handwriting as I made a fair copy gave me a splitting headache, but nothing in life is ever entirely perfect, not even chocolate profiteroles.

The copying-out took me a quarter of an hour. As soon as I'd finished, I put my answer paper carefully away, picked up the question booklet and prowled around in the corridors to nab the first person I met. This turned out to be a guy called Paul Schenk, who was virtually a friend of mine.

'Paul,' I said.

He stopped and turned to face me. 'What's up with you?' he said. 'You look awful.'

'Do me a favour,' I said, 'and have a look at this question sheet for me, will you?'

He glanced down at it. 'Sorry,' he said, 'haven't got time. Besides, I'm bloody hopeless at that sort of stuff.'

'No, that's all right,' I told him. 'I don't need any help with the questions, I just want you to look at the paper.'

He frowned. 'Is this a conjuring trick?' he asked suspiciously. 'Because if it's one of those things where you've got a hidden squirter that shoots a jet of water up my nose, I suggest you take it away and avoid months in plaster.'

'No trick,' I said. 'All I want you to do is tell me if you can see anything on there apart from the questions. Well?'

He looked at me as if I'd just walked through the wall with my head under my arm, wearing a frock. 'Apart from the questions,' he repeated.

'That's it. Any writing, that sort of thing.'

He made an exaggerated dumb-show of examining the paper, turning it upside down, shaking it, holding it to his ear, even nibbling off a tiny corner and chewing it. Great sense of humour, Paul had – according to Paul. 'Nope,' he said eventually. 'Nothing I can see except a big mess of quadratic equations with a tasteful white border. Are you sure you're feeling OK?'

'Much better now, thanks for asking,' I said. 'Be seeing you.'

I went back and stared at what I'd just written, as much as anything to satisfy myself that it was still there. It was; and bloody impressive it looked too, so much so that although I could see on a purely intuitive level that the answers were right, when I tried to follow the calculations they sort of bounced away ahead of me like excessively frisky dogs chasing sheep. One thing was for sure, namely that those answers had been figured out by somebody else, not by me. And if I hadn't done them, it stood to reason that someone else had. Someone with very small, neat handwriting.

The implications of that didn't really bear thinking about, but I thought about them anyway. If, as logic would have me believe, an elf had done my homework for me, that meant that my tiny, Spock-eared benefactor must've found the question paper in my folder on my shelf in this same room and had either done them for his own amusement, the way a human being might do a crossword puzzle, or else had done them in order to help me out, presumably by way of saying thank you for some kind deed or other. The former hypothesis posited the existence of a life form able and willing to do vicious, man-eating quadratic equations for fun – elves I could believe in, but some concepts are just too freaky for the brain to get a grip on. The other explanation required me to believe that there was an elf here, on the premises, and (there are concepts even freakier than maths-loving elves) that he liked me. A lot.

Now that really was crazy, particularly since to my certain knowledge I'd thoughtlessly killed a third of all the elves I'd ever met. But suppose it was true, and that the gracefully tumbling sheaves of numbers and mathematical symbols staring up at me from my sheet of paper were a token of grateful esteem. Surely that had to rule out the possibility of a local chapter of elves (unless my act of kindness had been entirely unconscious, like chucking away a seven-eighths empty crisp packet behind a bush under which cowered a family of starving elf orphans; but I'm careful about litter and I don't like crisps) and left me with the bizarre conclusion that when I came back after the Christmas holiday, I brought with me a minute, prodigiously numerate freeloader.

Yes, but how? In my pocket? Hidden deep in the folds of my innermost socks? Or maybe elves were invisible to everybody unless and until they wanted a specific person to see them, in which case the sucker could've travelled up with me, sitting on my shoulder like an invisible parrot.

Why, though? And, more to the point, where was he now? And what was he up to, apart from abstruse mathematical calculations?

I tried to sit still and put it out of my mind, but I couldn't: there was too much of it, and it wouldn't shut up. I needed to share it with somebody; but that was all right, because now (I realised) I had evidence. Hard, indisputable proof. I grabbed the question sheet and my answer and shot out of the study area like a politician pursued by newshounds.

Eventually, I ran Cru to ground in the library, of all places. She was sitting in a corner, apparently trying to barricade herself in with stacks of big, fat books. For a moment I wondered whether it was a protest of some kind; but at least it wasn't a hunger strike, since she was surreptitiously munching a fistful of Twiglets, one of which she swallowed the wrong way when I popped my head up over her literary battlement and said, 'Guess what!'

She jumped, scowled horribly, and shoved the Twiglet packet into her bag. 'What the hell do you think you're playing at?' she hissed. 'I could've choked to death.'

'Sorry,' I replied, with a rather obvious lack of sincerity. 'But it's important. Here, look at this.'

She took the question paper and glanced at it. 'If you think I'm going to do your stinking maths questions for you—'

'No,' I interrupted. '*Look*. Closely. What do you see?'

She looked. 'Well,' she said, 'if you ask me it looks as if someone's eaten too many numbers and then been sick into a photocopier. Take it away, I don't do maths.'

(Which was true: strictly an Eng Lit and History buff was Cru. Not that she wasn't perfectly competent at mathematical procedures, especially if the product was less than ten and she wasn't holding anything in her hands at the time.)

'You're missing the point,' I told her. 'Now, then. Apart from the questions can you see anything else on this page? Well?'

She gave me a fools-not-so-gladly look. 'Please don't tell me it's more invisible writing,' she sighed. 'Because if you do I'll have to smash your skull with a dictionary, and that'll mean spending all evening hanging about down at the police station.'

'You can't see anything, then.'

'No. It's one of the drawbacks to being sober and sane – it can be so limiting sometimes.'

'Fine,' I said. 'Now look at this.' And I handed her the answers.

She looked at the page for awhile, turned it right side up and looked at it again. 'It's beautiful,' she said. 'What's it supposed to be?'

'Think,' I said. 'I just wrote out those answers to those questions.'

She twitched her nose. 'You did. And?'

The penny landed and teetered round on its edge before flopping over. Yes, I had conclusive proof to back up my elf story; but she, not being a mathematician, couldn't understand the significance of it. I took a deep breath. 'Do you trust me?' I asked.

'No, of course not.'

'Try. Just this once. Please. I want you to go and find someone you know who's good at maths. Show them both the questions and the answers, and ask them what they reckon to it. All right? I'll wait here.'

A look of martyred patience dragged across her face. 'Have I got to?'

'Yes.'

'Really?'

'Really.'

'All right. Don't let anybody touch those books. That includes you. Actually, that includes you a *lot*.'

Cru was gone a long time. When eventually she came back, she had a pained, thoughtful look on her face.

'This is weird,' she said. 'In fact, this is the weirdest thing since Salvador Dali got a job as the speaking clock. This is your handwriting, yes?'

'You know perfectly well it is.'

'True,' she replied. 'I don't think there's anybody else in the world who can do such cruel and unusual things to innocent letters.' She checked her books were where they'd been, to the millimetre, then sat down. 'I found someone to ask,' she said. 'Melanie Harrison, not my favourite person and about as interesting as a gardening programme in Portuguese, but very good at sums. Then I found someone else, just to be sure.' She handed me the papers. 'If what they said is right, there's no way you could've done those answers.'

I grinned. 'I didn't,' I said.

'I'd guessed that.' She paused for a moment, and turned up the gain on her scowl.

'So,' I said, 'your friends confirmed it. These are the right answers.'

'Ah.' She looked at me as if I was a pane of glass. 'That's actually a very good question. You see, apparently whoever wrote that stuff doesn't do maths the way everybody else does it. That's what freaked our Melanie and our Sean. I couldn't follow all the technical drivel, but apparently, it's maths, Jim, but not as we know it. Completely new, different approach, is what they told me.'

I frowned. 'But I use a new and different approach all

the time,' I said. 'That's why I keep getting the wrong answer.'

'Ah, but that's because you're stupid,' Cru explained. 'Whoever did this stuff may be a lot of things, but stupid isn't one of them.' She leaned forward on her elbows. 'So,' she said, 'out with it. Who's the new Einstein?'

I looked at her and didn't say anything. No need.

'Thought so,' she replied slowly. 'Which is why you made me look at the question paper. There's something written on it that you can see and I can't.'

I nodded.

'Fine.' She breathed out slowly through her nose. 'Let me guess. This writing that you can see and I can't – it's not very big, is it?'

'Nope.'

'In fact, it's quite small. Tiny.'

'Virtually microscopic.'

'Jesus.' She clicked her tongue. 'Have I got to use the E word?'

I shook my head. 'But I think it'd be a gracious gesture if you did,' I added.

'All right, then.'

I waited for a few seconds, then drummed my fingertips ostentatiously on the table top.

'Elf,' she mumbled. 'Satisfied?'

'Thank you.'

'It was the least I could do,' she snarled. 'All right, so what's the story? What happened?'

I shrugged. 'Haven't a clue, really,' I replied. 'I went to do these questions, and when I opened the folder and took them out, there was this writing all up through the margin. So I copied it out, and came to find you.'

Cru glared at me. 'That's it?'

'That's it. The full story, complete and unabridged.'

'Oh.' She rubbed her eyelids, as if something was making her feel very tired. No idea what it could be. 'Theories.'

I nodded, and told her. She sighed.

'It's not getting any better, is it?' she said. 'You know, I think that's what's really getting to me about all this is the thought that after all the time and effort I put into trying to study hard and do well at my maths and science and stuff, just when I thought I was getting somewhere and really beginning to see how the universe works in an orderly and logical way, with no cheating – then you come along and the next thing I know is, I've got no choice but to believe in sodding elves. It isn't fair, is it? I mean, supposing I was doing a physics exam—'

'Unlikely,' I pointed out. 'You told me you stopped doing physics when you were fifteen.'

'All right,' she snapped, 'yes. But just supposing. I'd be having to sit there, writing answers that say yes, the cosmos is just one great big machine and if you wind up the spring and press the lever, such and such will inevitably happen and such and such inevitably won't – and it'd all be a load of old socks, because really there's magic and elves and things that some people can see and other people can't, for no bloody *reason*.' She looked up at me, bewildered as a chameleon on a paisley scarf. 'Come on,' she said, 'you're supposed to be into maths and science and stuff. How the hell can you bring yourself to lie to the examiners?'

Of course, I hadn't thought of it in that light, maybe because I had more sense. After all, things were difficult enough as it was without making everything worse by trying to *understand*. 'No idea,' I said. 'I guess you'd have to say that the elf stuff is all maths and physics we just haven't got around to discovering yet. Look, no offence, but I'd rather not go into that side of it right now, if it's all the same to you. I need to know what to do next.'

Cru shrugged. 'Well, I can see that,' she said. 'And I think that the first step should definitely be to find this elf. Agreed?'

'Er, I suppose so. But that's easier said than done. What did you have in mind? Infra-red motion detectors? Stop-motion surveillance cameras? A very large fly-paper?'

I'd offended her again. 'Sarcasm isn't going to help, now, is it?' she said. 'No, I was thinking of a more direct approach.'

'Really? More direct than a fly-paper?'

'Yes,' she said firmly. 'Think about it for a moment. There's this elf, OK, and he's doing your maths assignments for you. Consider that action for a moment. Can you tell me what it is?'

I shrugged. 'Bloody useful.'

'Yes, I know. Apart from that. I believe it's a way of getting your attention, saying "Hello, I'm here." Does that make any sense to you?'

'Seems like a reasonable assumption under the circumstances,' I replied. 'So what do you suggest?'

She steepled her fingers, 'Well,' she said. 'The elf wrote to you. Write back.'

Of course, I hadn't even considered that; I'd been too busy trying to figure out how to make a non-lethal mousetrap to contemplate the possibility that I could just sit down with the elf and talk. 'That's a very good idea,' I said.

'Being mine, that goes without saying. Mind you,' she went on, 'that's assuming you know where to put the letter so he'll find it. Also that he can read English. Big ifs.'

I shook my head. 'No, not really,' I replied. 'If he can't read English, how can he write it? As far as reaching him goes, I'll put a message in my diary and another one in each of my written work folders. If he wants to be reached, that ought to reach him.'

Cru was silent for a moment. 'Actually,' she said, 'that's quite sensible. Yes, you could try that, at least as a start. And if it doesn't work, we'll have to think of something else: messages painted on walls, adverts in the newspapers, sky-writing. I guess it depends on how badly he wants to get in touch with you.'

I thought of the tiny letters spelling out HELP. 'It's a lot of trouble and effort for him to go to if he doesn't,' I reasoned. 'And he's not stupid, after all.'

'What makes you think – ? Oh, you mean the maths answers.' She frowned. 'I don't mean to sound downbeat, but mathematical ability doesn't necessarily equate with common sense or intelligence. After all, look at you.'

'Well, quite,' I replied. 'Nevertheless, I think that's what I'll do.' I looked away, breaking eye contact. 'Thanks,' I said.

'You're grudgingly welcome. Thanks for what?'

I sighed. 'For listening. For not letting on that you're trying to humour a lunatic, even if that's what you're actually doing. For – well, lots of things, I suppose.'

'Whatever.' She opened a book and looked at it. I noticed it was the wrong way up. 'Well,' I said, 'I'd better get to it, then. As and when I find anything, I'll tell you straight away.'

'No, you bloody well won't,' she replied. 'Not if it's the middle of the night or I'm busy. Next time you see me will do just fine, thank you all the same.'

So there I was, biro in hand, diary open in front of me, trying to think of something to say.

Not a wholly unfamiliar sensation, at that. In fact, when I look back it seems to me that I've spent a depressingly large proportion of my life doing that sort of thing, starting with Christmas thank-you letters back when I'd only just grasped the concept that ink only came out of one end of the pen, on through hours of hunkering down writing history essays and geography essays and English essays and the like, to the point where my collected works would fill two shelves in the British Museum library and make Dickens look like a minimalist – and every line on every page ground out in spite of a writer's block you could've carved the pyramids from.

My literary compositions are very much like a ten-year-old Citroen: they're a pain to get started, and when they stop they stay stopped. Eventually, after ten minutes of staring blankly at the empty page, I'd decided to begin with *Dear elf* – but that was just plain ridiculous, so I crossed it out and substituted *To whom it may concern*. Once I'd crossed that out as well, my creative battery was effectively flat, and no amount of scowling at the paper or sighing tragically was going to get me up and running again. Unfortunately, I didn't have a choice, so I tore out the page and put down *Hello* instead.

Well, quite; but I told myself that there'd be plenty of time to go back and revise later. The main thing was to crack on and get something down, no matter what. *How are you?* I wrote.

That more or less drained me for the next hour; in fact, to be honest, I think I might have closed my eyes for a moment or so at some stage, because the next thing I was aware of was as light but insistent tugging on the lobe of my right ear; which had somehow wound up pressed to the desktop. *Odd*, I thought, and lifted my head. The tugging stopped, which was nice, but now I could hear a tiny voice calling my name, apparently from a long way away – the tennis courts, perhaps, or the cricket pavilion. I frowned as the sleep started to clear off the windscreen of my mind. Why would anybody be out on the playing field at this time of night?

'I said WAKE UP!' yelled the voice, gradually getting louder with each word. 'Are you deaf or something?' I looked round, towards the window, which was firmly shut. Weirder and weirder.

'No, you bloody fool, down HERE! Oh for crying out loud, can't you – ?'

Down? Down where? I glanced down under my desk, behind my chair; nothing. Maybe I was imagining it; in which case –

'Behind your elbow, bird-brain. No, not that one, the other –'

And there it was. There she was. Shorter than the genuine accept-no-substitutes Barbie and with shorter hair and a rather less pronounced bust; wearing, if memory serves, a light green sleeveless cotton blouse and something that was either a fairly short skirt of a fairly wide belt, depending on how you define such things. She was stunningly lovely and she was holding an unfastened safety pin, which she was just about to stab into my forearm.

'About bloody time, too,' she growled. 'Jesus, you're

stupid. If you had two more brain cells, you'd have a pair.'

I didn't say anything: I was too busy gawping, while what was left of my mind was wondering why at least some of the world's annual allowance of weirdness couldn't happen to somebody else, just for once. For her part, she dumped the safety pin, and stood glowering at me with her arms folded, tiny blue eyes loaded with an infinity of contempt; Sergeant Major Barbie, or My Little Fascist Dictator.

It looked like I'd just got myself a walking, talking, shouting, swearing, living doll.

CHAPTER FIVE

'Excuse me,' I said diffidently, 'but who the hell are you?'

She looked up at me out of two forget-me-not-blue eyes and called me an arsehole. 'How can you say that?' she said. 'After everything I've been through to get here—'

'Sorry,' I interrupted, 'but you've got to tell me this. Are you an elf?'

She sighed. 'No, I'm a chartered actuary. Dressing up in green miniskirts and being only six inches tall is just something I do in my spare time. Of course I'm an elf, you idiot. You should know that,' she added bitterly, 'better than anybody.'

Oh God, I thought, *another of those niggling little oblique references.* Unfortunately, there were more important issues waiting to be addressed, so clearing up that particular mystery was going to have to wait. 'OK,' I said, 'you're an elf, thank you. So – what are you doing here, and why are you doing it?'

For some reason that seemed to annoy her a lot. 'Oh yes,' she said, 'wonderful attitude. That's really going to help, if you keep it up.' She grabbed hold of a book, dragged it three inches across the desktop (remarkably strong, for her size; it must've been the equivalent of a full-sized human hauling a dead cow), and sat down on it as though it were a park bench. 'Serves me right for imagining you'd be different,' she went on. 'But that's me, hopelessly naive, as usual.'

Before I could call her on that, I noticed a shadow falling across the desk, suggesting that someone was standing between me and the light, directly behind me. I froze; no time to do anything.

'Here,' said a voice, 'have you seen my German grammar?'

Neil Fuller – his desk was two down from mine. In fact, the elf had just sat down on the book he was looking for.

'Sorry,' I answered, keeping my eyes fixed on a crack in the plaster on the opposite wall, 'no idea where it could have got to.'

A tongue clicked, and a hand appeared at the extreme edge of my peripheral vision. 'Are you blind or something?' Neil said, and I closed my eyes, so as not to see what was going to happen next. 'It's right here. Look,' he went on, 'under your stupid nose.'

I glanced down, to see a highly vexed female elf sprawling on the desktop where the book had been. But of course it wasn't what I could see that mattered. 'Oh,' I mumbled, '*that* book.'

'Idiot.' Neil sighed and he walked away. I waited till

the door swung shut behind him before looking back.

'He couldn't see you,' I said.

'What?' The elf made a great show of rubbing a purportedly bruised elbow. 'No, of course he couldn't, you fool. He's human.'

I ignored that one, too. Sooner or later I was going to have to deal with this issue, whatever it turned out to be. Later, for choice. 'So,' I said, 'is this anything to do with nobody else being able to read your writing?'

She grinned. 'No magic in that,' she said. 'I don't suppose many of them can read *your* writing, either. Talk about your inky-footed spiders.'

'I'll rephrase that. *See* your writing.'

'Ah.' She nodded. 'Yes, pretty much. There's a whole lot of physics that explains it, but I've had a quick flick through your physics notes, and there isn't a chance in hell that you'd be able to understand any of it. Same goes for whoever dictated those notes, if that's any consolation. I don't know,' she sighed. 'And they call themselves a dominant species.'

'They' in this context presumably being humans. It was getting harder and harder to ignore, but I managed it. Amazing what you can do if you try.

'So only I can see you,' I said. 'Well, that's something, I suppose.'

She lifted her head. 'You sound pleased.'

'You bet I'm pleased. God only knows how we'd keep you hidden if you were visible.'

A tiny eyebrow twitched upwards. 'You want to keep me hidden,' she said. 'Interesting. Why?'

I blinked twice before answering. 'Oh, because there's a school rule against keeping pets. And because if anybody saw you, they'd whisk you off to a government research lab so fast you'd be younger when you arrived than when you left. And before you ask, no, you wouldn't like it in a research lab. Trust me.'

That made her look thoughtful. 'Why should you care?' she said.

'What? Because - well, I just would. It's called compassion. Don't you have it where you come from?'

For some reason, she found that amusing. 'Oh *we*'ve got compassion all right. If you could bottle it and sell it, we'd have a bigger GDP than California. I'm just surprised to find you've heard of it, that's all.'

I nodded. 'I need to talk to you about that sort of stuff,' I said. 'Only not now, if you don't mind. First priority is to find somewhere you'll be safe and out of the way. Then maybe you'll tell me what the hell you're doing here.'

She sighed. 'Escaping,' she said. 'All right, where do you suggest?'

Good question. Excellent question. Where *do* you stash a six-inch-tall humanoid where she won't get squashed, asphyxiated, frozen, eaten or bored to death? 'I know,' I said. 'Look, would you mind getting into my pocket?'

'Yes,' she replied. 'First because I don't entirely trust you, the same way I wouldn't entirely trust a starving hyena. Second because I'm prepared to bet money that in any pocket of any garment you own, there'll be at least one square of squished and melted chocolate impregnated with grit and lint. Third, not on a first date. If you want to give me a lift somewhere, I'll go on your shoulder. Hold still, this might tickle.'

Before I could query or object, she'd jumped onto the back of my hand, run up my arm in defiance of stuffy old gravity, like a spider, and disappeared from my field of view.

'I'M UP HERE,' thundered a deafening voice in my ear. The way in which I winced sharply must've suggested to her that lowering her voice a tad was the polite thing to do. 'I'm sitting on your shoulder,' she said, 'looking straight into your earhole. To my surprise, I can't see the opposite wall, or hear the sea, but at some stage you're either going to have to get your ears syringed or start a candle factory. All right, ready when you are.'

I still think it was a good idea.

'Are you out of your mind?' she said, a few minutes later. 'I'm not getting in that.'

'But it's ideal,' I protested. 'Nobody ever uses it, and you can open the door from the inside.'

'No.'

'Why not?'

'Because,' she snarled. 'Understood?'

I shook my head; a strangled scream and a sharp pain, such as might be caused by someone with sharp fingernails hanging from my earlobe, suggested that it wasn't such a good idea. 'Sorry,' I yelped, and fished vaguely round the side of my head with my left hand. I didn't connect before the pain stopped, implying that she'd managed to get back on my shoulder without my help.

'It's a gas chamber,' she growled.

'No, it isn't,' I replied. 'It's a gas *cooker* – there's a difference. And this one doesn't work, which is why it's been hauled out into this shed. Seclusion, privacy, peace and quiet. You'll soon get to like it, I bet.'

It took her a few tries to get the hang of lifting the catch on the inside of the oven door, but she managed it in the end. 'It's horrible in here,' she called out after I'd shut the door on her for the fifth time. 'It's dark and greasy, the floor's got holes in it, and it smells disgusting.'

'Same goes for Manchester,' I replied, 'and thousands of people live there quite happily. Now come out, because I want to ask you something.'

The door swung open. I looked in, but I couldn't see the elf. 'Hello?' I called.

– Whereupon the elf suddenly appeared, out of thin air. Just like they do in *Star Trek*, only without the shimmering lights and the distinctive whoinging noise.

'Made you look,' the elf said, smirking.

'Oh great,' I muttered. 'You can make yourself invisible to me, too. Hey, will you please not do that? It really pisses me off.'

She shrugged. 'All right,' she said. 'It's an absolute pain to do, anyhow. And before you ask, no, I can't make it so mortals can see me. I can just make myself visible to other – well, to you. What was it you wanted to ask me about?'

I took a deep breath and shifted my weight onto my other knee. 'Let's start at the beginning, shall we? I suppose you've got a name.'

'Yes, but—' she hesitated.

'What's the matter?' I asked. 'Is there some kind of taboo about people knowing your true name?'

'No, I just don't like it very much.'

'Really?' I smiled. 'Come on, it can't be that bad.'

'You reckon?' she said, with a wry grin. 'All right, three guesses.'

I thought for a moment. 'Rumpelstiltskin, Peaseblossom. Am I warm?'

'No, just extremely annoying. Hurry up and use your imagination. You see, unless you've had your three guesses – properly, I mean, not just saying the first thing that comes into your head – it isn't going to work.'

'Fine,' I said. 'All right: Thumbelina, and that's my best offer.'

'Nope.' Her shoulders hunched and she looked the other way. 'If you really must know, it's Melissa.'

'Melissa? That's a nice name. Well, quite nice. Nothing wrong with it, anyhow.'

'Nothing wrong?' She was angry now. Suited her better. 'Melissa's a *human* name, it's downright embarrassing. God, it was bad enough when I was at school, with all the other kids teasing and chanting. *Melissa is a hu-man, Melissa is a hu-man* every single bloody playtime. And making fun of my ears.'

'There's nothing wrong with your ears,' I said, crossing my fingers behind my back. 'They're very, um, pointy.'

'Well, of course they damn' well are. But the kids at school, they pretended they weren't, just to be hurtful. You get sick of that sort of thing really quickly, believe me.'

Well, she wasn't going to get any arguments from me on that score. Nevertheless, I didn't have time for angst, even if legitimately acquired. 'Now,' I said, 'will you please tell me – in terms I can understand - what you're doing here. Please?' I added, on the off chance that she'd respond well to abject pleading.

She sat down on the oven floor, her chin resting on her hands. 'Like I told you,' she said, 'only maybe you didn't hear me with all that wax in your ears. I've escaped. And,' she said quickly, 'I'm not going back, and you can't make me.'

'I wouldn't dream of trying,' I replied. 'Escaped from where, exactly?'

This time she looked at me slightly differently; still the same level of contempt per kilowatt of stare, but a different sort of contempt. 'You don't know, do you?' she said. 'You really don't know. Well, bugger me. I wouldn't have thought anybody, not even a human – dammit, not even a small rock at the bottom of a disused mine shaft – could be that unobservant, but clearly I was wrong. Only goes to show,' she concluded, with a shrug.

'Show what?'

'Huh?'

'Only goes to show what?' I repeated. 'What is this thing I obviously don't know about?'

Long pause. 'If you don't know,' she said, 'I'm not sure I ought to tell you. Let me think about it for a moment, OK?'

I sighed. 'Please yourself,' I said. 'All right, so you've escaped from somewhere, and now you're here. So why did you do my maths questions for me?'

That provoked a tiny but ferocious scowl. 'If that's your idea of gratitude—'

'Oh, I'm grateful,' I interrupted. 'Really, it was very kind of you. But why did you do it?'

She shook her head. 'Bored, mostly. Besides, it was pretty bloody easy. Only took me five minutes.'

I managed to keep the soft growling noise down to an inaudible level. 'You were bored.'

'Well, yes. And,' she conceded, 'after you made it possible for me to escape – not intentionally, I know, but who gives a damn? All that stuff about it being the thought that counts is just a load of old socks spread around by people who got really lousy Chrissy presents when they were kids. Sorry, where was I? Oh yes. You let me escape, and you gave me a lift down here, so I felt I ought to do something, just by way of saying thanks. Though I should add that it's bloody dark and horrible inside your briefcase. You ought to give it a good clean-out. There's small, nasty things living in it.'

'Apparently so. You, for one.'

'Not living,' she pointed out, 'just passing through. And don't be so horrible to me. Especially after I did you maths for you.'

Well, it had to be said. 'Thanks, anyway. It was a nice thought, and I appreciate it. Only—'

'Only?'

'Only it's sort of missing the point. I mean, how'll I ever learn to do that stuff if you do my problems for me? And if I get picked on in class and told to explain my workings, I'll just be sat there opening and shutting my mouth like a goldfish singing karaoke.'

There was enough concentrated venom in the look she gave me to poison a major reservoir.

'Well, thoughtless old me,' she said. 'Actually, it's your own fault for being too bone idle or boneheaded to learn the stuff yourself, so don't you go blaming me. Bloody hell, if you can't manage simple stuff like this, maybe you ought to consider switching special subjects and doing something a bit more on your wavelength, like media studies or woodwork.' She stopped and scowled. 'Why are you looking at me like that?'

I hadn't realised I was. 'Like what?'

'Like you just found me in the bottom of your lunch-box and you can't decide whether to eat me or call in the Air Force. Something's on your mind, I think. Of course, it'd have to be something pretty small, or it'd overbalance and fall off, but—'

'Ah yes,' I said. 'Now I think I know what it is. You remind me of someone.'

Suddenly she seemed to shut down, as though I'd switched off the power. 'Really?'

I nodded. 'You don't look much like her,' I said. 'And I'm not just talking about size, she's not as – well, she looks different. But you sound a lot like her – voice, and turns of phrase, that sort of thing.'

'How fascinating. I don't believe you, of course. I mean,' she added, trying to sound bored and superior, 'from what I can gather, you've lived most of your life among *humans*, so any resemblance'd have to be fairly superficial.'

She was lying. Well, lying's maybe the wrong word, but she was definitely trying to misdirect me in some fashion. 'Oh, I don't know,' I said. 'Now you're doing just what she'd do if I got onto a subject she didn't want to talk about. You're being extra-specially obnoxious, so I won't notice you change the subject.'

'Who the bloody hell are you calling obnoxious, you tall . . . ?'

I let her rant on for a moment or so while I considered what I'd just said. I suppose I hadn't really noticed the remarkable similarity between the elf's way of talking to me and Cru's, presumably because I was so used to being insulted by girls that it just seemed normal. Now I'd made myself aware of it, however, I couldn't see past it: there were differences, sure, but the resemblance was too close to ignore. 'All right,' I broke in, interrupting her in mid-tirade, 'let's deal with this human thing. Who the hell are you, and what do you know about me that I don't?'

She sighed, a long, rather musical sigh that seemed to start somewhere down around her ankles. 'We-ell,' she said, 'if you really don't know, I suppose it's only fair to tell you, before you make life really difficult for yourself. Not to mention for us,' she added, in a distinctly odd tone of voice. 'Only problem is trying to get the idea across to you in human terms. It'd be like trying to explain quantum theory to a water vole.'

I frowned. 'Try me,' I said.

She thought for a moment. 'No,' she said eventually, 'it'll be far easier to show you. I'm not supposed to,' she added, 'but we won't worry about that now. Besides, I'm going that way anyway. And,' she said, looking away awkwardly, 'I need your help to get there.'

'*You* need *my* help?'

'All right, don't make a six-part miniseries out of it,' she snapped. 'You'll be amazed to hear that I'm not actually all that thrilled about having to go begging and pleading with a tall – with a compactness-challenged person about anything, let alone something as important – oh, the hell with it. Are you going to help me or not?'

I shrugged. 'Depends,' I said. 'Is it dangerous? Will it hurt? And how long's it going to take, because if I'm not careful, I'm going to be late for—' I paused. She was laughing. 'Sorry, what's so unbearably amusing about that?'

'Nothing,' she said around a mouthful of giggles. 'Nothing at all. Elf stuff. Don't you worry about it. As far as you're concerned—' Big snigger. 'Far as you're concerned, it'll take no time at all.'

Well, that didn't sound so bad. 'And it won't hurt?'

'You won't feel a thing. Promise.'

'All right. And then you'll explain.'

'It'll all become as clear as crystal, just you wait and see. Well, don't just stand there like a lovesick prune. This way.'

I had my doubts, of course. Unfortunately, the Pavlovian urge to obey overrode the soft whinnying of my vestigial self-preservation instinct. 'Okay,' I said. 'Where are we going? There's nothing out this way but sheds and dustbins.'

'That's what you think,' she replied without looking round, as she strode out of the door like a cross between Tinkerbell and Xena. 'That's because you're pathetically unobscrvant, as I think I may have mentioned already. Ah, here we go. I was sure I'd seen it on the way over, and here it is.'

I looked down, and saw a circular bald patch in the scruffy grass where, by the looks of it, a dustbin had stood until very recently. 'That's it?'

'I just told you, yes.' She stood on the edge of the ring, rubbing her chin thoughtfully. 'It's going to be a hell of a squeeze getting you in there with those ridiculous great big feet of yours, but we'll just have to manage somehow. That's it,' she continued, as I went and stood where she was pointing. 'Now, make sure that your whole foot's inside the ring.'

She was right, it was a tight fit. Believe me, it's a bizarre feeling having a very attractive six-inch-tall woman nestling in a hostile manner close against the calf of one's leg.

'Is that all right?' I asked.

'Absolutely not, you've got the big toe of your left foot three-eighths of an inch over the line.'

'Have I really? Does it matter?'

Force six scowl. 'Up to you,' she said. 'Just remember, while you're making your mind up, anything you don't take with you gets left behind. This includes clothes, footwear and, most of all, toes. Now, then: on three. One, two—'

I twitched my foot back just as she said the T word, and on balance I'm glad that I did, even though it meant that I inadvertently kicked my small companion in the stomach and knocked her over. Now, this wouldn't have mattered particularly (to me, at least, except on ethical and social grounds) if she'd stayed six inches tall; there would have been a small, irate girl yelling at me down at ankle level, but I've put up with far worse than that in my time. Where it all started to go wrong was the point where she started to grow.

Melissa put on five and a half feet in about a quarter of a second.

This complicated matters. Where, not so long before, there'd been something weighing maybe a pound and a half pressing against my ankle, there was now a mass roughly equivalent to that of a medium-sized farrier's anvil. Curiously enough, I heard the snap before I felt the pain.

More agonisingly late than never, though, if you see what I mean; when the pain eventually came on line a whole microsecond later (we apologise for the late running of this service &c &c) there was enough of it to fill up my senses like a well-presented pint of Guinness. I'm only mentioning this, not out of some rather pathetic attempt to gain sympathy, but to explain why I wasn't really paying much mind to the extraordinary miracle going on all around me.

Pity, really. And typical of my luck, needless to say. At

the precise moment when everything changed out of all recognition (while staying exactly the same in virtually every respect), I was squirming on the deck in agony, yelling, 'Get off me, get off me!' to a six-foot-tall female sprawling across my right thigh. Like I just said, typical; dammit, the sprawling alone should've been the most fun I'd ever had in my life, and of course I missed out on that, too.

I guess she must've removed herself, because the pain grew slightly less unbearably awful. Reconstructing the order of events with the benefit of hindsight, my guess is that she rolled sideways and scrambled up before she started yelling at me. At any rate, I tuned out the yelling (years of experience) and concentrated on the suffering and self-pity aspects, where at least I was doing something I was good at.

Then, quite suddenly, there was another click; except that this one was, for want of a better word, an unclick, the same sound as before only reversed. The pain stopped – of course, pain doesn't do that, it fades out like the end of a track on a record, but this time it was immediate, as though nasty Mr Pain had driven into a brick wall. And serve him right.

'Uh?' I said.

'Idiot,' she replied. 'Anyway, we're here.'

I wasn't expecting a comment like that, since I hadn't been aware of travelling any distance, unless you counted a short, fast journey in the Y axis. 'My leg,' I said. 'It's better.'

'I fixed it,' she said, with the air of someone getting an irrelevant detail out of the way. 'Double green-stick fracture of the left shin. That's perfectly all right, don't mention it, you're very welcome.'

'Thank you,' I said. 'What the bloody hell do you mean, you fixed it? and how do you know what sort of a—'

'Shut *up*, for pity's sake,' she said. 'We're here.' Her voice was suddenly different. 'I'm here. Home.'

'But you can't just fix a broken leg just like—' Then I noticed something out of the corner of my eye and sat up to look about me; after which I stopped worrying about my leg, or how come it was suddenly unbroken. Priorities, you see. Legs are all very well in their place, but there's other things in life.

I knew where I was, of course; I could've drawn a map blindfold, and marked the place where I was sitting with an X. There was the shed we'd just come from; behind that were the other outbuildings, and fifty yards or so in the other direction were the tennis courts and the football pavilion, all exactly where they should be.

Except that they weren't.

Let me try and hook my fingernails over the edge of coherence here, and try to explain. In the places where there should have been buildings, there were buildings, and the buildings were more or less the size and shape they should have been. But where there ought to have been rather crummy creosoted timber and galvanised steel sheet (that's our school for you: all Victorian Gothic out front, and scruffy as Albert Steptoe's junk-yard round the back), there was mellow golden stone and new thatch the colour of Dutch salted butter. Likewise, the grass should've been thin, patchy and scrawny, covering the mud like the residual traces of hair on Daddy George's bald patch. Instead, it was thick, even, and I think the word I'm looking for is ver-dant: Hollywood grass, costing more per square metre than best-quality Axminster carpet. Even the sky - the sky, dammit, was this amazingly *blue* shade of blue, like a very unconvincing background matte on a film. In England, in January? Get real, will you?

'What?' I asked.

Melissa was looking at me. She hadn't changed at all, except that now she was much, much taller, and somehow, during the thirty seconds or so since she'd said the word 'three', her hair had formed itself into a ferociously complicated-looking plait. There was another change, too, now I come to think of it, even more drastic and improbable than the instant hairdo. She looked happy.

'Well,' she said, 'here we are. Welcome to Elfland.'

CHAPTER SIX

'Don't be silly,' I said. 'this is round the back of the main buildings. We're in the Home Counties. England. Earth.'

Melissa laughed; and although she was laughing at me, there wasn't any cruelty in it. 'You're absolutely right,' she said. 'That's precisely where we are. Isn't it *wonderful*.'

I didn't say anything for a moment. All right, yes, she'd obviously gone barking mad at some point in the last couple of minutes, but there was an argument for saying that this was no bad thing, since it seemed to have done wonders for her attitude. On the other hand, anybody who could use the word 'wonderful' to describe the wasteland round the back of the school sheds was quite possible a danger to herself and others and oughtn't to have been out loose.

'Sorry,' I said mildly, just in case her mental condition

involved sudden extreme mood-swings, 'but I'd rather got the impression that you said we'd gone somewhere. And didn't you just . . .?'

She nodded, beaming like an angel (or, depending on your point of view, an imbecile). 'That's right, she said, yes. This is Elfland, where I come from. Do you like it? Isn't it fantastic?'

Well, the weather was an improvement and the architecture wasn't bad; likewise the grass, if grass is something that really matters to you. But it was still round the back of the sheds, or so she'd have me believe. 'Please tell me what's going on,' I pleaded. 'This is beginning to worry me.'

'I'm sorry,' she said –

Just in case you're as amazed as I was, I'll just repeat that.

'I'm sorry,' she said. 'I'm being thoughtless. It's just – well, being back here after such a long time . . . And I'm just starting to feel like I'm *me* again. You've no idea how utterly wonderful that is.' She frowned, with a side salad of guilt. 'Do I sound different?' she asked.

I paused. 'Do you want me to answer that?' I asked.

She nodded. 'It's very important that you're completely honest,' she said.

'Ah, right. Fine. In that case, yes, you do sound different. Nicer. Less of a horrible sarcastic bitch, if you follow me.'

She nodded gravely. 'That's how I see it too,' she said. 'You know, that's awful. It must mean that all the time I was there I was this really nasty unpleasant person—' She stopped, and a tiny teardrop welled up in the corner of her eye, like a small leak in a sink trap joint. 'I can remember,' she said unhappily. 'I'm remembering some of the horrid things I've said to you.' Pause. Sniff. 'Oh Michael, I'm so very sorry—'

Just a minute, I thought, *what's going on?* 'That's very nice of you,' I said, 'but I only met you about an hour ago, so I don't suppose it's done me any lasting psychological damage. Besides, compared with what I'm used to—'

'An hour ago?' She looked utterly bewildered. 'Oh, of course, you don't know yet. Oh dear.' Then, just to complicate things, she started crying.

People who cry when they're sad – well, they're a pain in the bum most of the time, but at least you can see where they're coming from. People who cry when they're *happy*, on the other hand, are an unmitigated nuisance and it's high time something was done about it. Now. I don't know; the government spends millions of pounds of your tax money on guided missiles and clogging up perfectly good roads with speed bumps, but can you persuade them to part with a bent nickel to deal with the growing menace of happy cryers? Can you hell as like.

Difficult to know what to do for the best. Quite possibly it was one of those situations that calls for the arm round the shoulders and the reassuring hug; but maybe it wasn't, in which case well-intentioned physical intervention might earn me a busted jaw followed by a long holiday in a mailbag factory. My theory is that until you know the locals' habits, customs and culture to Ph.D. level or preferably beyond, you're best off not pawing them about if there's any doubt in your mind whatsoever concerning how such contact's going to be interpreted.

On the other hand, standing there like a short, defective telegraph pole while the poor girl sobbed her eyes out was as clear a case of boorish male insensitivity as you're ever likely to see, and if there's one thing women can't be doing with (trust me on this one) it's boorish male insensitivity. Which would be worse – a boot in the nuts followed by a jail sentence, or long-term ongoing aggravation on the missed-birthday level - has got to be a matter of personal taste rather than objective judgement.

A tricky one, in fact. I decided that the best I could do was stand by and hope she'd notice and appreciate the waves of unspoken but palpable sympathy and support I was broadcasting straight at her, like some kind of emotional Bush House. Luckily, the tear-fest only lasted about a minute.

'I'm sorry,' she said (that made twice, in one day), 'it's just that I've been away for so long and there were times when I thought I was never going to get back here, and I'd be stuck there for the rest of my life, and – well, that my life was going to have a rest, instead of just—' She paused. 'None of this is really making any sense to you, is it?'

I shrugged. 'Well, no,' I replied. 'But sense isn't everything, God knows. Still, if you could see your way clear to giving me just a small explanation . . . Doesn't have to be the true one,' I added quickly, as another dangerous surge of snuffles threatened to sweep in from the northeast, 'just so long as it makes me feel better, and I can go home.'

And that, believe it or not, made her *laugh*. Bloody hell fire in a bucket; you know, on balance I think bewildering laughers are possibly an even worse menace than happy cryers. Round up the lot of 'em and nuke 'em till they glow, is my recommendation.

'You can't go home, silly,' she said.

'Can't I?' That didn't sound good. 'Oh.'

'No, of course not. You can't *go* home when you're already there, can you?'

Under any other circumstances, that would be the sort of ambient weirdness level that would prompt me to make a quick scuttle for the nearest exit. Tragically, that option wasn't really available; my leg was better, sure, but I now had more pins and needles in it than all the John Lewises in Christendom put together. That only left the back-up plan, namely staying put and trying to get some sense out of the dozy bitch. Well, I say back-up plan. It was a back-up plan the way hitting the ground after falling off the top of the Empire State building is a back-up plan for forward-thinking hang-glider pilots.

'Home,' I repeated. 'That's not here, that's in South Bucks. This is school. Home from home, maybe, but—'

'No, listen,' she said, and in spite of everything I had to take the time out to savour the difference. Ever so many girls have said 'No' to me since in a dazzlingly wide range of contexts, and quite a few have also said 'Listen'. But the way she said it was completely different. Nicer, if you get my meaning. 'Sorry,' she went on (third time!), 'I didn't mean to interrupt. But I do think it'd be much better if I started from the beginning. What do you think?'

What did *I* think? Bloody hell. Now I knew I wasn't in Kansas any more. 'I think that'd be wonderful,' I told her. 'Please, go on.'

'Well, if you're sure.'

'I'm sure. Really.'

'All right. Here goes. This is Elfland. I'm an elf. My

name is Melissa.' She paused. 'How are you doing?' she asked. 'All clear so far?'

I pursed my lips. 'Almost,' I said. 'There's just one small point, though. We were round the back of the sheds – those sheds,' I added, pointing. 'I don't seem to remember going anywhere.'

Another laugh. Silvery, possibly even quicksilver. 'That's not how you get to Elfland,' she said. 'It's more a case of staying where you are and hoping you can lure Elfland into coming to you.'

Now that conjured up a sheaf of mental images that I'd probably have enjoyed flicking through if things hadn't been so fraught. Worlds that come when you call. Planet-training classes. *Here, Elfland*, I thought, *good Elfland, down, boy; leave; leave it, for crying out loud, sit . . .*

'Hello?' she said. 'For a moment there you were miles away.' She grinned suddenly. 'No pun intended,' she added.

'I'm here,' I replied. 'And Elfland can't be gone to, it just sort of comes and gets you. Right so far?'

'I knew you'd get the hang of it, an intelligent person like you. The fact is, Elfland and where the humans live are really all just one place. The difference is only a matter of perception, like how things look different with and without sunglasses: same thing you're looking at, but what you see isn't quite the same. All right so far?'

Furtively I tried moving my leg, but it was still doing the ingrowing-porcupine bit. 'I think so,' I replied. 'You're saying that Elfland and the, um, other place, they both occupy the same spot.'

'Exactly.' Big happy beaming smile. Enough to scare a man to death, seeing so much quality ivory stacked up in one place. 'Like, there's only one radio but you can get loads and loads of different channels in it.'

'I see,' I lied. 'All right, so now I know about Elfland. How do I leave?'

She laughed. Double silvery with extra silver. 'Do you want to?'

Hadn't thought about that. 'Well,' I said, 'I can't stay here, can I? Can I?'

'Of course.' She took a deep breath, as if she was trying to inhale the whole sky. 'Oh, it's so *wonderful* to be back, and to be *me* again . . .' She paused, as if she'd just realised she'd said something extremely tactless. 'Not that there was anything wrong with – I mean, I know you were very fond of her, but—'

'Hold it,' I said. (I know, since when was I all forceful and self-confident and able to talk to girls without trying to swallow my tongue?) 'Who's this 'her' you're talking about?'

She looked down at the ground. And very nice ground it was too, but I don't think that was why she was looking at it. 'Me,' she said.

'You?'

She nodded. 'Cruella Watson.'

Do you ever get days like that, when you wake up and it seems like all the rules have subtly changed while you've been asleep, and everybody else except you knows the new version? I hate it when that happens, mostly because I can never quite get past the instinctive feeling that it's somehow my fault. I don't know what you're supposed to do about it. It'd all be so much easier if I could find the instruction booklet that should've come with me when I was born.

'Please,' I said, 'don't take this the wrong way, but you

aren't Cruella Watson. You can trust me on this one, really. For a start, you're taller and your hair's a different colour and you aren't a—'

She smiled, and shook her head. 'You don't understand,' she said. 'I'm Cruella Watson *here*.'

'All right,' I said doubtfully. 'So, who's Cruella Watson *there*?'

'She is, of course. Cruella Watson. And here, I'm Melissa. Don't you see?'

At least I knew the answer to that one. 'No,' I said.

She sighed. 'It's my fault,' she said. 'I knew it was going to be tricky to try and explain it in words, and it's not something I'm terribly good at, so I decided I'd bring you here and hope that'd make you able to figure it out for yourself. and now I think you're even more confused than you were. Sorry.'

Four times now. Definitely not Cruella; not my Cruella, at any rate. Sure, Cru did know the word, and I'd even heard her use it a few times, but only in conjunction with phrases like *excuse for a human being*, referring to guess who.

Then, suddenly I understood. No, that's overstating the case. But suddenly I could just about imagine a potential scenario where understanding might just possibly occur. 'Excuse me,' I said. 'I want to think for a moment. Is that all right?'

'Sure,' she said. 'I'm in no hurry.'

I turned away and looked round, trying to take in what I saw. She'd been right, of course. It was the same place, only different.

Of course. It was that simple.

For example; about sixty-five yards away due east there was a tree. Now I knew that tree pretty well;

nothing special, taciturn, morose, lousy conversation-
alist, just a tree under which I occasionally sat when I
was in a miserable mood and wanted an appropriate
setting. That tree was exactly where it had always been,
and as far as I could tell (I don't know much about that
stuff) it was the same type or variety or breed or make
of tree that it's always been. But here, it was also totally
different; here, it was a cheerful, optimistic, empow-
ered tree. Its branches seemed to be pushing upwards
instead of drooping under the unfair burden of gravity.
Its leaves were just a little thicker and greener – it
didn't give the impression of having bald patches with
leaves carefully combed over them. Same tree, only
different.

Okay. If it worked for trees, why not for people?
Maybe this place, or this version of the same place (I
steered my mind round that one before it got bogged
down in it) had exactly the same people as the place I
came from, but they were all different. Quantitatively
similar, but qualitatively divergent. Nicer.

Much nicer.

Well, there was one way of testing this hypothesis.
'Excuse me,' I said, 'but are there other people here I'm
likely to know?'

She laughed. 'Of course there are. Go on; name
someone, and we'll go and see if we can find him.'

You know what it's like when you've got to pick a
name at random; my mind went so blank you could've
projected movies on it. After an embarrassing pause the
only name I could think of was Neil Fuller (you remember Neil; he was the one who was looking for his
German grammar, when Melissa was sitting on it), so
that was who I nominated.

She thought for a moment. 'Ah yes,' she said. 'I expect he'll be in the west cloister.'

'Oh' Highly unlikely place for Neil to be, a cloister. Not unless there was something there he could steal, or he was meeting some girl. 'Can we go and look?'

'Sure,' she said; and as soon as she'd said it, there we were, back in the study area. Except that it was (also/instead) a definite and unmistakable cloister, with big arched unglazed windows looking out on a central courtyard and a rather attractive marble fountain.

'Hey,' I objected, 'how the hell did you do that?'

She looked startled. 'What do you mean? Oh,' she added, 'you mean how did we get here. We walked.'

I closed my eyes and tried to count to ten, but it didn't work. 'No we *didn't*,' I said. 'One moment we were out there, next moment we're here.'

She clapped her hands, as if applauding. '*Exactly*', she said. 'There were two moments, one there and one here. Plus a lot of other moments in between, during which we walked across the grass, in through the back gate, across the lobby, up a flight of stairs, across the scriptorium, past the dorter, down another flight of stairs and out under a low arch where we turned right to reach this place. But they were rather dull and boring moments and I got the impression you're in a hurry and want to get all this stuff sorted out in your mind, so I left them out.'

I gave up trying to stay cool and just stared at her. 'You left them out?'

She nodded. 'That's right. We can do that here. Time works in a rather different way.'

'Different.'

Another nod. 'Nicer.'

'Ah.' this time I tried taking a deep breath; waste of time and effort. 'You mean to say that if you don't want to bother with the dull and boring bits of your life, you can just sort of fast-forward them? Like the adverts on TV?'

'Precisely.' She sighed again. She was very good at sighing. Graceful melancholy, very tastefully done. 'You know,' she said, 'when I was stuck in – well, in your place, I thought I was going to go mad, having to live through every second of every day. How you people can stand it, I really can't imagine. You must be so brave.'

I'll admit, I'd never thought of it in that light before. Typical: I get to be a hero and never know it. 'So,' I went on, trying to clarify, 'I've just been for a two-hundred-yard walk which I don't remember a thing about—'

'Don't you?' She looked surprised. Her surprise wasn't quite up to her sighing, but it wasn't bad. 'Are you sure about that?'

'Well, yes. No,' I corrected myself, because I'd been wrong; I *could* remember it, once I'd found the right place in my mind to look. I could see myself trotting up the stairs, down the stairs, past the wrought-iron lamp sconces set into the walls—

Weird. Where the hell had wrought-iron lamp sconces come from?

'You can remember it, can't you?' she said, with a gentle smile.

'All right,' I conceded, 'yes. But it never happened. Did it?'

'Of course it did. Tell you what – after we've found your friend, we'll walk back, and he can be a witness. Will that do?'

I'd forgotten all about the quest for Neil Fuller. 'First things first,' I said. 'Where is he? I can't see—'

And suddenly, there he was, complete with a full memory of having stood around for half an hour waiting for me; but I skipped over that. One thing at a time, after all.

Neil Fuller. Unmistakably Neil Fuller – only he was six foot two, with light brown hair tied up in a ponytail, wearing what looked to me like a Robin Hood outfit from a rather upmarket fancy-dress hire place and – much more bizarre – looking pleased to see me.

'There you are,' he said. 'I was beginning to wonder when you'd show up. Oh, hi there, Melissa,' he added, with a polite little wave. 'Glad to see you're back with us.'

I cleared my throat nervously, as though I was about to make a speech in front of the whole school. 'Excuse me,' I said, 'but are you Neil Fuller?'

His grin was so broad that I was surprised his face didn't unzip. 'Of course I am,' he replied, whereupon he grabbed my hand and started shaking it enthusiastically. 'My name's Arganthonius, by the way,' he added. 'Welcome to Elfland.'

Now there comes a point – and God help you if you ever reach it – when the lunatic drivel starts making sense. Well – let me qualify that a little. It's sense, Jim, but not as we know it. I looked the newcomer in his clear, bright golden eyes, smiled as pleasantly as I could, and said, 'Did you manage to find the book you were looking for?'

He laughed. 'You know perfectly well I did,' he replied. 'You were there, remember? And so was Melissa. She was sitting on it.'

'Ah,' I said. 'Thanks.'

I turned to walk away, but the Fuller elf wasn't done with me yet. 'Well,' he said, 'how do you like it here?'

Tact; always tact. 'It's just fine,' I said. 'Very nice architecture. Good sky.'

The Fuller elf nodded. 'It'll take you a while to get settled in,' he said. 'Hardly surprising,' he added. 'It must be pretty disconcerting, coming home for the first time.'

I didn't reply to that, and he let me alone and turned to the Melissa female. 'Welcome back,' he said gravely. 'You were gone a long time.'

She nodded. 'Too long. But I'm back now. All that stuff is just – memories.'

Funny way she said the last word, though one more piece of weirdness was like a very brief shower of rain in mid-Atlantic as far as I was concerned. 'Precisely,' he said. 'So, what're we going to do about—?'

About *him*, he meant – referring to me. I swung round – I hate it when people talk about me behind my back to my face, if you see what I mean - and said, 'Can I make a suggestion?'

'Of course,' said the Fuller elf.

'Fire away,' the Melissa female confirmed.

When it actually came to it, I couldn't think of a better way of putting it than, 'Take me to your leader.' So that was what I said. I didn't add on the bit about coming in peace, because that would have been just plain silly.

'Ah,' Melissa said, 'that could be awkward. We don't have one.'

I shrugged. 'All right,' I said. 'Then take me to your national assembly, parliament, congress, board of directors, general purposes committees or Christmas thrift club. Please?' I put in, because it always helps to be polite.

'Haven't got any of those,' the Fuller elf said. 'That's not how we do things here, I'm afraid. Will we do instead?'

I sighed. 'I don't know,' I admitted. 'It's hard figuring out who's the best person to ask when you don't really know what the question is.'

'Tell us what you think the question is,' the Fuller elf suggested, 'and maybe we can help you.'

'All right,' I said. 'Who am I?'

The two pointy-eared ones looked at each other. 'Good question,' the Fuller elf said. He was starting to get on my nerves.

Melissa took a deep breath. 'Here goes,' she said. 'In your world, that's easy. You're Michael.'

'Thank you,' I replied. 'How about here? Since everything and everyone in my world seems to have a counterpart here, I suppose I must have one too. Yes?'

'No.'

Yeah, right. Just when you think there's a tiny thread of spider's web connecting the monolithic blocks of weirdness. 'There isn't,' I repeated. 'Oh.'

'That's the whole point,' Melissa said, with a slight catch in her voice. 'That's why it's all so difficult, in your case. You see, you're Michael here too. You're the only person in the whole world—'

'Both whole worlds,' the Fuller elf interrupted, presumably under the impression that he was helping.

'– Both whole worlds, thank you, who's the same on both sides.' Melissa bit her lip; not something you see every day, your actual perplexed lip-biting, but she did it exceptionally well. 'It's what makes you unique.'

Me. Unique. Probably just as well, of course. 'Really,' I said, and if I sounded just a tad sceptical, can you really blame me?

'Yes,' Melissa said. 'Which is absolutely wonderful, of course, because it meant you were able to save me. Nobody else in the world could've done that, and I'm really, really grateful. But it does—'

'Complicate things rather,' put in the Fuller elf. 'In fact, we aren't quite sure what to do.'

I sniffed. Well, if they could all do melodramatic gestures, so could I. 'Tell you what,' I said. 'You could appoint a leader and ask him.'

Yeah, well. It was supposed to be bitingly sarcastic, but I guess I wasn't exactly at the peak of my form.

Melissa took a step forward, then stopped. She looked extremely uncomfortable, and my diagnosis was either an intolerable moral dilemma or itchy underwear. 'It's because of what you are,' she said. 'Who you are. I think it's about time I told you.'

The Fuller elf gave her an are-you-sure-that's-wise look. I decided I didn't like him one bit. She replied with a little dip of the head. It made her hair sway in a quite enchanting fashion, but I really wasn't in the mood.

'Well,' I said.

Melissa looked at me gravely. 'I think perhaps you should sit down first.'

'How?' I objected. 'There aren't any—'

'—Chairs,' I continued, leaning back against the extremely soft and comfortable cushions of this really neat old-fashioned armchair. We were sitting on either side of a roaring fire in a gorgeous old oak-panelled hall that was, bizzarely, also the school gym. I clearly remembered getting there. 'All right,' I conceded. 'Look, would it be too much to ask for you to warn me the next time you do that? It makes my head hurt.'

'Sorry,' said the Fuller elf. 'My fault, I forgot you aren't used to it.'

I shrugged. 'That's all right,' I said. 'And now I'm sitting comfortably, can we begin?'

I could tell from the look of Melissa's face that she really didn't want to. Tough. I scowled at her, and she nodded.

'This may come as a bit of a shock,' she said.

Didn't say anything. No point.

'The thing is . . .' She paused, squeezing her left hand with her right – her dazzling repertoire of truly corny gestures was probably the most amazing thing I encountered in the whole of Elfland.

'Your father,' she said. 'Your real father—'

'Yes, I know all that,' I said. 'Daddy George isn't really my dad. My real father buggered off when I was just a kid. Was that what you were going to tell me?'

'You're sort of warmish,' Melissa replied wretchedly. The Fuller elf, meanwhile, was gazing at a small grey stain in the carpet as if it was the most amazing thing he'd ever seen in his life. *Coward*, I thought. Have I mentioned that I didn't like him very much?

'So,' she went on, 'you don't remember your real father?'

I shook my head.

'There's a reason for that,' Melissa said. 'You see, the man you call Daddy George - well, he actually *is* your real father.'

I started to get up, but it was one of those chairs from which you have to gradually work yourself free, like a bit of shrapnel in an old war wound. 'That's not true,' I said. 'My mum told me—'

'I'm afraid she wasn't being absolutely straight with you,' Melissa said. 'Daddy George really is your father. In a sense,' she added.

'In a sense?'

'In a sense,' she repeated. She was so obviously upset about something that under any other circumstances I'd have felt sorry for her. 'Oh dear, how can I put this? *A* Daddy George is quite definitely your father. But not perhaps the one you'd be likely to think of first.'

A very nasty, creepy thought was beginning to scamper across my mind. '*A* Daddy George?' I parroted.

'That's right. You see, there's two. Just like there's two of everybody. One in your world,' she said, the words coming out like pulled teeth, 'and one in ours. And the one who actually – well, your real father . . .'

I closed my eyes. I'm not the world's most naturally intuitive person, but I didn't want to see it coming.

'Your real father,' Melissa said, 'is our Daddy George. The one from our side of the line, not yours. Which makes you—'

My hands started towards my ears, but I have pretty slow reactions. Explains why I've always been lousy at catching things, or tennis.

'Which makes you,' Melissa said, 'an elf.'

CHAPTER SEVEN

I have this recurring nightmare. It's the one where I'm asleep and I'm dreaming that I'm a fairly average normal sort of a guy, meandering along quietly through life, nothing much happening – wake up, slice of toast and cup of coffee, then out into the world to do whatever it is I do. And just when this part of the dream is getting so normal as to be screamingly dull, I wake up and discover that I'm not a human being at all, I'm a small green bug hanging upside down off the underside of a leaf, *dreaming* I'm human.

Don't you just hate it when your dreams come true?

Well, yes. Elves aren't bugs. But it's a dream, damn it, not a simultaneous equation.

'What did you just say?' I asked quietly.

'You're an elf,' Melissa repeated. To her credit, she seemed very upset about it all. 'Or at least, half an elf. Your mother's a human, of course, so—'

'Half an elf,' I said.

'That's right, yes,' the Fuller elf cut in. 'Which means, you see, that there can only be one of you; not a human version on the other side of the line and an elf version over here, like everyone else. Which is also why you can go across the line from there to here. Which is wonderful,' he went on, trying to sound cheerful, 'because you were able to bring Melissa back with you. Isn't that great?'

'I'm half an elf,' I repeated. 'My mother's human, and my father's the elf version of Daddy George. Fine. *Now* can I go home, please?'

The Fuller elf squirmed a little bit in his chair. 'Melissa,' he said, 'maybe we ought to have told him all about it—'

I'm not usually very quick on the uptake, God only knows, but I noticed the tense of the verb *tell*. 'Hold on,' I said. '*Have* told?'

Neither of them said anything.

'I get you,' I said. 'You're too embarrassed to tell me whatever this story is that you think I ought to hear, so you're going to do your fast-forward thing, so I'll remember you telling me but you won't actually have to do it.' I shook my head. 'No dice.'

Melissa winced. 'It'd be much easier,' she said. 'And you'd have all the facts, and I wouldn't need to—'

'Tell me the bloody story,' I growled.

(Assertive little bugger I'd become, yes? I can only assume it was because they were being so polite and nice. If they'd been all snotty and brusque at me, I'd never have dared to speak to them like that. Typical.)

Pause, while souls were searched and consciences racked. 'All right,' Melissa said sadly, 'I'll tell you. It's a sad story, so you mustn't—'

'Get on with it already.'
'All right.'

It all started (she said) one Christmas.

Once upon a time, there was a little girl who believed in Santa Claus. Every Christmas Eve, she'd hang up her stocking from the mantelpiece before she went to bed, hoping that Santa would come and fill it with wonderful presents. And, sure enough, when Christmas morning came round—

'Excuse me,' I said.

She looked up. 'Yes?'

'I hate to criticise,' I said, 'but could you cut the saccharin levels, please? Otherwise when you get to an important bit I might be so preoccupied with throwing up that I could miss something vital.'

She frowned. 'But that's how it happened,' she said. 'Really.'

'Oh, for crying out—' I sighed. 'All right,' I said. 'You can do the fast-forward stuff.'

'Thank you,' she said – and suddenly the memory was there in my mind as fast as a bullet.

What I remembered was, basically, this.

Yes, sure enough there was this little human kid, and she believed in Santa. At least, she believed in what she'd been told about Santa, which is only a very small part of the whole truth, and not by any means the useful or essential part. I guess it'd be like being a Christian if the only parts of the Bible to have survived down the ages were Noah's ark, the feeding of the five thousand and the publishers' address.

All right, here's the important stuff about Father Christmas. He's an elf, too; that is, his natural habitat is the Elfland side of the line. He's also the greatest quantum physicist the elven race has ever produced (and, as I think you may have gathered from the ease with which Melissa did my quadratic equations, elves are hot stuff at sums). One of his many discoveries, and by no means the most significant, is the secret of faster-than-light travel.

Once you've grasped that, of course, a lot of the stuff you've heard about Santa Claus and dismissed as ludicrously implausible needs to be re-evaluated. Yes, he *can* travel right across the world in the space of a single night, no trouble at all; faster than a speeding bullet, in fact, (which is another elf-story we won't go into right now), and yes, he does have time to visit all the good little boys and girls and load their hosiery with consumer goods, because of (a) the relativistic temporal distortion resulting from the faster-than-light stuff and (b) this annoying but undoubtedly useful elf trick of being able to skip the boring bits of one's life and just live through the interesting stuff. In other words, it's all true, even the sleigh and the reindeer. Furthermore, the act of breaking the light-speed barrier opens a window in the barrier dividing Elfland from the human side, just large enough for an old fat guy in an overgrown wheelbarrow to slide through.

The first year, apparently, he did it as a bet; and it went down so well with the kiddies that he thought it'd be nice to make a regular thing of it. After a few years it all started to be a bit of a bind and he wished he'd never got involved, but all the kids in the Western world had come to expect it, not to mention the toymakers and the turkey farmers, and it was too late to back out without causing a considerable amount of grief and bad feeling, which elves aren't inclined to do.

(The thing about elves is that, because they can choose which bits of their lives to experience in real time, so to speak, quite apart from making a lifespan last ever so much longer than humans can, they tend only to bother with the nice stuff. This has had the effect, over many thousands of years, of making them nauseatingly cheerful and pleasant and charitable and good-natured, while poor human suckers have to put up with all the tedious garbage, which is why they're all so miserable.)

Anyhow, enough about that. Back to the little girl. There she is, one Christmas Eve, lying in bed waiting for it to be morning so she can scamper down the little wooden hill and start shredding wrapping-paper. She hears a clunk, down below in the living room. *Hooray*, she thinks, *It's Santa!*

Now, 999,999 times out of 1,000,000 she'd be wrong. Because of the various phenomena cited above, the actual amount of perceptible time Santa spends in any one house is something like a ninety-millionth of a nanosecond. In, get the job done, gobble the mince pie, swill the milk, out again like a rat up a kilt. But sometimes, in, say, one household in twenty million, he'll stop for a minute or so just to catch his breath, check his list, blow his nose, whatever. Throughout this time, of course, the transdimensional rift is wide open, which means that if an inquisitive and extremely stealthy little girl creeps downstairs and sneaks into the living room just as Santa's finished his breather and is all ready to get back to work, there's a risk, slight but real, that she might get sucked into the hyperspatial anomaly by the backwash of depolarised temporal ions (I'm making all this pseudo-technical garbage up, but you get the general idea) and find herself stuck in Elfland before she knows what's hit her.

Her name, by some sublime irony, was Carol. She was five years old when the vortex gobbled her up. As soon as the nice elves on the other side found her and realised what'd happened, they knew she'd have to go back, though of necessity they'd have to wait until next Christmas before it'd be possible to return her. A whole year in Elfland.

Being responsible and caring, the elves knew that the best thing for her would be to fast-forward her through her year of exile and fiddle the temporal divergence calibrations so she'd arrive back no more than five seconds after the moment in real time when she'd left; she'd still be five years old, her memories would seem like a pleasant dream, and everything would be OK. But, being loving and sweet to the point where they'd constitute a lethal threat to a diabetic, they couldn't bring themselves to do this. After all, a year in Elfland – how could they deprive this innocent wee mite of such a wonderful experience? Whisking her through it in a fingersnap and then effectively invalidating her memories? Too cruel, they felt, too callous and unfeeling.

Well, as I mentioned a moment ago, elves are red-hot when it comes to maths and physics. In most other respects, they've got the intelligence and common sense of educationally subnormal plankton.

Time passes, you see, even in Elfland. Especially in Elfland. One year on their side of the line can work out as anything from twenty to a thousand years on the human side, depending on a lot of technical stuff that I don't think even they understand. Furthermore, because Time is so profoundly squiffy there, the process of ageing works rather differently: everybody zooms to the age between eighteen and thirty that suits them best, and there they stay. There are no children and no wrinklies in Elfland, and no ugly or sick folks either – just healthy, beautiful young people. Imagine California, or the offices of a television company.

You can see where this is going, can't you? About ten minutes after setting pink-slippered foot on elf turf, little Carol was a gorgeous twenty-three-year-old, albeit with the outlook, experience and world-view of a wee tot. This would've been a problem if the same wasn't basically true of everybody else there.

And the highly predictable happened, as it so often does: she met a cute elf and they fell in love. Everybody in Elfland, without exception or excuse, is in love, needless to say, and everybody's love is perfectly requited, without any of the angst and mess that humans have to put up with, and they spend about ninety per cent of their time drifting vapidly from enchanted grove to fern-trimmed lake, hand in hand, gazing into each other's eyes like deranged optometrists.

Had Carol and her lover both been elves, of course, there wouldn't have been a problem. Without getting into the embarrassing details, little baby elves don't happen the same way that little baby humans do. (Actually, the stork brings them. Honest.) Accordingly, elves are rather less fussy about certain aspects of amatory relationships than humans are since the worst and most inconvenient thing that can happen is grass-stains on the elbows of their shirts. And, since most elves know approximately as much about humans as humans do about them, they naturally assume that it works the same way for *Homo sapiens*.

Unfortunately it doesn't.

So; when Carol – my mum – returned to the human side a year later, wafted back across the line on a flying sleigh drawn by eight light-speed-capable reindeer, she unwittingly brought with her a little souvenir of her visit, which soon grew into a big souvenir, namely me.

When she reached home, there were a few more surprises waiting for her. No sooner had Santa deposited her at chimney's end than she noticed that her living room had changed somewhat since she'd last been there. Different wallpaper, different carpets and curtains, different furniture, not to mention five unshaven men in shirtsleeves sitting round a table playing stud poker.

There was, inevitably, a certain initial awkwardness. The card-players, who were sports reporters working for a certain tabloid newspaper, weren't nearly as surprised as members of almost any other calling might have been at finding a beautiful girl in a very short skirt and green tights suddenly in their midst, and for a few minutes Carol couldn't make herself heard about the baying sound of the four guests thanking their host for his extremely imaginative hospitality. Eventually, several spilled beers and slapped faces later the truth was gradually winked out of its shell. Carol's parents didn't live there any more; they'd sold the house over ten years ago, and the present owner had been living there ever since – 'ever since', in this context, meaning eight years.

Needless to say, the story made the front page of a certain tabloid newspaper the very next working day. A quick rummage in the files had turned up the story of the little girl who'd vanished without trace on Christmas

Eve eighteen years ago, and one glance at the archive photos and the girl who'd come down the chimney was enough to confirm the latter's identity. In the limited time available the reporters weren't able to locate Carol's parents, but it was a fair bet that wherever they lived now, a copy of the paper would reach them before the day was out.

When Carol's mummy and daddy saw the picture under the inspired headline –

I WAS ABDUCTED BY ALIENS, CLAIMS ESSEX BEAUTY

– they could hardly believe their eyes. As you can imagine, the disappearance of their only daughter had done a fairly thorough job of screwing up their lives, and getting her back – radiant, healthy and clutching an exclusive-rights contract that was worth three times as much as their house - was truly the stuff of dreams and fairy tales. At once her father threw in his job sweeping floors at the local abattoir in order to become her business manager, and they settled down in confident expectation of a golden future of love, togetherness and lucrative product endorsements. Even the discovery that a little stranger was on the way was greeted as a marvellous blessing (I'M CARRYING ALIEN'S LOVE CHILD, REVEALS TV'S CAROL). In short, despite all the pain and loss and confusion surrounding the unfortunate affair, everything seemed as firmly locked on to the happy ending as a wire-guided missile when an unexpected visitor showed up at the gatehouse of the family's new 4,500-acre Wiltshire estate.

You've guessed it. Humans, being born to sorrow,

expect love not to last and are accordingly equipped to get over it. Not so elves. After pining as tragically as a restaurant critic on a diet, Carol's elven lover had turned desperate. He hijacked the sleigh, rustled the reindeer and punched a nasty jagged hole in the spatio-temporal whatsisface big enough to drive a century through.

Being an elf – sheer tabasco at long division but otherwise thick as a brick – he hadn't planned any further ahead than actually breaching the barrier and getting to the human side. I guess he assumed that once he was across, kindly humans would pick him up, give him some warm bread and milk, and take him to see his beloved. As luck would have it a bunch of humans did find him almost immediately; with the result that, ten hours after leaving Elfland and trashing the sleigh, he found himself sitting in a glass tank in a strange, rather grim-looking building in the middle of nowhere, while serious men in white coats and carrying clipboards drew off syringefuls of his blood and attached electrodes to various parts of his anatomy.

It was all rather unpleasant to begin with - which was strange, because the serious men turned out to be scientists (in the broadest sense of the term; he soon discovered that by elf standards their knowledge of science was ludicrously elementary) and so they should have had a lot in common and been friends, especially after he taught them a few junior bite-sized gobbets of basic theory that just about blew their minds. But the more he told them, the more needles they stuck into him and the less inclined they were to let him go. He tried asking nicely, then asking nicely but forcefully, then insisting. They took no notice. Finally, twenty-four hours after landing, he was forced to the conclusion that the people on this side of the line weren't as nice as elves, not by some considerable margin.

Whether it was because he was upset at the way he'd been treated, or whether it was something to do with gradually adapting himself to his new environment, the elf started to get annoyed. Annoyance escalated into irritation, irritation erupted into outright crossness, and the resulting explosion gouged a crater three-quarters of a mile wide and blew out windows in three adjacent villages. A cross elf is a dangerous entity, not to mention a cartographer's nightmare.

Once he realised what he'd done, and that the building disappearing in a sheet of red and yellow fire was all his fault, the elf was filled with horror and dismay. He sat at the very centre of the crater, watching the twisted steel girders dropping out of the sky like autumn leaves and wondering, for the first time, whether he might not have been better advised to stay at home and find someone else. But the feeling passed – remarkably quickly, in fact – and in its place was a little raw patch of resentment. *Dratted humans*, he said to himself, *being all nasty and horrid like that*. In a sense, it almost served them right, picking on a visitor from another dimension and making a pincushion out of him. Sure enough, he was very sad about the damage he'd done, especially the scientists he'd reduced to a fine red mist, but it had to be said, if they didn't want to be vaporised they shouldn't have shone lights in his eyes and prodded his tongue with wooden sticks. What was more, if any of them tried any more of that stuff, he'd probably do it again.

Now then, let's see if you've been paying attention. Elfland and our world are exactly the same (except for the differences). Consequently, every elf has a human counterpart, which does everything exactly the same (only differently). Therefore it follows that the lovestruck elf who'd gatecrashed our side of the line had a counterpart too, and that when the elf suddenly popped into existence and crash-landed in a field near Swindon, the counterpart had to be in precisely the same place.

Fortunately for him, the human counterpart (later known to me as Daddy George) had the good sense to leave that place, albeit only by about twenty yards, as soon as the fiery sleigh burst out of the sky and plummeted like a meteor or a dot-com share towards the ground. At the actual moment when the sleigh crashed into the exact same square food of grass he'd been standing on twenty seconds earlier, Daddy George was on the ground, rolling like a croquet ball, the unfortunate result of having put his foot down a rabbit hole as he scampered for cover. His head happened to coincide with a tree root, and he went to sleep for a while. When he woke up, the air was buzzing with helicopters, their floodlights scything the ground all about him and creating bizarre kaleidoscopic effects when they happened to coincide with the flashing blue lamps of the police's panda cars and the local hospital's ambulances.

Now, as everybody knows, the innocent citizen has nothing to fear from the police. Daddy George, on the other hand, was not an innocent citizen. The only reason he was in a cold, muddy field on a dark night was because he was on his way to steal a tractor, left lying around by some over-trusting farmer. The *son et lumière* of police helicopters evoked some painful memories in various strata of his subconscious, and as soon as he was able to get to his feet without falling over, he ran away as fast as he could in the first direction that came to hand.

Ah, you're saying, how could he do this? Surely if the cops and the guys in white coats and carrying clipboards had marched his elven oppo off to the freak-dissecting plant, he had no choice but to be there too.

Full marks for being the kind of observant, nit-picking, fault-finding reader who gives poor narrators ulcers. But you've failed to take into account (maybe because I haven't told you about it yet) the fact that once a stranger comes over from the other side, the link between him and his identical-except-for-the-different-bits twin is severed, although a strong subliminal urge to be close to him remains buried deep among the other submerged wiffin in the bottom of the shoebox of the mind.

Quite possibly it was this latent impulse that led Daddy George to try and burgle the secret government research station about ten seconds before the elf reduced it to widely dispersed brick dust. It's hard to think of any other reason why he should try and do such a bloody stupid thing.

As luck would have it, when the elf finally lost his rag and brought the house down (not to mention up and sideways) he'd just failed to get a foothold on the drainpipe that ran down the side of the biochemical weapons laboratory. The blast reduced the lab (and, fortuitously enough, its entire contents) to a cloud of disparate molecules, but the eight-foot-thick concrete wall that Daddy George had been vainly trying to scale held together long enough to deflect the main force of the explosion upwards and off to one side, with the result that, although everything else in the vicinity vanished like a pay cheque in December, he was left sitting on his bum among the ruins, trying to cope with the nagging suspicion that he'd just set off a truly serious alarm system.

A moment later he was on his feet again – just as well, because a substantial chunk of the administration-block roof swiftly snuggled into what had been his personal space about ten seconds previously – and running like hell towards the skyline. It was at this point that his personal doppelelf first caught sight of him.

'It's all right,' yelled the elf.

Liar, thought Daddy George, and carried on running. I don't know, maybe his body language was a little too obvious and he was running in an offensive manner, but that just made the elf angrier. He reached out with his transdimensional third arm – don't ask me, I'm just remembering what was downloaded into my head – grabbed Daddy George by the collar and hauled him right back.

'I was talking to you,' he said.

Amazingly, even while dangling by his collar from the elf's hand, his feet six inches off the deck, Daddy George's reply to that was, 'Fuck me, you've got pointed ears!' Only goes to show, I feel, the extraordinary strength of the innate human thirst for knowledge.

'Sure I have,' the elf replied. 'And you haven't, you freak.'

Have you noticed, by the way, that the elf's tone and general manner is getting steadily less couth and reminiscent of a Canadian hotel manager, and more in line with what you'd expect to hear this side of the line? Yes? That's all right, then – I'm trying not to hammer it into the ground, but subtlety is wasted on some people.

Anyway, Daddy George, suspended in the air like a

very large fairy on a smallish Christmas tree, didn't quite know what to make of that. True, people had been making disparaging remarks about his appearance ever since his other car had been a pram (and with good reason, God only knows) but this was the first time he could remember ever being berated for the unpointed-ness of his ears. In this regard, a change wasn't really as good as a rest.

'Huh?' he said.

'You heard,' the elf snarled. (Did you catch it that time? Snarled? This display of carefully modulated incremental snottitude brought to you by courtesy of Flaubert Integrated Dialog Systems Inc.) 'Your ears aren't pointed, they're sort of round at the top. Like all you people. All you *freaks*,' he added, with a pronounced spitty hiss on the final S. 'What the hell's wrong with you, anyhow? Cut yourselves shaving?'

To which Daddy George said something entirely appropriate and well chosen, like 'Urgh!' It should have been borne in mind that he hadn't been able to breathe very well for the last fifty-odd seconds, and the air in his lungs was getting distinctly unfashionable.

'Fuck you, too,' growled the elf. 'Right, then, where's the girl?'

'Girl?'

'Yeah, the girl, snot-for-brains. The bimbo. The chick. The skirt. Where've you hidden her?'

All throughout history wise men, from Pythagoras to Aristotle to Confucius to Lao Tzu, right down to St Thomas Aquinas and Descartes, have warned of the dangers of arguing the toss with a pissed-off elf with his hands round your throat. It's a tragedy that generations of over-fussy editors forced them to cut those bits for the mass-market paperback editions, because it's left so many of us unprepared for a rare but nonetheless very serious threat to life and health. Fortunately, Daddy George's wonderfully tuned survival instincts were able to work the whole thing out from first principles, in less than a sixteenth of a second.

'Ths wy,' he whispered.

The elf relaxed his grip by a few tons per square inch. 'Say again?'

'This way,' Daddy George wheezed, jerking his head due east. Quite by chance, he was indeed nodding along a direct flying-crow vector towards Carol's new home. 'Take you there if you like,' he added.

'You do that,' replied the elf. 'And if you're lying, I'm going to suck your brain out through your filthy round ears and blow it up your nose, *capisce*?'

Daddy George replied to the effect that that sounded perfectly reasonable to him, and the elf put him down, though he maintained a firm grip on Daddy George's collar with his third hand. Daddy George started, nervously, to walk.

For his part, the elf was getting grumpier with every step he took. Round ears weren't the worst thing about this neighbourhood, not by a long way. Even the getting prodded and electrocuted in the research lab hadn't been all that much of a problem for a life form practically impervious to physical pain. What was really bugging him was the boredom; second after second, minute after every boring minute, they were walking as due east as they could manage, and every step was practically identical to the one before. Back home, of course, all he'd have needed to do was fast-forward and he could've moved on painlessly to the end of the walk, where the girl would've been waiting for him, and a second or so of perceived time later, he'd have been home again, the rest of the century his own. Instead he was repeating the same action over and over again, and it wasn't even a particularly nice action, at that. It was enough to fry an elf's brain.

Enough of this, he decided. 'You there,' he snapped, yanking back hard with his third hand and stopping Daddy George dead in his tracks. 'Isn't there a faster way of getting to where we're going?'

'Sure,' Daddy George replied. 'Lots of different ways. Plane, train, bus, car, motorbike, skateboard—'

'What?'

(None of that sort of thing in Elfland, of course, unless you count Santa's sleigh. After all, why bother inventing things to help you move faster when you can just edit out the dull and uneventful journey, just like they do in the movies?)

'Machines,' Daddy George replied (and at that precise moment, a tiny speck of inspiration dropped into his mind). 'You climb up onto them, and they carry you. We've got loads of them, all different types.'

'That's more like it,' grunted the elf. 'Right, let's find some. I've had enough of this stupid walking.'

'No problem,' Daddy George replied. 'Provided you can get it unlocked and started, that is.'

'Locked?'

'It's something we have to do,' Daddy George explained. 'Otherwise some scumbag'd be in there stealing our stuff while we aren't looking. So there's these little machines called locks. They hold doors and things so tight shut, not even a germ could get in. Same with cars: you can't open the door or start the engine – sorry, the bits of the machine that make it go – unless you've got a little knobbly lever, called a key, which undoes the lock. It's really very—'

'Shuttup,' the elf yelled. The sound of Daddy George's voice was another tedious experience that just seemed to keep going on and on for ever. 'Look, just sort it out, will you, before I start rotting from the feet up.'

Purely by chance, they'd come to the main road. It was pitch dark by now, and the usual nose-to-tail procession of heavy lorries was trundling up and down the carriageway, each lorry pushing its own pool of light along in front of it, like a photon-scavenging dung-beetle. Insofar as Daddy George had a plan, it involved luring this freak to the side of the road, where with any luck the unaccustomed glare of some trucker's heavy-duty halogens would dazzle him stupid just long enough for Daddy George to get away, preferably after shoving the prickle-eared arsehole under a sixteen-wheeler. It was more of a blueprint or IOU for a plan, but Daddy George believed that inspiration is like a knackered grandfather clock: it only strikes if you force it. Besides, he was too scared to come up with anything too elaborate.

'What the hell are those?' the elf demanded. 'Those racing boxes with the bright eyes?'

'Lorries,' Daddy George replied. 'For moving large quantities of stuff from place to place.'

'Extraordinary,' the elf muttered. 'You people are so weird it's creepy being around you. Why would anybody in their right mind want to move things? If you're in the wrong place to use something, you should just go where it is. Otherwise, how in hell's name will anybody else know where to find it if you keep shifting it about?'

Daddy George replied that he'd never considered the matter in quite that light before, and when he'd finished helping the elf with his quest, he'd most certainly write to the United Nations and get them to pass a law changing it all around.

'Right,' said the elf. 'So I should hope.'

Then Daddy George shoved him under a bus.

It was one of those intercity coaches, the long, sleek ones that look like Cubist cigar tubes. It was hammering along at a smartish sixty-something, and it weighed a lot; accordingly, when it hit the elf, something was bound to get severely bent.

In this instance, the coach. The front end crumpled up like a squashed beer-can, and the engine coughed and died. It was a minor miracle, on a par with changing water into ginger beer or the Feeding of the Five, that no one was killed. The elf, meanwhile, hardly seemed to have noticed the impact.

'Watch what you're doing, moron,' he said, and his tone of voice was almost gentle. 'You nearly had me over that time.'

Daddy George was too stunned to be able to do more than mumble an apology; furthermore, the elf's third hand was still firmly attached to his collar. Back to the drawing board, he decided.

'Right,' the elf was saying. 'So, if we get on one of these things, it'll take us where we want to go?'

'That's right,' Daddy George replied. 'Not that one,' he added, looking at the coach's mangled front end. 'I'm afraid it's a bit broken, I don't think it'll go.'

The elf scowled. 'Fragile bloody things, aren't they?'

'Extremely so, yes.'

'Really can't see the point,' the elf muttered under his

breath, as he reached out and grabbed a passing motor-bike by the back wheel. 'Here,' he said, lifting the bike up and shaking the rider off like someone dislodging an earwig from a lettuce. 'Will this do instead?'

'Um,' Daddy George replied.

'It'll do,' the elf grunted. 'Now, how do you work this thing? No, don't tell me,' he went on, 'I should be able to figure it out for myself.' The rider got up off the ground, observed the way the elf was holding the bike upright with one hand by the rear swinging arm so as to get a good look inside the chain guard, and hobbled away as fast as he could go. 'Yes, all seems to be pretty straight-forward. Centrifugal force, and there's a sort of box inside to contain the explosions. Fairly ingenious, I suppose, but it's a hell of a lot of fuss just to get somewhere. Why you people insist on doing everything the hard way—'

He took the bike in both hands, wheels parallel to the ground, then threw it down hard, like a basketball player bouncing a ball off the court. The heavy coil springs in the front and rear shock absorbers compressed and expanded, and the bike jumped back into the air, salmon-on-a-waterfall fashion. While it was still airborne the elf vaulted into the saddle, third-handedly dragging Daddy George up onto the pillion. The bike landed and bounced again; by dabbing down with his feet, the elf managed to turn it through twenty degrees, so that it was pointing across the carriageway when the springs expanded again and launched the bike upwards like a leaping bullfrog. It cleared the entire width of the road on that bounce, and the next one carried it seventy yards into the field beyond.

'Not bad,' the elf conceded, as the springs bottomed out under full compression. 'More efficient than I'd imagined,' he added, pulling the front end round as it started another titanic bunny-hop. 'So tell me, what's the grey bit with all the explosions in aid of?'

'Unnnng,' Daddy George replied, as the bike touched down and his spine tried to shoot up through the back of his skull.

'What?'

It's an amazing tribute to Japanese engineering that the bike lasted for as long as it did; the poor thing went well over a mile before the frame finally gave way, with a terrible graunching of sundered welds that sounded like icebergs scraping together. The elf, however, wasn't impressed, maybe because when the dead bike threw him off, he landed in a very large, well-matured cow-pat.

'Pathetic,' he growled. 'Are they all as trashy as that, or was that one just a rotten example?'

Daddy George tried to explain that, although the elf's interpretation of motorcycling technique was entirely valid and every bit as good as the regular method (in many respects better) it wasn't really the nit-pickingly orthodox approach, and accordingly the machine hadn't been built to withstand the effect. Short-sighted people, these motorcycle designers. No imagination.

They left the shattered corpse where it lay, and walked on. The elf was making louder and more querulous are-we-there-yet noises with every step they took, and Daddy George realised that pretty soon he was going to have to think of some cunning plan or other, before the elf realised what he'd been up to and lost his temper. Unfortunately Daddy George's creativity and imagination appeared to have been shaken out through his ears at some point in the bike ride. In fact, he'd have been hard put to it to tell you his own name.

What neither of them knew, of course, was that the meadow they were tramping through was part of the grounds of the large and magnificent house that Carol's dad had bought with the newspaper money. All they saw was a big grey shape looming up at them out of the night.

'Now how far is it?' the elf demanded.

'Nearly there. Really nearly there,' said Daddy George, in one of the most accurate and truthful statements of his life. 'In fact, if it wasn't so dark you could practically see it from here.'

The elf sniffed suspiciously. 'You'd better be right,' he said. 'Because if I find out you've been playing games with me—'

One of the features of this particular house that had most impressed Carol's dad when he was considering buying it was the security system. Infra-red beams latticed the perimeter; once triggered they switched on more floodlights than Wembley Stadium and set off a devastating array of bullhorns, sirens and other musical instruments. To an elf, accustomed to the Arcadian calm of pastoral, unmechanised Elfland, the effect was extremely offputting. He dropped to his knees, hands clamped firmly over his pointy ears, while with his third hand he tried to find whatever it was you turned, pulled, pushed or pressed to turn the damn' things off.

Daddy George, by contrast – well, he wasn't in his element exactly, but he'd been a distinctly third-rate burglar long enough to be able to cope with a suddenly triggered burglar alarm and a few bright lights. As soon as the elf relaxed his invisible grip, he was off like the electric hare at a greyhound track, heading straight for the house. In consequence he had his back to the elf at the crucial moment, when the elf contrived to wrap all ten of his highly conductive fingers around the main live cable.

This was a slice of luck as far as Daddy George was concerned, since looking directly at a flash like that could easily have left his retina as crisp and charred as a transport café fried egg. Having guessed what'd happened, he slowed down, grinning hugely, and gradually turned round.

'Fuck', said a small voice from somewhere under the mushrooming pall of smoke that hovered a few feet above the ground.

'Are you all right?' Daddy George called out.

'Do I sound like I'm all bloody right?' the voice whimpered. 'What the hell was all that about, anyway?'

'Where are you?' Daddy George asked. 'I can't see you.'

'Down here.'

It took him about thirty seconds to figure out where the little squeaky voice was coming from. 'You've shrunk,' he observed.

'You don't say. Dammit, I think you may be right. Of course I've bloody well shrunk, you stupid tall—'

The elf got no further. Daddy George had picked him up between forefinger and thumb, and was shaking him. He was being quite gentle, at least by his standards, but the elf didn't like it at all.

'Well, well,' Daddy George said. 'Now this changes things rather, don't you think? A little jolt of electricity, and suddenly you're not nearly as big and mean and nasty. Doesn't look like your super-special magic powers are working too well, either.' He flipped the elf over into the palm of his hand and was about to close his fingers and squeeze very had when someone shone a powerful torch in his eyes and recommended that he keep absolutely still.

As far as Daddy George was concerned, it was love at third sight. First sight was mostly just blinking, thanks to the powerful torch I just told you about; second sight didn't get any further than the two large, malevolent-looking bull terriers straining at the leash gripped in the speaker's left hand. Third sight, however, got past the light and the dogs to the extremely beautiful, if unsympathetic, girl who'd just spoken to him, and apparently it liked what it saw.

The logical explanation is that the mutual attraction between Carol and the elf somehow adapted itself to the transdimensional shift, with the elf's human-side counterpart taking his place. My personal theory is that the vast majority of drive-by shootings by the kids with the wings and the arrows are unaimed area fire, and it's anybody's guess where the shots are going to land. I'm not sure that either hypothesis fits all the facts of the case; regardless of that it was undeniable that no more than two minutes after first setting eyes on each other, Carol and Daddy George were deeply and inextricably in love, a state of affairs, no pun intended, that carried on more or less unchanged throughout the sixteen years that followed, right up to the point where I'd waved them goodbye in the station car park on my way back to school for the new term. Nor did I have any reason to believe, as I reviewed the downloaded memories in my mind, that anything had happened to change it since.

'All right,' I said. 'Now I remember. So – what happened to the elf?'

Melissa pulled a sad face. 'As far as we can judge,' she said, 'your stepfather just shoved him away in his coat pocket, under a handkerchief and a roll of peppermints, and forgot all about him.'

I frowned. 'He just sat there in the pocket, did he? No shouting or screaming or trying to cut his way free through the lining.'

'He never got the chance,' the Neil elf put in. 'Apparently he bashed his head on the peppermints and passed out. When he woke up, your stepfather'd got him securely imprisoned in a jam jar. There wasn't any risk of him suffocating because your stepfather had poked some holes in the lid with a nail to let the air in, but there was absolutely no way he could unscrew the top and get out. Luckily, your stepfather hadn't bothered to clean the jar out properly before stuffing your father in it, so he was able to stay alive by licking the last traces of the jam off the walls and floor while he was waiting for the effects of the electric shock to wear off.'

'And did they?' I asked. He shook his head.

'No chance,' he told me. 'Not without another electric shock. What's more, it'd have to be exactly the same, not stronger or weaker. Not enough power and nothing'd happen; too much amperage and you'd get toasted elf. At least, we think that's what'd happen. Melissa here's the only elf who's ever been zapped and managed to get back home again, so you'll understand that our data's all a pit patchy and vague.'

CHAPTER EIGHT

'Hold on,' I said. 'Are you saying there've been others? Apart from you and my real father, I mean.'

Melissa smiled very sadly indeed. 'Oh yes,' she said. 'Ever so many. As you well know,' she added. 'You've seen at least two of them for yourself, in your own back garden. And that's only the tip of the iceberg. There's hundreds of them – of *us* – trapped there, and all because of him. Which is why,' she added, turning and facing the Fuller elf with a sort of grim, determined look on her beautiful face, like a supermodel who's just quit smoking, 'I've decided I'm going back.'

The Fuller elf was horrified. 'You can't,' he gasped. 'You've only just escaped, after all this time. What if he catches you?'

She shrugged. 'I'll have to make sure he doesn't, that's all. I'll be careful,' she added. 'At least this time I'll know what I'm up against. But I can't just leave them there. You do see that, don't you?'

'Just a minute,' I interrupted, 'I don't remember any of this. What's she talking about?'

The two elves looked at me as if I was a four-year-old four days before Christmas who'd just found out where all the presents were stashed. 'We didn't give you that memory,' Melissa said. 'We thought – well, you've got enough to come to terms with already, finding out about your mother and your stepfather, and coming here for the first time. Besides, none of this is your fault, you can't be expected to get involved.'

That sounded like an entirely reasonable argument to me. Unfortunately, the way I saw it, I was already involved up to my unpointed ears. 'Won't you let me be the judge of that?' I said.

They looked at each other. 'No,' they said.

'Ah.'

'Really,' Melissa went on, 'you definitely don't want to know, because it truly is very—' She shuddered, with such a magnificently expressive gesture that I could almost visualise an imaginary ice cube slithering down the back of her neck. 'You've got an expression on your side of the line, I remember: you don't want to go there. That puts it very well.'

I shook my head. 'I didn't want to come here, either,' I told her, 'but I don't recall being given any choice in the matter. Not since I was a little kid, and I saw one of your people in the vegetable patch. Ever since then, I've been the boy who saw an elf – have you any idea what it's been like, living with something like that? Don't you dare talk to me about getting involved.'

The look of genuine pity, remorse and regret on both

their faces was enough to break your heart. And as for sincerity – if only there'd been a way of extracting and bottling the sincerity of those sad expressions I'd be rich and politics would never be the same again.

'We're sorry,' Melissa said. 'Truly we are, and if there'd been any other way – or if I'd been me, instead of the rather nasty person I turned into while I was there . . .'

That reminded me of something, but I tagged it and put it aside for later; this was no time to get sidetracked. 'That's really nice of you,' I said. 'And you know, if I was really me – the meek, gutless, won't-stand-up-for-himself, lets-everybody-walk-all-over-him little weed I seem to remember being all my life, though how I could've been so pathetic I really can't understand – if I was still that same me, I'd tell myself that you two know best and let you get away with it. But I'm not, and I won't. You're going to tell me the rest of the story, or there's going to be big trouble.'

There was enough hopelessness in the looks they exchanged to fuel a whole fleet of Booker Prize runners-up. 'We're only thinking of what's best for you,' said the Fuller elf. 'Please don't make us do this.'

Well: I may have suddenly sprouted a tungsten carbide backbone and a will of high-carbon steel, but I could still feel compassion. 'All right,' I said, 'I guess I'll just have to find it out for myself. Which I'll do,' I added, 'just as soon as you send me back where I belong.'

To judge by the way they looked at me, I might as well have been talking in Klingon. 'But that's where you are,' Melissa said. 'Where you belong. Home. Here.'

I scowled. 'Absolutely not,' I said. 'This is some crazy

place, the Disneyworld that time forgot. If you think I'm staying here—'

'But you've got to,' Melissa said. 'You can't leave.'

'Thanks,' I replied, 'and I appreciate the hospitality, but I've got an English essay to write, for one thing. So, which way's the exit?'

The Fuller elf shook his head. 'No,' he said, 'I think you're missing the point, or we haven't explained properly. It's not just that we don't want you to go – though of course that's entirely true, we don't – but you *can't*. It's impossible. There's no way back across the line. I'm sorry.'

I was beginning to get seriously annoyed with both of them. Odd, in retrospect, how easily it came to me, back in my old life and my old personality, other people got annoyed with me, not the other way around. But here I was losing my temper like a seasoned professional.

'Bullshit,' I said. 'She just said she's going back, so it's got to be possible. If she can go back, so can I.'

Long silence, extremely awkward and embarrassing. Eventually, the Melissa elf heaved a huge sigh.

'We'd better tell him,' she said.

The Fuller elf frowned. 'Are you sure?'

'Hey!' I yelled. 'What about asking *me* if I'm sure? Because I am. Absolutely fucking positive. So tell me.'

I don't think elves use bad language – unless they pick up the habit when they find themselves over on the human side – though they would appear to know what it signifies. They stared at me disapprovingly, as if I'd just farted in the nave of Westminster Abbey in the middle of a royal wedding. 'All right,' the Melissa elf said. 'But don't blame us if you don't like what you hear.'

'Thank you,' I said.

Another pause; I think each of them was waiting for the other to go first. I guess the Melissa elf must've drawn the telepathic short straw, because she was the one who eventually broke the silence.

'Back home,' she said, 'where you lived; that's a really nice garden, don't you think?'

I nodded. I had a feeling I knew what was coming.

'But your stepfather,' she went on, 'doesn't do much to it himself, does he?'

I shook my head. 'Nor does Mum,' I said. 'I've wondered about that myself.'

She nodded. 'And your stepfather's business,' she continued, looking at a spot in the air about two feet to the left of me, 'he does quite nicely at it, doesn't he?'

'I suppose so. To be honest I never took much of an interest.' I grinned. 'I didn't want to give him the satisfaction.'

'Understandable,' the Melissa elf acknowledged. 'But you'll agree, he must be making money at it. I mean, your standard of living's pretty high.'

'In material terms, I suppose so, yes.'

The Melissa elf dipped her head a couple of times. 'And that's never struck you as odd?' she asked. 'At a time when all the shoes you see in the shops are cheap imports, from China and Eastern Europe and all those other places where they can make them so cheaply because their labour costs are so much lower than in Britain, your stepfather's making a good living running a small shoe factory in the Home Counties. That's never struck you as just a little bit curious?'

Now she'd lost me. 'I suppose so,' I said. 'Like I said, I've never really thought about it.'

'I don't suppose you've ever visited the factory?' she said.

'Never wanted to.'

'I'm sure that's right. But did he ever offer?'

I didn't reply. Come to think of it . . . 'Diplomatic relations between us have never been exactly wonderful,' I said. 'He doesn't like me, it's as simple as that.'

She looked at me. 'Nevertheless,' she said. 'You'd have thought that once, just once, he'd have offered. Wouldn't you?'

She'd set me thinking, sure enough. 'You don't know him,' I said. 'I do.'

A very strange expression appeared on her face. 'Oh, I know him, all right. Haven't you figured it out yet? Or do I have to spell it out for you?'

This time, I was the one who looked away. 'I think Daddy George has got elves doing his gardening for him,' I said. 'That's where I've seen elves, and neither him nor my mum ever do a hand's turn out there. But what's that got to do with the factory?'

She clicked her tongue. 'When you were a child,' she said, 'didn't your mother ever tell you the story of the shoemaker and the elves?'

The penny didn't drop exactly, but it teetered on the edge, like the coach on the cliff edge at the end of *The Italian Job*. 'Actually,' I said, 'no. First time I heard that story was at school. And,' I went on, 'it was in a book someone gave me for Christmas one time, but before I could read it for myself, someone cut those pages out with scissors. Never could understand that.'

'Do you understand it now?'

I nodded slowly. 'You're telling me he's got elves

working at the factory as well.' I turned and looked at her. 'Is that it?' I said. 'The big secret?'

'Partly.' She looked at me very solemnly, as if she was just about to launch me or declare me open. 'Yes, there are elves working in your garden. And in the house, too. In fact, they do all the housework. Haven't you ever wondered about that?'

Well, no, I hadn't. True, I'd never seen anybody wielding a Hoover or washing a dish in our house, and this had never struck me as worthy of notice. Big deal. Well, have you ever met a teenage boy who didn't assume that housework gets done by magic?

'The factory,' I said.

She sighed a little. 'All elves,' she said. 'Hundreds of them. Maybe a thousand, by now, I don't know. I was there for, what, ten years, then I was transferred to the house, and I haven't been back since, so I couldn't tell you.'

I frowned. 'You were in the factory? And in our *house?*' She nodded.

'But that's . . .' My mind was spinning, like a gerbil in a blender. 'But you just said elves can't cross the line. They can't go backwards and forwards between our side and home. So how can there be . . .'

She laughed, but not a funny-joke sort of laugh. 'There is one way,' she said. 'Your stepfather discovered it. You might say it's been the cornerstone of his success. Not so great for us though.'

She stopped talking, and the expression on her face was enough to make a bailiff weep. But I'm not a bailiff. 'Well?' I said. 'Get on with it, for crying out loud.'

Instead, the Fuller elf took up the story, while Melissa

pulled herself together. 'The fact is,' the Fuller elf said, 'all elves are curious.'

'That's putting it mildly.'

'All elves,' he amended, frowning, 'exhibit a high degree of curiosity, and one of the things they're most curious about is what it's like on the other side of the line. Being elves, though, when they're told by older, wiser elves that the human side is, well, not quite like our side, and humans do things in a way that we might well find hard to get along with – being elves, they accept what they're told and don't even try to get across.' He paused. 'Most elves, anyway.'

'Most,' I repeated.

'Most, but not all, I'm sorry to say: there're always a few who persist in believing that the other side is some kind of Paradise, and the stories about it being, um, unsuitable are just to put them off and stop them going there, because some unidentified cadre of selfish elves want all the nice things for themselves. So, inevitably, they look for a way over. And when your stepfather went snooping round the place where the sleigh crashed through, and found a way of opening a door from his side . . .' Now the Fuller elf was at it, making funny noises and turning his head away, as if it was all too much and floods of tears were only a split second away.

'A door,' I repeated firmly.

'We haven't the faintest idea how he does it,' snuffled the Melissa elf, and I saw her eyes were red – attractively red, of course – from crying. 'If we knew, we could put a stop to it. But we don't; and every time he needs more workers – oh, let's not fool ourselves, every time he needs more *slaves* – he opens the gate, and there's always one or two silly, silly elves who go tripping happily through, convinced they're on their way to a better life and a fresh start in a wonderful place full of opportunity, where they'll be *understood*.'

Ah. So that was it. 'Such as you,' I said.

She nodded. 'Once upon a time,' she said. 'Everybody warned me about it, but no, I had to know best. Which is how I ended up stitching uppers on men's fashion moccasins for ten years. Ten years real time,' she added. 'You can't begin to imagine . . . and being small, too. That was probably the worst thing about it. You see, the first thing that happens to you, when you pass through the gateway, is this sudden terrible bright light and this burning, tingling sensation right up through you, like someone's shaking you to bits—'

'Electric shock,' I guessed.

'That's right. And when you've stopped shaking, all the things you used to be able to do just don't work any more, and you're six inches tall. The same as happened to your father. And he can keep on and on doing it and getting away with it, because on the human side, of course, the humans can't see us, or hear us – there's no way of letting them know we're there.'

Trying to keep up with all this was like running for a bus with lead bars strapped to your ankles.

'Hang on,' I said. 'If you're invisible, how can he keep track of you?'

She smiled. 'Oh, he can see us all right. Again, we don't know how, but he can. What's more, he's done something that stops us getting out of the places where he keeps us – you know, tunnelling or climbing out through ventilation shafts, that sort of thing. We get so far and then it's like there's an invisible wall, and when you touch it, it's like being hit with a huge bell. All the time I was there, at the factory and then at the house, only two of us ever managed to get out. The first one was one of the gardeners: he said he'd found a way but it was terribly dangerous, he wouldn't tell us about it in case we tried it, but he'd have a go and if it worked, he'd come back for the rest of us.' Massive sniffle, at least six on the Richter scale. 'He got out,' she said, 'but he never came back.'

A very unpleasant thought formed in my mind. 'Out of interest,' I said, 'when was that, exactly?'

'Just before you came home from school last time,' she replied. 'In fact, I think it was the same night.'

'Ah,' I said. 'So, who was the other one? You, I suppose.'

'That's right,' she said. 'It was because you'd fallen in love with me – with *her*, I mean, the other me, my counterpart. Don't ask me how I knew, but I did; if you were in love with me – me as I am over there, really . . .'

'A real snotty bitch,' I supplied. 'Yes, go on.'

'Well,' she said, 'if you could love *her*, deep down you must be a really good, decent, perceptive person who'd want to help me get away and work out how to free the others. And of course, with you being half-and-half, so that whatever he uses to keep us in doesn't work on you – all I had to do was climb into your pocket, and I was away. Free and clear. Of course,' she went on, 'I was taking a huge risk, that you really weren't like your stepfather or your mother—'

'Hold it,' I said. 'Is she in on this?'

Melissa nodded. 'I'm afraid so,' she said. 'Like I told you, she practically worships your stepfather.'

'I'd noticed,' I grunted.

'But you,' she continued, 'you we couldn't be sure

about. You see, we all assumed you knew, that you were a part of it and you'd turn us in to *him* if you knew we were trying to escape. But then, when you started putting out the bread and milk, and then the beer, that didn't seem like someone who was part of the family business, or even someone who was aware of what was going on. So I thought, why not? I mean, the worst that could happen was that I'd be caught, horribly tortured and finally killed.'

'No big deal?'

She shook her head. 'If it was that simple,' she said, 'you'd have seen your stepfather hoeing his own spinach fifteen years ago. But it isn't. We can't just die over there, you see. On your side, we're practically immortal.'

Once again, I couldn't help thinking about someone small I'd tripped over once in a dark lane. 'Practically,' I said.

'That's right,' she said. 'On your side, we can only be killed by a close relative, or someone we love. And of course, that's pretty unlikely, isn't it?'

I smiled rather thinly. 'I guess so,' I replied. 'So, that explains why suicide wasn't an option. And now,' I went on, 'you're talking about going back there. Won't that mean getting zapped all over again, and ending up six inches tall and getting plonked down in the factory, punching lace-holes for fifty years?'

She looked at me. Big round blue eyes. It worries me when they do that.

'Maybe,' she said. 'But I've got to try. You can see that, can't you?'

Speak the truth, my mother always told me, and shame the devil; though whether, given what I'd just found out about her, she was any kind of role model for an impressionable youth, you can best gauge for your-self. 'No,' I said, 'I don't see that at all. That's like saying the best way to heal a cut thumb is to slice open a toe.' A little forty-watt inspiration flipped on inside my head. 'Now if we're going to be sensible and logical about this, surely the obvious person to go back and try and get things put right is me. After all, I've got the run of the place. More or less,' I added, in keeping with the spirit of the new Unvarnished Truth Initiative I seemed to be locked into. 'Anyway, a darn sight more of the run of the place than your lot, according to what you've been telling me. And that trick with the circle in the grass, where I just sort of went from there to here without moving . . .'

The Fuller elf nodded. 'It's because you're half-and-half,' he said. 'Just the one of you for both sides.'

'So I can go across the line the way you lot can't?'

'It means that in practice, where you're concerned, there is no line,' he replied.

'Well,' I said, 'there you are, then. You lot can only get across by signing on for height reduction therapy and a career in footwear or horticulture. I can just stroll across with my hands in my pockets.'

'Yes,' said Melissa, her face screwed up like she had toothache. 'But—'

'But?'

'But you can't leave.'

This was getting confusing: past electric-toothbrush-instruction-leaflet confusing, way past income-tax-return explanatory-notes confusing and into the language-bending domain of Windows Online Help confusing. As bad as that.

'Don't be ridiculous,' I said. 'You just said I could.'

'No,' Melissa said emphatically, 'you're missing the point. Yes, you can *leave*. But no, *you* can't leave. It's all to do with—'

No, I thought, *the hell with all this*. For some reason, these two were dead set on making me stay there, either out of some weird idea that I belonged there or for some other reason I really didn't want to find out about. In any event, time I wasn't there.

All it took, if I'd understood them correctly (yes, I know, don't hurt yourself by sniggering too much), was a circle, like the mark of the missing dustbin back in the school grounds. Now, as it happened, there was a circle just one pace to my right. True, it was quite narrow and completely encircled by a foot-high wicker rim – it was, in fact, a nice old-fashioned waste-paper basket – but it was quite definitely circular, and I was in a hurry.

'I'm off now,' I said. 'Thanks for everything, and I promise I'll do what I can. Goodbye.'

So saying, I jumped with both feet into the bin –

– And found myself in an exactly similar place and position, namely standing rather precariously inside a wickerwork waste bin about ten inches across. Now, you're going to tell me there simply isn't room to stand up in a tiny space like that.

You'd be right.

I toppled over quite slowly, like a factory chimney being demolished, except that I didn't fall down nearly as gracefully or accurately. Fortunately, the arm of the chair broke my fall when my forehead hit it.

Ouch, I told myself, and looked down. The waste-paper basket had split like a peeled banana, poor innocent thing, scattering bits of screwed-up paper and pencil sharpenings all over the rather fine red, blue and yellow carpet. Lovely to look at, but not very practical. (In our house we always had coffee-coloured carpet. Guess why.)

I hauled myself to my feet and had a quick look round. The first thing that caught my eye was the complete and, let's be honest, refreshing absence of elves. The room was empty, in fact, apart from me and all that really cute old furniture. Unmistakably the same room, apart from the differences.

Which were . . .? I knew there were some, but they were so subtle I couldn't identify them straight off. Maybe a chair-leg an inch or so to the right, a cushion slightly more faded and frayed, different books on the shelves of the glass-fronted Edwardian mahogany bookcase. Oh, and I knew where I was – the memory came back quite suddenly, leaving me wondering how the hell I'd failed to pick up on it before. I was at school again, in a place I'd been to many times, never for anything nice. The headmaster's study.

Spiffing, I thought. *And I've just squashed his waste-paper basket. He won't take kindly to that.*

There was, of course, the sensible option; namely flight. I was only about ten paces from the door; through that, up the stairs, across the top landing, down the other stairs and out into the back courtyard and relative safety. Sounds easy, put like that. I expect you could make a trek to the South Pole sound like a cakewalk, too, if you set your mind to it.

Still, if I was going, I'd better go. A fraction of a second later I was by the door, hand on the doorknob, the long road to freedom only a wrist's turn away. I stopped dead in my tracks, not even trying to move.

Because I'm stupid? No, not on this particular occasion. I think that if you'd been in my shoes, you'd (a) have done the same (b) have blisters on both heels.

What prompted me to stop was a mirror, hanging just to the east of the light switch. My guess is that our beloved headmaster hung it there so that he could make a final check on his appearance – fine-tune his scowl, get his eyebrows really meshed together in the middle – before going out where we could see him. Not my favourite person, our headmaster.

Anyhow . . . what do you suppose I saw in that mirror? Correct, a reflection. And everything I'd learned in physics about reflection and refraction of light led me to conclude that it couldn't help but be *my* reflection, an accurate – albeit reversed – depiction of my appearance.

And therein lay the problem.

The face looking back at me was recognisable, sure. There were my lorry-wing-mirror ears, my superfluous length of nose, my turkey neck and Kirk Douglas Lite chin, exactly the same as they'd been the last time I'd seen them; apart, that is, from the differences.

Now, it wasn't the strange and subtle rearrangement of features, the strengthening and softening and blurring of edges and drawing in of bits that stuck out, though they were remarkable enough. God knows, they were an improvement. You could pay a cosmetic surgeon a year's wages and you still wouldn't get such a complete and flattering make-over. Just consider that, will you? In the time it'd taken me to go to Elfland and back – no time at all, since *there* was *here* – I'd shed the unlovely appearance I'd been hatefully self-conscious about all my life and acquired a face that'd earn me a living doing aftershave commercials. And I didn't even realise it until some time later, because I was too preoccupied in a completely stunned sort of way, with the other difference, the one that made me retrace my steps back to the desk, where I happened to remember there was a calendar.

It was one of those thought-for-the-day calendars, and the pearl of wisdom it offered me was *You're only as old as you feel*. I pulled off the leaf, stared at it, laughed bitterly and dropped it into the ruins of the bin.

The date on the calendar was 12 January, just as it would have been when I left. But I'd left in 1985, and the calendar said 1995. Which was bad, because it meant that the clean-cut, distinctly good-looking twenty-five-year-old dressed in a brown suede waistcoat and green tights that I'd just seen in the mirror was indeed me.

CHAPTER NINE

That was when I heard footsteps.

Sometimes, you know, I wonder about evolution. As I understand it, the general idea is that over millions of years the process of natural selection has weeded out those traits that are useless or counter-productive and favoured those that tend towards success in Life's demolition derby. Fine; it sounds reasonable enough until you get down to cases. For instance: can anybody tell me why the hell blind, limb-freezing panic got included in the package, at the expense of, say, wings, or a back-up central nervous system, or telepathy?

So there I was, frozen to the spot, unable to think anything much except *shit fuck help buggery* (and it was only because I still had some of that wonderfully forceful, abrasive Elf-side-acquired personality left that I was able to think in swear words; but even that was slipping away, and before my microsecond of panic was over I'd already started replacing the strong language with *oh dear oh my help oh Lord*) and the footsteps got closer and closer; and before I could get a grip on myself and start scanning for useful stuff such as windows or built-in wardrobes or sofas I could crawl behind, the doorknob turned (in perceived time, it rotated as slowly as a large hourly paid planet) and the door opened, and this stranger walked in.

'Who the bloody hell are you?' he asked.

If my other personality hadn't more or less completely drained away into the floor by then, leaving me with the rotten old non-boo-to-geese-saying default personality I'd had before I crossed the line, I might easily have asked him the same question. I'd been expecting (dreading, to be pedantically correct) the headmaster, a seven-foot-tall, vicious, steel-haired bastard with enormous eyebrows and a bald head like the Kremlin dome. This joker was shorter than me by a head, in his mid-thirties and wearing a Microsoft T-shirt. Of course, I didn't know about Microsoft, but my headmaster would rather have worn a barbed-wire shroud than a T-shirt of any description. This bloke was no more a headmaster than I was.

'Well?' he repeated. 'And what are you doing in my office?'

'Um,' I replied, and all things considered, I reckon it was a pretty good effort.

'What?'

I tried smiling. A smile defuses even the most tense social situation, as well as releasing endorphins or something of the sort into the bloodstream, making you more relaxed and better able to cope. At least, that's what I read in a dentist's waiting room once, though I have to say that I tried smiling at the dentist shortly afterwards, and it didn't work then, either. 'I'm sorry,' I said. 'I think I may be lost.'

The short man didn't seem very impressed by that. 'I'm going to call the police,' he said. 'Stay right there. If you move, I'll smash your face in.'

He'd have needed a stepladder to make good on that threat, but I wasn't looking for a fight, even if for once there was a one-in-a-million chance that I might win. 'Please,' I said, 'don't do that. Is this – I mean, I was at school here.'

That seemed to calm him down just a tad; at least he didn't reach for the phone on the desk. 'So what?' he said. 'This place hasn't been a school for nearly ten years. What gives you the right to go prowling round my office like you owned the place? And how did you get in, anyway?'

That last one was going to be tricky, I could tell, and I was just wondering, in a very abstract and theoretical way, whether bashing the bloke on the head and running for it might not be such a bad idea at that, when he took a step back and looked at me.

'Hold on,' he said, 'I know you.'

Well, I wasn't going to call him a liar to his face, even if his face was on a level with my collar-bone, but if we'd met I didn't remember. 'Do you?' I asked.

He didn't answer straight away. Then a sort of combination one-size-fits-all smile and frown lip up his fairly commonplace features. 'You're him, aren't you? Bloody hell, you *are* him. Where did you suddenly pop up from, then?'

Not terribly helpful, you'll agree. 'I'm sorry,' I said, 'but I don't quite follow. Who do you think I am?'

He laughed. 'You're my special benefactor,' he said, relaxing perceptibly (but he was still firmly between me and the door). "It's all thanks to you I was able to buy this place. Well, bugger me. Where have you been all this time?'

I was morally certain he didn't want to know that. 'Please,' I said, 'will you tell me what you're talking about? Only I've been, um, away, and—'

He laughed. Heartless git. 'Oh, you've been away all right. Don't you know what happened?'

The urge to belt him one on the nose was getting stronger by the second, and it didn't have much to do with effecting an escape. 'No,' I said. 'Will you tell me, please?'

'You vanished,' he replied, grinning. 'The way I understand it, one minute you were there, one of the pupils at this exclusive toffee-nosed private school, and the next you'd gone. No clues, no ransom note, nothing. Cops turned the area upside down for a fortnight, your picture was on the news and in the papers, and they never had a clue what'd happened to you. Course, once they'd given up the search, the smelly stuff really hit the fan – your family sued the school for ten million, the school had to close and sell up; I was lucky, I nipped in and did a deal with the receivers, got this joint for pennies. Thank you,' he added, beaming. 'You did me a right favour there. Now fuck off out of here before I have you arrested.'

'Yes, but—'

'Yes but nothing,' he growled, his grin dying away suddenly. 'I'm not a bloody lawyer, don't know about these things; for all I know, your turning up again and not being dead after all might mean the whole deal's off or something.' He scowled at me. 'How do I know you're really him, anyway? For all I know, you might just be some con artist pretending to be him, just to get money off me.'

He was going a bit too fast for me. 'It's all right,' I said, 'I don't want any money from anybody, I just wanted to know where everybody'd gone. My parents,' I added, as what he'd just said finally permeated through my thick skull. 'They think I'm dead?'

'Everybody thinks you're dead,' he replied. 'Come on, get real. Do you honestly think you'd be worth ten million quid to anybody if you were alive?'

An entirely valid observation, if tactlessly phrased. 'Everybody,' I repeated. 'Oh.'

You're way ahead of me, I expect. Well: if it'd been ten years, and everyone was sure I'd snuffed it, there was absolutely no reason to think that she might have waited for me. Probably married with two kids by now, and who wasn't to say she hadn't had a lucky escape? Which was assuming the relationship would've lasted beyond the puppy-love stage, which of course it wouldn't, because how many people do you know who married their childhood sweethearts? Nevertheless and even so; *shit*, I thought. *Bloody interfering elves*.

'You still here?' the short man said.

'What? Oh, I see what you mean.' I tried to remember how to move. 'I'll be going now, shall I?'

'You do that, sunshine. And listen: if you so much as breathe a word about being him and not being dead after all, my lawyers'll be all over you like flies on a dog turd, so you just watch it, understood?'

He got his gardener, a very large man called Kurt, to show me to the end of the drive; in case, presumably, I'd forgotten the way. One thing that was definitely new since my time was the radio-controlled twelve-foot-high gates and the razor-wire fence. Getting back in was definitely not going to be easy, assuming I ever wanted to. Which I didn't. Probably.

The railway station in the small town five miles down the road from the school had closed and been turned into a tyre-and-exhaust outfit; not that it mattered, since elves apparently don't use money. I sat down on a low wall as the rain started to drizzle, and reflected on what the Melissa elf had said. Sure, I could go back, but the person who arrived could never be me, just some old guy inconveniently returned from the dead. Did I still exist, I wondered; was the me who'd crossed over into Elfland stranded somewhere in some spatio-temporal waiting room, twiddling his thumbs in a vortex of warped chronology and reading back issues of *Scientific Aztec*? I couldn't see how that could be possible. He'd gone, been blitzed out of existence when I crossed over; not like the bits of data you're supposed to be able to retrieve from a crashed hard drive, but lost for ever. Properly speaking, he'd been lost when I *entered* Elfland, when my personality changed from pathetic little weed into arrogant, aggressive jerk. Now I was back home, the jerk was fading away and the weed was, so to speak, growing up again through the cracks; but I was now a twenty-five-year-old pathetic weed, which was a very different kettle of scampi from the fifteen-year-old variety. After all, I didn't feel all that different, I still had the mindset and database of experiences and overall gauche unloveliness of a teenager. (*You're as young as you feel*, quoth the calendar), which wasn't going to sit well in the body of a man who was meant to be ten years older, wiser and more mature. As far as I could see, I was inevitably doomed for a life of solitude, inadequacy, stunted emotional growth and working in local government.

Now to be fair, it's not as though I'd been anticipating a wonderful life and a glorious career even if I hadn't been scooped up and dumped in a deep pool of weirdness; I was, after all, the kid who'd seen the elf – I wasn't ever going to amount to very much. But . . . all right, I'd have been pathetic and sad no matter what happened, but at least I'd have been pathetic and sad with Daddy George's money to fall back on – was he going to welcome me home with open arms if it meant parting with ten million quid? Somehow I had my doubts about that one – and there was at least the slender possibility that I had actually found true love, if only for the short period of time that it took Cru to grow sick of the sight of me. As it was, I hadn't even had that.

Not fair, I thought. *Not fair.*

So I could jump under a bus (not a train, since there weren't any), or I could drift aimlessly through life getting trodden on and serve me bloody well right; or I could do what I'd promised Melissa and the Fuller elf I'd do as soon as I got here – in fact, wasn't that supposed to be the main reason for returning, this frightfully important wrong to be righted that mattered so desperately much to me that I'd clean forgotten all about it until now?

Yeah, right. Might as well. Nothing better to do.

Almost immediately, of course, I realised that there was now a problem with the original plan. The notion that I was the person best suited to rescue the enslaved elves depended on me being on the inside; and now, of course, I wasn't. In fact, I wasn't anything any more; my whole life, such as it was, had been wiped out by a pesky chronological anomaly, and all because of those rotten, interfering, we-know-what's-best-for-you-even-if-you-don't elves (the same ones I'd been dead set on rescuing a few hours ago; well, they could forget that, for a start). Now, for the first time in my life, I had *real* problems. It wasn't just a case of my parents not loving me or not being popular at school or having a face like a prune and the physique of a Lowry portrait of an anorexic; right now, I had nowhere to sleep, nothing to eat, no money and no means of getting any. Those aren't just a few specks of dust in Life's ice cream, those are real problems, as faced by millions of real people every day right across the world.

Fuck, I thought. *I'm screwed.*

Not a pleasant situation to find yourself in, at that. Of course, there was one other option: I could find some grass with a circle in it, and go crawling back to the elves. Somehow I got the feeling that starvation and homelessness and stuff like that didn't happen over there; and even if economic disaster was possible on the other side of the line and they were temporarily hungry or broke, all they had to do was fast-forward until they reached the point where the found gold dust in the bed of a stream or their number came up in the premium bonds draw. *All right for some*, I thought resentfully, *they just don't know they're born.*

(And all this anger after I'd been penniless and destitute for about three-quarters of an hour. God only knew what I'd be like after, say, an hour and a half. Storming the Winter Palace single-handedly, probably.)

No, I told myself, *you're being melodramatic. All right, maybe Daddy George won't be overjoyed at seeing you again, not to mention forfeiting his ten million quid, but he's still family, blood is thicker than water, the prodigal lamb goes most often to the well, and there's no place like home.*

Assuming you can get there.

Not so much of a problem as the penniless-and-destitute thing, but still a problem. No train; no money for a ticket even if there had been one, so forget buses too. My sturdy yeomen ancestors (on my mum's side; my father, of course, was a bloody *elf*) would've sneered at me and told me that's what the flat-bottomed things on the end of my legs were for. But it was over a hundred miles from school to home and I didn't even know what direction to start walking in. How the hell was I supposed to find my parents' house if I didn't even know whether to turn left or right at the bottom of the road?

But of course. How stupid of me. All I had to do was hitch a lift.

Oh sure. Well, in this era of wandering serial killers and smiling little old ladies with axes in their shopping bags, do you stop and pick up hitch-hikers any more? Of course you don't. Back in 1985, however, things were different, and I was still thinking in those terms.

After a bit of aimless wandering I found a main road with lots and lots of big lorries and cars swooshing up and down (the cars looked odd, as if they'd been left on a hot radiator and started to melt; I assumed that was because of Progress), and I walked beside it for a couple of hours until it got too dark to see and my thumb hurt from being waggled. By this stage I was painfully aware that my last meal had been a school breakfast in 1985, and the blisters on my heels weren't helping much, either. I sat down on a little patch of grass between the crash barrier and the chain link fence, leaned up against a fence post and closed my eyes for a minute or two.

When I opened them again, someone was pointing an offensively bright torch in my face and telling me to get up. It took me a few seconds to boot up my sorely fragmented memory and figure out who and where I was – I'd been having this wonderful dream where I was back at school, with nothing worse to contend with than an unprepared-for maths test – during which time the voice behind the torch repeated its request, only louder and not quite so graciously. *Policemen*, I realised. *Wonderful*.

Of course, they asked what I thought I was doing, dossing down beside a main road in a designated something-or-other area, but I got the feeling they didn't really want to know, and I quite definitely didn't want to tell them anything remotely resembling the truth. Car design wasn't the only thing that had changed since 1985; these days, it appeared, police fashions tended towards thick belts with loads and loads of scary-looking toys dangling off them, including a few obscure-looking gadgets I felt sure that any self-respecting Imperial Stormtrooper would give his right prosthetic limb for. These weren't the cuddly, helpful bobbies of my youth (they weren't even then, but at least they didn't clank when they walked), and my instincts told me they were probably a bit short on patience and understanding, and not at all minded to be told interesting stuff about elves.

'Sorry,' I said.

They helped me into the back of their car by the scruff of my neck, stuck the siren on (whatever happened to DAA-dum, DAA-dum, by the way? If you ask me, this modern cat-in-a-combine-harvester noise they've got these days isn't a patch on the old one) and off we went for a ride.

At first I just sat there, hating Fate and God and the world in general (not to mention bloody elves); and then it occurred to me that at least I wasn't still walking, risking chronic carpal tunnel syndrome by wiggling my thumb like a loon, and that where I was going it'd probably be warm and dry, and they might well give me a cup of tea, and possibly food as well. That felt like a promising avenue of thought, so I followed it up by recalling something about being allowed one phone call (or was that only in America?), not to mention the right to have a lawyer present . . . Not that I wanted a lawyer, of course, but by the time we reached the cop-shop and they'd asked me my name fifteen times and taken my photograph and confiscated by bootlaces it'd probably be cracking on for midnight, and the thought of rooting some fat git of a lawyer away from his fireside and TV and making him trek in from the suburbs and sit around for an hour or so on an uncomfortable chair gave me a distinct glow of sadistic pleasure. Misery should be like Quality Street, something you share with those around you.

More to the point, I could phone home, or if it really was just America where they let you do that, I could get the solicitor to phone home for me. (That'd be better: an experienced orator, he'd be far more likely to know what to say than I would.) Looked at from that perspective, I began to realise that getting nicked was in fact the best possible thing that could have happened to me, and that the grim-faced kydex-fetishist sitting beside me was really my best friend in all the world.

Well, maybe not that; but it could be worse, and there

was at least a fair chance that things were going to turn
out all right. I smiled (it was dark in the back of the car,
so there was no risk of them seeing me. I have an idea
it's a serious offence, smiling in a police car without a
licence).

About twenty minutes later the car stopped, they
extracted me from it with what I'm sure was the minimum of reasonable force, and took me to say hello to the
desk sergeant. He turned out to be a pleasant enough
fellow if you happen to like Nazis, and even let me keep
my socks after he'd snipped them lengthways with a pair
of scissors to make sure I didn't have an Uzi hidden in
them. I thanked him for his kindness and asked about
the phone call thing.

Turns out it *is* only in America; but when I explained
that really it was all a mistake and I hadn't been dossing
down by the road, it was really a very important and
sacred ritual that was essential to my religion, and
hadn't there been that case recently where they awarded
record damages for wrongful arrest, I guess he decided
that if letting me use the phone would induce me to
shut up, the quality of mercy wasn't strained and
anyway, it wasn't his phone bill.

My main fear was that there'd be nobody home; typical, I thought, for them to be out on the razzle –
probably getting smashed out of their minds at some
criminally expensive restaurant before driving drunk-
enly home, wickedly irresponsible and dangerous –

'Hello?'

Apparently not; at least, there was someone at the
end of the line. Wasn't sure I recognised the voice, but it
could be a new live-in handyman or other peon. 'Hello?'
I replied.

'Hello.'

No, not a voice I was familiar with. 'Is that Norton six seven six five eight?'

'Yes. Who's this?'

Um, I thought. 'Could I speak to George Higgins, please?'

'Ah, right,' the voice said. 'I know that name. They're the people who had this house before the people we bought it from.'

My mind spied with its little eye something beginning with S, in which the rest of me was enmired up to the kneecaps. 'Oh,' I said. 'Look, I don't suppose you happen to have their new number, do you?'

'Sorry,' replied the voice. 'I used to have the Perkins' number – that's who we bought from – but I seem to remember hearing they'd emigrated to Tasmania. 'Course, you could ring their old number, if I can find it, and the people who bought their old house – the old house they had after this one, I mean – they might have their number in Tasmania, if that's any help.'

The desk sergeant was scowling and tapping the dial of his watch; somehow, I got the feeling he wouldn't be enthusiastic about playing hunt-the-Higginses across two hemispheres. 'No, that's OK,' I said. 'Thanks, anyway.'

Thanks, anyway, unhelpful bastard was what I really wanted to say, but I didn't, not with a police officer watching. Instead I put down the phone and looked glum, something that came naturally to me.

'Well?' said the desk sergeant.

'They've moved,' I replied.

'Really.' His expression communicated more clearly than words ever could his belief that if I'd been out of circulation for so long that my next of kin had moved away without bothering to tell me, I must've been in prison, probably for a crime so heinous that even my own mother wanted to make sure I'd never be able to find her. 'Right, this way.'

'Can I see a lawyer, please?'

A dab hand at non-verbal communication, this one; his look of weary distaste was quite remarkably eloquent. 'Yeah, all right,' he said. 'I'll ring the duty solicitor when I've got a minute.'

Since I appeared to be the night's only customer, and there didn't seem to be anybody else in the place except him and me, I wasn't sure what there was to keep him from ringing through right away. Still, I wasn't going to say that to his face. 'That'd be really kind and helpful,' I said. 'Thank you.'

Flattery got me somewhere in this instance; a small whitewashed apartment with a bed and a sink, and an extremely burglar proof front door. The view wasn't up to much, but you can't have everything. 'Any chance of a cup of tea?' I called out, just before he left me to it. The what-did-your-last-butler-die-of way in which he slammed the door on me put his previous efforts to shame.

There's a certain light-headed relief that comes with being locked up in a police cell; the feeling that it can't possibly get any worse than this, so whatever happens next is bound to be an improvement. I guess that's a warped echo of the eternal optimist in all of us, the man falling out of a plane at 50,000 feet and muttering 'So far, so good,' every second of his descent. Deceptive, of course; if there's one unalterable truth in the universe, it's that something, at least one aspect of your current situation, can always get worse, no matter how lousy everything may already seem. Nevertheless, I'll admit that as I lay down on the bed I still had a few little snippets of hope left, wrapped up, as it were, in the table-napkin of innocence. All right, so Mum and Daddy George had vanished into the unchartable wastes of the telephone directory and it'd probably take Philip Marlowe five years, working full time, to find them. Could be worse; the silver lining was that now I wasn't going to have to be beholden to them ever again. I was, in a sense, free.

Odd choice of place to be free in, the nick; but that was a purely temporary thing, I felt sure, because after all I hadn't actually done anything wrong, and this was England, a free country, cradle of parliamentary democracy and birthplace of trial by jury, habeas corpus and the presumption of innocence. Ten minutes after my solicitor arrived, I'd have my bootlaces back and be at liberty to go about my lawful occasions. No sweat.

I guess the soothing nature of these reflections must've lulled me to sleep, because the next thing I remember was being woken up by the scraunch of the lock. The door swung open – you may find this distressing, but in police stations room service doesn't knock before entering – and my friend the desk sergeant shuffled in.

'You,' he said. 'This way.'

After a short walk down a dreary-looking corridor (it seemed longer because of the pins and needles I'd woken up with) I ended up in a small room with a table and three chairs. As far as the aesthetics were concerned, I preferred the cell. The desk sergeant dumped me in one of the chairs, and a moment later we were joined by a young woman who was introduced to me as the duty solicitor.

No introduction, however, was necessary. We'd already met.

CHAPTER TEN

'You bastard,' she said.

I smiled; or at least I twisted my face into something more or less smile-shaped. 'Hello, Cru,' I said. 'Fancy meeting you like—'

'You *bastard*!' she repeated. 'You horrible, thoughtless, worthless scumbag. What the hell are you doing here?'

Well, I thought; fine solicitor she turned out to be if she didn't know that. 'I've been arrested,' I explained.

I think I may have missed the point of her question. 'I know that, you moron,' she snapped. 'What I mean is, what the bloody hell happened to you? One minute you were there, the next you'd gone. We were looking for you for days, we thought you were dead. Where on earth did you go?'

'Ah,' I said. 'Do you really want me to answer that?'

'Oh, for crying out loud,' she said, snuffling through

her rage. 'What a stupid question. Of course, you always were singularly thick; in fact, you could build a three-masted schooner out of the short planks you're as thick as. But even by your standards, that's a very stupid question.'

I nodded. 'All right,' I said. 'I got kidnapped.'

'Really.' She leaned back and folded her arms. Her eyes were a bit red; maybe someone had been smoking in the room earlier. 'By aliens, I suppose.'

'No,' I replied. 'By elves. Want me to go on?'

She shrugged. Apart from a few superficial changes, most of which I approved of, she looked much the same. Exactly the same, as it were, apart from the differences. 'Sure,' she said, 'why not? I like listening to deranged drivel. You were kidnapped by elves. What for?'

I laughed. 'They thought they were doing me a favour.'

'I see.'

'Well,' I qualified, 'one of them, the one who . . .' *The one who's you on the other side* was what I'd started to say, but I decided against it at the last moment. Weirdness, like soy sauce, should be introduced sparingly to anything you want someone else to swallow. 'The one who did those maths answers,' I said (*Good recovery*, I thought). 'You remember, the ones I showed you . . .'

A thoughtful look crossed her face. 'I remember,' she said. 'But don't sidetrack me. This elf.'

'I was going to hide her in one of the sheds out back,' I went on, 'but instead she sort of grabbed me and next thing I knew we were in Elfland—'

'She,' Cru repeated.

'What? Oh, right. It was a female elf, yes.'

'I see. Sorry, you were saying.'

Captain Scott could've survived in the same room as that *I see*, and possibly Amundsen or a fairly hardy yeti. Too chilly for me, though.

'It wasn't like that,' I said. 'For crying out loud, she was only six inches tall. What do you take me for, a contortionist?'

She frowned. 'Let's get this straight,' she said. 'You were overpowered and abducted against your will by a six-inch-tall female?'

'Well, yes.'

'And you've spent the last ten years in a faraway land entirely populated by tiny little people?'

'No, of course not,' I snapped. 'Once you're over there, everybody's sort of normal-sized.'

'Well, of course,' she replied. 'After all, like you said, you're not a contortionist.'

Of the two contests a man can never ever win, I think on balance, I prefer playing chess against a computer. 'It wasn't like that,' I reiterated. 'You see, they reckon I'm one of them.'

'You're an elf.'

'Yes. Well, half an elf. You see—'

'In that case,' she said, 'wouldn't half of you be three inches tall? Or is it just certain parts of you that are very, very small? Like, for example—'

'No.'

She grinned. 'Actually,' she said, 'I was going to say your brain. Anyhow, that's beside the point. Well?'

Awkward silence.

'So,' I said, 'you're a solicitor now, then.'

'Yes.'

'Enjoying it?'

'No, not really.'

'Oh. Is it boring? Stressful? You meet lots of disagreeable people?'

'The worst part's probably being dragged out of bed at two in the morning to listen to clinically insane, legally dead people babbling about being kidnapped by six-inch-tall nymphomaniacs,' she said. 'The rest of it isn't so bad, actually. It's my life that's dreary and horrible and wretched and screwed up beyond all hope of redemption, rather than the job itself.'

I kind of got the feeling that she was subtly steering the conversation back to the topic I didn't really want to discuss any further at that point. 'I'm sorry things aren't going so well for you,' I said – yes, I know, incredibly stupid thing to say. But dammit, the day before that I'd only been fifteen, how the hell was I supposed to know?

'You're sorry,' she repeated. 'Oh, well then, *that*'s all right. I can stop sleepwalking through my life in a state of dull agony and have some fun now, I suppose. So kind of you.'

The traditional cartoon light bulb started to glimmer faintly in my head, and I glanced down at her hands. Ring-free zones from knuckles to nails. Certainly not conclusive, but not without evidential value. 'Look,' I said, 'can you get me out of here so we can talk properly? I really don't feel right in here.'

She shook her head. 'Nope,' she said, 'I think I'm going to leave you here. After all, that way at least I'll have some idea where you are.'

Well, I couldn't be sure: Cru did make jokes, from time to time, but she had the sort of deadpan delivery that made Buster Keaton look like Jim Carrey; and if anybody of my acquaintance was capable of leaving me in prison out of raw pique, it was her. 'If it's all the same to you,' I said, 'I'd really rather leave now, if that can be arranged.'

She breathed out slowly, through her nose. 'As it happens,' she said, 'there's another element in the equation that you don't know about yet; at least, I'm assuming you don't. All right; stay there, keep your face shut, don't go digging any tunnels. I'll see what I can do.'

She went out, and a copper with an expression you could've sharpened chisels on came in to keep me company. I asked him for a cup of tea, and he called me an uncouth name.

Half an hour later, she came back. 'All sorted,' she said. 'I explained that you're an amnesiac millionaire, and if they don't let you go, I'll have no option but to wallpaper the place with QCs and file a hundred-million-pound harassment suit. Let's get out of here before they change their minds.'

I frowned. 'They bought that?' I queried, as we scuttled out into the corridor.

'They did when I told them who you are,' she replied.

I didn't quite get that, but I wasn't going to argue. 'Where are we going?' I asked.

She sighed. 'Back to the office,' she said. 'You can doss down in the stationery store for tonight. After that – well, there are various options, as you'll find out. And stop dawdling, for God's sake.'

She had one of those Salvador-Dali-watch cars too; it was parked outside among the Pandas, like a solitary lamb in the middle of a pack of wolves. At first I felt extreme reluctance at getting in (after all, Cru was my age, far too young to drive a car . . .). But she explained that it was all right – 'Get in, or I'll leave you here' – and it turned out she was quite a good driver. Very good indeed, in fact; only an expert could've judged a gap of ten thousandths of an inch between us and a parked Transit by eye alone. Nevertheless, I was too preoccupied trying to remember various prayers I'd learned in school assembly to chat much while the car was in motion.

We stopped outside a big, impressive-looking glass tower. She got past the door by sticking something that looked like a library ticket in the lock. More progress, I assumed. After all, why bother with clumsy old metal keys when you can have a flimsy, easily scratched piece of plastic?

The office proved to be on the twelfth floor, and the lift was out of order, so it was several minutes after we'd reached her firm's office before I was fit to speak again.

'So,' I said, pushing my overdraft limit at the breath bank, 'what's all this about, then?'

She raised an eyebrow at me. Of course, she wasn't the least bit out of breath. 'You're asking me that?' she said. 'After vanishing into thin air and then suddenly materialising on a grass verge beside a major arterial road?'

I shook my head, to save breath. 'You said there was something I didn't know.'

'Loads of things,' she replied pointedly. 'But the main thing—' She paused. Odd. Couldn't ever remember seeing her at a loss for words before. 'You mentioned it yourself, while we were in the interview room. Those maths questions.'

'What? Oh, right, yes. What've they got to do with anything?'

She grinned. 'You'd be amazed,' she said. 'Look,

when you disappeared, they scooped up all the papers in
your desk, just in case there were any clues; and in due
course, when they reckoned you must've snuffed it and
there had to be an inquest, those equations of yours
were included in the evidence bundle. Somehow or
other, they got passed on to a mathematician of some
description; and as soon as he saw them, he freaked out
and got on the phone to Cambridge. Of course,' she
went on, 'we both know that you contributed about as
much to those answers as a footballer writing his auto-
biography; the maths wizards didn't know that, though,
which is how come you won the Nobel Prize.'

'I did?'

'Oh yes. Twice. The father of modern mathematics, I
think they called you the second time. Or was that the
first one, and the second one was the greatest mathematical genius since Newton? Can't remember. Anyway,
it was something like that.'

'Oh,' I said.

She nodded. 'That was just the start of it,' she went
on. 'I mean, Nobel prizes, they're all very fine and splendid but at the end of the day it's just another bit of
clutter on the mantelpiece every time you dust. The
money, on the other hand—'

'The money,' I parroted.

'Ah, you've woken up. And good morning to you, too.
Now if you want precise details, I can fish around in the
library for today's *Financial Times* and we can see what
Higginsoft shares were worth at close of business yesterday. If you're prepared to make do with a quick and
dirty estimate, I'd say your twenty per cent must be
worth, oh, two billion. Give or take ten million. Will
"lots" do to be going on with?'

'Two billion pounds?'

She shrugged. 'Or thereabouts. Not,' she added, 'that it'll do *you* much good. After all, like they say, you can't take it with you.'

'Huh?'

'Oh for God's sake, have I got to draw Venn diagrams? You're dead, silly. Or had you forgotten?'

I took that personally. 'No, I'm not,' I replied.

'According to one coroner, one High Court judge and five Lords of Appeal in ordinary, you're as dead as the Monty Python parrot – which may explain, come to think of it, why you will insist on repeating everything I say. You want to tell all those important people that they've cocked it up and they're wrong, you go ahead. Of course,' she added, 'when your stepfather finds out, he'll undoubtedly see to it that the Court was right after all. If only retrospectively. In case you didn't know, Lord Higgins isn't a very nice man.'

'*Lord* Higgins?'

She nodded. 'For services to industry,' she said. 'Ten million of them, direct to party funds just before the last election. Cheap at half the price, everybody said at the time.'

'My God,' I whispered. 'And I thought the shoe trade wasn't doing too well.'

She giggled. 'Higginsoft doesn't make shoes, you idiot,' she said. 'And neither does Higgins Integrated Systems or HiggInside. Your stepfather's gone into the hi-tech business, thanks to your maths homework. In just over a month, he'll be launching Higgins ™95, the biggest software event in history.' She opened a desk drawer, took out a roll of peppermints and ate one. Didn't offer me one, of course. 'Can't recall offhand what the projected sales figures are, but it's a moderately safe bet that by this time next year, he'd be able to buy Australia out of his pocket change.' She stopped to crunch the peppermint, then went on: 'So you can see why he wouldn't be terribly keen to have you show up again.'

My head was spinning too much to allow me to do nuances of meaning and stuff like that. 'Can I?' I asked.

She clicked her tongue, a manoeuvre that resulted in an atomiser-fine spray of peppermint juice. 'You know,' she said, 'for a double Nobel laureate, you're a bit slow on the uptake. Come on, think about it. You own twenty per cent of everything he's got, plus the technology it's all based on. You don't get to be the third richest man in the world by caring and sharing. And from what I've heard about him, his business methods are – well, businesslike.'

I shrugged. 'Oh well,' I said. 'What you've never had you'll never miss, I guess.' I stood up and walked a couple of steps, for no apparent reason. 'Lucky for me you're so clued up about high finance and stuff.'

'I'm not, you fool. I just follow this one particular company.'

I was touched. 'What, because of me?' I asked.

She threw a typewriter at me.

Well, I say typewriter; back in 1985, they still had them, you know. But what she threw was something a bit more advanced, though obviously not advanced enough to matter if it got bounced off a few walls. Screen printer, I think they call them.

'Hey,' I objected, reasonably enough.

'Bastard,' she replied, and tried to follow up the screen-thingummy with a telephone. Fortunately, they don't make ideal medium-range missiles, on account of being tethered to the wall by a finite length of cable.

'Sorry,' I offered, ducking behind a filing cabinet. 'Was it something I said?'

Her next selection was a stapler; far more practical and aerodynamic. I can only assume that the reason she missed was the tears in her eyes. 'Yes,' she snuffled angrily. 'Quite a few things, actually. God, I wish I'd left you in that cell. What did you have to go coming back for, anyhow? Everything was so much better without you.'

Well, now she'd actually said it out loud, though of course I'd had my suspicions from the moment I saw her in the interview room. All perfectly reasonable, of course. There she'd been, getting on with her life after I went away; presumably she'd found someone else - well, she would, wouldn't she? - and just when everything seemed to be coming together, I suddenly reappear like a Klingon bird of prey decloaking off the starboard bow. What's she supposed to do about that? She can't bring herself to tell me to get lost, she isn't interested any more; not someone with a wonderful, compassionate nature like Cru. It must've cost her a lot in terms of emotional airmiles to say it straight out like that. I admired her for it, really.

'Oh,' I said.

She paused, her arm drawn back to launch a black plastic desk tidy. 'What the bloody hell do you mean, "oh"?' she snarled tearfully. 'For pity's sake, at least make an effort instead of grunting like a sick pig.'

'It's all right,' I said. 'I understand, really I do.'

'Understand what?'

I took a deep breath. Wasn't easy, because even

though it was ten years or forty-eight hours since I'd last set eyes on her, I realised I still felt exactly the same about her (a sort of nervous devotion, like those people in South America who worshipped volcanoes) and having to admit it was all over between us hurt like careless dentistry. 'That it's time we got on with our lives,' I said, 'recognised that – well, we've grown apart, basically. I mean, you've got your career, you've obviously achieved so much in the last ten years—'

'As opposed to a measly brace of Nobel prizes?'

I shrugged. 'That wasn't me, we both know that. I'd only hold you back. To be honest, I never was good enough for you – *shit*, that hurt.'

'Good.'

I'd been wrong about the plastic desk tidy: it flew pretty straight, and turned out to be chunkier than I'd thought. 'So,' I went on, skipping down behind the desk, 'I guess it'd probably be for the best if I just sort of wander off now and let you get on with what you were doing.'

Pause, during which she didn't throw anything or even sniffle. 'All right,' she said.

'You're OK with that, then?'

'Sure. And you can come out now. I've put down the file-card box.'

Well, the basis of any lasting relationship is trust; and she had, too. Just as well. One of those things could give you a nasty bump on the head. I straightened up and looked at her. The expression on her face was – well, neutral, really.

'So,' she said, 'what're you planning to do?'

I scratched my ear, not that it was itchy or anything. 'Haven't thought about it,' I confessed. 'Really, I don't think I've got that many options to choose from. I'll have to go back.'

'Back? Where back?'

'The other side of the line. Elfland. I mean, there's nothing for me here any more.'

'I see.' Her stare would've kept a woolly mammoth oven-ready for a million years. 'Back to your six-inch friends, huh?'

'Sorry, didn't I explain about that? Over there, you see, they're normal height. In fact, normally they'd be normal here, it's just that my stepfather electrocutes them as soon as they arrive.'

'Ah.' She nodded. 'That'd account for it. So this lady friend of yours—'

'She's not—' I started to say, then I realised what she was doing. In order to cancel out her own guilt about having found someone else, she needed me to have done the same thing. Brilliant, the way I figured that out; no formal training, sheer intuition. I honestly believe I could've had a career in psychology if I'd had the chance. 'Normal height, that's right,' I said.

'Cute, is she?'

I shrugged. 'All right,' I said. 'Blonde, They all are, in fact.'

'How unspeakably Aryan. Well, there you go. Best of luck.'

'Thank you,' I said, looking away. 'The same to you, too. Thanks again for everything.'

'Just doing my job, really.'

'Doing it very well,' I replied, because it's always a good idea to help people maintain their self-esteem. 'Oh, you won't get in any trouble, will you? With the police, I mean. If I go away again.'

She shook her head. 'Nothing to worry about,' she replied. 'So, how do you do this going-back thing? I've never seen real magic before.'

'It's very simple,' I told her. 'All I need is some grass, and a circle. In fact, for all I know the grass isn't necessary and carpet will do just as well. No special effects or anything.'

'I see. Well, I'd better let you get on with it, then.'

'All right. Though,' I added, 'I'm not in any particular hurry. Over there, you see, time has no meaning.'

She sighed. 'Wouldn't suit me, then. In this office, time costs between two and seven pence a second, depending on whether you're a partner, an assistant solicitor or a legal executive. I suppose lawyers on your side have a completely different charging structure.'

'I guess so,' I replied. 'Assuming there *are* any lawyers over there. To be honest with you, I wouldn't have thought they had any use for them.'

She looked at me oddly. 'No use me going there, then,' she said.

I wasn't quite sure why we were talking about legal fees, but my intuition told me she was just making conversation to ease over the high residual awkwardness levels. 'I suppose not,' I replied. 'Actually, I don't think you'd like it much. Things are very different there. People, too.'

'Oh? In what way?'

Nicer, I didn't say; neither did I explain that since everybody there was gentle and polite and almost lethally pacifistic, she'd stick out like a lion in a den of Daniels. 'It's very quiet,' I said. 'Dull, really. You'd be bored stiff in five minutes.'

Which of course wasn't true, since all the boring bits

got edited out; and I had my doubts about whether she'd be all that out of place, bearing in mind the abrupt personality change I'd experienced while I was there. If Elfland made me assertive, loud-mouthed and uppity, surely it'd turn her into a baa-lamb. In fact, I knew exactly what she'd be like there, since I'd already met her.

Eeek, I thought.

If I really was a Nobel-prizewinning maths genius, I'd probably have been able to figure out what'd happen if Cru and Melissa, identical twins apart from the differences, were ever to meet face to face. But I wasn't, and I really didn't fancy the possibility that the result would be a very loud and destructive explosion. Besides – cards-on-table time – Cru being all sweet and gentle just wouldn't be right, I'd been there and seen that and, as far as was concerned, you could keep it. The Cru I wanted, the one I was in love with—

Anyway.

'You wouldn't be happy there,' I said. 'That's assuming you'd even be able to get across, which I doubt – there's all sorts of rules and science stuff that reckons it's not possible. I can, of course, because I'm half an elf already, but as far as you're concerned I just don't know. Anyway, not worth the risk, really.'

'No, I suppose not.'

I looked at her sideways. Total absence of emotion, like a waxwork Vulcan. The sort of look that makes you think that if you whispered something in her ear, you'd probably end up being deafened by the echo.

'Well, must fly,' I said. 'You wouldn't happen to know where the nearest lawn is, do you? I think I'd better stick to grass for the time being.'

'Down the stairs, out through the main doors – just press the button, they're electric – then keep bearing left until you come to a flight of steps going down; at the bottom of those take a right, under a sort of portico thing, left there, straight on about twenty-five yards, straight ahead of you, can't miss it. Sort of cloister arrangement where the typing pool eat their sandwiches in summer.'

'Thank you,' I said, trying to remember what came after the electric doors. 'Oh, and can I borrow a dustbin or something? To make a circle in the grass with.'

'Help yourself. That one big enough, or do you need the next size up?'

'No, that'll do fine. Thanks.'

'You're welcome.'

Neither of us moved. Part of me, approximately ten per cent by volume, was wishing there was some way to make all this easier on her. The remaining ninety per cent was wishing there was some way to make it all easier on me. No dice on either account, seemed to be the consensus of opinion.

'You'd better empty it first,' she said.

'What?'

'The dustbin.'

'Oh, yes, right.' I looked round. 'Where?'

'Outside. Where you're going to turn, turn right, then right again, that'll bring you to the trash chute. Then to get back, instead of left then left again, which'd just be retracing your steps, go straight on, then left and just follow the alleyway round till you come to a sort of sunken floor arrangement; there's a left turn directly opposite where you'll have come in, take that, then the third right, brings you back to where you started from.'

'Ah,' I said. 'OK, I'll find it.'

Did I mention that my sense of direction is so amazingly acute I could get lost in a telephone box? Sad but true. I made a mental note to dump the few pieces of screwed-up paper nestling inside the bin into another bin on my way back through the office.

'Anyway,' she said. 'I guess this is goodbye, then.'

'I suppose so.'

'I mean,' she went on, 'from what you were saying, it doesn't sound like you'll be coming back.'

I tried a nonchalant shrug, which turned out like a mudslide off a giant blancmange. 'No way of telling, really,' I said. 'Who knows, I may really hate it. After all, last time I was only there for what, three-quarters of an hour. I may decide I can't stick it and come back.'

She frowned at me, clearly debating whether it was worth the hassle and weirdness involved in getting me to explain how I'd disappeared ten years ago but only been away for forty-five minutes. An untroubled mind and a quiet life must've won out, because she sniffed and started fidgeting with a plastic cup full of paper clips. 'Don't suppose you will,' she said. 'Oh well. Have a nice life, wherever you finally end up.'

'You too,' I replied, and picked up the dustbin. I guess it must've stood there a fair old time, to judge by the way it'd marked the carpet. I was ready to go now, but I couldn't resist one last cheap parting shot. 'Whoever he is,' I said (head averted, in fact straight into the dustbin, which imparted a wonderful booming resonance to my words. Cross between God and a railway station announcement), 'tell him from me, he's a lucky man.'

She gazed at me with an expression of bewilderment,

understanding, contempt and joy, all mixed together and steeped in relief. Then she called me a rude name and threw the paper clips at me.

As a half-elf and a serial Nobel prizewinner, I can probably explain just why a plastic cup full of paper clips makes such a rotten missile. The ballistics of it are actually quite interesting; it's all to do with the weight-to-surface-area ratio of the cup and the way in which the shifting contents alter the centre of gravity while the arc of the trajectory is still developing. But we'll leave that on one side for now, maybe come back to it later once we've got the next chunk of narrative out of the way. The net result, which is what we're concerned with here, was that I ducked to get out of the way but, because the cup's flight path described an outswinging curve, I contrived to put my head where the cup finally decided to go.

On a scale of one to ten, where ten is a right cross to the chin from Mike Tyson and two is a greenfly landing on your nose, I guess the impact of the cup registered a solid 0.0000000000000000000000001. In other words, it wasn't the cup that knocked me off balance at all. If anything, it was my trying to get out of the revised line of fire at the very last minute that made me wobble on the ball of my left foot, overbalance and go plunging forward like a badly felled tree. Cru, it turned out, had far better reflexes than me. She cleared out of the way with a very impressive standing jump, which left her with both feet in the dustbin. Unfortunately, the confinement of her movements caused by the sides of said dustbin meant that she couldn't move her feet to adjust her balance. So, after a moment of perfect equilibrium during which she stood perfectly upright, like a ball on top of the stick perched on the trained sea lion's nose, she toppled sideways like a felled bowling pin.

I'd like to claim that it was a combination of true love and instinctive chivalry that made me reach out and grab her before she cracked the side of her head on the edge of the desk. The rather less attractive truth is that I was trying to fend her off me, and missed. Besides, I wasn't giving the falling-about aspect of things my full attention. I was too preoccupied with the implications of that look, and the ensuing bombardment. Could it possibly be the case, I was wondering, that I'd completely misinterpreted everything she'd said and seemed to imply, and that there wasn't a somebody else after all, and that maybe, just possibly, she was still in love with me? If so, It changed everything, because . . .

And while I was figuring out exactly what it changed. while tottering backwards into the incuse ring pressed into the carpet by the waste-paper basket with my arms full of Cru, everything suddenly stopped for a brief but perceptible moment; and when it had stopped being stopped, if you follow me, I was lying on my back in lush, dew-moistened grass with a beautiful girl in my arms.

Everything exactly the same, in other words, apart from the differences.

'Cru?' I said.

The girl looked at me. She was looking overpoweringly lovely, with her straight golden hair hanging forward over her shoulders, her lips slightly parted, her eyes wide open and deep as unfathomable pools of pure cobalt blue. In other words, the wrong bloody chick.

'Melissa,' I said.

'Michael!'

Typical. The sort of poetic justice you'd expect to get if Judge Dredd wrote sonnets. I noted in passing that I appeared to have broken my leg; but that was just the free plastic toy at the bottom of the cornflake packet of my afflictions.

CHAPTER ELEVEN

I closed my eyes. 'Fuck,' I said.

'Well,' Melissa replied, 'all right. But first, shouldn't we—?'

I sighed. 'No,' I said, 'not like that, I meant - oh, forget it. And would you mind getting off me? My leg hurts.'

'Oh.'

'In fact,' I went on, 'I think it's probably broken. Ouch,' I added, just to drive the point home.

'Sorry,' Melissa said.

'No use saying you're sorry, is it?' I snapped. 'Get off me, for crying out loud.'

She seemed to shoot upwards, like a Harrier off the deck of a ship. 'It's all right,' she said. 'Your leg, I mean. It'll fix itself.'

'Will it? Well, that's something, I suppose—' A nasty thought struck me. 'How long will it take?'

'Oh, no more than a month, if it's a clean break. And—'

'And you'll fast-forward me through it, so I won't have to endure all that lying around in traction eating grapes? No, thank you very much. From now on, my time's my own. You got that?'

She frowned. 'You want to spend a month in hospital? Actually live through it, I mean? But it's so *boring*—'

'Yes!' I shouted. 'And no, I don't enjoy being bored. In fact, I have an abnormally low boredom threshold, I can't even sit still during the weather forecast. But I will not have you pointy-eared freaks snipping out great big chunks of my life. It's not right, and I won't stand for it. Understood?'

She looked at me thoughtfully for a moment. 'I hate to have to say this, but you won't be in any fit state to stand for anything until your leg's healed. Are you sure you wouldn't rather edit it out? I mean, it's not as if there's anything useful you can do, lying on your back with one leg in the air.'

Unfortunately, she was right. I hate it when people are right at me like that; it's like having a cat that insists on fetching in dead mice and laying them at your feet, like loyal subjects bringing tribute to the Sultan. 'Oh, all right then,' I said. 'But this is the last time, understood? I've got to get back there as quickly as possible, before she changes her mind.'

'She?'

(And I could remember the whole thing; days and weeks of staring at the ceiling, nothing to do but see how many times out of ten I could hit the lampshade with a precision-spat grape pip. If I'd had to go through all that – with the irascible, short-temper, pain-in-the-bum personality I appeared to be stuck with on this side of the line – I'd have gone stir-crazy in a week. Somehow, though, acknowledging that Melissa had been absolutely right didn't make me feel any better-disposed to her at all.)

'She,' I repeated. 'Cruella. The girl I'm in love with. The wonderful girl who waited for me for ten years, even though everybody told her I was dead. The angel in human shape who now thinks I've pissed off over here for good, thanks to you and your ridiculous magic circles. Right,' I added, 'I'm off. Let's hope this is the very last time I ever see you or this loathsome place.' I looked about me for something circular to tread in. Fortunately, there didn't seem to be any cows in Elfland.

'Oh,' she said.

It was the way she said it, of course. Now if I'd been me, instead of the miserable-self-centred-jerk me, that particular expression would've made macramé out of my heartstrings. As it was, I just felt mildly uncomfortable without really knowing why.

'Trust me,' I said, 'you'll be better off. I mean, be honest. Just listen to me, would you? I'd be the sort of husband who'd come home drunk from the pub and yell the place down because his dinner wasn't on the table.'

'It would be,' Melissa replied quickly. 'I'd make sure of that. I'm a good cook,' she added. 'Why don't you let me fry you up some bacon and eggs? You like bacon and eggs.'

Well, yes, I do; and let's not forget, it'd been well over a day, going on ten years, since I'd had anything to eat. 'With fried bread?'

'And black pudding and baked beans and hash browns and sausages and fried tomatoes—'

'No, I can't stand fried tomatoes. And why aren't there any mushrooms?'

'I was just coming to them,' she said. 'Followed by toast and marmalade, with plenty of fresh coffee—'

'Proper coffee,' I pointed out, 'not that decaff rubbish.'

'Of course. We don't have decaff here; after all, we don't sleep, so who needs it?'

Talk about your temptation beyond endurance. I have a notion that if Satan had crept up to Jesus fasting in the wilderness and offered him a full cooked breakfast and a big pot of steaming Blue Mountain, we'd all be going to the pictures on Black Sabbath Eve and sending each other Walpurgis Night cards. But man shall not live by bread alone, even fried bread. 'No,' I said, 'don't bother. I'll grab something to eat once I'm back where I belong.'

'Oh.'

'Will you stop saying that, for crying out loud?'

'Sorry.'

She reminded me of someone, just as I reminded me of someone. Different someones, naturally. 'All right, you're sorry, big deal. Now, get me something I can make a circle with. Well, don't just stand there like a prune.'

'Right. Of course. Won't be a moment.'

She set off like a guilt-stricken hare, and that was what made me realise who she put me in mind of. Me, of course; human-side me, the poor fool who'd jump through six hoops backwards and land on my head in a neglected cesspool if Cru told me to. As to who I reminded me of – three guesses ought to be two too many.

Everything exactly the same, in fact, apart from the differences.

While I was still working this out for myself, she came scuttling back with a small barrel. 'This ought to do,' she said.

I looked at it. 'You couldn't find anything larger?'

'Sorry.'

I scowled at her. 'Oh's bad enough,' I said. 'Sorry's worse. Don't do it, understand?'

'Sor— I won't. Promise.'

Even then a little tiny part of me was saying, *Sweet Jesus, am I really that wet and pathetic?* And coming to the conclusion that if I was, maybe I'd be better off staying here after all. Going back to being *that* after tasting the exuberant freedom of this commanding, authoritative if rather annoying-to-other-people – but then, who gives a stuff about *other people* anyway? – personality: it wouldn't be fun. In fact, it'd be horrible. Furthermore, I'd still have all those dreadful problems to contend with - down and out, no job, Daddy George most likely out to get me and conceal my remains in the footings of a flyover, no money to buy cooked breakfasts with. And for what? Some bird who'd always treated me as commandingly and authoritatively as I was treating Melissa. *No way*, I thought. *Bugger that for a full-scale NATO training exercise.*

'On the other hand,' I said slowly, 'where's the rush? I mean,' I went on, 'if she waited for me ten years when she thought I was dead—'

Something clinked. It was Melissa sliding the coffee pot onto an already overcrowded trestle table. Of course, I should have shouted at her for doing another of those dumb time-slip things when I'd expressly ordered her not to; but the bacon was beautifully golden-crisp round the edges, and the fried eggs were exactly the way I liked them, and the sausages—

'Chair,' I pointed out.

'Ooops. I forgot.'

'Stupid woman.'

'Here you are,' she said, drawing the chair back so I could sit down. 'I'll just go and get the salt and pepper.'

'Of course, a bottle of brown sauce'd be too much to ask for,' I said with my mouth full.

'And the brown sauce,' she said. 'Shall I pour it for you?'

I shook my head. 'Give it here,' I said. 'I don't want you drowning everything in it.'

They were excellent sausages, I had to give her that, though the mushrooms were a tad underdone. Even so; maybe I *could* grow to like it here, if I tried really hard. The ability to compromise is the hallmark of a truly evolved personality, I always say.

'Here,' I mumbled through a faceful of semi-chewed toast, 'get rid of that damned barrel, will you? Somebody could trip over that and break a leg or something.'

'Sorry. I mean, right away.'

Remarkable how a good meal changes one's perspective. I guess it all goes back to our primitive hunter-gatherer instincts. A hungry man is tense, on edge, nervous, prey to all manner of doubts and worries. A man with a few thousand calories straining his shirt buttons is, by contrast, relaxed, at peace, able to sit back and take a calm, rational view of the situation at hand. Not so bad here after all, I reflected; at least, the grub's all right and it's free, you aren't forever getting arrested by over-zealous fuzz when you choose to take an al fresco nap, the locals seem polite enough, and the scenery's not bad at all. True, you've lost the only girl you've ever loved – again - but at the end of the day, what you've never had you don't miss; whereas this Melissa – not in the same league as Cruella, of course, but you wouldn't kick her out of bed, either, at least not unless you wanted something fetched from downstairs. Actually, to be brutally honest, a bloody sight better-looking than Cruella (and that's not saying much) and not nearly so bloody stroppy. If there's one thing a wise person avoids when selecting a future helpmeet, it's bloody stroppiness.

'Here,' I called out without looking round (no need),' can you get Sky Sport in this godforsaken dump?'

She didn't answer (they get moody sometimes; the best thing is to take no notice), so I kicked off my shoes and closed my eyes for a nap.

Not a sensible thing to do in Elfland, where they don't sleep but where they can fast-forward you. As far as I was concerned, I'd hardly closed my eyes when someone prodded my arm. I did the eyelid routine in reverse and muttered, 'Now what?'

To my surprise, I was surrounded by elves. Hundreds of the buggers, all looking at me as if I'd just kicked my football through their greenhouse window.

'Not now,' I grunted. 'Piss off, all of you, I'm trying to get some sleep.'

'Sleep?' said an elf I hadn't seen before.

'Yes,' I replied, 'it's where you shut your eyes and keep them shut. I used to do a lot of it at one time, but then you clowns ram-raided your way into my life, and I haven't managed to get any kip for over ten years. Go away.'

Silence, and plenty of it. Somehow, a couple of hundred people not saying anything all at the same time is a damn' sight quieter than an empty room. Spooky, too.

'Well?' I snapped – I wasn't in the mood to play games with a bunch of Enid Blyton characters. 'Do you actually want something, or have you all come here to gawp at me?'

An elf in the front row cleared her throat. Cute little thing, if you liked blondes. 'There was something,' she said.

'Oh joy,' I grunted. 'Well, spit it out then, if you must. Then I can sort you lot out and get back to my snooze.'

'It's about—' The spokeself fidgeted with the sleeve of her tunic. Very irritating. 'It's about you,' she said.

'Yes?'

'You see—'

'Oh, for pity's sake. Get on with it or go and play hopscotch in the minefield.'

'You see,' the spokeself said, 'you've been here a while now, and—'

'Don't be ridiculous. I only just got here.'

Immediately she looked down at her feet, obviously unwilling to contradict me. Another elf stepped forward. 'Actually,' he said,' that's not strictly true.'

'Huh?'

'Not strictly,' said the elf, slowly turning purple with embarrassment. Very strange effect it was, too, given the greenish tinge of the elfin complexion. 'In actual fact, you've been here six weeks, and during that time—'

'No, I bloody well—' I hesitated. No, dammit, the bugger was perfectly correct. I could remember every detail of it. Good fun, too; lots of sitting about being waited on hand, foot and finger by a bunch of obedient if exquisitely dull elves. The thought that I'd missed all that made me very angry indeed. 'You bastards,' I growled. 'What the hell did you want to go and do that for? I'd have enjoyed all that.'

'Yes,' said the elf (he was now the colour of a ripe plum, didn't suit him a bit), 'that's more or less the point. You enjoyed it very much indeed. We didn't.'

I couldn't see any problem with that. 'So?'

The elf shuffled his feet. Never actually seen anybody do that before. 'Look,' he said, 'no offence, but to be brutally honest with you, we're all a bit fed up about it. You see, because the last six weeks have been - well, not a whole bundle of laughs for any of us, it means we've all had to miss out on them. And, well, it's a bit inconvenient, actually.'

I shrugged. 'Tough shit,' I said. 'Hey, don't look at me with that constipated-yak expression. If you didn't want to miss out, you shouldn't have fast-forwarded. Especially,' I added, remembering how very, very angry I was, 'without asking my permission first. Bloody annoying habit of yours, and if you do it again I'll kick your bum. Got that?'

No answer; in fact, the concerted absence of answer was deafening.

'And you can pack that in while you're at it,' I said. 'From now on, anybody who stands there looking at me without saying anything will be deemed to be asking for my boot up their backside. All right?'

Melissa sort of nudged her way to the front of the crowd. About time, I said to myself. Why is it they're never around when you want them? 'We're very sorry,' she said, 'but it isn't.'

'Talk English, you stupid woman. It isn't what?'

Honestly. To judge by the look on her face you'd think I'd just eaten her cat. 'It isn't all right,' she simpered. 'In fact, it's not very right at all. We think—' You could see she was all tensed up about something; probably that time of the month. 'Well, we think you should go back.'

I tell you, you could've blown me down with a fart. 'You what?'

'It seems to us,' Melissa went on, averting her eyes like I was a road accident or something, 'that you haven't really fitted in terribly well since you arrived, which makes us think you probably aren't all that happy here—'

'Only because you buggers won't give me the chance,' I pointed out. 'Bloody hell, every time I try and have a bit of fun, or even just put my feet up and veg out for half an hour, some daft clown zaps me into the middle of next week. Idiotic thing to do, and I won't stand for it. Apart from that, though, I could probably get used to it here.'

Somehow, I got the impression that the elves didn't want that to happen.

I wouldn't have thought it was possible for me to get angrier than I was already; but, as so often, I surprised myself by my ability to rise to the occasion. 'For God's sake,' I snapped, 'I wish you green-faced bunch of freaks'd make your stupid minds up, once and for all. One minute you're practically kidnapping me, and you—' Meaningful scowl at Melissa. 'The moment I got here, you were trying to tear my clothes off. You don't need a degree in psychology to figure out what was on your mind.'

Melissa made a tiny whimpering noise, like a small dog whose tail's got sucked up the Hoover. 'It wasn't like that at all, I thought we were—' She stopped and pulled herself together, or at least, she managed to rally some of the outlying areas. Pulling herself together would've netted all the king's horses and all the king's men some pretty juicy overtime. 'I think we both got hold of the wrong end of the stick,' she said. 'You see—'

'Impossible,' I pointed out.

'Sorry?'

'We can't both have got hold of the wrong end of the stick,' I explained. 'Stick's only got two ends, so one of 'em would have to be the right one. Do try and express yourself a bit more clearly, otherwise it's bloody wearing trying to make out what you're trying to say.'

Reasonable enough observation, I thought; but that bunch of goggle-eyed mutants just looked at each other and shuddered with refined disgust. If I'd had the energy I'd have given them something to shudder about.

'My apologies,' Melissa said frostily. 'What I meant to say was, we feel that we've made a serious error of judgement by encouraging you to come and settle here, when it's quite obvious that this environment really isn't at all suitable for someone with your temperament and attitude. So we all think—'

I waved a hand in a vague gesture of reassurance. 'It's all right,' I said. 'Please, don't get your knickers in a twist on my account. Look, if it makes you feel any better, I forgive you. There, now you can all stop wetting yourselves with sublimated guilt and shove off.'

'Actually,' Melissa said, with a little tremor in her voice, 'not us. You.'

All I could do for a moment was stare. '*Me?*'

She nodded. 'You,' she said. 'We'd be very grateful indeed if you could possibly see your way at some point in the nearish future to going sort of away. Please,' she added.

'What? You're telling me to fuck off?'

Melissa sighed; the sigh seemed to be coming up out of the ground, like a geyser with wind. 'Yes,' she said. 'If you wouldn't mind too awfully much.'

'Oh really? And if I *do* mind?'

'Then we'd all feel terribly upset about it and blame ourselves for making you so unhappy.'

'But I'd still have to fuck off?'

'Yes.'

I didn't know what to say. I'd never been thrown out of a parallel dimension before. 'But where am I supposed to go?' I demanded. 'Fuck it, this is my home. I haven't got anywhere else. All thanks,' I pointed out,' to you lot.'

They didn't like that one bit; I could see them all squirming in unison. Enough to give a bloke vertigo.

'Well, actually,' said an elf in the second row, in a teeny-tiny little voice, 'you have sort of lived most of your life over the other side, so—'

'Oh sure,' I grunted. 'And what a life it's been. Ever since I was a kid it's been sheer hell, and you want to know why? Because of you. Because, when I was still a little snotnose brat, I saw an elf. Have you any idea what that did to me? And that was just the start; since then I've vanished, been declared officially dead, lost a staggeringly huge amount of money and the only girl I ever loved; and if I ever show my face on the other side again, Daddy George'll have me hunted down like a cockroach in the Ritz and killed. Oh, and while we're at it, I'm half an elf. Half of me is one of you creeps, so I've got every bit as much right to be here as the whole bunch of you put together. So there.'

'Actually,' Melissa whispered, 'that's not entirely true either. Not if we all say you've got to go.'

'Don't be ridiculous,' I shouted. 'Or are you trying to tell me that your laws allow you to sling someone out of your poxy little world just because you don't like his face?'

'We haven't got any laws,' Melissa said.

'Haven't got any . . . ? Pull the other one, it's got a big heavy boot on the end. Of course you've got laws. Everybody's got *laws*.'

'We haven't. We don't need them, you see, everybody here's civilised and nice. Everybody except—'

'Except me.'

'Nearly everybody,' Melissa said glumly. 'So yes, if we say we think it's be quite a good thing if you were to go somewhere else, then, strictly speaking, you've got to go.'

'Really,' I said, folding my arms defiantly. 'And if I decide I don't want to go, who the bloody hell's going to make me?'

'Um,' Melissa said. 'Well, us.'

I laughed. 'You. Oh, right. My God, I'm so scared.'

'It's all right,' another elf broke in hastily, 'we won't hurt you. It'll all be done as quickly and painlessly as possible. You honestly won't feel a thing.'

'Too frigging right I won't,' I snorted. 'Because the only thing I'll be feeling is my fist pushing your teeth down your poxy turkey throats. And don't say I haven't give you fair warning.'

Melissa looked so sad that if I hadn't been boiling with righteous fury I couldn't have helped feeling sorry for her. 'Please,' she said, 'just think of all the good you could do over on the other side. Rescuing all those poor elves trapped in your stepfather's factories, for a start. It'd be such a wonderful thing to do, we'd all be ever so grateful, and there isn't actually anybody else who could do it – well, apart from Santa Claus, of course, but he's ever so busy choosing toys for the children—'

'Hey.'

'Sorry?'

'Stop drivelling,' I told her. 'It's bad enough you coming here with a lynch mob trying to run me out of town without you drivelling on as well. I can't hear myself think for your incessant bloody yattering.'

'Sorry.'

'And don't keep saying you're sorry. I told you before—'

While I was still talking (how rude can you get?) they tried it on; I could feel the force of their united will-power pressing down on me like a vast soggy weight, beginning to push me down through the interface the way you'd stick a pen through damp blotting paper. No chance; I was, after all, half an elf, and half-human too, which gave me a huge reserve of bloody-mindedness and annoyability that their more rarefied genetic make-up denied them. I dug my extradimensional heels in and pushed back. They stopped shoving and stared at me.

'Pathetic,' I said. 'You're going to have to do better than that if you want to get rid of me. Now quit pissing about, before I lose my temper.'

Picture serried ranks of six-foot elves all sagging in unison. Funniest thing you could ever hope to see. Of course, I said to myself, two can play at that game. I reached out with whatever it was I'd been pushing back with, and sent the front two ranks sprawling in the grass. 'I'm warning you,' I said. 'Or do you want me to find out just how hard I can swat with this thing? I'm up for it if you are.'

It was rather satisfying to watch all those elves scrambling up and scurrying off to the sides, clearly scared out of their feeble wits. I'd often wondered what it'd feel like to push people around, after a lifetime of being on the other end of the procedure; for the first time, I could fully understand where all the kids who'd bullied me at school got their kicks from.

'Please don't do that,' said an elf. 'We have a saying here, a punch is the shortest distance between two victims. You're hurting yourself more than you're hurting us.'

I grinned. 'No, I'm not,' I said. 'Here, I'll show you,' I added, scattering another swathe of the buggers. 'See? Didn't hurt me a bit.'

Before that lot had picked themselves up off the deck and legged it into the wings, I felled another tranche, and another one after that. Resistance? They were too scared. And to think I'd been missing this much fun all my life!

'Stop it Michael, please!' There was Melissa, or at least her head, sticking out from under a pile of toppled elves. 'Stop now, before it's too late!'

I ignored her and launched another sweep at the last few still standing. Down they went. But when they picked themselves up, they didn't run like the others. They just stood there instead. That struck me as off, and prompted me to wonder where the others had run to.

A quick look round answered that question. They hadn't run so much as regrouped; in fact, they had me surrounded. *Big deal*, I thought. Couldn't matter less to me which direction they came from, there still wasn't anything they could do.

'Well,' I sneered, 'what are you waiting for?'

They didn't move. Too scared, I reckoned, to do anything except stand there and cower. More chicken than Colonel Sanders.

By the time I realised what they were really up to, and that the real reason for their regrouping was to form a circle in the grass around me, it was significantly too late.

CHAPTER TWELVE

The first thing that struck me when I opened my eyes was that I wasn't in Elfland any more. The second thing was a boot.

It was a black boot, as I recall, with decorative white stripes stitched up the side, and several rows of studs moulded into the sole. It seemed to take an awful long time getting to me as I lay on my back watching it, and yet by the time it made contact with my jaw I got the impression that it was travelling really rather fast. One of those relativistic paradoxes, I guess.

About half a second after that, someone blew a whistle.

I was a bit too preoccupied with the pain in my face to be properly aware of what was going on around me, but there seemed to be a whole bunch of people in shorts and long woolly socks standing around, and I think I heard someone asking someone else where the fuck he – me, presumably – had suddenly appeared from. A wonderful thing, the human brain; even while I was still three-quarters stunned from the kick, a part of my brain was patiently, diligently sorting through the data and analysing various alternative hypotheses. Shorts, for example, might be taken to imply a hot summer on the beach; but the muddy grass and long socks suggested winter, which also happened to be the football season. Add in the whistle and the studded boots, unsheathe Occam's razor and there you have it. A football match.

'Yes, you,' said a voice directly over me, 'I'm talking to you. What do you think you're playing at? And how did you get on the pitch in the first place?'

It was at about this stage in the proceedings that I became aware of approximately twenty thousand people watching me. Yes, they were a long way away, behind a load of barriers, but even so it was a bit embarrassing.

'Well?'

Even if I'd had a plausible explanation all worked out and ready to roll, my jaw wasn't exactly in prime working condition, which made it pretty well impossible for me to say anything much apart from 'Aung'. This didn't seem to have occurred to the owner of the voice, who must accordingly have taken my silence for dumb insolence.

(That same scrupulously conscientious part of my brain that had figured out the football match solution now chimed in to point out that since everything in Elfland is the same as it is here, apart from the differences, if when I'd left Elfland I'd been surrounded by a huge crowd of people, it was only logical that a similar crowd would be all around me as soon as I reached the human side. Very well-reasoned and helpful, my internal research department; if only I'd known how, I'd have fired the lot of them.)

'On your feet,' somebody said; a different voice, though, but nevertheless familiar. 'I said, on your – oh, for crying out loud. You.'

A face appeared, looming up in front of me. Hardly surprising that I remembered him, since in my timescale it was only a few hours since the last time he'd arrested me. I was impressed, however, that he recognised me so readily. Still, I guess a policeman needs a good memory for faces.

'You know this clown?' muttered the first voice.

'Too right,' said the policeman, sideways. 'I nicked him five years ago for vagrancy.'

Five years . . . With my jaw still numb, all I could do was groan.

'Fine,' said the first voice. (I decided I didn't like him very much, whoever he was). 'Practice makes perfect, arrest him again. Assault. He head-butted my boot.'

It may just have been my imagination, but the policeman seemed to hesitate for a split second. Then he told me to get up.

I did try. In fact, I managed to stand sort of Neanderthal-upright before my knees gave out and dumped me in mid-air. Instinctively, I grabbed at the nearest object for support.

Not a case where instinct knew best, since the nearest object turned out to be the policeman's leg. He landed on top of me, his nose impacting on the top of my skull. I had a feeling I knew what was going to come next.

'Right,' said the policeman in a somewhat nasal voice, 'that does it. Resisting arrest, assaulting a police officer, obstruction. You're nicked.'

Blame it on the cuts, I guess; anyhow, they hadn't

redecorated my cell since I was last there. I remembered the little brown damp stain on the ceiling as if it was yesterday. Which, of course, it had been.

It was a different desk sergeant this time; a shorter, rounder model with a thicker neck. The drill was pretty much the same, though, giving me a distinct feeling of déjà vu. Set me thinking, too; what if all this flitting backwards and forwards across the line had set up some kind of causality loop? Had I contrived to lock myself into a pattern, always ending up in this cell, starting at that brown stain? I rather hoped not.

While the desk sergeant had been divesting me of my bootlaces, I'd mumbled something or other about wanting to see the duty solicitor. But either he hadn't heard me or he didn't hold with lawyers cluttering up his nice orderly station; it'd been five hours now, and no sign of anyone. Probably just as well, I told myself, since there was a slender chance that Cruella would still be working that particular beat. If she'd been annoyed with me the last time, I didn't really want to contemplate how she'd react to seeing me again.

While I was running after this train of thought, the door opened and the desk sergeant's head appeared in the crack. 'You,' he said.

'Me?'

'You asked to see the duty solicitor. Well, you can't.'

'Oh.'

He sighed. 'I been trying her number, but it's just the machine. Rang the senior partner of her firm at home – he wasn't happy about that – and he said she'd mentioned something about going to watch her boyfriend playing in a football match.' He grinned, as widely and unnervingly as the San Andreas fault opening up just outside Los Angeles. 'You've met him,' he went on. 'He's the centre forward for United.'

'Ah,' I said. 'Any chance of a cup of tea?'

'No.'

The door swung shut, and I heard the by-now-familiar sound of the lock scraunching home. Well, at least that answered one of my questions, though not the one I'd most have liked out of the way.

The sensible, logical reaction would have been relief; after all, I'd been the one who'd screwed up ten years of her life, so I should have been glad to hear that it had all turned out right in the end and that she'd found true love with a large, sarcastic man with big, hard feet. Curiously enough, I didn't see it that way; in fact, my immediate reaction was to think unkind thoughts about her. Silly, really, though I guess you could blame it on the last vestigial traces of my Elfland obnoxious-arsehole personality.

Irrelevant what I thought about it, anyway. Her future happiness was none of my business; my own, on the other hand, was an immediate and legitimate concern insofar as there was any chance of my having any, which seemed unlikely. As far as I could judge, I was back where I'd been five human-side years ago – broke, homeless, quite possibly in grave danger of being murdered on the orders of my stepfather – except that I no longer had the option of going back to Elfland, and I was facing a spell of jail time for an impressively chunky list of serious offences that I'd be hard put to it to deny. Put like that, if I'd had the opportunity to change places with a turkey in mid-December, I'd have been a fool not to take it.

Why me? I thought. *What did I do?*

I was just weighing up the potential advantages of

lying on my back and sobbing hysterically when the door opened again. This time, my friend the sergeant didn't even speak; he just jerked his head vaguely leftish and pushed the door a bit wider.

New chairs in the interview room: that rather bendy plastic instead of wood. Same table, though, and probably the same lino on the floor, though I've got to admit that one expanse of scuffed lino looks pretty much like any other to me. Not a cheerful place, all in all; maybe Lawrence and Carol and Andy could make something of it, but even they'd need a whole week and probably a bulldozer.

She was already there when I arrived.

'Sorry I'm a bit late,' she said crisply, opening her briefcase. 'I was having a furious row with my ex-boyfriend, and it took rather longer than I expected.'

One syllable in particular caught my attention. 'Ex?'

She nodded. 'As of two hours ago, yes. You'll be delighted to hear that you were the cause. Of course. Where the hell did you suddenly materialise from, by the way? As if I didn't know.'

Only one word seemed suitable and she'd forbidden me to use it; still, rules are made to be broken. 'Sorry,' I said.

'That's all right,' she said with more than a trace of weariness. 'Did me a favour, actually. Miserable, self-centred jerk. You can guess what we had in common.'

She looked exactly the same, apart from the differences. Somehow, the last fifteen years had managed to chamfer off the sharp angles in her face, the carrot-on-a-snowman pointedness of her nose, the vicious cutting profile of her chin; she didn't slump quite so much either. 'No,' I said.

'We both like football,' she replied. 'Or at least, that's what I kept telling myself. Over and over again.'

'I don't remember you liking football when we were at school.'

'Neither do I. But then, I'm just a stupid woman, what do I know? That's beside the point,' she said, snapping back into formal mode. 'Is this just a flying visit, or are you planning on sticking around long enough for a kettle to boil?'

I smiled. 'I'm here for good,' I replied. 'I got thrown out.'

'What? Oh, you mean out of Elfland.' She frowned. 'How on earth did you manage that? It sounds such a quiet place.'

'It is,' I told her, 'when I'm not there.'

She twitched her nostrils. 'Is that what they turfed you out for, then? Being noisy? Must be a very strange place. Do they make the ants wear carpet slippers, too?'

I shook my head. 'I don't suppose I explained it properly last time I was here,' I said. 'Basically, when I'm over there I'm a different person entirely.'

'Different? How different?'

'Rude,' I said. 'Loud-mouthed. Insulting. Insufferable. A bit like—'

She leaned forwards a little. 'Do go on,' she said. 'Like who?'

'Doctor Jekyll,' I answered smoothly, though she clearly wasn't fooled. 'And Mr Hyde. You know, the same body but two completely different people living in it.'

'Really. Well, I never. And they threw you out.'

'Yes.'

'Sounds like an interesting place – I'd like to go there sometime. Would I be different there too, do you think?'

'Oh definitely,' I told her. 'In fact, I know just what you'd be like.' I left it at that; I may be an idiot, but I'm not stupid.

'I'll take your word for it,' she said. 'So, this is interesting. You're telling me that when you're over there, you're a seething mass of attitude and geese huddle in corners for fear you'll jump out and say Boo! to them?'

'That's one way of putting it,' I said.

'Well, if it's true I suppose it'd explain the strange fascination the place seems to have for you. After all, you've spent longer over there than you have here.'

Forty-eight hours, give or take twenty minutes. More than half my life. Short-changed at Time's checkout, and no realistic chance of ever getting to see the manager and complaining. And that was, at least in the short-to-medium term, the least of my problems.

'Listen,' I said. 'The last time I was here, just before—'

'Just before you buggered off for half a decade. Sorry, please do go on.'

'Last time I was here,' I repeated grimly, 'you said something which seemed to imply—' The words were drying superglue-fast on my tongue; I felt like I was in the dentist's chair, trying to explain quantum theory in a foreign language with half my face anaesthetised . . . 'That seemed to imply that possibly you felt something for me rather stronger than ordinary friendship; and I was wondering—'

'You can forget friendship,' Cru said steadily. 'A friend is someone who lends you a spare hairdryer when yours packs up, and splits the price of a twelve-inch pizza with you after you've been to the movies. Or so I've heard,' she added. 'Somehow I've never seemed to have any for long enough to observe their habits, so I'm mostly going on hearsay and the TV soaps. Don't think we could ever be friends.'

'Oh,' I said.

'Enemies, on the other hand,' she went on, 'we could easily be enemies. The way I heard it, an enemy is someone who smashed into your life, screws up everything in sight, causes you endless grief and inconvenience and then buggers off before you can so much as bash his head in, leaving muddy footprints all across your future. Remind you of anyone?'

'Yes,' I said.

'Or,' she continued, 'we could be in love. Actually, I get a bit confused here, because the specifications for "in love" are so bloody close to those for enemy that I'm not sure how you're supposed to tell them apart. You wouldn't happen to know, would you? My guess is that it's something you have to get right up close to see, like a hallmark or a serial number. Unfortunately, there isn't anything about it in the instruction manual.'

I frowned. 'What instruction manual?'

'The one you aren't issued with when you're born,' she replied. 'Which is a really stupid thing, if you ask me. Buy a CD player and it comes with a chunky thing like the director's cut of *War and Peace* in nine languages at once, but when it comes to Life you're supposed to be able to figure it out from first principles. If I was a proper lawyer, I'd sue someone about it.'

Odd; I wasn't used to Cru gabbling. Talking a lot, yes, very much her default setting, but not in this aimless vein. 'I take it you mean no,' I said.

'No what? Oh, you mean did I love you back in

nineteen ninety-whatever-it-was? Yes, I did. I loved you so much that when you vanished off the face of the earth – this is the first time I'm talking about, not the second – I lost interest in my life more or less completely, just drifted along taking law exams and being horrible to people until they went away, because there had once been a moment when I was sure I'd found the one person I wanted to be with, and after that there really didn't seem any point in fooling about with substitutes. So, yes, I did. Ever so much. And look where it got me.'

I took a deep breath; it felt like inhaling lumpy custard. 'What about now?' I said.

Cru turned her head away, so far that I heard the tendons in her neck crinkling softly. 'You should be aware,' she said, 'that my time is being paid for out of public money, via the Legal Aid fund. Unfortunately, with the government being such a bunch of old skinflints, you can't actually get Legal Aid for problems of the heart - silly, really, because they'll happily pay for a slap-up divorce, but they won't fork out a measly few bob for a happy-ever-after. But that's the way the system works, and—'

'Cruella,' I said.

'And,' she carried on, pushing past my rather fatuous attempt to call the meeting to order, 'I should point out that if I'm caught misusing the Duty Solicitor scheme for selfish personal ends, it could mean our firm losing its Legal Aid franchise, and you wouldn't want that, would you? So – what on earth possessed you to go biting my ex-fiancé's toes. Even I never did *that*.'

'Cru,' I said, 'shut up and answer the fucking question.'

She shook her head. 'Sorry, but like I said, I'm not authorised to deal with that matter. Ask me again when I'm off duty. Getting back to the charges—'

'All right,' I said. 'And when'll that be?'

'When we're outside the police station,' she said, 'and I'm no longer acting for you in connection with this case. Assuming,' she added, 'that I'm still talking to you, when I'm not getting paid for it. That's quite a big assumption. Anyway; when you hit the arresting officer the third time—'

'Please,' I said. 'It won't take you a second.'

She sighed. 'Well, all right,' she said. 'But not on the Legal Aid Board's time; I'll have to treat you as a fee-paying client and charge you separately. Usually, of course, we as a firm don't accept private client work without an up-front payment, in advance, of £250 plus VAT, but—'

'It's OK,' I said. 'I'm a millionaire's son, remember?'

'Cash is better,' she replied, 'but I guess that'll have to do. Now, then. Yes.'

Some opportunist bastard had nipped in while my mouth was hanging open and stolen all the air out of my lungs. 'Yes, what?' I croaked.

'Yes, I suppose I'm still in love with you,' she replied. 'For what that's worth,' she added quickly. 'I mean, I don't think we've got any kind of a future together, because even if you are planning on staying unvanished for long enough to hear the weather forecast, there's a fairly good chance you'll be going to prison for a while, particularly if you will insist on ruining my concentration when I'm trying to prepare your defence, and even putting that on one side—'

'You mean it?' I said.

'No, I only said it to see if your ears turned pink. Of course I mean it. Would I have said it otherwise?' She shut her eyes, then immediately opened them again. 'You still here?' she said. 'Good, that's an improvement. Now, if we can finally get down to these witness statements—'

I stood up, leaned across the table and kissed her. I didn't make a wonderful job of it – lack of practical experience, plus the excitement of the moment and all that government furniture getting in the way; there was a nasty moment when our teeth clashed and she called me a clumsy moron but it passed.

'Right,' I said, having disentangled myself, 'what were you saying about witness statements?'

She gave me a look you could have kept polar bears in. 'This isn't going to work, you know,' she said. 'Not you and me, actually *together*. I mean, being in love with you when you weren't there, God knows how many million miles or light years or whatever in a different dimension, I could cope with that. Well, so I should hope; after all, I got enough practice at it over the years. But being in love with you when you're actually here—'

'We'll manage,' I said.

She hadn't moved since the kiss. 'And then there's this half-an-elf business,' she went on. 'Without getting crudely biological, surely that's going to present all sorts of difficulties. Take citizenship, for example. Immigration law isn't really my area, but there's all sorts of complicated rules. Are you even allowed to be in the country, properly speaking? And if we were to have children – Look, I'm just talking hypothetically, anticipating all possible contingencies. It's a lawyer thing, we're trained to think like that.'

'One of each,' I said. 'A boy and a girl.'

She shook her head. 'It'd have to be four,' she said. 'Boy/girl, human/elf. Or is it more than that? I can't remember if it's two squared or two cubed—'

'Four would be OK with me,' I said.

'*Look*.' She was scowling at me as if I was something she'd found on her shoe – exactly the way she always had, ever since I'd met her. For the first time since I could remember, I felt *happy*. 'Look,' she repeated, 'you're racing on way too far ahead, we've got to get you out of this dump first before we can even start thinking about where we go from here.'

I grinned. Didn't want to particularly; couldn't help it. 'I'm not worried about that any more,' I said. 'So what if I go to prison? I'm sure it wouldn't be for long – and after living all my life in our house with Daddy George, when I wasn't at an English boarding school, I'm not sure prison wouldn't be a pleasant change. Besides, if I'm in there he can't get at me. Then, when I come out, you'll be there waiting for me—'

'Oh yes,' she said. 'I'm *good* at that.'

'Yes, well,' I said, 'at least you'll know where I am and when you can expect to see me again. It's not perfect, but it's got to be better than the last fifteen years. And that way, we'll all know where we are and what we're supposed to be doing, and we can make plans—'

'Great. I can come and see you on visiting days and we can discuss pension schemes. I'm going weak at the knees just thinking about it.'

She was doing her best, but her heart wasn't in it. There comes a time when even the feistiest pessimist has to face up to the ineluctability of the happy ending.

'Well,' she said, 'at least I'm going to try. If we go for a guilty plea, bearing in mind it's a first offence—'

'Just tell the judge we're getting married,' I said. 'Bound to do the trick. He'd have to be really miserable to send me to jail then.'

She gave me another one of those looks. 'I think I'll keep that in reserve as a very last resort,' she said. 'I don't want to get the reputation of being one of those lawyers who'll do anything to win a case. Now, will you stop gushing pink hearts and shut up for a minute while I go through these witness statements?'

I let her get on with her legal stuff, nodding at intervals to give the impression that I was listening; but I wasn't in the mood for anything like that. Well, would you have been? You can't just turn off joy like shutting off the water when you go away from home for a week. Since I couldn't dance around the room skipping and shouting, for fear of attracting unwelcome attention from the bogies, all I could do was to sit still and marinade in the pleasure of the moment, the first thing that'd ever actually gone right since the doctor snipped my umbilical cord. At last – I know, it was a complete non sequitur, but you've got to allow me my moment of intuitive clarity – at last I was free of the one thing I'd become that day when I'd seen my first elf. I'd finally managed to join the human race, even if I'd had to sneak round the back and climb in through the toilet window in order to do it. You can have no idea how much that meant to me.

And Cru – if we were together, what else could possibly matter?

I was so preoccupied with wallowing about in this self-inflicted quagmire of soppiness that I missed most of what happened next: a damned shame, but typical. One moment I was gazing idiotically at Cru's left ear, listening to her voice reciting some statement or other in a Dalek monotone and remembering the first time I'd noticed how small and neat her ear lobes were (yes, I know; but these things matter to you when you've got a mental age of fifteen and you're in love for the first time); the next, the door was just a few splinters hanging off bent hinges, the room was full of horrible white smoke, and someone was pulling me out of my chair by the scruff of my neck and propelling me towards the doorway. I didn't have time to be frightened until I was pushed out into the corridor, just as a thunderflash went off at the other end.

'Excuse me,' I started to say.

I didn't get any further than that. A man wearing a black balaclava was kneeling down in front of me, fiddling about with a rectangular grey metal box about the size and shape of an arc welder. The man who'd grabbed me out of the interview room took hold of my hand just below the wrist and shoved it forward, whereupon the kneeling man snapped a couple of crocodile clips onto my index and third fingers. Another thunderflash went off somewhere beyond where the corridor took a sharp turn to our left, and a fine sprinkling of plaster dust drifted down, like icing sugar. Then the kneeling man flipped a switch.

It was the classic Frankenstein moment; or, if you prefer, the Cistine chapel bit where Adam reaches up and touches God's outstretched finger, having foolishly neglected to put his rubber boots on first. The nearest I can get to describing it - you're in the dentist's chair and he's drilling away and his hand slips a bit, so that his evil little drill digs right into the exposed nerve. It was something like that, if your whole body was the bit of raw gum, except that it didn't hurt exactly; I'd take mere pain over that sensation any day. It was very weird, and no fun at all; and after it had been going on for at least a sixty-fourth of a second, possibly even longer than that, there was also this other sensation – equally impossible to describe, but just suppose you were a cardigan sleeve, and someone pulled you inside out and then stuffed you into a jam jar. Exactly like that, apart from the differences.

But that wasn't the really freaky bit. Oh no; that came later, when I opened my eyes and looked down, and realised that I was something in the region of six inches tall, standing in the palm of someone's hand.

CHAPTER THIRTEEN

A very different sensation; not one I'd necessarily recommend, except to a long-term enemy. The most disconcerting thing about it, apart from the vertigo and stuff like that, is that there's no way to get your mind to accept on anything but the most superficial level that you've shrunk. No, what your brain wants to believe is that you're the right size and everything else has suddenly got very, very big. This may seem like a minor academic quibble to you, but believe me, it isn't. It affects the whole way you see things, because to us poor idiot humans, who bring our children up on stories of giants who live at the tops of beanstalks and eat people, anything and everything that monstrously outsize must be actively hostile. As a result, the mind locks up immediately with fear, and all you can do is stand there and quiver helplessly.

Didn't I speculate a while ago about why Nature should program us hapless life forms to do the whole panic thing at the first sign of danger? Well, I think I've got it figured out. It's a good idea from the point of view of running a successful ecosphere; not a lot of use as far as helping small, defenceless creatures to survive is concerned, but pretty well essential for the well-being of the predators. At the bottom of the food chain there are only two categories, the quick and the dead. Hence the phrase, fast-food chain.

So: instead of thinking on my feet, assessing the risks and taking quick and decisive action, like jumping off the hand and scuttling for cover under a low table, I just stood there like a prune as the fingers rose up around me, London Bridge fashion, and pinned me down so I couldn't move. That was a really rather unpleasant moment, like the bit in the first *Star Wars* film where they're trapped in the garbage crusher; worse for me, since I didn't have a contract promising me work in two sequels. My innate fear of heights didn't exactly help, either, as the hand lifted alarmingly quickly into the air, flipped over and let go of me.

I didn't fall far, and I landed uncomfortably on a chunky metal object that turned out to be a car ignition key. Next to it I could just make out a disposable Bic biro without a cap, and beyond that a big green cylinder that I identified, after a couple of wild and incorrect guesses, as a roll of Polo mints. I was in a pocket.

It was dark in there, and the ride was horribly bumpy; and to make matters worse, I could distinctly hear noises off through the lining: thunderflashes and muffled shouts and what were probably gunshots. Being caught up in a battle is one thing; being caught up in a battle when you're six inches tall and trapped in the coat pocket of one of the combatants has to be the absolute pits. It gives you a whole new perspective on armed conflict, because you realise that nobody, not even a police marksman, could possibly fail to hit something *that* big.

One thing I wasn't bewildered about – quite atypically, for me – was what was going on. All my life, I'd known that Daddy George's idea of subtlety was the bank robber who doesn't take his gun out of his jacket pocket when pointing it at the cashier; also, I suspected, the sheer nerve of snatching me out of a police cell was entirely in line with his view of himself as a swashbuckling pirate king. (It was embarrassing going to the pantomime with Daddy George: he cheered for Captain Hook and laughed hysterically when Tinkerbell asked if anybody believed in fairies.) Also, the small matter of the making-elves-smaller machine was pretty well conclusive, if the memories Melissa had uploaded into my head were at all trustworthy.

I don't know exactly what happened there in the police station, but whatever it was, it didn't last very long. While I think of it, a word of advice: if you suddenly find yourself, please excuse the expression, suddenly taken short, try to avoid getting put in the pocket of someone who subsequently does quite a lot of running up and down stairs. That particular experience gave me a lot of valuable insights into how much unnecessary suffering there is in the world, and one of these days I'm going to found the Milk Shake Liberation front and the League Against Popcorn.

One of the things you're supposed to do when you're kidnapped is to try and be observant, take careful note of your surroundings, anything you see or hear that will help the authorities to figure out exactly what's been done to you and where you've been taken. I did my best; but since my surroundings consisted of coat lining, a grubby handkerchief and a dangerously heavy roll of mints, I eventually got bored with it and gave up. I think I was in a car for a long time; and then there was some brisk walking (not as bad as the running, but still no fun), and then the pocket filled up with huge pink things and I was fished out and dumped on a vast expanse of mirror-polished brown wood. The last bit jangled my brains quite a lot, and it was only when I recognised the scratch I'd made when I was nine – to me, of course, it looked like the San Andreas Fault on a bad day – that I realised I was standing on Daddy George's favourite desk.

That made me look up, but I couldn't get my head back far enough to see anything helpful. There was a huge white thing with what looked like a frozen waterfall of garishly coloured cloth cascading down it – I stared at it for quite a long time before I figured out it was a shirt-front and tie – but I couldn't see anything above the collar line.

I could appreciate why the captive elves I'd talked to used 'tall' as their worst insult.

'Good Lord,' said a voice above me, apparently speaking through a PA system borrowed from God and hooked up to a speaker the size of Jupiter. 'Look who it is.'

I didn't recognise the voice, because it was too loud to be anything but an enormous noise; but the *tone* of voice, that was unmistakable. 'Hello,' I said.

'Hello yourself.' Laughter, loud as an artillery barrage and about as friendly. 'Usually, the next line would be, "My, how you've grown." Trust you to be different.'

That struck me as the kind of remark that doesn't need a reply. Daddy George was working himself into his Evil Overlord persona. (The only time he ever regarded me with anything remotely approaching affection was one Christmas when I bought him a Darth Vader coffee mug. He really liked the thing and made a point of using it for years.) He appeared to be at the Being-Funny-At-The-Prisoner's-Expense stage - you know, the bit before he has his minions lock up the hero in a storeroom with a flimsy grille leading to a ventilation shaft twice the height and width of the New York subway. I only hoped he'd follow the script faithfully.

'You're also looking remarkably well for someone who's been dead for fifteen years,' he went on. 'Obviously death agrees with you. Well, it must do; I mean – two Nobel prizes, a vast fortune, a major shareholding in the fastest-growing major corporation in the world; look at everything you've accomplished since you died, and then compare it with the miserable hash you called a life before that. Being dead's been the making of you, son.'

Still no answer required; and I was damned if I was going to be the straight man in this comedy routine. If he wanted to do stand-up, he'd have to do all the work himself.

'But,' he went on, with a sigh like a Kansas twister, 'much as I'd like to encourage you in your career in not living, I'm afraid this is one time when I can't afford to indulge your every whim. It's a distressing fault of mine, but having people killed just isn't my style – even,' he added thunderously, 'people I could squash flat with one well-aimed swat and a rolled-up *Independent on*

Sunday. There'd be this little voice in the back of my mind telling me I'm a rotten bully and why don't I pick on someone my own size? Besides,' he went on lugubriously, 'you may be annoying and pathetic, not to mention a potential source of considerable embarrassment, but you're still the nearest thing I've got to a son of my own, and I suppose I'm just a great big softie.'

Well, two out of three, anyhow. I wasn't reassured by this declaration; if Daddy George had decided to keep me alive, it could only be for the purpose of finding out by controlled scientific experiment whether there really was a fate worse than death.

'So instead,' he went on, 'I'm going to be merciful and kind and even generous above and beyond the call. I'm going to start you off in the family business. At the bottom,' he added, 'on the shop floor. But that's all right, isn't it?' he said. 'It's so traditional it's practically compulsory. You'll enjoy it there. Plenty of your own kind, for one thing.'

I'd thought as much when he said the words 'family business' – he was going to lock me up in the shoe factory with the rest of the slaves. As a future, it had a slight edge on being killed, but I'd sort of guessed that wasn't an immediate threat from the fact that I was still alive, albeit considerably condensed, like a *Readers Digest* potted novel. Why bother to bring me all the way here, instead of simply having his employees kill me back at the police station? No, he was too deeply into his James Bond villain trip; at the very least he'd keep me alive so I could watch him launch his secret master plan. (Utterly safe bet to assume he had one; a supervillain without a plan is as unthinkable as a headmaster without trousers.)

'Thank you,' I replied. It was the first thing I'd said since my nasty slide down the Y axis, and although it sounded just normally loud to me, I don't think he heard me or even knew I'd spoken. No big deal; it wasn't exactly the cleverest thing I'd ever said. I think it was just a very deep-seated reflex prompting me to be polite to my elders and betters.

'I'm assuming,' he thundered on, 'that either you've figured out what happens here for yourself, or one of your prickle-eared relatives has told you the whole sad story. Just in case you're in any doubt, just think of it as the old folk tale of the shoemaker and the elves, updated and put on a sound commercial footing. Now I know you're far too feeble and chickenshit to cause me anything interesting enough to merit the term trouble, but just in case you're minded to make a pest of yourself here's a couple of things you might care to consider. First, the height thing isn't the only useful effect of my electric elf-zapper. I won't bore you with the technical stuff and you're too ignorant to understand it anyway, but what it boils down to is that the zapper freezes you in a state of interdimensional flux, whereby about ninety-five per cent of you is on this side of the line, and the other five per cent is over there among the Kate Greenaway types. Not only does this limit you to a much smaller slice of our airspace – there's a diminishing-returns effect that you'd find utterly fascinating if you were really enough of a mathematician to spell Nobel prize, let alone win one, but you're not, so screw it; it also means that the only people who can see you are either humans with amazingly complicated light-band filters built into their contact lenses – of whom there's presently one and you're looking up at him – and other elves. So,' he continued with an edge to his voice that you could've performed surgery with, 'if you think you can give me the slip, make a run for it and go find your mother, who'll save you from me and make everything all right again, forget it. For what little it's worth, she hasn't got the faintest idea how I earn my living; she thinks I'm just exceptionally good at running a business, which is true but not nearly enough in these hard times. *She* thinks you were kidnapped by aliens, which is why she gives millions of dollars a year to the flying-saucer freaks in hopes they'll find the bug-eyed critters who took you and persuade them to bring you back.' He sighed, nearly blowing me off the desk. 'Your mother may be as thick as a lorryload of bricks, but she has an extraordinarily compassionate nature. In fact, she's a truly wonderful person, and it's a very great shame that she's had to go through so much sorrow and pain on account of a worthless little gob of snot like you. Oh, and in case you were wondering, because we never ever got around to having one of those quality-time step-father-to-stepson chats that can make all the difference in an awkward family structure, I don't like you very much. Never have, never will; and if you think I enjoy having to pretend that what measure of success I've had in the last fifteen years or so is down to your incredibly prodigious talents rather than my own hard work, scientific genius and sheer dogged determination, then you take after your mother when it comes to thickness quotients. Any questions?'

All the time he'd been talking, I'd been fidgeting around inside my mind, looking for a volume control. I knew there had to be one, because I could remember how Melissa had been able to speak up so I could hear her, when she'd been over this side of the line. Eventually I did find it, purely by fluke; I have no idea what I did, but it worked.

'Yes,' I said. 'If you don't mind my asking. What happened to my *real* father?'

He laughed. 'I was telling you how clever I am,' he said, 'and there's a case in point. Now, if you were good enough at maths to be able to do long division without a calculator, you'd have figured out for yourself that having me and him together in the same dimension wouldn't be a good idea; a bit like mixing matter and antimatter in a cocktail shaker with a sprig of mint and an olive. It was only the fag end of the original interface that saved England from getting blown into orbit, that night when I nobbled the creep; whittling him down to your present size helped a bit, because the five per cent of him on the other side helped stabilise the whole mess a little, just long enough for me to invent an unbelievably cool and brilliant dimensional-implosion stabiliser – think of it as a magnetic acroprop wedged under the crumbling foundations of the cosmos – that sorted the problem out once and for all and also gave me a stable interface with a wonderful source of cheap labour.' He laughed again. 'Bless their feckless little hearts,' he added. 'No matter how much evidence snowdrifts up to the contrary, there'll always be a healthy supply of utterly stupid people, your side and this, who truly believe they can get a fresh start and a new, wonderful life just by crossing a border. Greenbacks, I call 'em, and long may they continue to trickle through. Anyhow, your old man. Well, I needed a specimen for some fairly essential tests I had to do in order to calibrate the interface controls, so I sent him back. All of him,' he added cheerfully. 'Eventually.'

I suddenly felt cold, as if I'd just stepped out of a warm house into the snow. 'You killed him, then,' I said.

The great laugh rolled out once more. 'You bet I did,' he said. 'In fact, saying I killed him is a bit like saying America is bigger than the Isle of Wight. I killed him a *lot*. Partly for sound commercial, just-business-nothing-personal reasons, because he'd been the one who burst through the interface and might have used his elves-being-good-at-sums brains to figure out a way of jamming it up. Partly because of what he'd been and done with your mother – and bringing you into my life, let's not forget that. Partly, I suppose, because by the very nature of things he was my exact equal and opposite, so it's just straightforward physics that I'd have to cancel him out. But mostly because he was a pointy-eared green-skinned freak, and I hate elves. Always have, ever since I was a snot-nosed brat. I was drawing horns and blackening teeth on pictures of elves in my *First-Ever Story Book* before I could walk, and if Tolkien was alive today I'd have him executed for crimes against humanity. That's mostly why I killed your dad. That, and I needed something to do my experiments on, like I said. One thing I've never ever been guilty of is random, senseless violence. Don't hold with it – complete waste of time and effort.'

'Oh,' I said. 'Well, thank you for explaining.'

That made him laugh even louder. 'Oh yes,' he said, 'that sort of thing puts it beyond a shadow of a doubt, you really are one of them. Only an elf could thank his father's murderer for taunting him with it. You people, you're worse than Canadians. Well, as bad as, anyway.'

I couldn't really think of anything else to say to him; the sheer size of what he'd done was so unimaginable, like he was himself, that even hating him seemed faintly ridiculous, like trying to exact a terrible vengeance on the sea by pissing in Morecambe Bay. In fact, just being in the same space as him was starting to make me feel almost embarrassed. He was overdoing the Evil Overlord stuff so painfully that he was undercutting his own credibility. To be helpless and at the mercy of a vicious, sadistic monster is one thing; being in the power of a vicious, sadistic *silly* monster, the sort who'd prompt you to yawn and switch channels if you saw him on the box, is something else entirely. It's a very bad sign when you can't respect your arch-enemy.

(And he was being so like himself, too; that may have been the worst thing of all. The harsh mocking laughter, the melodramatic exaggerations, the brutal insults – these were all things I'd fidgeted and stifled yawns through all my life, in respect of such issues as broken windows, untidy rooms and unfinished mashed potato. It was all so dreadfully familiar, and familiarity was breeding what it always tends to breed with the speed and efficiency of a state-of-the-art rabbit factory farm.)

'Anyway,' he said, 'this is a moment I'm going to savour for a very long time. I'd like to say that all through your childhood I tried to like you, or at least get to the point where I could be in the same room with you without wanting to throw up; but we can't have everything we want in this life and that's all there is to it. Like I said just now, you're the closest thing I've ever had to a kid of my own, and that's still too bloody close for me.

So I guess this is goodbye for ever, you horrible little shit.'

There he went again: I don't know, maybe he believed it himself. But the plain fact was that he hadn't always been like that – oh, sure, he'd never exactly been a TV-commercial father, playing football in the backyard and taking me fishing at weekends, but there had been times, not many but some, when he'd forgotten he was the arch-villain wicked stepfather and been quite normal, even relatively pleasant. When I was ten, he'd made me a kite and helped me build a plastic scale-model kit of the *Ark Royal*. You'd never have caught Darth Vader doing that, or at least not in the version I saw.

If this really was the last time I'd ever see him, I had a feeling I'd miss him.

'Bye, then,' I said. 'And thank you for the kite.'

'Kite?' He blinked, then nodded. 'Oh,' he said, '*that* kite. The one I got you just so as to lull you into a false sense of security, and then you flew it slap bang into a tree first time out and shredded the bloody thing.'

I wondered if he'd been resenting that all these years. Well, obviously he had. But really it was his fault, he'd mucked up the airframe and the kite wouldn't fly straight. But that was typically him, too, rewriting history so everything was someone else's fault and done regardless of his best efforts to avert disaster, usually just to spite him.

If he hadn't been twelve times bigger than me and about to send me to a forced labour camp to die, I'd probably have felt sorry for him.

He must've pressed some kind of hidden bell or buzzer, because I heard the door sweep open behind me, and tyrannosaurus footsteps padding towards me from behind. Call me a pessimist if you must, but I had an idea that this probably wasn't a positive development, seen from my perspective.

'Well,' boomed Daddy George, 'I suppose this is it. You know, things just won't be the same without you hanging round the place – I mean, they'll be better, absolutely no question about that, but they'll be different. Not all that different, of course, because you've been away fifteen years, but somehow knowing you'll be gone for good – it's like the place where the aching tooth you had pulled out used to be not hurting any more. The end of an era, if you like. Goodbye.'

'Goodbye,' I replied, half a second before a giant hand closed around me and hoisted me into first the air, second a Marks & Spencer plastic carrier bag. (One instance where putting your name and logo on your give-away peripherals proved to be counter-productive; for some reason I blamed them for their unwitting complicity and swore an oath never to buy another pair of socks from them as long as I lived.) I hit the bottom of the bag squirming, gave that up as a bad job and flopped.

'All right,' said Daddy George, 'he's all yours. Here you go.'

A rustle and a vertiginous vertical take-off suggested that he was handing the bag over to whoever it was who'd just come in. Some thug, I supposed, or hired myrmidon. Still—

Still, I said to myself, mostly in a vain effort to take my mind off the stomach-churning unpleasantness of being carried around in a plastic bag. (Guilt spanned a chasm of years, whisking me back to a ten-year-old me carrying home a goldfish I'd won at a fair; in particular the moment when I nearly dropped the poor wee sod, and only managed to retrieve it inches from the ground with a rather remarkable juggling catch.) Still, this wasn't so much an ending as a new beginning. True, it was the beginning of a long and probably horrible career in the shoe manufacturing business, and I'd have had to be as optimistic as twelve short planks to believe that it was going to be fun, challenging, fulfilling or a barrel of laughs. But at least I'd be somewhere, doing something, able to go to sleep at night with a moderate chance of waking up the next morning in the same place in the same dimension, the same size and only a few hours older than when I'd gone to bed. And yes, I'd just lost the only girl I'd ever loved, just when I was on the point of uncrossing the galaxy of crossed stars we'd somehow managed to blunder into; and yes, this time it did rather look as if I'd lost her for ever, since even if we did ever meet again, I'd be six inches tall and she wouldn't be able to see me. But – actually there wasn't a 'but' to that one, it was a silver-lining-free zone and immune to all forms of positive thinking and bright-side visual inspection. *Damn*, I thought. *Still, better than being dead. Probably.*

Now the chances are that you, poor underprivileged stay-at-home that you are, will probably never get to travel for several hours in a plastic bag. Instead, you want me to describe what it was like for you, so that you can live the experience vicariously by means of the small miracle of imagination.

Believe me, you don't want to know. If you're the sort of reckless contaminant floating on the scummy surface of the gene pool who makes a habit of ignoring the well-meant advice of wiser sufferers, you'll probably have a shot at imagining it anyway, so here's a few pointers, just to steer you towards the right kind of nightmare. Think of a football-pitch-sized trampoline, or a Bouncy Castle of Doom, or a zero-gravity padded cell that has suddenly come alive and decided it's hungry. Think of all this happening for a *long* time, and please also bear in mind that there are no toilets in carrier bags, not even Marks & Sparks ones. In other words, think scary, painful, undignified, unpredictable and extremely sordid.

Still, most bad things come to an end, and eventually the hamster-in-a-blender sensation slowed down and stopped. I was still trying to make up my mind whether or not this was a good thing or just something even worse getting ready to happen when the world suddenly flipped upside down and shot me out onto a cold, hard, concrete floor.

At least that cleared up one point for me; to paraphrase Lennon and McCartney, you dunno how lucky you are, boy, back in the Marks & Spencer carrier bag.

Most of what I dislike about cold, hard floors can be summed up in the two words 'cold' and 'hard'. My physics education was rudely interrupted just as I was getting to the good bit, so I can't actually lay my hand on my heart and tell you for certain that a hard surface is harder when you're knee high to a Cabbage Patch Doll than it would be for, say, a seven-foot-tall professional basketball player, and the same reservation obviously applies to coolth. It just feels that way, that's all.

No point in moving around; in fact, being small and invisible and therefore at extreme risk of being trodden on if I started wandering around like a one-man nomadic tribe, the only sensible course of action was to stay put and wait for someone to come and tell me what to do. So I did, and they didn't; not for a very long time. If you've ever wondered whether it's possible to be scared into a jelly and bored stiff at the same time, let me assure you that it is. In fact, it's dead easy; no previous experience or specialist equipment necessary.

To my surprise, when the Main Cop finally did show up, it turned out to be an elf; on the large side, sure, at least six and an eighth inches tall, maybe as much as six and a quarter, but not the agonising strain on the neck tendons I'd been anticipating. When I heard his voice behind me, of course, I instinctively looked straight up in the air.

'No, you clown, down here,' the voice corrected me, and I got the impression that maybe I'd started off the foreman/junior-assistant-nonentity relationship on the wrong foot. 'So you're him, then,' the voice went on, as I lowered my chin looking for its source. 'The freak.'

Bear in mind that I'd met elves, rather more of them than I'd ever wanted to, and the ones I'd been hanging out with recently were all pleasant, friendly, hospitable, kindly folks, gentle and polite to the point of violent nausea. They were also, of course, on the other side of the line; on the side where I was a loud-mouthed, overbearing jerk. Of course I should have anticipated the effect of that syndrome, like changing the signs when you take away the brackets in algebra; but I didn't. Tsk. And me a Nobel prizewinner.

'Freak?' I repeated. 'Oh, you mean—'

With that size and complexion and those ears, he was indisputably an elf, couldn't have been anything else.

But not only did he sound different from the ones on the other side, he looked different too. Where the Elfland elves had been long and thin, like supermodels hung over a radiator to dry out, he resembled your stereotypical Alabama police sergeant, only with added neck density and smaller, beadier eyes. I can't say I took to him.

'Freak,' he said, with lots and lots of emphasis. 'You got a problem with that?'

I thought about it and decided I didn't. Eminently fair and admirably concise, I reckoned. I shook my head. 'No, sir,' I said. I guessed he was probably the sort of person who liked being called 'Sir'. Most thoroughly unpleasant people do, in my experience.

'And don't call me that,' he snapped, making me wonder if perhaps I'd misjudged him. 'You call the manager 'sir'. You call me 'boss'. You got that?'

'Yes,' I replied. 'Boss.'

He frowned; it was like watching a rockslide on Mount Rushmore, to the point where you expected to see miniature Cary Grants and James Masons slugging it out on the bridge of his nose. 'OK,' he grunted, 'but you're still a freak, and I've got my eye on you. Understood?'

I wanted to assure him that he'd explained all the relevant factors so lucidly that even someone of my limited intelligence had no trouble at all in grasping all the salient points; but it occurred to me that if I said all that in words he'd probably think I was being funny and kick my ears inside my head, whereas if I stuck to body language, the worst that'd happen if I cocked it up would be him thinking I'd got epilepsy or a nervous tic or something. So I nodded.

He didn't react to my nod, so I suppose I judged it about right. 'Just remember, though,' he grunted, 'the first sign of trouble from you and I'll know what to do. All right, follow me.'

Well, it wasn't as if I had a non-lethal choice. So I followed him.

CHAPTER FOURTEEN

The first thing that struck me about my new surroundings was the scale, and boy, was I relieved.
Everything was the proper size – well, not everything;
the doorways loomed overhead like triumphal arches,
and the windows were set neck-crickingly high in the
soaring walls, giving me the feeling I was in a cathedral.
But the stuff that actually mattered, like chairs and
tables and benches, were all the right height, and so
were the people.

There were a *lot* of people. All elves, needless to say:
pointed ears, greenish complexions. They were far
greener than Elfland elves; I eventually found out that
there was a sound scientific reason for this, something to
do with light travelling at a different speed over there –
either this was the reason the locals could play games
with linear chronology, or else their continual faffing
about with time had resulted in it getting seriously bent,
with knock-on effects to several other constants. In any

case, the Elfland spectrum isn't nearly as inflexible as ours, which may also have something to do with the fact that their rainbows really do have ends, and pots of gold to go with them. According to the elf who told me about this stuff, all the time I was in Elfland, the locals would have perceived me as being a garish shade of orange, though naturally they'd been far too polite to mention it.

A lot of elves, then; and all of them without exception dead miserable and snotty. To what degree this was due to them being the opposites of the sweet-natured folk they'd have been on their own side of the line, and how much of it was the result of being banged up in a sweatshop and forced to make shoes for a psychotic Nazi, I never did find out. Six of one, I guess. It didn't take me long – about five seconds, in fact – to realise that they didn't like me, either.

The first four of these five seconds were taken up with the foreman telling the congregated workforce that I was the new guy, and as they could see from my ears I was only half an elf and therefore a freak, but even so he'd rather they didn't kill me outright, since he was accountable to management for staffing levels. The fifth second was a moment of complete and utter silence as they all turned round and stared at me. At the end of that second, I'd pretty well got the message.

Whether it was because they didn't want to get the foreman into trouble, or because they were too demoralised and generally pissed off to bother, they didn't immediately rise up and lynch me or beat me to a pulp. When they'd finished staring – a second and a half was all it took to download all they needed to know about me, apparently – they turned round and got on with what they were doing, namely their mid-morning break, which they spent standing around in small, wretched groups with their hands by their sides, muttering in low, unhappy voices. I soon discovered that this was pretty much the high point of their day.

The foreman looked at me, shook his head sadly, and wandered off, leaving me standing there on my own on the edge of the mob of sad elves, and I decided that it was now my turn to look at them. There wasn't really a lot to see, since it was well-nigh impossible to tell them apart. They were all more or less the same height, dressed in extremely similar shabby green boiler suits and clumping engineers' boots, and they all slumped in more or less the same way (head forward, shoulders drooping, knees very slightly bent, hands dangling on the ends of arms like defeated conkers). It's hard to imagine a sadder, more disheatened and despondent collection of life forms anywhere in time and space, with the possible exception of the Conservative party after the 1997 general election.

I suppose I hadn't been there for more than ten minutes (which, in context, felt like slightly over a million years) when a sadder-than-average-looking elf peeled off from the crowd and trudged towards me, moving with all the snap and vigour of an exhausted man wading through waist-deep semolina. He looked older than most of them; his hair was getting thin and tufty on top, and even the points of his ears looked like they were wilting. 'You,' he said.

There's not a lot you can say by way of reply to 'You', sighed at you by someone who looks like he's spent the last hundred years down the back of a sofa. I tried to look respectfully alert and attentive. I'm morally certain he didn't notice.

'You're with me,' he said, in a tone of voice that suggested that that was the most depressing and dismal fact he'd ever had to come to terms with. 'I'm putting you in the stockroom.'

'Ah,' I said. Right.' I toyed with adding *thank you* or something like that, but decided not to, in case he took it the wrong way. I'd got the distinct feeling that in the prevailing culture, pretty well any remark over two syllables long would probably be interpreted as a mortal insult requiring settlement in blood.

'Right, then,' he replied. 'You'd better follow me, then.'

He led me across the huge floor towards a Marble Arch-sized doorway in the opposite wall. It was a long walk, but at least it gave me the opportunity to look about me and take in the scenery. Under other circumstances, I might even have been impressed; the sheer size of the place, as seen from my perspective, lent it a certain air of grandeur. Imagine St Mark's in Venice after a raid by a bunch of really dedicated bailiffs. Other aspects, however, weren't quite so impressive; the dust was OK, it was almost like walking along a sandy beach, but the cobwebs started my imagination off along distinctly unsettling avenues. When you're six inches tall, arachnophobia is less of a psychological disorder and more of a survival trait.

As I followed the sad elf I did make a real effort to get my bearings, or at least try and remember which way we'd come, but it wasn't long before I gave up. The trouble is that when you're walking through a succession of spaces so overwhelmingly huge that you have trouble seeing the opposite wall until you're halfway across the room, it's quite hard to maintain a sense of direction.

Think what it'd be like trying to navigate if you were travelling through intergalactic space from the Milky Way to Andromeda on foot.

The upshot was that after an hour or so I fell into a sort of dazed trance, and when the sad elf suddenly stopped and said, 'Well, we're here', I'd lost track of pretty well everything. I couldn't actually see what differentiated *here* from anywhere else; the place we'd stopped in was a double-Wembley-sized concrete-floored desert, and although I could just about make out vague shapes on the horizon, I didn't have a clue what they were. Could've been pyramids or mountains or medium-sized cities, for all I knew.

'Right,' I said. 'Um, where is this?'

'Stockroom,' whispered the sad elf, as if acknowledging a deadly secret he'd managed to keep hidden for the last forty years. 'It's where we keep stuff.'

Oh, I thought, *that sort of stockroom*. 'What would you like me to do?' I asked.

The look in his eyes answered that question more eloquently than words ever could, and if he'd insisted, the result would have been extremely uncomfortable and ultimately fatal. But what he said was, 'You can start on loading trolleys. Try not to bugger it up, it's hard enough as it is.'

'Okay,' I said, making it sound a bit like a major concession during international trade negotiations. 'Um, can someone show me what to do, or . . . ?'

His head slumped even further forward, implying he had a triple-jointed neck. 'Yeah, why not?' he replied, as if to suggest that everything was so far gone that nothing really mattered any more. 'Come with me, I'll show you myself.'

'Thanks,' I said, but he managed to rise above it.

We walked on in silence for a few minutes, to the point where I began to make out recognisable shapes in the distance. On the walls there were shelves, the usual steel angle-iron type bolted together like good old-fashioned Meccano, except that each shelving unit was the size of the Pompidou Centre. Fortunately there were lifts from the ground to each shelf, and running along each shelf a little railway line, beside which gangs of elves, each gang between twenty and fifty strong, were hauling about such things as cardboard boxes, reels of thread and rolls of canvas. Each item was mounted on a sled and tied down to stop it toppling off and flattening the crew, and the gangs were hauling on ropes like students re-enacting the building of Stonehenge. When they reached the railhead there were derricks and cranes to hoist the load off the sled and onto a flatbed truck, which waited in a siding till a locomotive arrived to haul it to the lift shaft. I noticed that all the railway stuff – track and rolling stock and engines - was the same Hornby Dublo I'd had in my train set when I was a kid.

'There you go,' said the sad elf. 'Watch what you're doing, don't fall off the shelves or get under the loads when they're shifting. 'Snot fair to the rest of the lads, having to scrape you off the deck.'

'I can see that,' I told him. 'I'll try and be careful.'

His shrug suggested that he'd heard that one before. 'Right,' he said, 'I'll be getting back. If you get any problems,' he added, and rounded off the statement with a vague hand gesture.

'Thanks again,' I said.

He sighed, shook his head and walked away.

As I set off to plod the remaining distance to the foot of the nearest shelving unit, I tried to imagine what all this lot would look like if I were a story-book giant, five feet six in my bare feet. It'd all be completely different, I realised (though, of course, essentially the same), and all I'd see from my towering, thin-atmosphere height would be a poky little store where they kept a few things. If I needed something off the shelves, I'd just reach over and lift it off. No sweat.

A bit like being God, really.

But such speculations were foolish, because (as I recognised, probably for the first time) this was *it*; I'd never be five-six again, let alone a scrape under six feet, I'd never see things from that kind of Olympian perspective, and I'd quite definitely never get out of this dump alive. I was here for the duration, and I was what I'd become, the lowest grade of slave labourer in a vast, uncaring enterprise run by creatures immeasurably more powerful than I was. Something of a novelty for me, a spoiled kid from a rich and privileged background, and therefore even more of a culture shock. Suddenly, without warning or preparation, and without possibility of reprieve or parole, I'd been cut down to size. I was now, for ever and always, just one of the little people.

That's life for you. When I was at liberty and the world was a counter overflowing with free samples of wonderful new experiences for me to try out, I lost fifteen years as quickly and easily as you lose a screw or fiddly little spring out of some dismantled household appliance. In Daddy George's shoe factory, by contrast, each second of each minute of each hour of each day had to be got through, like those dinners I sat in front of when I was eight and really not in the mood for eating, but the plate had to be cleared before I could go upstairs and play, and no matter how furiously I munched and chewed, the measureless carrot mountains and Alpine mounds of mashed potato never seemed to get smaller.

I guess it was even worse for the elves, who were used to being able to fast-forward through Life's adverts and trailers; like South Sea islanders who'd never been exposed to flu, they had no inherent immunity to boredom. Now I'd been bored for a significant proportion of my time on this earth, what with school and family Christmases and Sunday visits to relatives; I could shrug off the regular kind of boredom, the sort that starts around ankle level and slowly works its way up your spine to your head, and the frantic if-I-don't-get-out-of-here-soon-I'll-explode fidgety boredom, and even the molybdenum-steel-acroprops-won't-keep-my-eyelids-apart narcoleptic boredom, or Brookside Syndrome. The boredom in the factory, however, was new to me, it was a deadly blend of extreme tedium and bowel-loosening terror, whereby quite often you're scared witless and bored silly at the same time. Unless you're a collector or compiling a Ph.D. Thesis I really wouldn't recommend that variety.

And yet; although every second of every minute was endlessly prolonged, to the point where I reckoned I could trace the path of every sluggardly photon, because every hour of every day was like every other hour of every other day, the whole experience soon melded seamlessly into one interminable continuum, and before I knew it, it was a whole lot later. I guess that losing track of time isn't so far removed from the Elfland fast-forwarding trick, at that.

So what did I do all day? Well, at five-thirty a.m. every morning the screamer went off, and we all rolled off our thin pile of threadbare blankets, yawned and trooped off to breakfast – one-fiftieth of a stale Ritz cracker and a Barbie-shoeful of brackish water. Ten minutes to grind the masonry-tough biscuit into swallowable paste, then the long march from the dormitory to the stockroom, a trailing grey-green crocodile, no talking, keeping step. Once there, we shuffled off into our respective groups – no need to tell us what to do, it took a whole thirty seconds to learn the trade to grand master level. Take a firm hold of your assigned eighteen inches of rope, and when the worried-looking elf with the clipboard shouts, 'Pull,' you pull. When he says, 'Stop pulling,' you stop pulling. So simple you could train Arts graduates to do it, given time.

Even within this rather sparse framework there was scope for a certain amount of variety. Some days we worked in gangs of a hundred, pulling rolls of canvas or vinyl. Other days, we worked in gangs of fifty, hauling reels of sewing thread. Occasionally we were assigned to intimate little crews of fifteen or twenty, shifting cardboard boxes full of eyelets and laces and tissue paper and other evocatively labelled commodities straight out of a Masefield poem – at least, the boxes were marked 'eyelets' or 'laces' or 'tissue paper'. We never actually got to see any of these fabulous artefacts, but it was just nice to believe they were in there, soft and shiny and smooth. Talking, singing, whistling and other forms of unproductive gaiety were strictly forbidden, needless to say – it wasn't clear who was enforcing the forbidding, because nobody ever broke the rules and I never got to find out; my guess is no one could be bothered to try.

At some unspecified hour the screamer went and we had our mid-morning break. I've already described that, and I won't enlarge on it, for fear of getting snotty letters from Dante's lawyers wanting to know what I think I'm playing at, plagiarising bits of the *Inferno*; suffice it to say that all my fellow-workers had long since abandoned Hope with the decisive speed you'd usually reserve for used styrofoam hamburger boxes. Please dispose of Hope tidily.

Time and the hour runs through the dreariest tea break, however, and the rest of the morning was spent pulling on topes, or not pulling on ropes, as directed by those with a broader perspective. Lunch (a fiftieth of a Ritz and the other Barbie-shoe of water) came and went and you just had to grit your biscuit-abused teeth and bear it before shuffling back to your assigned gang and your rope and whatever hoarded sliver of a dream you still had left. For a long time (don't ask me how long, something like a year, or two weeks; let's say the time it'd take for a glacier to slide three times round the world, and leave it at that) I kept going by thinking about Cru, remembering shy fragments of smiles, the sunlight glinting on her hair, the shape of her fingertips, selected insults, put-downs and cutting remarks. But memory wears out under heavy use quicker than a cheap crossply tyre, and it wasn't long before the image of her face got polished away into a silhouette, like the portrait on an old copper penny. As soon as I became aware of this effect I made a conscious decision to ration my as yet uneroded Cru memories and save them up for later. Instead, I tried remembering the happy, carefree days of my childhood (both of them), and after I'd worn through the chrome of them, I just remembered stuff – Pythagoras's theorem, camels' humps, the Tottenham Court Road in winter, the colour scheme of WD-40 tins, the tunes of soap-powder jingles, the arrangement of aisles in supermarkets I'd known over the years, the birthdays of aunts, bit-players in Coronation Street through the ages, the height of telegraph poles, the mid-night murmurs of domestic plumbing. They all helped, a little; but the longer I was there, the more the very act of remembering became like chewing a piece of gum long after you've ground out the last vestiges of the flavour, and your jaws are just kneading putty. After all, where was the point? As far as I was concerned, none of that stuff existed any more. The whole of reality was confined to the dormitory, the stockroom and my per-sonal eighteen inches of blue nylon rope.

Pain, they say, has the merit of reminding you that you're still alive; the time to start worrying is when it doesn't hurt any more. Now I'm prepared to go along with that view up to a point, preferably a very sharp point which I'm pressing against the neck of whatever wiseacre thought up such a stupid maxim. My personal take on pain is that it's very painful, and I'll do pretty much whatever it takes to make it stop. As far as I could tell, there were only two ways of achieving this highly desirable goal. I could drop down dead (tempting, but probably not very good for you) or I could escape.

Having decided to escape, the first issue to be addressed was why all the other inmates in this house of fun hadn't already done so. Double Nobel laureate or not, I doubted that I was the only poor sap in the place who'd thought how nice it'd be to get out of there, so there had to be a fairly good reason why none of them seemed particularly eager to give it a go. As far as I could see, the security arrangements weren't enough to merit even half a searchlight in the Colditz Guide; no human guard, no bars on the windows, there didn't even seem to be locks on the two or three doors I'd had occasion to see during my stay. There weren't morning and evening roll-calls, or dormitory inspections, or warders prising up floorboards looking for escape tunnels. Nobody, it seemed to me, gave a damn.

You, of course, being an insufferable cleverclogs, have already worked it out for yourself; if you're six inches tall and invisible, where the hell do you go that isn't likely to be worse than a weathertight building with regular meals? Outside in the world, everything was scaled up for the convenience of the indigenous race of giants. Supposing you got away without being trodden on or run over by a lorry (it'd take *days* to cross a dual carriageway), the undergrowth was positively teeming with furry predators who hunted more by smell than sight. If the term of these perils was finite, if it was just a matter of evading death or capture long enough to nip across the Swiss border and find the nearest town hall, it might be worth taking the risk. But there was, quite literally, nowhere to go to, this side of the line, unless you got really lucky and found your way to Legoland or somewhere with a good old-fashioned doll's house.

True; but you're forgetting something. All the other elves were stuck here, true enough, because they could never get back across the line. Not so in my case. Admittedly I'd been slung out of Elfland on my non-pointy ear. But if only I could get out of the factory, I'd be able to find a patch of grass and something to make a circle with. Then I could get to Elfland, and if they threw me out again, at least there was a sporting chance I'd re-enter the human side my proper height and visible, which was all I could possibly ask of Providence at that stage in my career.

(Before you ask: yes, I'd tried the circle trick, it was practically the first thing I did when I arrived. On one of the stockroom shelves there were traces of an ancient coffee-mug stain, a ring of blackened stickiness still clinging to the grey metal. I'd jumped into it and done what I reckoned were all the things that had worked the previous times, but nothing happened other than some very odd looks from my co-workers. The obvious conclusion, from that and stuff I remembered from Melissa's downloaded history lesson was that Daddy George had set up some kind of technobabble field or incomprehensibility generator that damped down any and all elven superpowers. Well, he would, wouldn't he? A simple thing like that, even an Evil Underling should be able to hack it, let alone a full-blown Overlord. Needless to say, there was also the possibility that the anti-superpowers fix was something to do with the big electric shock, rather than a territorial thing, and that even if I got outside I'd still be fixed every bit as good as I'd been back in the stockroom. But I passed a unilateral resolution to forget I'd ever thought of that, since it was far too discouraging.)

Escape. Well, according to my observations, it might well be as easy as heading for a doorway and keeping going. I couldn't see that playing hookey from the work gang for a day while I did some essential reconnaissance was going to get me into any fatal kind of trouble, since I hadn't as yet seen any evidence to suggest that anybody else remembered who I was or where I was meant to be. Admittedly it might all end in tears and six weeks in solitary, but what was six weeks – or six months, or sixteen years – in a place where time was about as relevant as degree-level pure maths in a Latvian brothel?

Nothing to lose. Go for it.

So, the very next day (I couldn't quite bring myself to let go of my rope and walk away in the middle of the afternoon) I put my plan, or at least the big fuzzy hole in my mind marked as SPACE RESERVED FOR PLAN, into operation. When the screamer went and the elves trooped out for breakfast, markedly not singing hi-ho, hi-ho, I hung around at the back of the crowd and, when I was fairly sure nobody was looking, I sneaked off as fast as my wee short legs would carry me, due east. I had an idea I knew where east was because of the angle of the light slanting in through the windows each morning, and it seemed likely that there was an external door somewhere in the east wall because I fancied I'd heard the revving of artic engines coming from that direction, albeit filtered through many inches of brick.

Nothing like being proved right, even if your road to the correct conclusion was paved with false premises, as mine was. A morning spent snooping around the eastern elevation of the factory (I managed to snag a clipboard and a pencil – add a worried expression, and walk quickly at all times) didn't reveal the loading bay or the factory gate or any of the apertures I'd been expecting to find; but there was a small door with frosted glass in the top half, through which leaked palpable daylight. Trouble was, of course, that the handle was seven times my height off the ground.

But I was feeling pretty good about finding a door of

any description; added to which, I had a huge reserve of pent-up energy to spend on anything that looked like a good idea, and a chocolate-free diet and hauling on ropes had left me in pretty good, though miniature, shape. A bit of hunting around unearthed a ball of string, a pocket tape-measure and an old-fashioned metal ruler. The rest was sheer ingenuity, though I say so myself.

Before I tell you what I did next, a word of warning: *don't try this at home.*

Step one was to haul the ruler over to the skirting board, where a pair of copper pipes ran in parallel, level with the floor. With an awful lot of effort and bad language, I got the ruler upright, scrambled up onto the top pipe and hauled the ruler up after me; then I wedged it between the upper and lower pipes and tied it down as best I could with nine inches of the string. Cutting the string proved to be a real pain; there was a pair of scissors on the seat of a human-sized office chair about a yard away, but when I eventually managed to scale the chair-leg and drag myself up by my fingernails on to the seat, I found that the scissors were way too heavy for me to move, so my chances of getting them over the pipes and operating them were effectively zero. In the end, I managed to saw through the string with the edge of the tape-measure; but the whole string-cutting thing took over an hour and used up a lot of my reserves of strength and positive attitude.

Now came the really difficult, fiddly part. The idea was to use the ruler as a catapult to shoot the ball of string over the door handle. As if making such a precise shot didn't promise to be tricky enough, I also faced the fairly monumental problem of getting the ball of string – which I could just about lift over my head if I really tried – to stay on the ruler while I pulled it back (how was I going to pull it back?) far enough to achieve the necessary airspeed and arc of trajectory.

There is always Sellotape in a British office, just as there's always water a few feet under the desert; the trick is to find it. Eventually I tracked it to its lair in the second drawer of a desk five minutes' walk away across the limitless floor. Climbing up there, prising the drawer open with a fortuitously abandoned metal-barrelled biro, elfhandling the roll of tape up onto the lip of the drawer until it overbalanced and dropped to the ground, these were enough to wear me down to the point where I was running on the last knockings of emergency adrenalin. Getting the Sellotape roll back to the launch site, however, turned out to be far easier than I'd anticipated, once I'd hit on the cunning wheeze of climbing inside the roll and imitating the action of the hamster.

The Sellotape made all the difference. As soon as I'd mastered the art of fraying it into lengths against the tape-measure edge, I was able to construct a double-sided sticky pad to go on the top of the ruler, into which I was able to press the string so it'd stay put. With another length of sticky tape, I secured one end of a foot of string to the top of the ruler; after all this time, I was fairly confident that I'd be able to do the business with the other end of the string, and for once my confidence wasn't misplaced. When I'd bent the ruler as far as I could get it to go – a healthy thirty degrees of deflection, more than I thought I'd be able to get – I tied it off on the pipe with a slip-knot and collapsed, hardly able to move at all, for a very long time.

Aiming my improvised siege engine was going to have to be a matter of intuition and blind guesswork. Whether

I'd get another shot if I missed was a point of the utmost mootness, so I took my time, considered the angles, the air-resistance factor, the speed and direction of the wind (there was a small electric fan whirring away on the other side of the room: details *matter* . . .) and every other possible variable I could think of, did the maths, double-checked my answers, realised that I really didn't have a clue what I was doing, closed my eyes and yanked on the string to release the slip-knot.

The recoil from the discharge of the bent ruler knocked me off the top pipe. When I was through picking myself up off the floor and indulging in concussion-induced astronomy, I looked to see where my shot had gone and was both amazed and thrilled to see the string forming a wonderfully graceful right-angled triangle – pipe (where one end was securely fastened) to door handle, door handle to floor. I'd done it.

Well, I'd done part of it. Next came the *really* fiddly bit.

Hauling on ropes may have become my career, even my vocation, but I was fairly sure I wasn't going to be able to scramble all that way up to the door handle from the floor just by doing the Indian Rope Trick. This, of course, was where the tape-measure came in. You may not have noticed this, but at the extreme tip of a tape-measure, where there's a right-angled piece of flat plate which serves as the hook for securing the end to what you're measuring, there's always a rivet to hold the hook in place; and on your better class of tape-measure (which luckily this example was) the rivet takes the form of a hollow eyelet, just wide enough to admit a piece of string.

I lugged the tape-measure over until it was directly

under the end of the door handle, and threaded the string through the hole. Then it got awkward. What I had to do was haul on the other side of the string – the section forming the hypotenuse of the right-angle triangle we admired so fulsomely just now – so as to pull the tape out of the casing, which I'd taped securely to the floor. The hook part was festooned with multiple tendrils or pseudopods of training Sellotape, and the idea was that when I hoisted it up to the handle, the Sellotape would wrap itself around the projecting aluminium horn of the handle – you now how Sellotape loves to attach itself to things, particularly when you don't want it to – and create a secure anchor-point. The rest would be (relatively) easy.

My strength gave out completely on the second attempt; I was pulling against the coiled spring inside the tape-measure, and I'd already exhausted myself setting the whole apparatus up to reach this point. So I rested for as long as I dared – of course, I had no guarantee that a party of quisling elves wouldn't happen along at any minute and drag me away to the solitary-confinement shoebox – then tried to figure out a way of bringing mechanical advantage to bear on the problem. I have to say this, and screw false modesty; my solution was little short of serendipitous genius. Admittedly, I was in two minds as to whether it would work; I pondered and fretted, racked with doubt, like a man offered a cigar by Bill Clinton. On the floor near to where I'd tied up to the pipes, neglected and unloved like all its kind in these cyber-crazed times, there huddled a good old-time Remington manual typewriter. Now, if you're old enough to remember them, you'll recall that when you got to the end of a line, you had to pull back the carriage; and there was a little key you pressed that made the carriage shoot back at great speed, propelled by a hidden spring.

So: the end of the string, made fast to the carriage return lever. The carriage, laboriously forced back step by arduous step (like trying to push-start an eighteen-wheel lorry) until it locked. All set, whereupon I jumped with both feet on the shoot-the-carriage-back key.

It worked; when the carriage crashed back into place, it had raised the end of the tape-measure a good twelve inches. Onwards; tie up the slack of the string to the pipe, shorten the line and tie it to the carriage, repeat the procedure, and jump once more. Repeat the operation four times; job done. The tape-measure hook was right up level with the door handle, and the trailing strips of Sellotape had wrapped themselves round the handle horn like half a dozen starving pythons attacking a water buffalo. I untied the string, holding my breath, and – behold – the tape-measure was still there. Success.

Which only left the piss-easy part; namely, to swagger across to the tape-measure, sit astride it, tease off the ends of the Sellotape that secured the tape-measure casing to the deck, and ascend, as if on a magic carpet, to the door handle under the firm power of the tape-measure spring.

Firm. You betcha. My main concern had been that the spring would prove to lack the necessary welly to get me up there, and I'd been left stranded astride a tape-measure three feet off the ground. As it turned out, I needn't have worried about that, not one bit. In fact, I distinctly remember thinking, *well, that's all right, then* as I sailed past the door handle at something approaching the speed of sound. It was only when I hit the ceiling like a fly swatting itself against a windscreen that I realised that dangling comfortably in the air isn't the worst possible fate that can befall a person in this uncertain world.

By pure chance, having rebounded with extreme force off the ceiling I landed in a plastic beaker filled to the brim with rubber bands. Half an inch either way and I'd have broken my silly neck, but either the Force was with me for once or it decided I was too stupid to die and lower the tone of the afterlife. It took me quite some time to get my breath back, though, and even longer to scrounge up enough strength to scriggle backwards out of the beaker and drop numbly to the floor. As I lifted my head and stared at the firmly closed door, I reached a definite and irrevocable decision. I was giving up.

I have no idea who the human who walked in through it was. I guess he was a lorry driver making a delivery, something like that. At any rate he walked in, gave the tangled mess of string hanging off the inside door handle a quick, bewildered glance, dumped a load of papers on the seat of the office chair and hurried back the way he'd just come, banging the door behind him. And, since he was in a hurry to get out of there – the place seemed to give him the creeps, God alone knew why – he didn't look round to see if the door had actually closed, or if something (the casing, say, of a broken tape-measure) had fallen into the jamb and blocked it as neatly and effectively as the proverbial salesman's foot.

For several minutes I just lay there and gawped. The door was ajar. All I had to do was walk through it.

Simple as that.

So I did. I may even have had my hands in my pockets as I crossed the threshold. I may even have been whistling a jaunty tune. Whatever; it made no odds, because as soon as I emerged into the sunlight on the other side of the door, something invisible but very, very, very heavy and hard bashed me on the head and I went straight to sleep.

CHAPTER FIFTEEN

I woke up with a migraine, a bump on my head the size of a roc's egg, and a feeling of grim determination quite unlike anything I'd experienced before. At last, after a life of aimless and uncommitted drifting, devoid of any real meaning, I had a purpose. I was getting out of there; not only that, I was taking the enslaved elves with me. Whether they liked it or not.

Someone I used to know when I was a kid – I think it was the man who came to service the water heater; anyway, he was singularly unmemorable, whoever the hell he was, apart from this one thing – used to say that the quickest and easiest way to do something is properly. By this, I've always assumed that what he meant was, if you go for the quick fix and the botched-up job, you'll spend twice as much time, ingenuity and effort getting it wrong and then struggling to put it right again than you'd have done if you'd gone about it in a calm, methodical fashion to begin with. On balance I've got to say that if he was the guy I'm thinking of, he was a better philosopher than he was a heating engineer, because the water heater used to make the most amazing noises in the middle of the night, and as far as hot water was concerned we'd have been better off warming up a tin bath over a large candle. That, however, shouldn't detract from the shining truth of his one great statement; and besides, it could just as easily have been the tree surgeon or the man who emptied the septic tank who said it, and not the water-heater bloke at all. I mean, I was only twelve at the time and I wasn't taking notes.

So; no more half-baked why-not-just-stroll-out-the-door-whistling-'Greensleeves' escape attempts for me; from now on, it was going to be all meticulous planning, with lots of timing people with stopwatches and scale drawings and every possible contingency allowed for. After all, there was no desperate rush. Life in the factory went on; it was miserable and boring and there was nothing nice to look forward to and all the other people who worked there were about as much fun as severe piles, but never mind. If such conditions as those were enough to kill you off, the human race would've died out a thousand years ago and there would never have been any accountants.

I was still quite a long way off perfecting my escape plan – to be mercilessly honest, I hadn't even started it yet – when I got my promotion. Apparently, I'd caught the supervisor's eye, with my deep-rooted work ethic and uncomplaining diligence, to the point where he couldn't stand the sight of me any more. So I got a transfer: out of the stockroom and into packing.

Yes, definitely a promotion; and in an environment where such things were considered extremely rare. It wasn't even a case of dead elves' shoes, since the elves appeared to live for ever in spite of the exhausting work and rotten food. You were assigned to a job and you stayed put and did it. Only the very best, brightest and most insufferable actually progressed up the golden ladder.

Mind you, I had to keep telling myself it was a promotion, usually through gritted teeth. True, the work in packing was lighter, you got to sit down instead of being on your feet all day, there was none of that back-breaking, tendon-wrenching hauling on ropes we got in the stockroom. But it was boring. Very boring. Very very boring. Very very very boring. Very very very boring indeed.

Packing centred around a long conveyor belt, a sort of ghastly satanic parody of the yellow brick road. At one end there was a small, dismal colony of elves who took cardboard boxes out of large cartons and hoisted them with a winch and a derrick onto the belt. Downstream from them was where I was stationed, along with a dozen or so fellow craftsmen; our job was to lay a sheet of tissue paper over the open top of each box. Further down from us, another group inserted a single left shoe. Still further down the line, the next batch folded one end of my tissue sheet over this shoe, so that the next outfit could lower the right shoe, whereupon the next mob folded over the other end of the sheet and the bunch of tiny specks in the far distance put the lid on. Adventurous travellers who claimed to have been all the way down the belt, presumably in the spirit of Sir Richard Burton seeking to discover the source of the Nile, asserted that after the lid went on the boxes just vanished down a chute, like medieval mariners falling off the edge of the world. It was far less trouble to believe them than to argue, so I did.

My first job as founder, chairman and sole member of the escape committee was to recruit some support. This turned out to be extremely difficult. Naturally enough, the first people I tried to enlist were the twelve or so other wretched souls who worked with me on tissue-sheet insertion, partly because they were essential to the plan that was just starting to take shape in my mind, partly because they were the only ones close enough for me to make myself heard without shouting.

Talk (if you can really be bothered) about apathy. I had to explain the plan a dozen times before they were even prepared to acknowledge my existence, and their initial reaction was a not-particularly-encouraging *piss off, you noisy bugger*. But, being a man with a mission and having absolutely nothing else to do, I persisted, and eventually five out of the twelve declared that they were with me to the death, provided they didn't actually have to do anything and that if they agreed, I'd shut the hell up.

Ah well, I thought; it was probably the same for Martin Luther and Lenin and Peter Tatchell; unless you've got a nerve like a ship's hawser and skin thick enough to withstand a direct hit from a wire-guided missile, you aren't likely to get far founding Movements. Eventually I persuaded them to have a go at recruiting the next lot down the line. It was several weeks before anyone said anything (apart from *piss off, you noisy bugger*); then one day, quite suddenly, the thin gormless-looking character who stood next to me on the line – I have no idea what his name was – happened to mention that Left Shoes were with us, Left-Shoe Folds were about half-and-half, and Right Shoes were thinking about it. A terrible beauty was born.

Of course, I hadn't been idle all this time. I'd been banging away fornlornly about life, liberty and the pursuit of happiness to the delivery crews who brought us the sheets of tissue paper, and seven out of ten of them were pledged to the cause, albeit with a high level of resigned pessimism; life, they reckoned, was all right but highly overrated, liberty was a nice idea but it'd probably never catch on, and the pursuit of happiness as practised by humans was probably a blood sport. Still, they reckoned, they had nothing better to do, and the worst that could happen was that we'd all be found out, rounded up and horribly tortured to death, so yeah, why not?

From that point on, the movement spread like butter straight from the fridge, until the day came when Packing was a hundred per cent solid, Cutting was right behind us (cowering), Stitching was prepared to give us all the moral support we could use so long as they didn't have to get involved, and the Stockroom was practically singing the 'Marseillaise', albeit quietly under its breath. Admittedly, I got the distinct impression that most of my support was conditional on the whole project fizzling out within a month or so with nothing to show for it, but I tried not to let that bother me. They'd all be smirking on the other side of their faces when I led them forth into the Promised Land, even if it did turn out to be the Threatened Land by the time we actually got there.

That was an aspect of the matter that did worry me, I confess. Just suppose we did somehow contrive to get a whole load of elves out of the factory and into the world – what the hell were we supposed to do then, in an environment in which everything larger than a young

earwig would have to be regarded as a dangerous pred-
ator? The idea, if you could call it that, was that we'd
find an out-of-the-way corner somewhere, settle down,
build an itsy-bitsy-teeny-weeny settlement and grow our
own food – mustard and cress, probably, and possibly
dwarf spinach once we'd achieved the level of techno-
logical skill needed to build elf-sized chainsaws to
harvest it with. In all honesty, since none of us really
believed we'd make it that far, we didn't dwell on the
subject. The certainty of failure can be a great comfort,
sometimes.

With all the support I could handle without suc-
cumbing to terminal depression, I was ready to initiate
Phase One. This bit was going to be crucial, and for a
very long time I couldn't figure out how to go about it.
I needed to weigh (a) an elf (b) a left-hand shoe.

Ah, you dirty great big bastards, you don't know how
lucky you are. You want to weigh something – piece of
cake: just totter into the kitchen and drag out the trusty
Salter, or lug your unseemly bulk up the stairs and fire
up the bathroom scales. So easy. Nothing to it.

It's all very different when you're small, and the evil
overlord who's using you as slave labour hasn't seen fit
to equip your factory with any kind of weight-measuring
device. You have to improvise; tricky enough at the best
of times when you're six inches tall, virtually impossible
when you have no off-duty time to speak of and nothing
much to improvise with. In fact, the escape project
would've foundered there and then, if it hadn't been for
Spike.

I first came across Spike during my time in the stockroom. Maybe I should point out that Spike wasn't her
name, or if it was, it was only because of a monstrous

coincidence of the kind that ought to be outlawed in all civilised nations because of the risk of extreme bewilderment. Spike was the name I attributed to her in the back of my mind, because she had the pointedest ears ever – twin stilettos sprouting upwards like the first crocus shoots of spring, the sort of thing you could envisage Count Vlad Dracul impaling his least favourite people on. Spike was short even by our standards, not much more than five and a half inches, and built like Sumo Barbie or My Little Bouncer, and her best friend (if she had one, which she didn't) couldn't have described her as cheerful; but she had a gift for engineering design that was outstanding even among the scientifically-inclined elves. Imagine a female Isambard Kingdom Brunel who's shrunk in the wash and then been compressed under a pile of very heavy weights, and you'll get the idea.

'Problem,' said Spike, 'call that a problem?' According to Spike, we wouldn't recognise a problem if it bit us on the nose. All we had to do in order to ascertain the weight of an elf, a shoe or any bloody thing was to construct a simple balance – two plastic coffee cups, a ruler and some string, poised over a makeshift fulcrum, such as the top ridge of a Sellotape dispenser – and put the thing we wanted to weigh in one side and the requisite number of items of known weight needed to achieve equilibrium in the other. Easy peasy.

Yes, we argued, but. It was all very well to chatter blithely about multiple items of known weight, but how were we supposed to go about knowing the weight of the multiple items without a set of scales to weigh them with?

Spike wasn't impressed with this line of argument.

All we needed, she said, was one thing whose weight we knew; everything else we could calculate, with a bit of hard work and application. Just one thing, and everything else would follow.

First, we retorted, catch your thing. Spike's response to that was distinctly crude, so we set up a subcommittee; and after a good deal of furtive searching, we struck gold, in the form of a packet of chocolate digestives.

They were old chocolate digestives; veteran bordering on vintage. My guess was that they'd been stashed away by one of the previous (human) occupants of the building so as to avoid having to share them with his or her voracious colleagues come morning-coffee time, and for some reason never retrieved. The important thing was that on the cellophane wrapper were the words *net weight 454g*.

Those choccy bickies were our Rosetta stone. The packet contained thirty biscuits. Four hundred and fifty-four divided by thirty is (as any elf will tell you in the time it takes to pick your nose) fifteen point one three recurring, so one biscuit weighed fifteen grammes, close enough for jazz, allowing for crumbs and absorption of atmospheric moisture. Next step was to lug one biscuit across the stockroom floor into the office, where we'd set up our improvised scales, hoist it into the plastic cup and load the other cup with paper clips until the two cups balanced. It took twenty-nine paper clips to level up one biscuit; therefore, one paper clip weighed 0.51724137931 grammes, or half a gramme for ready money. (Not that the elves were satisfied with that kind of thinking. Oh no. If it didn't have ten digits after the decimal point, they wouldn't sully their minds with it. It may be worth pointing out that I got very, very tired of elves during this phase of the operation.)

Of course, you can't get an elf in a plastic cup, let alone a shoe; so we had to start from scratch and build a whole new, bigger set of scales before we could go any further. In the end we had to settle on shoebox lids, which turned the enterprise into labour-intensive heavy engineering and held up progress for over a fortnight. Even after we'd finished the thing, we were stymied by the discovery that we simply didn't have enough paper clips to counterbalance a left-hand moccasin, which meant we had to fool around weighing the things we did have – run-out biros, eyelets, shoelaces, reels of cotton – in terms of paper clips on the little scales before we were in a position to go back and rebuild the big scales (which we'd had to dismantle in the interests of security) and do the shoe. Since all these things had to be done during the part of the morning break when the supervisors (who weren't in on the plot, needless to say) were off writing up their dockets or having a wee, you can probably see why it too such a very long time.

But, like a touring glacier or a Virgin Atlantic jumbo, we got there in the end, which means that I'm uniquely qualified to tell you that one standard size 11 gentleman's left light-tan moccasin weighs the same as 672.5568 paper clips (or three duff biros, nine eyelets, one shoelace, three reels of white hand-sewing nylon thread and 226 paper clips); or (as you'll have figured out already, no doubt) 347.873 grammes; or, rather more relevantly as far as we were concerned, 1.391 average-sized male elves, or one male elf and fifty paper clips, give or take a tenth of a paper clip.

Ah. Now you're beginning to grasp the essence of my plan. The idea was quite simple, like all those wonderful ideas that seem so good at the time. My nasty experience with the doorway suggested to me that there was some kind of field, scientific or magical or what the hell you care to call it, that stopped elves from leaving the building – you'll remember that when I tried to cross the threshold I went out like a light, fell down and nutted myself, suffering a nasty bump on the head and an even nastier dent in my self-esteem. At first, this seemed to mc to be an insoluble hindrance to the whole escape project, especially when I thought back to all the useful stuff I'd had downloaded into my mind the first time I crossed the line into Elfland and was given the inside story of how Daddy George trapped my real father. I pieced it all together into a patchwork of factlings, checked out the basic science with a dozen or so more than usually eggheaded elves, and reached the conclusion that Daddy George had contrived a barrier that effectively stripped elves of all the useful attributes they brought with them from the other side (as a result of the time/space thing I muddled you to sleep with earlier in this story) and cut them down to the extremely small size we were all forced to endure inside the factory. How this barrier worked, we never could work out – we guessed it had something to do with the heavy dose of raw voltage that had shrunk me and all the rest of them at one time or another – but one thing we were able to do (something much more useful, in context) was calculate to within the nearest five hundred volts how much power it would take to run that kind of field all the way round a whopping great factory.

I can't remember the actual figures off the top of my head, but the gist of it was: a lot. A whole lot. A very large, chunky whole lot indeed. Here was where my expert knowledge of Daddy George came in so very useful; because electricity, as you've probably found out at some point in your life, costs money, and the more you use, the more money you have to spend. And if there was one thing Daddy George hated doing, it was spending money.

So, I argued, the chances were that the field didn't actually extend the whole way round the building; Daddy George, crown prince of cheapskates, would only have booby-trapped the parts of the building through which elves might reasonably be expected to try and go. Doors, windows, skylights, maybe even the drains; but I was prepared to bet that that was probably the full extent of his defences. Which was where my plan slotted in.

You'll remember me telling you that once the shoes had been boxed and the lids had been fitted, the shoe-replete box trundled on down the conveyor and disappeared down a chute. I sent a scouting party to investigate this, and they reported back that this account was substantially correct. The belt, they said, vanished into a hole in the wall; a hole, moreover, curtained with a trailing fringe of rubber strips (like an airport carousel, though they didn't make the comparison, never having heard of such things) that brushed all round the box before it disappeared, with the obvious objective of dislodging any recklessly brave elf who fancied riding a shoebox to freedom.

That rang very true indeed; it was just like Daddy George to devise a system whereby a few strips of old rubber mat did the same job as a fiendishly expensive hi-tech force field. In my mind's eye I could practically see him grinning all over his face and rubbing his hands together at the thought of all the money he'd be saving that way.

Fine so far; the idea was basically so sound that no elf had even tried to get out that way, thereby proving Daddy George's point. Well, then; if his rubber-strip idea worked so wonderfully well, was it likely that he'd waste good money fitting the loading bay gates with a costly and superfluous elf-zapper unit? Catch him doing that? No way.

But: supposing that instead of elves clinging to the tops of the boxes and getting duly swatted by the rubber strips, we had elves riding inside the boxes, like snails in shells or the crews of so many cardboard Panzers? All they'd have to do would be to bide still and quiet inside their cartons until they were sure they'd been loaded off the belt and into the lorries, and the lorries had driven through the factory gates and outside the compound. Then all they'd have to do would be to climb out and wait patiently until the lorry got to where it was going and the driver rolled up the tailgate whereupon they could sneak invisibly past him, hurl themselves off the lorry and run like buggery for the nearest safe cover. After that, of course, they'd be on their own, but that was one threadbare and fraying rope bridge across a vertiginous sheer-sided canyon that we could cross when we came to it.

Next problem: how to get the elf into the box. Packing was the obvious place to do it; instead of a shoe, insert an elf. It'd have to be the left shoe, of course, because the left shoe went in first, with a fold of tissue paper to cover it and then the right shoe and its cover. Substitute an elf for the left shoe and he'd be out of sight if the box lid happened to slide off after it'd gone through the chute, or if some nosy scumbag of a human lifted the lid to inspect the contents.

The weight issue: now, maybe I was being paranoid about this aspect, but I could foresee problems if we just did a straight swap. Because elves weigh less than shoes, the packed boxes would come up light – not enough, perhaps to notice in the case of a single box, but we weren't contemplating single boxes, we were talking about a whole lorryload of them. None of us had a clue how many boxes went into each lorry, naturally enough (since none of us had ever been in the loading bay, or seen inside the cargo compartment of a shoe lorry), but say each lorryload comprised a thousand boxes. With a weight shortfall of something like 25 grammes per box, that made for a differential of 25 kilos – half a hundred-weight – per fully-laden consignment. Would anybody notice a variation of that order? We didn't have the faintest idea, but it seemed reasonable to assume that if we turned a blind eye to it, chances were that someone would indeed notice and it'd be the factor that got us all found out and caught. Better, I figured, to take the extra time and effort, and get it as near gramme-perfect as we possibly could.

(Bear in mind also that the calculations so lovingly reproduced above posited an average-sized elf of standard sectional density. You and I both know that where individuals are concerned, the average is pretty well useless; build up a statistical definition of an average person and I'll bet you good money that half your sample will be shorter and lighter than the mythical Mr Average, while the other half will be taller and heavier. Weigh each individual elf, male and female, skeletally thin and grossly overweight, and make up the deviation from the norm with paper clips, packets of staples, typewriter rubbers and shagged-out pencil sharpeners. The easiest and quickest way to do the job is properly, because then you won't have to do it all over again. And so forth.)

All done in a sort of dream, needless to say, because the only way to rationalise this whole experience – being only six inches tall and trapped for life in a shoe factory with a whole lot of snotty elves – was to keep telling myself that really it was all just a dream (a thoroughly unpleasant dream, and that's the very last time I eat Canadian cheddar as a bedtime snack), that what seemed like months in the factory was just a few minutes of feverish REM sleep, and that any minute now I'd wake up and forget the whole thing by the time I'd pasted my toothbrush. As an explanation it made much more sense than the alternative – Occam's razor, and all that jazz - so, if it was all just a nightmare, it didn't actually matter what I did or what happened to me. If the scheme failed, so what? If I got caught and horribly tortured, it'd only be dream pain, and when I woke up I wouldn't be mutilated and crippled for life. Besides, it'd probably work, because in a dream the laws of physics are about as binding as speed limits to a cabinet minister. Nothing to worry about. All in the mind. If it's all going to be wiped from your memory as soon as you open your eyes, can it truly be said to have happened, existentially speaking?

All in all, it was going remarkably smoothly, apart from the obstacles and the disasters; too smoothly, of course. It's fair to say that the only well-oiled machines you're likely to encounter as you stroll through life are guillotines and out-of-control chainsaws falling on you out of tall trees.

Meet Sweetie-Pie. I don't for one moment believe

that that was his real name – well, even his real name wasn't his real name, because his *real* name would've been something elvish on the other side of the line; suffice it to say that the only place in any dimension or continuum where Sweetie-Pie was called that was probably the inside of my head. Doesn't matter in the slightest.

Sweetie-Pie was foreman of the cutting room, and I called him Sweetie-Pie because, out of the several thousand miserable, unpleasant, unlovely bastard elves crowded together under our communal roof, he was beyond challenge or question the worst. I didn't like him much, and neither did anyone else.

Obviously, conscripting him into the escape committee was about as sensible as buying prime time advertising on FM radio, so we didn't; we made a point of keeping him well away from anywhere we happened to be when we were doing escape stuff. In retrospect, of course, that was our fundamental mistake. In order to distract his attention, you see, we sent elves to engage him in conversation, tell him miserable stories (jokes just weren't in fashion in the factory), show him faded and crumpled postcards of large hotels in Barcelona that we'd excavated from long-forgotten desk drawers, and generally make him feel loved and wanted.

Which, of course, he wasn't, neither of them. Now, when the most unpopular person in the community suddenly finds himself the centre of a Parisian-style salon, with folks standing in line to canvass his views on everything from the Heisenberg uncertainty principle to Elfland Wanderers' chances in the League –

(Elf football is stunningly boring, in any case; competition implies conflict, conflict is just a fancy euphemism for violence, violence is not the elven way, so football matches in Elfland consist of twenty-two elves carefully avoiding the ball while discussing the aforementioned Heisenberg uncertainty principle)

– he didn't have to be a rocket scientist to figure out that something was going on. As it happened, he was a rocket scientist, like ninety per cent of all elves. He began to suspect.

As you can probably appreciate, the position of a fore-man in a slave-labour camp tends to be a little awkward, with more grey areas than a black-and-white movie. Management (in this case, Daddy George, who never visited the place and whose only contact with it was via a bewilderingly complex labyrinth of rerouted e-mails) doesn't trust him as far as he's sneezable through a blocked nostril, Sweetie-Pie's fellow-workers, needless to say, trusted him rather less than that. His authority was underwritten, at least in theory, by an unspecified number of unidentified human heavies who'd be sum-moned and sent in with baseball bats at the first sign of insurrection or civil disobedience. But we'd never seen them, because nobody had ever dared do anything that might cause them to be summoned, and there were cer-tain practical objections, such as how they'd be supposed to see us if they ever were called in, that cast more than a little doubt on their very existence; and we were all morally certain that prominent among the lead-ing sceptics was Sweetie-Pie himself. Not that any of us would've been prepared to call his bluff on this point, at least not before the escape project got under way; but Sweetie-Pie had to face the fact that if he was too heavy-handed in his approach he could easily find himself backed into a corner where he'd have no option but to send for the storm troopers, and if it turned out that there weren't any after all, he'd find himself in a distinctly awkward position, probably on top of something hot and sharp.

On the other hand, he couldn't very well do nothing at all, just in case we really were planning a rebellion or a mass breakout. Somehow, therefore, he had to get across the idea that he was onto us and closing in like wolves around a small, broken-winded piglet, while at the same time finding a way to avoid committing himself on the subject of precisely what he was closing in with. It was a pretty tactical problem, and anybody even slightly less miserable would probably have relished the challenge.

He resolved it, eventually, by the time-honoured method of cornering one small, timid, feeble-minded conspirator and telling her that she (and she alone) had a slim chance of avoiding the hideous fate in store for the rest of the conspirators, provided that she gave him all the relevant names, times and places by way of corroborative evidence. Not that any further evidence was needed, he had enough already to have the whole workforce clapped in irons, but it saved time and paperwork if there was just the one signed confession instead of a cellarful of affidavits and witness statements that the prosecution would have to spend days piecing together. Her choice, he pointed out; if she didn't want to cooperate he could easily find someone else, or simply not bother, but if she wanted to help she'd have to do it straight away, since he was on a fairly tight schedule –

Can't really blame her, of course, the treacherous bloody cow. Ask yourself what you'd have done in her shoes, and if your answer isn't *exactly the same as she did*, award yourself three bonus points for outstanding moral fibre, and five thousand anti-points for stupidity, survival-instinct deficiency and lying to yourself. In the event, I gather, she lasted about three times as long as I'd have done before breaking down sobbing for mercy – a full fifteen seconds, though three of those seconds were taken up with a loud sneeze, and I don't think that should be allowed to count.

The first we knew about it was some time later. We were in the stockroom, weighing the elves who were going out with the first escape party. I wasn't one of them, it goes without saying. No, I'd come over all noble and self-sacrificing and given away my reserved space to some pathetic loser or other. Me all over. Quite.

Don't get the idea that we hadn't given any thought to what might happen if we got busted; far from it. But one thing we were relying on, not unreasonably if you ask me, was the element of lack of surprise. Remember, in our terms the factory was vast, the size of a small country, and all the rooms were enormous. This meant, we figured, that sneaking up on us without us seeing the bogeys coming a long way off was pretty much out of the question. Also, talking about seeing people, humans couldn't see us, unless Daddy George had come up with another of his scientific marvels. Consequently, if they were coming to get us, we figured we'd have plenty of time to abandon whatever we were doing and run like blazes for the sort of cover in which it's very difficult indeed for a full-size human to detect and evict a tiny invisible elf.

Not much wrong with that line of reasoning, though I do say it myself, and that's probably why Sweetie-Pie didn't try the direct approach (that and a distinct lack of human security guards, if you ask me). Instead - well, you have to give him credit for a little genuine ingenuity, because his solution was pretty damned smart.

One minute we were standing there watching the balance swaying gently towards equilibrium, with an elf on one side and a saucerload of miscellaneous stationery on the other. The next, the air suddenly grew unnervingly thick, and it started monsooning shiny metallic paint, great splodgy dollops of the stuff falling out of the air and flooding us, like incie-wincie spiders when the rain set in. Once the paint hit you, that was it; you went out like a light. In my case, I vaguely remember thinking, *So this is what it's like to get rained on by a cloud with a silver lining.* Fortunately, before I could take that theme any further, I blacked out.

CHAPTER SIXTEEN

I don't think I was out for very long; just long enough for the paint to have dried into that gooey-sticky state where it's at its most objectionable. I was still on the stockroom floor, and my fellow conspirators were all around me as I woke up, lying where they'd dropped – like the closing moments of a Tarentino film set in Toytown.

Clever old Sweetie-Pie. He'd sprayed paint all over us through the sprinkler system. It struck me as a smart effort at the time, but it was only much later that I found out just how clever the strategy was.

When I came round and remembered what had happened, I immediately assumed – I think we all did – that the purpose behind the paint job was to make us all visible, so that the human security thugs would be able to see and arrest us. This wasn't even remotely the case – partly because the paint didn't make us even the tiniest bit visible (as far as humans were concerned, any paint that hit an elf vanished instantly; I guess that with a computer linked to a bunch of CCTV cameras, you could've used the patterns caused by disappearances of paint blobs to chart where we were when the sprinklers started up, but that wouldn't have been any practical help, since there was plenty of time to move a yard or so after the paint landed and before we blacked out) and partly because there weren't actually any guards to see us even if the paint thing *had* worked. The simple fact of the matter was that we hadn't been caught at all, but that Sweetie-Pie had cunningly tricked us into believing we'd been caught – just as good as the real thing, and in many respects even better. If you're convinced you haven't got a hope in hell of escaping, you don't bother trying. That was the security policy on which the whole enterprise was based – typical Daddy George: why spend money when you can cheat?

But of course, we didn't know . . . And while we were still twitching and groaning and rubbing our eyes and feeling - well, pretty much the way I always feel after I've just woken up, but I'm the archetypal Not A Morning Person – there was Sweetie-Pie, stomping up and down between the slumped carcases and shouting in the very finest traditions of law enforcement through the ages; and the gist of what he was shouting was, *You're nicked*.

With hindsight, it's worth considering the situation from his point of view. He'd just unmasked a conspiracy, but he still didn't know what we'd all been conspiring to do (except in the most general terms; I don't suppose he thought we were all skulking furtively about in order to plan his surprise birthday party) and as for what he was supposed to do with us next, I'm fairly sure he didn't have a clue. Having us all savagely executed wasn't remotely feasible, but if he didn't have us savagely exe-cuted, that'd be as good as admitting his severe lack of resources. On balance, therefore, I think he did the only thing he could do, in the circumstances.

'All right,' he said. 'On your feet. Line up. Come on, let's be having you.'

We did as we were told, albeit slowly and awkwardly, thanks to the semi-plastic paint we were all wearing. Nobody even considered running away. Why bother? They'd only be caught and dragged back again, and in the meanwhile they could fall over and bruise their knees.

'OK,' said Sweetie-Pie, facing the rows of dejected elves like a sergeant major. 'This conspiracy of yours. How do I go about joining?'

Like I said, the only thing he could do: he couldn't hold us, he couldn't let us go, and once we realised this it was a fair bet that he'd be severely dealt with, if not by us then by Daddy George, for letting us escape. It took him a while to get this across to the more suspicious members of the conspiracy, a faction that made up about a hundred per cent of the membership; but once we'd got our heads around it, I have to admit that it made pretty good sense. We were all sitting a bit upset about the nasty shock, of course, not to mention the silver paint, but in the end we had to acknowledge that it was about the only method open to him of getting our undivided attention.

That was when it started to get depressing.

We explained our plan to Sweetie-Pie. He listened carefully, nodding from time to time to show he was paying attention, a properly serious expression smeared on his face like peanut butter on a slice of toast. When we'd finished, he nodded.

'You're out of your skulls,' he said.

Understandably, I pressed him for details.

'Won't work,' he replied, 'simple as that. One, the dampening field goes all the way round. You try and get out in a shoebox, you'll wake up dead. If you're lucky,' he added, with a hint of doleful *schadenfreude*. 'When you tried to get out the door – yes, of course, I know about that, what do you think I do all day, knit baby clothes? – when you tried the door, all you got was the minimum setting, 'cos He knows there's always some clever bugger who'll try and get out, and He doesn't want to kill the whole bloody workforce. Hard enough to meet the delivery dates with all of you alive; if He was to let you go frying yourselves all over the place, there'd never be any work done. But the rest of the field, He's got the power cranked up to max. There'd be a little blue spark, and that'd be you.'

'Oh,' I said.

'And another thing,' Sweetie-Pie went on, in the extra-mournful voice he used when pointing out really crass errors. 'It's all very well you morons going around weighing each and making up the weight with paper clips and stuff, but didn't it ever occur to you that if you do that, the boxes are going to rattle like buggery? You ever heard of a shoebox that rattled?'

He had a point. It was a pity he insisted on shoving that point right up our self-confidence, but I guess he had the right.

'And,' he continued, 'that's not the worst of it, either.' He shook his head. 'The boss, see. He doesn't want his customers putting on their brand new shoes and finding 'em full of invisible elves. Could give someone a nasty jolt, that. So He's got all sorts of scanning gear out there in the loading bay, and if there's an elf in the box, it sets off this alarm—'

'My god,' I said, awed. 'Elf detectors.'

'Never used 'em, mind,' Sweetie-Pie pointed out. 'Never had to. I mean, you lot are a pretty sad bunch, but at least you aren't dumb enough to think you could get out of here. Or at least,' he added, 'up till now you haven't been. It only takes one smartarse to spoil everything.

Meaning me, naturally. 'Fine,' I said. 'So why were you in such a hurry to join us?'

He shrugged. 'Thought you'd actually found a way that'd work,' he said. 'Else, why's everybody suddenly got escape fever? 'Course, I was completely wrong. Haven't got a clue, the lot of you.'

My fellow conspirators were starting to look at me with less than friendly expressions on their little faces. 'All right,' I said, 'if you know so much about it, what would you suggest?'

'Forget it,' he answered, with a sigh. 'Can't be done, don't go breaking your heart over it. Oh, and before someone makes a fool of himself suggesting it, no, you can't switch off the field from inside the building, and you can't jam it or sabotage it either. All the controls and stuff are in a junction box on the north outside wall.'

There was a lot more of this sort of thing, all of it described with such miserable glee that you'd have been forgiven for thinking that Sweetie-Pie's real motive for joining up was to persuade us to forget about the whole thing and resign ourselves to the prospect of a life in the factory. But it wasn't like that, I'm sure. You couldn't have faked that triumphant told-you-so disillusionment in his voice. Besides, a few straightforward tests proved well enough that what he'd told us wasn't any kind of disinformation, it was the plain truth. Brand new form of counter-espionage: you infiltrate the enemy and tell him all your most closely guarded military secrets, whereupon he realises for the first time just how profoundly outmatched he is, and gives up. Not a bad idea, at that.

'What about up?' I remember suggesting, rather desperately, during one of our rather tragic brainstorming sessions. 'Or are you going to tell me he's booby-trapped the roof as well?'

'One of the first things He did,' Sweetie-Pie replied. 'On account of, it's exactly the sort of thing He'd expect you lot to try. So yes, the roof's wired to buggery, and so's the floor, and the drains. And whatever you do, don't try crawling out through the ventilator shafts. He's got stuff hidden in there'd give you screaming bloody nightmares just thinking about it.'

I sighed. 'All right,' I said, 'what about overloading this dampening field thing? If enough of us were to try getting through a door at the same time—'

'You'd be vaporised,' Sweetie-Pie replied, with an unwholesome glint in his eye that suggested that this might not be a bad thing, especially if one of the unfortunate souls reduced to his component atoms happened to be me. 'Bloody clever system – the more load you put on it, the higher the setting it adjusts itself to. I s'pose you might just overload it if you all tried leaving at once, but that'd sort of defeat the object of the exercise.'

'We could blast a hole in the wall,' put in Spike. (You remember Spike: small, ingenious female elf with an attitude problem, figured out how to do the weighing stuff.) 'I've been thinking about that, actually. That stuff they make the polycarbonate trainer soles from, I reckon that with a bit of time and some improvised lab equipment, I could get nitrocellulose out of that. Explosive,' she explained. 'We could blow the east wall out, where the masonry's not as thick as in the rest of the building. Don't tell me this dampening field'd still work if we took the wall away.'

Sweetie-Pie nodded gravely. 'You could do that,' he said. 'You could blow up a wall, no problem. Only trouble is, if you do that you'll set off the explosive charges stashed in the wall cavities, just in case someone ever find out about this place and he needs to get rid of the evidence in a tearing hurry. Nice idea, but I wouldn't try it if I were you.'

You can tell how much Sweetie-Pie's thoroughly depressing revelations had got to us from the fact that Spike didn't even argue; she just shrugged, muttered, 'Oh, screw that, then,' and went back to doodling symbolic logic equations on the concrete floor with a rusty nail. Someone told me later that her doodling was a breathtaking insight, a melting-down and recasting of the most basic conventions of mathematics that would finally allow Fermat's Last Theorem to be fully evaluated in a simple expression that could be easily understood even by a Californian high-school teacher. Presumably that meant she'd done something clever, but don't ask me what. I'm only a double Nobel laureate, for crying out loud.

'Oh well,' someone said (can't remember who; some elf or other), 'that's that, then. We stay here and rot. Well, you can't have everything, I suppose.'

Nobody said anything, and the meeting decomposed. ('Broke up' is too vigorous a term to describe the aimless way they all drifted off, shoulders drooping, heads lolling off necks, little heels dragging, like a bunch of Action Man dolls who've just learned that the ceasefire is now official.) The general unspoken consensus seemed to be that the great escape was off, postponed indefinitely because of lack of interest. I found this extremely annoying.

– All right, yes: I'd ended up here because I got caught, not because I'd actually carried through on my early resolve to rescue all the prisoners and bring 'em back alive to the promised land, like Rambo Moses. But it was that initial spurt of heroism (heroic as two short planks, me) that started off the landslip in my fortunes that ended up with me getting my collar felt, so in a sense I was there because of them, I had put myself in harm's way for their sakes, and to have them give it up as a bad job simply because escape was impossible and resistance was futile struck me as gormless cowardice of the worst possible sort. I'd have turned on my heel and stormed out in a huff if it hadn't been for the containment field and the booby-traps.

It was time I was back at my post on the conveyor belt; heroes of the revolution may enjoy a certain degree of latitude in matters of timekeeping, but leaders of failed uprisings had better be in their places when the whistle goes, or the foreman will want to know the reason why. *Damn,* I thought, *it shouldn't be like this.* After all, I'd managed the really difficult bit, getting all those pathetic, terminally apathetic losers to get off their bums and do something. Failing at this point was tantamount to having threaded my way through the labyrinth of doom and climbed the sheer cliff face to the temple housing the golden fleece, only to be turned back because I didn't have the right change for the ticket machine.

I was missing something, I knew that; something right down deep, something fundamentally important but so simple I was taking it for granted. All I had to do was recognise it for what it was –

I waited, but it didn't come. Maybe I was wrong after all, maybe there wasn't a way out, and I had just been wasting my time and raising everybody's hopes with nothing to show for it. Now that was just plain cruel, because I wasn't that sort of person. Me, a leader; me, the type that gets people moving, shapes destinies, sets off revolutions. As if. The very fact that I'd started this idiotic conspiracy only went to show it was doomed from the outset, like a literary quarterly in Australia.

And what had I done to deserve all this, and what was I being punished for? All my life I'd been the meek, patiently waiting to inherit the Earth –

(If the meek ever do inherit the Earth, by the way, you can be sure that they'll dutifully pay the inheritance tax and the capital gains tax and the stamp duty, and the thought of trying to dodge any of the due taxes will never even cross their minds; with the result that after the lawyers and accountants have had their bite out of what's left, all the meek will actually inherit is the unfashionable south-western quarter of Madagascar . . .)

Not fair, I thought, *not fair at all. What did I do? Why me?*

Why me?

And then it all clicked into place, like a jigsaw you've been staring at for three-quarters of an hour and suddenly you realise that if you turn round the little knobbly-edged bit, it'll go. *Why me?* Because nobody else could do it, was why. Fancy not realising that from the very start. *That* was what I'd been doing wrong. I'd been a man sullenly trying to bash a screw into a block of wood with a butt of a screwdriver while bitching about the poxy useless hammer I'd been issued with. I'd missed the point by such a wide margin that I'd got myself impaled on the next point across.

All I had to do was be myself, the person I was meant to be all along. You see, I wasn't born to be anybody important, clever, successful or even interesting. I was supposed to. be an insignificant, unimportant nonentity – I'd have been good at that. Instead, I was a Nobel prizewinner, a major shareholder in one of the world's biggest multinational corporations, the sole bridge between human-side and Elfland, the chosen one who'd lead the enslaved elves out of servitude. Either I'd misunderstood myself completely (but come on, you've shared my company and been inside my head for a while now, you don't need me to tell you there simply isn't enough in me to misunderstand) or the officer in charge of the duty roster had screwed up on a pretty staggering scale; or the duties, privileges, station and responsibilities I'd been called to demanded precisely the sort of person I was.

Maybe this was a battle that only a total loser could win.

The elves took some convincing, but you don't want to take any particular notice of that because the elves would've argued the toss if they'd been aboard a sinking ship and someone had suggested they get into the lifeboat. I convinced them, somehow. God only knows how I managed it. I mean, if I'd been one of them, I sure as hell wouldn't have convinced me.

Setting it all up only took about half an hour. If we'd done it properly so it'd have worked, it would probably have taken over a month, but we didn't need it to work. In fact, that was the very last thing we wanted to happen. The hell with stuff working. Stuff working is for winners.

Spike did all the wiring, while Sweetie-Pie showed me how to use the phone. It wasn't a regular phone, of course; it was more of a real-time digital video link, with special enhancements so that Daddy George could see an invisible elf on his screen, but all the elf at our end could see was a grim-looking loud speaker with a steel grille over it to prevent sabotage and vandalism. He wrote down the access codes for me on a piece of paper, told me which buttons I had to press, and which ones had to be held down when and for how long. I reckon flying the space shuttle would have been a piece of cake compared with making a quick call on Daddy George's special phone. Once I'd finally got the hang of the system (it took a while) all that remained was to get everybody else safely out of sight. This meant forcibly rounding up and herding all the hyper-miserable types who were still refusing to have anything to do with the escape project; they didn't fight or anything, but it all took time and effort when we couldn't be doing with the extra hassle, and the whole thing got very tiresome indeed. Sure, Moses had his problems along the way, but I'll bet he didn't have to put up with two dozen snotty elves from Cutting (and if he had, there'd have been no Exodus, and Egypt'd be knee-deep in extra pyramids).

But in the end, even the round-up somehow got done, and we reached the extremely unnerving point where there was nothing else to do except set the plan in motion. There was an enormous weight of reluctance hanging over us at that moment, like the heaviest, sulkiest pre-thunderstorm weather you've ever had to live through. I could see why. Up till then, we all had something to look forward to, something to believe in – even for terminally miserable elves, that's a wonderful thing. But if we did the plan and it all went horrendously wrong, we'd have nothing at all. It didn't help that all our meagre, fanatically hoarded savings of hope were sitting there in the pot, and all we had in our hand was a pair of threes. The fact that anything higher than that and we'd most certainly lose was no consolation at all.

Sweetie-Pie looked at the loudspeaker grill, then at me. 'Right, then,' he said.

'Right,' I replied. Neither of us moved.

'You're all set,' he said.

'Right.'

About five seconds of dead silence. 'You can start any time,' he pointed out.

'OK,' I said.

Another four seconds. 'Like, now, for instance.'

'Now?'

'Yes.'

'Right.'

He didn't frown; in fact, his face was as blank as a hard drive after the latest Windows upgrade has just done its worst. 'You don't want to do this, do you?' he said.

'Not really.'

'Can't say I blame you,' said Sweetie-Pie. 'It's a bloody terrible idea.'

'Yes,' I said.

'Well, then.'

'Quite. Oh well,' I said, 'here goes nothing.' And I pressed the button.

'Not that one, you clown,' said Sweetie-Pie. 'That's the one for setting the month on the digital clock.'

'Oh, right, sorry. This one?'

'That one.'

'Ah, fine, I see. All right, then, *here* goes nothing. Does it?' I checked. He nodded.

I pressed the button. For maybe a second and a half, nothing happened, and I was just starting to hope that perhaps we'd got it all wrong and the phone link wouldn't work for me and we'd have to call the whole thing off and go back to making shoes (which really wasn't as bad as all that, in fact it could be quite satisfying and ful-filling at times, there's a sort of pure Platonic beauty in a precisely folded piece of tissue paper) when the speaker crackled violently, and a voice I quite definitely recognised growled, 'Yes?'

Hearing him again – it went beyond a nasty turn and a quick flash of instinctive panic. I'd got used to those, over the years, they were almost reassuringly familiar and friendly (you know how it is when something, a sound or a smell, reminds you quite unexpectedly of something from your childhood). This time, though, there was something new, a quite different and alto-gether less pleasant isotope of fear – the kind that tells you you're going to die, very soon, very painfully, and there's nothing at all you can do about it. Acquaintances have told me that shopkeepers get the same sort of feeling when the excise men show up for a surprise VAT audit, but I wouldn't know about that.

'Hello,' I said.

Silence. A very long moment of dead silence. You know, I should have realised before then (what with elves' weird fast-forwarding ability and so forth) just how elastic and negotiable time can be. I may have lost fifteen years flitting back and forth across the line, but I reckon I caught up with them in full during that second and a half.

'Who is this?'

'Me,' I replied.

'Oh.' Very neutral tone of voice: no expression, no feeling. 'Thought I recognised you. What the fuck are you doing using the phone system?'

I took a deep breath. 'There isn't anyone else,' I replied. 'Look, you've got to come quick, before it's too late.'

Another pause. By my calculations, I was at least sixty-three years old by the time it was over. 'What are you drivelling on about now?'

'You've got to come here now and stop them,' I said, 'before they're all killed.'

'What is all this?' asked Daddy George. (And I thought, *Shit, he knows I'm up to something. I never could fool him, he knows me too well.* And then I remembered, that's why me, because he knows me too well.)

'Listen,' I said, 'please. There's no more time, they're all going to die unless you—' And then I hit the kill button.

I stood there for quite some time, my finger still down hard on the button, as if I was trying to smother it to death, or at least keep it from getting out of its socket and biting me. Or maybe I was afraid that if I let go, Daddy George himself would push his way up out of the control panel, squeezing his head through the button socket. Crazy.

'You think he bought it?' Sweetie-Pie whispered.

I shook my head. 'No idea,' I said. 'But he's coming.'

'You're sure about that?'

I nodded. 'Absolutely positive,' I said. 'Trust me. I know him too well.'

CHAPTER SEVENTEEN

Waiting for him to arrive –

It was the strangest feeling. Partly – partly, it was just like when you were a kid and your best friend was supposed to be coming to tea; and you'd sit by the window looking out for the car, and when it didn't arrive and didn't arrive you'd open the front door a crack and peep out through that. (How that was meant to make the car get there quicker I never quite figured out.) Partly it was hoping and praying that I'd been right and Daddy George had suspected something and wasn't going to come after all (but that didn't work, because if he thought I was up to something, he'd get here even quicker), and partly it was a dull, bleating voice in the back of my head repeating, *Seemed like a good idea at the time, seemed like a good idea—*

At least there was plenty to do to keep myself occupied; there were stray elves to chivvy into hiding, wiring relays to triple-check, unforeseen contingencies to plan for, lots of redundant and meaningless stuff that had to be done anyway; and all the time I was thinking, *Me and him, face to face, and whoever loses will be proved to have been wrong*. I guess that was the very worst part about it all; not the fear of death or pain, certainly not an abstract fear of losing (I've always been a very good loser, probably because I've had so much practice), but the very specific and unbearable fear of losing to *him*, because that would mean that in some vague but incredibly important sense, he'd be vindicated and I'd know for sure, in that last despairing moment, that he'd been right about me being worthless and no good all along, just as I'd always suspected—

If the bad guy wins, he isn't the bad guy any more, because everybody knows the good guy always wins. It's like the old gag about how in every election the government always gets elected. Victory is clarity, it defines everything.

Him and me, I told myself. *We know each other too well.*

I thought I'd gone over everything, visualised each moment, each possible version of each moment, in my mind's eye before I even made the call. But apparently not. Turned out I'd forgotten to prepare myself for the biggest moment of all, the door opening.

The door opened.

The way it should be is, the older you get, the smaller they become; the big people, the giants who stomped around and scowled down at you when you were a kid. Parents, teachers, headmasters, the older boys who used to kick you around; the idea is that you grow up and they grow old, so when you meet them again ten, twenty, thirty years later, you find yourself looking *down*, looking at this funny little guy who once scared you half to death just by scowling at you, but now you could lift him up and shake him like a pillow, except you don't want to any more – all the fear and the resentment and the hate melt away, because you who were once small are now big, and he who was once big has dwindled down into a little old man. You look down and see what you once were, one of the little people.

But the door opened, and he was absolutely fucking *huge*; he'd always been this big, broad, threatening ogre, American-footballer shoulders, hairy-backed hands like frying pans, the biggest face you ever saw in your life. Sure, I'd seen him from this angle before, once, the first day, when his goons grabbed and shrunk me and he'd loomed over me and sentenced me to the shoe factory. But I'd had other things on my mind at the time and besides, I'd really only been able to see his lower slopes (and at the time I wasn't used to being this size, I still didn't believe it had happened to me and most certainly didn't believe I'd be this way for ever, that this was actually the size *I'd always been meant to be . . .*)

He walked in, quickly shut the door and locked it behind him, then pulled some kind of remote-control thing out of his inside pocket and prodded a few buttons, making some little green and red lights flash. He hadn't seen me – fair enough, I was hiding behind a chair leg, and I was only six inches tall. Same as I'd always been.

He looked round, then lowered his head and looked down.

'There you are,' he said.

It was one of his phrases, I remembered it very well. 'There you are,' he used to say, when I'd done something bad. (I never meant to do anything bad, but a lot of what

I did turned out that way, because he said it was bad and he was bigger than me, so of course he must've been right.) I used to hide, but I was very bad at it and when he found me he'd always say, 'There you are,' in that same tone of voice, that same fundamental disappointment that I was so pathetic I couldn't even hide. 'There you are,' he said again. 'Now then, what's all this about?'

I took a deep breath. 'It's too late,' I said. 'You're too late. They're all dead.'

He raised an eyebrow. His eyebrows were as long as my arm. I'd have needed a crane and a winch. 'Just for once,' he said, 'try not to babble. Who's dead?'

He hadn't changed a bit; apart from still being so big, I mean. I'd hoped for a few comforting signs of ageing – some wrinkles, a little sagging of the skin, a token gesture or two in the direction of mortality, just one or two grey hairs would've done – but he hadn't given me the satisfaction. 'All of them,' I said. 'I tried warning them, but they wouldn't listen. They laughed at me.'

'Well, they would,' said Daddy George. 'You're very funny when you try and be serious.'

'They'd decided to escape,' I went on. 'Some of them were going to try going out onto the roof, another lot were going through the air vents, and the rest of them had decided on the drains. I told them you'd have booby-trapped all the ways out. I told them, I know how your mind works.'

He laughed. 'They should've listened to you.' He actually laughed. 'You chose a hell of a time to be right.' A long sigh. 'So,' he went on, 'they're all dead. Bugger. All of them except you. Why am I not surprised?'

I peered up at him from behind my chair-leg. He'd lost me.

'You know what you are?' he went on. 'You're a born survivor. Pity, that, but there it is. You know, you remind me a lot of a virus; you're small and insidious, and just when it looks like you've been wiped out and I'm finally rid of you, bingo! You mutate into an even more stubborn and annoying strain, and there you bloody well are again. I hate that.'

'Sorry,' I said.

He sighed; it was like a scale-model El Nino. 'I don't suppose you can help it,' he said. 'I mean, the worst you've ever done to me is to be alive – though it's always seemed to me that you've consistently managed to be alive *at* me, as if carrying on breathing and walking about was a gesture of insubordination, like refusing to eat your carrots. You turn up, you vanish, you turn up again – I knew you weren't dead, you know; even when you disappeared, I knew you were still hanging around somewhere, because you're the toothache in the tooth I've just had pulled. It wasn't enough that your mother and I couldn't have children of our own. Oh, no. We had to have *you*.'

'It's not my fault,' I said.

'Of course it's not your fault, you moron,' Daddy George snapped. 'Like it's not your fault you're his son, that fucking prickle-eared freak's nasty little act of preemptive revenge. It's not your fault that everybody thinks that all my work, all the absolutely amazingly brilliant discoveries I've made were all done by you, Mister Double-Nobel-Laureate. It's not your fault, as in you didn't do anything. Not a thing, not one bloody hand's turn, and yet you're part-owner of everything I've worked myself half to death to achieve, and I can't even kill you, because of not being able to look your mother in the face again if I did. I really do love her, you know, I'd never do anything to hurt her. And now they're all dead, except you. Just my absolutely bloody wonderful sodding luck.'

I came out from behind the chair-leg; not too far, in case I had to dart back under cover in a hurry. Those enormous junkyard-car-crusher feet of his could flatten me in half a second by pure and genuine accident. 'That's right,' I said, 'it's not my fault and I haven't done anything. I never did anything, and you've completely screwed up my life.'

'Excuse me?' He burst out laughing, like a jolly volcano. 'What harm have I ever done you? I brought you up as my own son, I sent you to the best school money could buy, and what did you do? You buggered off. *I* didn't send you away or sell you to a slave-trader or abandon you on a hillside for the wolves to rear - you fucked off and left us, worried your mother to death. She cried herself to sleep for the first six months, did you know that?'

I didn't; but all I thought was, *Only six months*? Besides, I never really liked her all that much, not after she let him send me away to school.

'And then,' he said, 'then you came back; and before I could reach you, you'd gone again. And what did you do for the brief few moments you were back? Did you call your mother and let her know you were all right? Did you hell; you were too busy slurping round that sour-faced lawyer bitch, setting her on me, as if I didn't have enough to put up with. And then you pop up *again*, and this time I manage to get you under control, put you away where you won't be able to hurt anybody or fuck up anything important—'

'It's a *labour camp*,' I shouted, at the top of my little voice. 'You make it sound like a bloody sanatorium.'

He grinned at me. 'You don't know you're born,' he replied. 'I give you a chance – all your life you've been useless, couldn't trust you to post a letter, but I give you a chance in the family business, start you off at the bottom, on the shop floor, the traditional way of going about it. For God's sake, look at yourself. When you were at that school you were a weedy, skinny, shambling little runt with the self-confidence of a water vole. A few months in here, and you're fit, strong, healthy, confident, assertive – dammit, you miserable little snot, I've done my part, like a good father should. I've made a man of you. A very small man, true, but a man. And how do you thank me? You bloody well *survive*. Again. It's enough to make a person spit.'

'You didn't mean to help me,' I said. 'You wanted me dead.'

'So what? It's the results that matter. You owe me everything, and all you've ever been is an unmitigated pain in the bum.'

Normally, of course, I'd have taken his word for it; after all, this side of the line, that's who I had to be, a quiet little twit who believes and does what he's told. Not this time; all those months in the stockroom and Packing had changed me, and probably for the better. Thanks, I thought. But—

'You arsehole,' I said. 'You shrunk me. You made me six inches tall.'

Big sneer on his big face. 'I did, didn't I, Mister multi-millionaire-mathematical-genius-without-even-trying? The way I look at it, someone had to cut you down to size. I'm glad it was me.'

Hadn't considered it in that light; didn't have time to consider it at that particular moment, other things I had to do. In fact, this whole conversation was unscheduled, unscripted and off-topic. On the other hand, it was the first time we'd ever, you know, *talked*. I guess you could say we were sharing a little quality time.

'You're jealous,' I said.

'Of course I'm sodding well jealous, you stupid little shit,' Daddy George shouted down at me. 'Why the hell wouldn't I be, when I've had to work all my life and you've had everything handed to you on a skewer dripping with barbecue sauce? I wasn't born in the lap of luxury, nobody ever gave me anything; and your mother always cared more about you than about me, and I could never have figured out those fucking equations, but some elf just gave them to you on a scrap of paper. And just look at me, I'm just a plain old regular human mortal, all I've got to look forward to is getting old and senile, and dying. I'm not half-immortal, I can't stroll backwards and forwards across the line as the fancy takes me. Fuck it, I should've wrung your stupid neck when you were three, and then none of all this would've happened and I could've had a life, instead of scrambling along out of breath just to keep up with you—' He stopped, cold and deliberate. 'But that's all right,' he said, 'you're here and you aren't leaving, not ever. So they're all dead, so what? The more dead elves, the better I like it. I don't need them any more; thanks to you, I don't have to do any of this secret creeping-around stuff any more. I can run a legitimate business and the hell with this poxy little factory. All I've got to do is walk out of here and lock the door behind me, and all my troubles will be over. Yours too,' he added, 'if you take the objective view. Me all over, that is, altruistic as a barrelful of eels.'

I took a deep breath. This was getting easier every second. 'So you're just going to walk out of here and leave me to starve to death.'

'Yes,' he replied. 'Or you can go and immolate yourself on the containment field, if you feel like going out with a bang. Entirely up to you – your choice.'

I shook my head. 'No, you're not,' I said.

He laughed. 'Watch me,' he said.

'No, you're not,' I repeated. 'You can try, but you won't make it. Want to know why?'

He frowned; for the first time since I could remember, he didn't seem a hundred per cent sure about everything. 'Go on, then,' he said. 'Astound me. What's the deal?'

'In the walls,' I said. 'Explosive charges, so you can blow the place up if anybody finds out about it.'

He shrugged. 'I like to cover all possible eventualities,' he said. 'And I've got this place very well insured. All the celluloid dust and crap like that we've got floating about in here, anything could happen.'

I nodded. 'That's you all over,' I said, 'shaving every margin till it bleeds; you couldn't use high-density neoprene like you say you do on the labels, you had to save a few pennies by making the stiffeners out of dangerous, flammable celluloid – which,' I added, 'when chopped up fine and wired up to a battery with a few strands of wire wool, makes a passable bomb.'

'Congratulations,' he said, still sounding mystified. 'I'm not sure I can see the relevance, though.'

'A passable bomb,' I continued (back into the scripted material; a great relief), 'stuffed down an air-brick and connected up to this handset, the one I'm holding. Can you see it all right from up there? You can? Splendid – I thought perhaps it might be a bit on the small side for a tall bastard like you. So, if I were to press this button, all that high explosive you crammed into the walls would go bang, and that'd be the end of you. Wouldn't it?'

He relaxed, smiled. 'But you aren't going to do that, idiot,' he said. 'Because if you did, you'd get blown up too, and where would be the point?'

'That would be the point,' I told him. 'In fact, that'd be *perfect*.'

His face went as white as a sheet. 'Bloody hell,' he said. 'You're bluffing. You'd never do a thing like that.'

'I wouldn't make a habit of it,' I replied. 'Just once, though. Once would do me.'

He was sweating. I could've filled a bath with what was dripping off his forehead. 'But you'll *die*,' he said.

'You make it sound like that'd be a bad thing.' Oh, I was wonderfully calm just then. 'And of course, for you it would be. Complete downer. But not for me. If I did, I don't have to go on being six inches tall.'

'But—'

And that was that: I'd got him. He knew I meant it, and that he was left with no options whatsoever. I knew him too well.

'All right,' he said. 'So, what do you want this time?'

My turn to smile. Couldn't remember having smiled at him before. No call to. 'Oh, not much,' I said. 'Simple stuff. Little things and little minds. Like, switch off the dampening field and unshrink me. Then we can call it quits.'

He shook his head. 'If I turn off the field—'

'If you turn off the field,' I said, 'I can clear off out of here and go back across the line, never to bother you again. Isn't that what you always wanted?'

He frowned. 'There's more to it than that,' he said.

'No,' I interrupted, 'there isn't. Oh sure, if there were any real elves left, I can see you wouldn't dare turn the field off, you'd be better off getting blown to bits than letting a whole lot of very angry elves get their powers back, start doing all that stuff we both know they can do on this side of the line when they're upset about something. But that's all right,' I went on, 'they're all dead, there's only me. I can't do that stuff, remember, I'm not a real elf. I'm just me.'

He thought about that for a moment. 'And that'd be it?' he said. 'You'd fuck off and leave me in peace?'

'Yes,' I said, 'I would. You'd have nothing to fear from me.'

'I dunno.' He rubbed his chin, something I'd never seen him do before. Either it was a recently acquired mannerism or something he only did when he was on the wrong end of the spike. 'You'd really let me go?'

'Yes. I'll even let you get well clear before I blow this dump to kingdom come.'

'That's big of you,' he said.

'I'm that sort of person,' I replied. 'Enormous moral stature. You could say I'm the world's shortest giant.'

He didn't comment on that. 'And then we'd be quits? No getting your own back, anything like that?'

I shook my head. 'Can't be bothered,' I replied. 'I'll be out of here, and I'll have taught you a lesson; in future, pick on someone your own size. If you can find someone that small.'

He didn't say anything. I think he reckoned the crisis

was over and he'd got away with it. A minor inconvenience, tax loss, insurance settlement. And no more me,
of course. Adjust a few definitions of victory, and he'd
have won.

'All right,' he said.

(And that, in case you were wondering, was the point,
about me knowing him too well. He'd rather have been
blown up than lose, but I'd given him a way of winning;
once I'd gone and he was still here, there'd be nothing
but a memory to be deleted – time is flexible, history is
negotiable – and an overpoweringly sickly smell of roses.
I knew him well enough to be sure he'd believe I was
loser enough to die just so I could take him with me; his
contempt would make him believe that. I knew him well
enough to know that he'd never believe I had the nerve
to bluff on the strength of a few strands of wire connected to a black plastic floppy-disk box at one end and
absolutely nothing whatsoever at the other – me, blow
myself up just to kill Daddy George? Catch me doing
that. Loser I may be, but I only lose when I have to. Oh,
he knew me all right, too well but not well enough. He
knew that the taller they are, the further they fall, while
the little people are only a few inches off the deck at the
best of times, so they don't care . . .)

'Fuck,' he said. 'Still, can't be helped. Always been
too soft-hearted for my own good.'

He reached in his pocket, and for a split second I
wondered if I'd got it wrong again; but when his hand
reappeared he was holding a slim dark grey box, like a
TV remote, and he thumbed a couple of buttons.
(Didn't have to look for them, knew where they were by
touch.)

It was as if I'd been trudging painfully up a long, steep

hill and someone had pointed out that I might find it easier if I took off the lead-weighted diving boots. It was like stopping breathing custard. It was like losing five stones instantly, in the same fraction of a second you shake off a month-long cold and a really traumatic hangover. It was like bursting out of a cocoon and discovering you're a butterfly, when all your friends and relatives have always told you that when you grow up you'll be a clothes-moth. It was like trampolining in zero gravity with a nose stuffed with cocaine. It was way cool. It was *me*.

It was also extremely painful, because I'd gone from being six inches tall and crouched behind a chair-leg to being six feet tall directly underneath a chair in the twinkling of an eye. Actually, it wasn't my head hitting the chair that really hurt, it was the chair falling off my head and landing on my right big toe. Absolutely no fun at all.

Just as well, though; because when I suddenly got tall again, I left my purported bomb trigger on the floor, and as soon as Daddy George saw that, he made a grab for my throat with his outstretched left hand. If the chair hadn't toppled off my foot and got in his way, he could easily have strangled me while I was still off balance. As it was, I was able to jump backwards out of his reach and put my foot over the pretend trigger thing. When he saw that, he slumped a little and stayed put.

'My,' he said, 'how you've grown.'

He had a point. Sure, I was disorientated by suddenly putting on sixty-six inches, but surely I'd never been this tall; or maybe he'd shrunk. Don't know; in any event, I looked at him and realised I could handle him. Any trouble and all I had to do was smash his face in. Easy as that.

'That remote-control thing,' I said. 'Give it here.'

'As if.'

I shrugged, stooped down, pulled off my left shoe and threw it at him. Good shot; not just the height, also the hand/eye coordination. The shoe hit him right on the point of the nose, and he was far too busy reeling about and swearing like a bad ventriloquist to stop me picking up the remote, which had fallen out of his hand. I put it in my pocket, for later.

'Id all ight,' he buzzed through his cupped hands, 'I got anudder.'

'Won't do you any good,' I said.

'Uck oo.' He took one hand away from his face and dipped it into his side pocket. 'I also god dis,' he went on, pulling out a small, shiny gun and pointing it at me. 'Wadn't goping to shood oo, bud oo shudded hab done dat.'

I looked at the gun, and it looked at me. We could see eye to eye on a large range of issues, unfortunately, one of them being my immediate future prospects. *Oh well*, I thought, *I did try.* Oddly enough, that was about as bad as it got: a calm acceptance of imminent death. I can only suppose it was because I knew I'd won really, and killing me was an acceptance of defeat on his part. Either that, or I'd run out of emotions.

'Please yourself,' I said. 'You'll be sorry.'

'Really?' He'd taken away the other hand from in front of his face, so at least he'd stopped sounding like Donald Duck. The incongruity of being murdered by a Disney character had been bothering me. 'Don't think so. When this building blows up, who's going to know you died?'

I took a step back. 'I wasn't thinking about that,' I replied, and damn it, my voice was quite steady. Mister

Cool, I was being, so the damp stuff trickling down the inside of my leg must've been sweat, because of the air conditioning being full of elves or something. 'What I meant was, if you hurt me, the elves are going to tear you apart.'

He laughed. 'Unlikely,' he said. 'I'm not planning on crossing the line any time soon, and all the ones on this side are dead. By your own admission.'

'Ah.' I smiled, or at least one side of my face twitched. Sort of smiled, anyway. 'I have a confession to make. I was lying.'

He frowned. 'Don't believe you,' he said.

'Suit yourself.' Now, the agreed signal was supposed to be a shrill whistle, but have you ever tried whistling when your face is paralysed by fear? Can't be done. 'All right,' I shouted – and it came out all reedy and croaky, like a chain-smoking frog. 'You can come out now.'

And they did. Loads of them, from all directions; great, big, tall, irritable-looking elves. A few of them were holding hammers and makeshift clubs, but I got the impression that by the time they got to the head of the queue, there wouldn't be enough left of Daddy George to hit.

'You bastard,' said Daddy George, quietly and with great feeling. 'You bloody well tricked me.'

'Sorry,' I said. 'But you asked for it.'

'Treacherous little snot,' he growled. 'I always knew you were a sneaky, underhanded bugger, but I never thought you'd do this to me. For God's sake,' he added, with a catch in his voice I'd never heard before, 'tell them to back off. Please.'

Another first.

'It's all right,' I said, 'they won't hurt you, so long as

you put that gun down and do as you're told. Oh, come on,' I added, 'just for once stop faffing around and be reasonable.'

He crouched down and laid the gun on the floor. 'Wait till your mother hears about this,' he said. 'She'll bloody skin you alive.'

'That's better,' I said. 'Much more like it. Well,' I added in the general direction of the nearest elf, 'if it's all the same to you, I'll wait for you outside. Don't take all day about it.'

A lot of elves took a step forward. Daddy George whirled round, to see even more of them coming up from behind. There was Spike, holding something (*Ah, I thought, maybe that explains how she got her nickname*), and there was Sweetie-Pie, looking distinctly unsweet. 'Hey,' shrieked Daddy George, 'where the hell do you think you're going?'

'Outside,' I told him. 'Squeamish,' I explained. 'Don't want to spoil their big moment by fainting or throwing up.'

'But you *promised*—'

'You know your trouble?' I said. 'You're far too trusting.'

He was terrified. Odd how fear always makes a person look smaller. I didn't feel sorry for him, though. Probably I should've, but I didn't. I suppose he brought out the worst in me.

'Stop,' he shouted. 'Help me. You can't let them—'

'Get real,' I interrupted, rather rudely. 'Do you honestly think I could stop them?'

(And I wondered, at that moment, about all the opposite numbers of all these elves, the humans they were paired with, on this side of the line. Who were they, I asked myself, and what were they like? Bloody strange thing to think of, quite suddenly at a time like that. Funny old critter, the mind.)

'*Please.*'

I stopped. 'Ah,' I said, 'that puts a different complexion on it. All right,' I said, in my sergeant-major voice, not nearly so thin and crackly as it had been a few minutes earlier, 'that'll do, leave him alone.'

I had no idea whether they'd listened to me or not. I suspect that if I'd been them, I'd have told myself to get profoundly lost. Luckily they were more amenable to reason than me.

'Right,' I said, 'here's what we're going to do.' I took a deep breath; because I'd only stopped them for the simple reason that, where they'd only had to put up with being kidnapped and turned into slaves, I'd grown up with the bastard as my stepfather, and seeing him ripped into mince just wouldn't have been good enough. I wanted to get *even*. So I took Daddy George's remote-control thing out of my pocket. 'Here, Spike,' I said, 'you're good with technical stuff. Tell me how you work this thing.'

She looked at me, and grinned. 'Pleasure,' she said. 'You know what,' she added, 'you're evil.'

'I learned from the best,' I replied, and handed it over.

That Spike – even for an elf, she was smart with electrical goods. I didn't actually see the moment when Daddy George shrank, because there was a dazzling blue flash that half-blinded me. One moment he was stood there, all six foot one of him. The next—

'I think you overdid it,' I said.

She shrugged. 'It's a tricky thing to calibrate,' she said. 'Still,' she added, as she put the remote carefully on the ground and jumped on it, 'no harm done.' I don't think I'd have liked to have been Daddy George just then. It must have been rather intimidating for him, not more than an inch and a half tall, looking up at all those gigantic elves crowding round him in a ring and staring. 'Now, then,' I said, 'mind your backs, coming through.' I edged my way past them into the middle of the circle, bent down, picked Daddy George up and placed him on the palm of my left hand. 'Guess what's going to happen now,' I said.

He was too small for me to be able to see the expression on his face, but I could hear him quite clearly. He was calling me all kinds of uncouth names. Not sensible, for a very small person in his position. 'Shut up,' I advised him, 'or I'll inhale you.'

'You think you're really clever,' he yelled inaccurately. 'You think you've won, and it'll be happy endings all the way. You wait and see.'

I frowned. 'Not all the way,' I replied. 'There's still flu and income tax and traffic jams and supermarket queues and stuff like that. Mostly, though—'

'I told her,' he said. 'Your girlfriend, that Cruella. She came looking for you, after I had you captured and brought here, she said I knew what'd happened to you and she wanted you back.'

'Really,' I said.

'Yes, really. So I told her, I hadn't got you, you'd gone back over the line. Not to get away from me, I said, to get away from her; because you'd got this elf girl over there, that was why you'd gone away in the first place, and stayed so long.' He laughed: tiny little laugh, all full of unpleasantness, full of victory. 'You know what? She believed me. Hook, line and sinker. Burst into tears, stood there on the doorstep sobbing her eyes out at me. Said she never wanted to see you again, in this world or the next. I nearly did my back in not laughing. So you see,' he went on, 'I really put one over on you; made sure she wasn't going to come sniffing round again, making trouble. And I know her sort, vindictive little bitch, nothing you can ever say or do'll convince her I wasn't telling the truth. You've had it as far as she's concerned. I just thought I'd tell you that, while I think of it.'

Clever man, my stepfather, but he didn't know me as well as he thought he did. He was sure I'd go mad with rage and close my hand tight, squash him to death, put him out of his misery, make myself the villain. But I knew him too well; I knew that he'd rather die than go where I was about to take him. Like I'd told Spike, I'd learned from the best when it came to inflicting pain and suffering, and at that moment I was all cruelty, all seventy-two enormous inches of me.

I glanced round at the circle of elves surrounding me and closed my eyes. *Here goes nothing,* I said to myself, and crossed the line.

CHAPTER EIGHTEEN

At first I thought, 'Where is everybody?' – and then I figured it out. The factory was miles from any-where, and there wouldn't be any Elfland equivalents for the guys in the factory, since they were all elves already; and I didn't have a counterpart, because of who I was, so that only left—

Nobody. Remember. Daddy George had killed his counterpart, many years earlier. I had a feeling quite a few people in those parts wouldn't have forgotten that.

We were in a building. Well, of course we were, we were still in the factory (the Elfland equivalent of it, anyway) and when looked more closely I could see that – same floor plan, same high walls, same wide-open plan. Except that here, the factory was a cathedral. *Crazy*, I thought. *I wonder what the Elfland equivalent of Westminster Abbey looks like.*

Daddy George was still in the palm of my hand; and that surprised me, because I'd expected him to have reverted to his proper size when he crossed the line, the same as Cru's elfin doppelgänger had done the first time I arrived there. Apparently not. I guessed it had something to do with Spike giving the shrinker too much welly – in any event, I wasn't unduly bothered.

I smiled; a big, warm smile that bounded out onto my face before I could stop it, like a friendly dog when you open the front door. 'Here we are,' I said. 'Welcome to your new home.' I held out my hand, and a tiny Daddy George peered out over my fingertips. 'This is your factory,' I told him, 'exactly the same, only different. We'll come back and look at it later. But first, there's some people I want you to meet.'

It was, of course, the cruellest punishment imaginable. Not just the being small – I hadn't even planned on that, it was just a bonus miracle given away free with the box tops of suffering. Instead, it was the torment of being for ever the exact opposite of himself, a timid, sensitive, caring, altruistic, pointy-eared freak, while a tiny part of himself would always remember (like I'd remembered) who he really was, back where he belonged. It had been far easier for me, of course, since in theory at least I belonged equally on both sides. For him—

It would be a long walk from the factory to the nearest village of settlement, and I was on a schedule. I didn't have the time. So, rather unwillingly, I fast-forwarded through the gruelling six-hour hike, to the point where we were standing in a village square, surrounded by friendly inquisitive elves.

'Hello,' I said. 'there's someone here to see you.'

(Too cruel, perhaps? Too cruel, even for him? But then I thought about the slaves in the factory and my

own real father, vivisected to death just because once
he'd loved my mother, and I thought, no. An eye for an
eye, a tooth for a tooth, a pointy ear for a pointy ear. It
was exactly right.)

I couldn't help noticing how my minuscule companion squirmed with terror as the elves came flocking
round, and tried to bury himself in the gully between my
middle and index fingers. Daddy George and I may not
have seen eye to eye in the past – I'd have needed a
stepladder, for one thing – but even I would never have
said he was the timid sort. True, there's a lot to be timid
about when you're knee-high to an action figurine, as I'd
found out myself the hard way, but even so.
Interesting—

'Oooh,' cooed an elf, extending a finger towards
Daddy George's abdomen. 'He's so *cute*. Can I pick him
up?'

I smiled. 'Of course,' I said. 'Here.' I tipped my hand
over, dropping Daddy George into the elf's cupped
palm. 'You do realise who you've got there, don't you?'

The elf nodded. 'He's the one who opened up the
gateway,' she replied, 'and lured all those poor people
across the line. Oosa ickle-wickle *sweetie*, den?' she
added, with apparent sincerity. *Hang on*, I thought, *this
isn't right. The greatest criminal in elf history, and she's
trying to tickle him under the ear?* 'You don't seem to
mind,' I said.

She didn't look up. 'He's been a very naughty boy –
haven't oo, vewwy bad, bad boyzlewoyzle – but that's all
in the past now. And he's such a little darling, with his
little feet and his dear little hands—'

And then I realised I'd been barking up the wrong
tree altogether. I'd brought him here on the assumption

that when the elves got their delicate, artistic hands on him, they'd deconstruct him slowly and painfully with the help of extremely fine medical instruments. Blame it on my lack of vision, my inability to see the full canvas, the big picture. What the elf female was doing to him now was, of course, far more agonising and excruciating than anything that could be achieved with mere clumsy, inefficient steel and nitric acid. Steel could only torture his body; acid could only gnaw away at his flesh. Two or three days, a week at most, and he'd be safely dead and beyond the reach of vengeance. What the elves would do to him – sweet, sentimental, forgiving, loving, caring, nurturing creatures that they were – would strip away his self-esteem and burn out his brain, and they could keep it up for years and years and years, while he cowered and hid and cringed like the cutest-ever little puppy dog, inciting his tormentors to greater and greater excesses—

(And inside? Just as inside every darling little bundle of fluff there's a very small sabre-toothed tiger frantically scrabbling to get out, so it would be in this case. The real Daddy George was still in there somewhere, always would be: trapped for all eternity in a frightened, help-less little body that practically yelled to all comers, 'Hug me! Pick me up! Stroke me! Love me!')

I felt sick. There're more ways of killing a fluffy kitten than drowning it in cream, but none of them comes any-where close as regards sheer inhuman cruelty.

An elf was hurrying towards the group with a saucer of milk in one hand and a ball of pink wool in the other. Seeing them, I felt like some kind of monster.

Time, I decided, *I wasn't here*. I still had a lot of work to do; there were elves trapped on the wrong side of the line to be rescued, for a start. I had no idea where

Daddy George's gateway was, let alone how to defuse the booby traps so that the prisoners could use it to get home. So the only way to bring them back would be one at a time, taking them with me by way of a circle in the grass. It could take years, for all I knew – not that I had anything better to do, God knew, not after Daddy George had played his last and quite possibly nastiest trick. He'd known Cruella far too well; figured out the surest and most infallible way to make sure she'd never speak to me again. And without her – well, I might as well be back in the factory, laying sheets of tissue paper over a thousand empty shoeboxes a day.

I turned my back and walked away. For some time, I could still hear the voices of the elves, exacting their unspeakable, unintentional revenge. When I couldn't hear them any more, I began at last to feel as if that unwelcome and unpleasant phase of my life that had begun all those years ago when I had first seen an elf in our garden was finally drawing to a close. But that wasn't a solution. Winning the war was one thing; coming home again afterwards is something else entirely. And what shall it profit a conquering hero to get off the troopship and catch the train back to his home town, only to find that while he's been away the whole street's been flattened by a land mine?

It didn't take years, as I'd feared, to repatriate the slaves. Once I'd got back into the swing of it, and organised the waiting elves into orderly queues, I found I could take back as many as five hundred an hour. The last elf I dropped off happened to be Spike.

'There you go,' I said, as we stepped out of the circle in Elfland. 'Home again.'

'Thank you.' As I may have mentioned earlier, on our side of the line Spike was short, stocky and built like a very small Sumo wrestler. On her side, she turned out to be a tall, willowy blonde with deep grey eyes and the face of an unusually solemn angel. In fact, she looked quite stunningly beautiful standing there in the deserted cathedral, with a shaft of pale evening sunlight glancing down through a high window and bathing her head and shoulders in a pool of liquid gold. But as I looked at her, with the look of calm serenity glowing in her eyes, I realised that this version of Spike would be great if you liked long, soulful silences and shared moments of total intuitive clarity, but she probably couldn't change a light bulb or rewire a plug if her life depended on it; and as for her acid tongue and the extremely grudging way she'd had of saying that for once you'd managed to get something almost sort of right, which made you feel so much better than mere praise could ever have done, because Spike never said anything nice if she could possibly avoid it—

I looked away. Different, and not the same at all. Cute as they come, sure enough, but she just wasn't Spike any more; and Spike had been my friend.

'Well, so long,' I said, looking at the ground. 'Thanks for your help. Couldn't have done it without you.'

'Oh, I didn't do anything, really,' Not-Spike replied, in a low, breathless voice that would've set my heart tap-dancing if it hadn't been for who she now wasn't. 'You saved us all. We'd never have escaped if it wasn't for your courage, your intelligence, your compassion.'

'You're welcome,' I mumbled. 'Don't worry about it. Anyway, it's time I was getting back. You know, things to see to.'

'You're leaving?'

I nodded.

'Oh.' She sounded like an angel who's just seen the value of her investment portfolio tumble in a stock-market panic. 'I'm sorry, I'd rather got the impression you were going to stay. Are you sure—?'

'Yes,' I said. 'No offence, but I'd better be getting back. I mean, it's really nice here, but it's not me. Really.'

'Oh.'

Amazingly versatile word, 'oh'. With the right inflec-tion, it can mean anything from 'I'm not listening, shut up and go away' to 'Jesus fucking Christ, we're all going to die!' to just plain 'oh', with a million gradations of subtle significations in between. In this case, it was, 'You're going away and it's all my fault and I've ruined everything and even if I managed to struggle through the rest of my life without slashing my wrists, I'll never smile again.'

'Cheerio, then,' I said, and stepped back into the circle.

On the other side of the line, the factory was empty, and quiet, and desolate. Sure, it had been a terrible place when it had been full of elves and the hum of busy machinery and the unique stench of tanning fluid and shoebox cardboard; but at least there had been people in it, and some of them had been my friends, even if they were difficult, annoying and dead miserable ninety-nine per cent of the time. Now it just felt empty, as if there was nothing there at all.

All my fault, too. Because of what I'd done, all those people, the elves, my comrades-in-arms and in afflic-tion – and Daddy George himself, of course – they'd all changed so much that by all meaningful criteria they simply didn't exist anymore. They'd gone away for ever, and been replaced by people who were totally unlike them. You could say I'd killed them all, and you wouldn't be far wrong.

I was so lonely, I even missed Daddy George.

The factory: whose was it now, I wondered? It's rightful owner was gone for good, but there was no way of proving that. Time would pass and he wouldn't come back (and my mother, who loved him, would be worried sick; she'd loved me, too, and I'd never come back) and presumably after a while the law would say he was dead, so Mum would own the factory, and the huge multinational business empire, and the nice house and all the money, not to mention the little plaques or statuettes or whatever it is they give you for winning a Nobel prize . . .

(Hers by right of inheritance; they'd belonged to her dead son . . .)

I couldn't stay in the factory. There wasn't anything to eat, and I was starving hungry; it was over forty-eight hours, I realised, since I'd had any food, and even then it had been a meal precisely calculated to provide the minimum nourishment necessary for a person six inches tall. What I wanted most of all, I discovered, was a hamburger the size of the Sydney opera house, and enough chips to pave the Champs d'Elysée.

I didn't have any money, of course. Come to think of it, all I had was the clothes I stood up in, namely a leaf-green jerkin, a pair of thick green woollen tights, and brown shoes with a silver buckle; my demob outfit, the equivalent of a Marks & Spencer navy pinstripe suit in Elfland, but a tad conspicuous on this side of the line. I really didn't want to go out into the world and get arrested *again*. If it was the same policeman as last time, I'd die of embarrassment.

Wouldn't it be nice, I thought, if I could just fast-forward . . .? To where? To the moment after I'd just had my next square meal; to when I'd sorted out all my many, many problems and complications, and my life was back to normal; to when I was finally happy; come to that, to the end of the tape. (Be considerate; please rewind this life for the benefit of the next person living it.) What I really wanted to do, of course, was wind *back*, but there didn't seem to be a facility for doing that, even in Elfland. No back, only forwards. Sorry, but that's how it is, and please direct any complaints to the ghost of Albert Einstein.

So I walked out of the factory gates – strange experience, that – and found myself in a narrow country lane, with grass growing up the middle and untended hedges that met across the top, sculpted into a flat-roofed arch by the tops of heavy lorries. It was just getting light (I'd forgotten about day and night after *x* months in the factory) and somewhere offstage a wood pigeon was cooing. I wondered what it was saying—

' . . . Sevens are forty-nine, eight sevens are fifty-six, nine sevens are sixty-three, ten sevens are seventy. Eleven sevens . . .'

Bugger me, I thought, *I can understand the language of birds*; and then I remembered (couldn't remember having found it out, just remembered the memory) that all elves can understand the language of birds when they're over this side of the line, but it's a singularly useless ability, since all birds ever do is recite their times tables, or the dates of the kings of France, or the Periodic Table – all the stuff that must be extremely helpful and important, because we all learn it at school, but which we never ever seem to find ourselves using once we've escaped. Being able to understand the language of birds doesn't mean you can speak it, of course – you can't ask a passing sparrowhawk the way to the nearest all-night café or anything useful like that. All you can do is listen to them grinding out the Ten Commandments or the prime numbers or French irregular verbs, until eventually you develop a mental spamblock that edits all the gibberish out and replaces it with melodious warbling noises.

Enlightenment, I thought. *You can stuff it.*

So I walked on a bit further, and eventually I heard a lorry rumbling up the road behind me. I'd never hitch-hiked successfully in life before, needless to say (don't accept lifts from strange men, and all that) but I stuck my thumb out anyway. The lorry thundered past me, then stopped.

I trotted up the lane towards it, and noticed the name stencilled on the side in tall white letters: *HigginStyle Footwear* – Daddy George's company. I ordered myself to calm down. Perfectly reasonable to come across one of his lorries in the lane leading to his factory and nowhere else.

'Bloody hell,' said the driver, staring down at me. 'What the fuck are you got up as?'

'Don't ask,' I growled. 'If you must know, I'm a film extra – we were doing this big kids' film with elves and brownies and pixies and all that crap. Last night was the wrap party, and when I woke up they'd all gone, left without me. So here's me, stranded in the middle of nowhere, dressed as an elf. You got a problem with that?'

The driver grinned. 'Hop in, then,' he said. 'I can take you as far as Northampton.'

I'd never ridden in a lorry before, either. Interesting perspective you get from the front passenger seat of one of those things; you're much higher off the ground than you'd be in an ordinary car, and the feeling of being whisked along over the heads of the traffic, like a Roman senator in a sedan chair, is rather fine.

'Bloody strange day,' the driver was saying. 'Went to pick up a load of shoes at the factory, nobody about. I banged on the gate till I hurt my hand, but it's all shut up. Then I went round the side, there was this door open, and the whole place is deserted, like the Mary Whatsername. Bloody strange.'

'Hadn't you heard?' I said. 'They've closed down the factory, going to buy in all the stock from Poland from now on. Cheaper, they reckon. We got talking to some of the locals down at the pub while we were filming. They're very upset about it all, as you can imagine.'

The driver shook his head. 'Marvellous,' he said. 'Makes you think. What's this country coming to? The accountants up at head office, they do their sums and reckon they can shave a few quid off costs, but they don't stop to think about the little people.'

'Who does?' I said. 'That's the problem with business today. Same in my line, of course,' I added, and held forth for several minutes about the trials of being an lowly spear-carrier in today's motion-picture industry. I was making it all up as I went along, of course, but the driver didn't seem to notice or mind; in fact, it struck me that I was sounding particularly plausible and convincing, not to mention putting across my message with style and a certain passion. Suddenly it was great fun

330 • Tom Holt

being my improvised persona, my imaginary friend
called me; I could clearly see every facet of his life, every
stitch and purl of his character. His name was Steve,
originally he was from Romford but he'd been brought
up in Sheffield (now *there* was a dead-end place), and
he'd always wanted to be an actor, but of course unless
you're really lucky there's absolutely no way to break in;
so instead he tried this film-extra gig, and once you got
your name known and assistant directors knew you
could be relied on to show up on time and do as you
were told, actually there was a living to be made at it –
not a wonderful living, sure, but it was better than
plucking chickens, and of course you were constantly
rubbing shoulders with the stars, like for instance
Robert de Niro; shared a mobile field latrine with him
once, just outside Melton Mowbray – well, there was a
crowd of us, and there were about seven other extras
standing between him and me, but it's something you
can tell you kids when you're old and grey—

(*Listen to yourself*, I thought, *this is complete garbage*.
But it passed the time, and this Steve's life was so much
more interesting than mine that I wasn't really in any
great hurry to leave it and go back to my own; and
then I realised that it wouldn't take very long to make it
true. So long as I was content to be just an extra, a
nobody-much, one of the little people, nobody would
ever listen carefully enough to figure out that I was
lying through my teeth; and after I'd really been an
extra on three or four films, the wind would change and
I'd stick like it. And wouldn't that be absolutely bloody
fantastic—)

'Whereabouts in Melton Mowbray?' the driver asked.
'Sorry?'

'Whereabouts in Melton Mowbray were you doing this film? My wife's lot come from round there.'

Never been to Melton Mowbray in my life, of course. 'Don't ask me,' I replied. 'Ours not to reason why, ours but to get on a coach at Pinewood and get out the other end. Some field in the middle of nowhere, with a row of Portaloos and a chuck wagon. One location looks pretty much like another, after a while.'

He nodded. 'Her mum and dad live in this village called Saxby,' he said, 'and her sister – that's her older sister, not the one who married a Yank – she lives in Stapleford. All sort of flat and open. Very slow driving all round there, specially when there's caravans.'

'I can imagine,' I said, and I wasn't kidding either; suddenly I *could* imagine. In my mind's eye I could see a straight, narrow road, quite possibly a Roman road, like a line drawn with a ruler across the map, and on either side a hazy golden panorama of newly cut wheat stubbles, pigeon-haunted and rook-spotted, broken here and there by brusque square castles of straw-bales; behind me and in front of me as I drove my mighty sixteen-wheel Daf was a pilgrimage of slow cars following a squat white caravan, towed by an elderly Mercedes. Overhead the sky was blue, dusted with small patches of scruffy white cloud, and the sun's warmth through my greenhouse windscreen made the skin of my forearm glow pleasantly. *God*, I thought, *what an absolutely wonderful life, how idyllic, how perfect*: the road, winding slow and sure to a certain, reliable destination, through the very heart of unspoilt England on a glorious late-summer day, Tammy Wynette on the tape deck and the promise of a fat mug of strong tea and the all-day breakfast at some truck-stop or Little Chef just a few miles down the way – how could anything possibly be better than that?

'I said,' the driver was repeating, 'I'm going to stop for breakfast in about five miles, all right?'

I pulled a face. 'You go ahead,' I replied. 'Just wish I could join you, only the bastards took all my stuff with them, and my wallet was in my rucksack.'

'You haven't got any money?'

I shook my head. 'No pockets in these bloody stupid clothes,' I pointed out. 'Otherwise you'd have elves with mobile phones and bunches of keys sticking out of the sides of their legs, it'd screw up the whole film.'

'Yeah,' the driver said, 'I can see that. 'S OK, breakfast's on me. Only,' he added, 'I'll fetch you yours over and you can stay in the cab. I'm not going anywhere people can see me with a bloke wearing green tights.'

His unexpected generosity nearly broke my heart. So this was what *real* people were like, I told myself: spontaneous, compassionate, filled with the simple fellowship of the road. All my life, and I'd never known anything like it. 'Thanks,' I said, managing to keep my voice steady. 'I could murder a bacon roll.'

He was as good as his word; he brought me out a bacon roll wrapped in a paper napkin and a styrofoam cup of very hot dark brown tea, looked round furtively to make sure nobody was watching him talk to me, and scuttled off back to the café. For a while after that, I didn't have any attention to spare for the world around me. I was too busy relishing the amazingly subtle and exotic flavours of bacon, the delicious softness of white bread, the overwhelmingly savoury tang of vintage cooking-oil, lovingly matured in the bottom of a constantly used frying pan. My senses drowned in them, like kittens in a bucket; *Oh brave new world,* I said to myself, *that has such butties in it.* I'd finished the last exquisitely crusty crumbs of the roll and was peeling the plastic lid off the cup of tea when I became aware of someone hammering on the cab window with a clenched fist.

I wound down the window and looked out. There were two policemen, looking up at me. The taller of the pair reached up and put his hand on the door handle. I knew him from somewhere.

'You're nicked,' he said.

CHAPTER NINETEEN

'I don't quite follow,' I said.

I was lying, of course. I lie very badly, certainly not well enough to deceive policemen, and quite definitely not well enough to convince this particular flatfoot, who'd last seen me being hauled out of an interview room by an armed man in a balaclava. Truth was, I followed like a cat chasing a piece of string. Still, one has to go through the motions.

'You,' said the policeman. 'Out of the cab. Slowly. You have the right to remain silent—'

I'd have liked to say goodbye to the lorry driver, but there didn't seem to be time. I'd also have liked to drink my tea, but when I asked if it'd be OK if I brought it with me, they put me in handcuffs. At least I'd finished my bacon roll. Small mercies, and all that.

It'd been a while – several months, at least – since I'd ridden in the back of a police car, and I'd hoped they might have upgraded a bit, invested in a model with a bit more knee-room. But they hadn't; a pity, really, because when Daddy George unshrank me I think he must have overdone it a touch. My legs were unquestionably longer than they'd been the last time I took a trip in a government taxi, and I spent most of the ride with my knees up around my chin.

In difficult situations, it helps if you know the drill, and by that point I could've booked myself in without any prompting from the desk sergeant. They put me in a different cell this time though. I can say that with total confidence, since there were a thousand and twenty-four bricks in the wall opposite the bed, compared with a thousand and seventy-eight in my previous studio apartment.

Ask Marco Polo or Cervantes or Sir Walter Raleigh or Oscar Wilde – they'll all tell you the same thing. Being in jug provides you with a first-class opportunity for taking stock of your life, thinking things over, honing and fine-tuning your world-view. In fact, it's about all there is to do once you've run out of bricks to count, and person-ally I'd be inclined to count it in as part of the punishment schedule, under the sub-heading 'cruel and unusual'. Of course, it'd be different if your life was happy and successful and nothing but blue skies; but if that was the case, you wouldn't have ended up in nick in the first place.

So I did the customary stocktake, and the results weren't encouraging. True, I'd contrived to get myself sprung from the shoe factory. On the other hand, com-pared with a small whitewashed cell, the shoe factory hadn't been all that bad. At least there'd been some-thing to do and people to talk to, even if mostly they'd either not answered or told me to bugger off. True, I'd freed the slaves and settled the score with Daddy George, but that hadn't actually got me anywhere, and nobody on this side of the line would ever know about it or believe it if the story ever did get out. On the negative side, I had no home, no money, no job, no identity, no recent past, no friends and no Cru, and quite soon I was going to be asked to explain what had happened the last time I was in police custody, something I wasn't going to be able to do. Pretty bleak, really.

I had one option. I could figure out a way of marking a circle on the floor, and go back to Elfland. Technically, of course, I was still banned for life, but it seemed pretty likely that the ban no longer applied, particularly with the rescued slaves putting in a good word for me, not to mention the fact that I'd changed a certain amount while I'd been in the shoe business. So, yes, I could go back there, stay there for good where the police and the DSS and the social services and God only knew who else couldn't find me. I could do that just by wanting to, it'd be no big deal; and once I was back in the place where there really was no hunger, homelessness or poverty (what you might call the elfare state) I'd be more likely than not to settle down there and get on with it. Fine; except that wasn't what I wanted to do. I'd be there, but it wouldn't be me. I'd be exactly the same, but different.

No, thanks.

Fine. That helped put everything else into a vague sort of perspective. No matter what kind of unholy pig's ear my life might turn into from this point on, at least it'd be *my* life, not the edited highlights of an existence being lived by someone else on the other side of the looking-glass. Besides, even if it was worse than the shoe factory, it couldn't be all that much worse. I'd just made it through an unknown number of months, years for all I knew, surviving extremes of hunger, deprivation, solitude, fatigue and boredom, and here I still was. So long as they didn't cut off any major limbs or line me up against a wall and shoot me, I figured I could handle it.

In which case, there really wasn't all that much to worry about. I leaned back – it felt odd to be resting in the middle of the day like this, but it was growing on me – closed my eyes and went peacefully to sleep.

I think I was dreaming about chicken, marinaded in spices and yogurt, cooked to perfection in a hot clay oven and served on a bed of saffron-scented rice with chickpeas, spinach and okra. Strange thing to be dreaming about, since I'd only ever had one Indian meal, back when I was about thirteen, and I hadn't liked it much. Anyway, at some point towards the end of the main course, someone grabbed my shoulder and started shaking me, making me spill my beer. When I turned my head, I found I couldn't quite see how it was, probably because my eyes were shut. I opened them and saw a policeman.

'Your lawyer's here,' he said.

Odd thing to serve for dessert, I thought, could I skip that and just have a coffee? 'Huh?' I said.

'Your lawyer. Waiting to see you.'

'Oh. Yes. Right. You mean the duty solicitor?'

He nodded. 'Come on,' he said, 'this way.'

As I walked down the corridor, I thought about that, as far as I could think about anything with a mind still clogged up with tandoori chicken, soft grey fluff and sleep. All these lawyers know each other, I said to myself, so maybe this one'll know what's become of Cru, assuming she hasn't packed in the legal profession already and gone straight. Maybe he'd turn out to be from the same firm, and could pass on a message. One thing that didn't occur to me was that I'd find Cru sitting behind the table in the interview room. Too unlikely, even by my rather rarefied standards.

She was reading a magazine – *Practical* something-or-other, boat-building or bee-keeping or some other activity starting with B – and I noticed she was wearing reading glasses: they suited her, somehow made her look a bit less likely to bite you in the leg if you annoyed her. Other than that, she looked exactly the same.

'Bastard,' she said.

The copper grinned and went out, leaving us alone together.

'Hello,' I said.

'Bastard,' she repeated, putting the magazine down. Out of curiosity I squinted at the title.

'You're looking well,' I said. 'Since when have you been interested in bee-keeping?'

'I'm not,' she replied. 'Where the bloody hell have you been?'

'Well—'

She rolled the magazine up and twisted it, like she was trying to strangle it. 'Don't tell me, I know perfectly well where you've been, and what you've been up to. So what happened? She throw you out or something? Can't say I blame her.'

'Actually,' I said.

'There I was,' she went on, as if I hadn't spoken, 'enjoying my day off, nice warm fire, cup of tea, cream slice, footstool, magazine, Classic FM, and the phone goes, which I was expecting because it always bloody goes when I've just got completely comfortable, so I crawl out of the house and drag down here, expecting it to be just some harmless arsonist or serial killer, and guess what, it's you. Should've guessed. You know why I should've guessed? Because every time I get comfy the phone rings, and every time I manage to get the shattered wreckage of my life rigged up into some sort of improvised shelter, you turn up. So am I surprised to see you? No, of course I'm not. Hence the magazine.'

'*Practical Bee-Keeping?*'

She threw it at me. Good shot. Ouch. 'Heaviest one I could find in Smith's on my way here,' she replied. '*You and Your Pentium 4* was thicker, but they print it on that flimsy paper. Also it was a pound dearer. I ought to bash your lying, treacherous head in.'

, 'It's nice to see you again,' I said. 'I've missed you.'

She made a strange noise at the back of her throat. 'Glad I didn't miss *you*,' she said, 'else that'd been £2.75 down the drain. Hold still while I get it and I'll not-miss you again.'

But she didn't get up to fetch the magazine. Instead she just sat there, staring at me, as if she was trying to wring my neck by telekinesis.

'So,' I said, 'what've you been up to since I've been away? Any interesting cases?'

She looked at me as if I'd just announced that I couldn't stay long, the mother-ship was about to leave orbit. 'You bet,' she said. 'There's this lunatic I used to act for, convinced he's a garden gnome or something of the sort, and he keeps vanishing for years at a time. And when he turns up again, he's always managed to get himself arrested for something or other. Nothing major, of course; just mounting commando raids on police stations, trivial stuff like that. You can't begin to imagine the things they say about me down at the Legal Aid board when I send in my bill.'

'Ah,' I said. 'So you're keeping busy, then?'

'You could say that, yes. Pushing around meaningless bits of paper all day, crying myself to sleep all night, and on my day off I get called out to the police station. I guess that's a pretty good example of what Thomas Jefferson called the pursuit of happiness. How about you? Keeping well?'

I nodded. 'Can't complain,' I said.

She narrowed her eyes a little. 'You know,' she said, 'if I didn't know you better, I'd swear you've grown since I last saw you.'

'Could be,' I replied. 'So far I've come up with two theories. The second theory is that in real time I'm still only sixteen years old, so maybe I haven't stopped growing yet.' I frowned. 'I don't suppose you want to hear the first theory.'

'Oh, go on,' she said. 'I enjoy a bit of gibberish now and again.'

So I told her all about it, from the moment when Daddy George's men had burst into that very room, right down to the transport café and the same policeman. 'And my theory is,' I went on, 'that when he reversed the shrinking process, he got the calibrations a bit skew-whiff and gave me a couple more of inches of leg. Not what I'd call full and fair compensation, mind, but I guess it's better than nothing. To tell you the truth, I haven't got a clue what I look like these days. I think I saw my reflection in a polished surface once or twice in the factory, but I wasn't really paying attention; and since I got out, I haven't been around mirrors very much. You wouldn't happen to have a mirror on you, by any chance?'

'Sure,' she said, and took one of those round plastic face-powder things out of her briefcase. There was a mirror inside the lid.

Whoever he was, he didn't look a bit like me. Or rather, there was a noticeable resemblance, such as you'd expect to see between two first cousins. But he was clean-cut, boldly nosed, Kirk Douglas-chinned, with a stylish fuzz of designer stubble that couldn't have been more canonically correct if it'd been applied with an aerosol in the best hair care establishment in Beverly Hills. To be honest, I was jealous. *Lucky old him*, I thought, *I wish I looked like that*.

'And I hope you two will be very happy together,' she said, thereby bringing to my attention the fact that I'd been gazing into said mirror for rather longer than was seemly. 'Can I have my compact back now? It's all right,' she added, 'it'll still be there even if you can't see it. Like the light inside the fridge.'

'I'm sorry,' I said. 'But really, it's been a while.'

She took the powder thing back and closed it with a snap. 'I think they have mirrors in prison cells these days,' she said, 'so you'll be able to see it whenever you want. In fact, you'll have all the time in the world to admire yourself in; that and slopping-out'll be the high-lights of your day.'

Downbeat, I thought; accentuating the negative to a rather unwholesome degree. 'You think it'll come to that?' I asked.

She looked thoughtful for a moment. 'Ordinarily, no,' she replied. 'Under other circumstances, I'd be fairly confident that you'd get off, since there's no real proof to suggest that you were anything but an unwilling victim of abduction. All a lot of fuss over nothing, in fact.'

'Ah,' I said. 'You said "under other circumstances". What's the problem here?'

She leaned back in her chair. 'Oh, just the fact that I'm handling the defence and I'm going to do everything I possibly can to throw the match. By the time the jury retires to consider its verdict, you'll be lucky if they let you out much before April 2030.'

I took a deep breath, then let it go slowly. 'So you believe what he told you, then.'

'That's right.'

'Fair enough,' I said quietly. 'How'd it be if I took you to the factory so you could see for yourself? It'll all still be there; the dormitories and the conveyor belt and the ladders and such all designed for use by six-inch people. I can show you all sorts of stuff I couldn't possibly know about if I hadn't been there.'

She shook her head. 'No, thanks,' she replied. 'On account of you can't go there unless I somehow manage to get bail for you, and even if I could I wouldn't. You seem to have forgotten you're under arrest. Would you like me to write it down for you, or would a knotted handkerchief be better?'

'All right, then,' I said, 'I'll draw you a map and you can go there yourself. It isn't hard to find.'

'No,' she replied. 'I haven't got the time or the energy to go around living out your fantasies. You know what? I think this whole elf thing is a figment of your imagination. I think you made it all up as a bizarrely roundabout way of giving me the elbow. Thanks, but if I want my intelligence insulted I'll visit Parliament or read a news-paper.'

'If you're that sure I'm lying,' I said, 'why don't you go and take a look for yourself? Then you'd know for sure I'd made it all up. Or you'd have no choice but to believe me. That's why you don't want to go, isn't it? Because you know it'll corroborate what I've told you, and then you'll have to face the fact that you've been wrong all this time, and I'm innocent.'

She sighed. 'If I had a fiver for every time someone sitting where you are now's told me a story like that, I'd be able to buy Wales. And still have some over for a cup of tea and a macaroon. No, I'm not going to go wandering about testing out stories that are so pathetic, even I'd end up wondering why anyone'd ever believe it. Nope, I'm going to stay here and make absolutely sure you go to prison. I see it as my civic duty.'

She was starting to annoy me. 'Listen,' I said. 'There was no girl. Not in Elfland, not anywhere else.' Yes, I didn't think about Spike when I said that, but that was between me and the past, nobody else's business. 'I've spent the last – oh God, I haven't got the faintest idea how long it's been. Do you happen to know, offhand?'

'Eighteen months, two weeks, three days, fourteen hours and, let's see, nine minutes. There or thereabouts.'

Eighteen months. Jesus. 'I've spent the last eighteen months working in a combination shoe factory and concentration camp, along with a couple of thousand other enslave elves. You want to know why I didn't phone or write? Because all that time I was six inches tall, and besides, there weren't any phones or letter boxes. And you know this is true, because you know me.'

'I know you too well,' she said.

'You know me,' I repeated. 'You know I've never lied to you. It'd have been far easier to lie, right from the start, when I told you about that first elf, but I didn't. You believed me then, and nothing's changed. And you also know what kind of man Daddy George was—'

'Was?' Suddenly she sounded interested. 'What do you mean, "was"? Is he dead or something?'

I looked at her. 'You think I've killed him or something?'

'For crying out loud, don't play games. Have you or haven't you?'

'I've settled up with him,' I replied slowly, 'and he won't be coming back.'

Her eyes were huge and round. 'For God's sake, Mike. What've you done?'

Interesting; she never called me by my name. 'He had it coming, after what he did to me. Don't you agree?'

'Yes, but—' She stopped. I smiled.

'So you do believe me,' I said.

'No. Well, yes, all right; I believe he treated you appallingly badly when you were a kid, and then he stole your maths discoveries and all that money that should've been yours.'

'Yes,' I interrupted, 'but that's not what either of us meant. You do believe me, about the factory. I know you do.'

'All *right*,' she snarled, 'yes, I do believe you about the stupid factory and being six inches tall and everything like that. That's beside the point. If you've killed him—'

'And you know he was lying,' I ground on. 'About there being a girl, I mean.'

'I already said so, yes. Look, that doesn't matter right now. If you've committed murder—'

I shook my head. 'I never said I'd killed him,' I replied. 'I haven't. I said I'd dealt with him and he's gone for good, but he's still alive. Do I look like someone who'd go around killing people?'

She sagged a little. 'I suppose not,' she said. 'But a lot of people who kill people aren't killers – I mean, they aren't professional hit men or crazed serial murderers or anything like that, they're just ordinary people who find themselves in impossible situations, and someone ends up dead. And after everything he's done to you - well, anybody could just go snap under those circumstances. I'm pretty sure I could.'

'I know you better than that,' I told her. 'You wouldn't, and neither would I. Oh, I was tempted, and not just for a split second, either. But I couldn't kill him. It wouldn't be enough.'

She was very quiet for a moment or so. 'Go on, then,' she said. 'What've you done?'

So I told her. It was some time before she spoke, or even moved.

'You're kidding,' she said eventually.

I looked away. 'All right,' I said, 'I'm not particularly proud of what I did. It was vindictive and cruel, and I did it because it was the nastiest, most vicious punishment I could think of. But I didn't kill anyone, and besides, he – what are you laughing about?'

She made a valiant but futile attempt to choke back a snigger. 'Sorry,' she said, 'but—'

'I don't happen to think it's very funny.'

For some reason, that just cracked her up even more. 'It's bloody hilarious,' she said. 'Oh, come on; the chairman and CEO of one of the world's most powerful corporations, one inch tall and being cooed over like a gerbil—'

'I'd call that tragic, not comic,' I replied stiffly.

She put her hands in front of her mouth. 'Yes,' she said, 'I guess you probably would. You know, we're going to have to find some way of getting you to lighten up. Otherwise, we're going to have an awful lot of rows in the years to come.'

In a way, it was a bit like that old bottom-of-the-escalator thing, when you're expecting a step and there isn't one. Also there was a sense of having turned over two pages at once, subtly blended with getting hit on the head by a rapidly descending sack full of wet sand. 'Are we?' I said.

'I should think so,' she replied. 'Because if you're going to be all po-faced and stuffy, you'll be a real pain to have round the house, and I'm not going to put up with it without a fight.'

'Yes, but—'

It was also a bit like waking up one morning to find that you've been elected Pope – a wonderful thing and a really stupendous honour, but really, really unexpected. She was smiling at me, and part of me was saying, she can't do that, how dare she, she's taking the mickey; and the rest of me was pointing out that it couldn't care less if she accused me of dressing up in women's clothes and molesting sheep, because what she was mostly saying was that it was all right, she loved me right back, and everything was going to be just fine. In any event, one thing that even I could figure out was that talking about it, trying to clarify the grey areas and maybe work towards hammering out a joint communiqué and statement of intent, simply wasn't going to cut it this time. It was a situation where nothing except strictly non-verbal communication would get the job done. So I kissed her.

It's a confoundedly tricky operation, kissing someone, especially if you're not used to it. Stuff like noses and teeth get in the way—

'Ouch,' she said. 'Watch what you're doing, you clumsy idiot.'

– But if you take both hands off the wheel, so to speak, and let instinct take over, I assure you, it can be done. Good fun, too. If you've never tried it, you should.

'All right,' she said, some time later, 'you've made your point. Get off, someone could come in any minute. I don't want some bluebottle to stroll in and find me snogging the suspect, they'll report me to the Legal Aid.' She frowned. 'Which reminds me,' she said.

'Oh.' To be honest with you, the being-under-arrest side of things had slipped my mind rather. 'But that's all right,' I said. 'Like you told me, they haven't got any evidence. You can point that out to them, and they'll have to let me go.'

She nodded thoughtfully. 'Sure,' she said. 'But by the time I've done that, word's going to get about that your rotten stepfather's disappeared; and you stand to benefit from his death, obviously, because you still have a big stake in the company; and they'll ask you where you've been and what you've been doing.' She frowned. 'And even if you've got the sense not to mention the shoe factory, that still leaves us with a hell of a problem. Like, if you tell them about the elves and crossing the line and all, they'll stick you in a padded cell; and if you don't, you've got no way of accounting for your movements or explaining where you've been or what you've been doing all these months – all these *years*, rather.' She sighed. 'This is very bad,' she said. 'I really don't like the look of it one bit.'

That wasn't really what I wanted to hear. 'Aren't you being just a tad alarmist?' I said. 'I mean, it could be days before anybody notices he's not around any more—'

'I'd say a maximum of six hours,' Cru interrupted, 'from the time you sent him away. After that, he'll be missing appointments, not showing up for important meetings, not being there when his flight to New York takes off without him. Could be much sooner than that, of course. Depends on how his diary was looking for the rest of the day.'

She had a point; and the way she seemed to be insisting on driving said point through my skull into my brain with a big hammer didn't detract from its patent validity. 'Then you'd better get me out of here quick,' I said. 'I don't know, you could threaten to sue them for wrongful arrest of something.'

A little sideways flick of the head, to indicate that my suggestion was too fatuous to deserve a response; typical Cru gesture and quite endearing, in an extremely annoying sort of way. 'Listen,' she said, 'if you were on fire, carrying a contagious disease and had a ticking bomb stuffed down the front of your trousers, it'd still take over an hour just to fill out the release paperwork. It's what Shakespeare calls the law's delays, and what we in the trade prefer to think of as the law's fucking you about from here to next Whitsun with a blunt tent peg. Sorry, but that's how it is. No fast-track checkout, and you can't get a table by tipping the head waiter.'

'All right,' I said, 'but if I've got to lighten up, you've

got to stop being so damned negative. We'll just have to escape, that's all.'

She sighed. 'What a wonderful idea,' she said. 'All right, what's it to be? Do we dig a tunnel, or were you thinking more along the lines of the old riding-a-motor-bike-across-the-Swiss-border routine?'

This time, I smiled. Or rather, I smirked. Can't say I remember ever having smirked before. It's OK, but it puts a strain on the muscles at the corners of your mouth. 'Piece of cake,' I told her. 'All we need is a circle.'

'What do you mean, a circle?'

'Round thing,' I said. 'A plane figure bounded by a single line equidistant at every point from its centre. Got a lipstick?'

She shrugged, and produced one from her bag. 'It's not really your colour,' she pointed out. 'You're more of an Autumn, if you ask me. Can I ask what you think you're doing?'

'I'm drawing a circle on the floor.'

'That's not a circle,' she objected. 'More of an irregular ellipse. Well,' she added as I pulled a face at her, 'you're the one who started up with the maths stuff. What's it supposed to be for?'

Another smirk; I'd have to be careful I didn't stick like it. 'You'll see,' I said. 'Now, if you'll just come over here—'

She stopped. 'You're going to Elfland, aren't you?' she said.

'*We*'re going to Elfland,' I corrected her. 'Come on, it doesn't hurt or anything.'

The scowl she gave me would've stripped chrome. 'No,' she said, 'absolutely not. I hate foreign travel. I've only been abroad once, on a school trip, and I had a tummy upset for weeks afterwards. If you think—'

Uncharacteristically, she didn't finish her sentence. Which may have been because I grabbed her by the arm and pulled her into the circle.

CHAPTER TWENTY

'Here we are,' I said.

Apparently, the Elfland equivalent of a police station was a farmyard. There's probably a perfectly rational explanation: either the only place on their side of the line where living creatures are detained in a confined space is a hen-coop, or it's something to do with the fact that we ended up standing next to a trough full of swill.

'Where the hell,' Cruella demanded, 'is this?'

'Same place that we were a moment ago,' I said wearily. 'Only different.'

'Elfland?'

I nodded.

'Thank God for that,' she replied with feeling. 'For one awful moment I thought I'd died and gone to Ambridge.'

I realised we weren't alone. There was someone standing right behind us; a tall, slim, golden-haired girl with shining blue eyes, an angelic expression and pointy ears. *Oh snot*, I thought.

'There you are,' she said. 'We were wondering where you'd got to.'

Not really the most helpful thing to say, after I'd spent a fair bit of time and energy persuading Cru that there wasn't a tall, slim, golden-haired, blue-eyed, pointy-eared babe waiting for me at the end of the rainbow. For her part, Cruella jumped a foot in the air and said, 'Eeek!'

Oh well, I thought. 'Cruella,' I said, 'I'd like you to meet Melissa. Melissa, Cruella. I don't suppose either of you are going to be happy about this, but you've both got a lot in common.'

Melissa's eyes opened wide. 'Gosh,' she said. 'You mean, this is her? I mean me?'

Just goes to show; thinking things can't possibly get worse is pretty much an infallible way of proving yourself wrong. 'Mike,' Cru hissed loudly at me, 'who is this strange woman and why is she staring at me? I'm not the one with deformed ears, for crying out loud.'

Sisters under the skin, I thought, yes, well. 'Cru,' I said, 'you remember me telling you that everything and everybody on our side – except me – has an equal and opposite over here?'

Cru made a small, bewildered noise in the back of her throat. 'You mean, *that*—'

'Yes,' I said unhappily. 'Over here, that's you. And Melissa, um, likewise. OK?'

Melissa was goggling at Cru with the most extraordinary expression on her face. The closest I can get to describing it is: imagine how Sir Lancelot would've looked if he'd finally managed to find the Holy Grail, and he'd pulled off the lid and looked inside and found a small, fresh dog turd. 'This is extraordinary,' Melissa said. 'You see, none of us has ever met our other half before, at least not on this side. Really, this is quite—'

'Yes,' Cru growled, 'isn't it? But don't worry, it's purely temporary, because we're going back again now. Straight away,' she added pointedly.

'Um.' Melissa's face clouded over. 'Actually,' she said, 'I'm not sure that's going to be possible. At least, it's possible but I really don't think it'd be terribly wise. I'm sorry,' she added, with perhaps a tad more feeling than necessary.

'Mike, what's she talking about?' Cru snapped. I winced. If this was going to turn into one of those please-tell-your-friend conversations, I'd rather have stayed in the nick.

'It's rather complicated,' Melissa replied, 'and we aren't terribly sure of the details, because of course nothing like this has ever happened, and we didn't dare do experiments, even virtual simulations, for fear of what might happen. But—'

'And tell her to stop waffling,' Cru interrupted.

'But,' Melissa went on, 'the theories say that if one of us meets his or her opposite number on this side of the line, there'd be a terrific build-up of latent transdimensional potential energy, a bit like matter and antimatter. Obviously just bringing the two together isn't enough to cause any problems—'

'Matter of opinion,' Cru growled.

'But we're very much afraid that once the two opposites have come together, any attempt to separate them would cause a quite dreadful fracture in the phase interface, which in turn would set off a multiphasic chain reaction releasing enormous quantities of differentially charged paranexal particles into the resulting fissure—'

'What's she talking about, Mike?'

'Boom,' I explained. 'Very loud, followed by the world coming to an end. That's right, isn't it?'

Melissa nodded. 'That's what we're afraid of,' she said. 'Effectively an interface meltdown followed by a complete annihilation reaction. It could be—' She hesitated for a moment. 'Very awkward,' she said. 'And we'd rather it didn't happen.'

Cru's jaw dropped so fast it nearly burned up in the atmosphere. 'Now just a minute,' she said. 'Mike, is she trying to tell me that unless she follows me about wherever I go for ever and ever, the world will blow up and we'll all be killed.'

I thought about it. 'I think so,' I said. 'Something like that, anyhow.'

'And if I go back to our side and she doesn't come with me—'

Melissa coughed very softly. 'Actually,' she said, 'we're fairly sure that if you went back to your side, even if I came too, the ensuing repolarisation of the latent geomagnetic field—'

'You mean I'm *stuck here*?' Even with all this weirdness to contend with, I couldn't help being just faintly amused to see that the shock had jarred Cru into recognising Melissa's existence. 'I'm stuck here in *Fairyland* and I can't ever go home? Bloody hell, Mike—'

Another very faint cough, this time with overtones of shock and extreme distaste. 'Actually, Cru,' I whispered, 'if you could possibly avoid the B word while we're over here—'

'What?' She blinked twice. 'You're saying I'm

marooned in a world populated by Disney characters and I can't even *swear*?' She shook her head vigorously. 'Sorry,' she said, 'no way. No deal. I'm getting out of here, and if it means the world gets blown up, it'll just have to be an omelettes-and-eggs job.'

I shuddered a little. Of course I loved her, passionately and with all my heart, but there were times I couldn't help wishing a tree would fall on her head or something. Not a big tree, of course, and it'd have to be appropriate. A lilac or a flowering cherry, something like that.

'Cru,' I said. 'Shut up.'

I think it was probably just the shock, not my commanding personality or my newly acquired self-confidence. Worked, though. 'And you, too,' I added, as Melissa opened her rosebud cakehole. 'Be quiet, both of you. I'm trying to think.'

Of course, when you say that, your mind immediately goes blank. You could've projected movies on the inside of my skull. Still, the silence alone made it worthwhile.

'All right,' I said, 'I think I know what we're going to do.' I was lying, of course – clueless as a blind detective in an isolation chamber. But it was imperative that we did something, before Cru and Melissa both started talking simultaneously, rapidly and at length. 'The way I see it,' I went on, 'personality's got to be at the root of it. Must be. Because,' I went on, and this time I knew I really was on to something, even if it turned out to be the extreme edge of my gourd, 'of everything being the same, only different. Where's Daddy George, do you know?'

Melissa looked at me, as if asking for permission to speak. Hard to say which of them was more irritating, her or Cru.

'I'm not absolutely sure,' Melissa replied. 'I think they're building a little house for him on the village green, so he's probably around there somewhere.'

'Village green,' I repeated. 'Right, take us there. You,' I added, turning to Cru, 'keep up, for crying out loud.'

'Yes, all right, there's no need to shout.'

So, off we went; and for all her brave words about omelettes, eggs and Armageddon, I noticed that Cru kept so close behind Melissa that another cigarette-paper's breadth would've constituted assault. *Good*, I thought, *one less thing to worry about* – which goes to show, I guess, how the fear of death can really skew the way you stack your priorities.

We had to walk, of course; I recall that it was a long and exhausting trudge, up stony hillsides and across treacherous marshes, through dense briar thickets and over rickety, swaying, canyon-spanning rope bridges—

'What happened?' Cru demanded. 'And where the hell are we?'

'The village, presumably,' I replied (and if this was the village, I thought, bags I be Number Six).

'But we haven't moved,' Cru protested. 'About two seconds ago we were in that farmyard—'

I sighed. 'I'll explain later. Think about it, and you'll remember the whole thing.'

'What whole thing?'

'Doesn't matter,' I snapped, 'we're here now. Where's—? Oh, right.'

We were on the edge of a large-ish triangle of immaculately tonsured grass, neatly trimmed at the edges with substantial black-beamed thatched cottages, all of them heartbreakingly quaint to the point of nausea. The cold, rational part of my mind pointed out that if you were to

superimpose a sketch of the green over a similar-scale
plan of Victoria Square in Birmingham you'd most likely
get an exact match. 'Excuse me,' I asked Melissa, 'but
what's this village called?'

'Littleton Snowdrop,' she replied.

'Ah,' I murmured, 'right. Thanks, I won't ask again.
So where would this little house be?'

'Over there, look. Just next to the duck pond.'

She pointed. The duck pond was easy to see, and
beside it there was a huge, exceptionally fine statue of a
reclining water nymph. Victoria Square, I thought; the
same but different. Well, it's always nice to have some
idea of where you are.

And, sure enough, when I looked more closely, there
was the little house. It was a *little* little house, and I don't
suppose I'd have noticed it if it hadn't been for the substantial mob of elves crowded around it, necks craned. It
took a fair bit of sidling and shoving to get to the front.

Did you ever play with Lego? I did; and I used to
build these ambitious, if rather unsound, red-white-and-
blue plastic castles, like a pre-teen Mad King Ludwig.
My castles weren't thatched, but that aside, the little
house could've been one of them; in which case, I sin-
cerely hoped that any life form inside was wearing a
hard hat.

'Excuse me,' I asked an elf, 'but is this where they've
put the midget? You know, the one from the other side
of the line.'

The elf nodded. 'He's in there right now,' he replied.
'Hope he likes it, it's very nice in there. He's got his
own little table and chair, and we're going to make him
his own tiny miniature dinner service as soon as
Rhydichen gets back with some acorn cups.'

'Thanks,' I said. 'All right, coming through.'

Fortunately, both Cru and Melissa had stayed at the back of the crowd (for fear of getting separated, presumably) so I didn't have to wait for them. I leaned over and lifted off a small detachable section of roof.

'Hey,' said a tiny voice from inside. 'What's going on?'

'It's OK,' I replied, 'it's only me.'

'Oh. Please go away.'

'I want to ask you a question.'

'Do you really have to?'

'Yes,' I replied. 'Where are you?'

'In the toilet, actually. If you could possibly see your way to coming back in five minutes—'

'That's all right,' I said, 'I don't need to bother you any more, you've told me everything I need.'

'Ah. That's all right, then.'

'Cheerio.'

'Be seeing you.'

Just as I'd thought, I reflected as I slid my way through the elf cordon. The trip across the line had changed his personality out of all recognition – just like it'd changed mine, if you remember. But Cru had come through with all of her considerable reserves of personality unchanged. Strange, I thought, but pretty much what I'd expected. Anyway, it gave me the answer I'd been looking for. Didn't have a clue what it meant, of course; but you don't have to know how something works in order to use it. Mercifully.

'Well?' Cru demanded.

'It's awful,' I told her, with a slight involuntary shudder. 'It's got sweet little lace curtains on the windows and a teensy-weensy three-piece suite with darling little pink satin cushion-covers and a tiny scale-model dustbin and everything. It's the sort of thing Dante might've dreamed up if he'd had a really serious LSD addiction.'

'Not the house,' Cru said irritably. 'What did he say? Have you—'

'I think so,' I said. 'The crux of it seems to be, he and I experienced a major personality change when we crossed the line; I became all assertive and brash and a real pain in the bum, and he's turned timid and shy-woodland-creaturish. You, with all due respect, are still the same.'

'Good,' Cru said firmly. 'So what?'

'Ah,' I said, 'I'm coming to that. Interestingly, the elves in the shoe factory were all miserable as hell and un-elflike. So was Melissa, when she was over our side. Everybody changes, in fact, except you. All right so far?'

She shrugged, while Melissa stood perfectly still and attentive, the model listener. I found that extremely annoying, though I can't really explain why.

'So,' I went on, 'what's different about you? Any ideas?'

Cru thought for a moment. 'I'm not a snivelling pointy-eared freak?' she suggested.

I nodded. 'Yes,' I said, 'but right now you should be, that's the whole point. Now, what's different about our crossing the line, as opposed to all the others who've done it?'

'Go on,' she said, 'impress me.'

'I'll try,' I promised. 'It's because every second you've been over here, you've been in the company of your alter ego. Now, when I brought Daddy George across, he wasn't – he'd killed his opposite number, my dad, years ago, over on our side. Likewise, I guess, when all the elves who ended up in the factory – nobody's said anything about their opposite numbers being there to meet them when they came through, though of course that's what should have happened. I'm guessing that Daddy George's gateway contraption somehow screwed up the equivalencies, and the equal-opposite effect didn't happen, because they were sort of pulled out of context when they came through. Really wish I knew more about that, but right now I can't face all the aggravation of asking Daddy George about it; it'd be like interrogating Minnie Mouse, and I haven't got the energy. So we'll just have to assume, for now.'

'You assume away,' Cru growled. 'Drivel's drivel, after all. Is there a point to all this?'

'I think so,' I said. 'I think that when things are all normal and everyone's got their opposite number on the other side of the line – well, they're all taking up the amount of space they're supposed to be taking up, and everything's fine. It's like a see-saw, and it balances. But when you take someone off one end of the plank and simultaneously plonk them down on the opposite end, it throws everything out. All right so far?'

She wrinkled her nose. 'I suppose so.'

'All right,' I said. 'But if that's the case, the big explosion should've happened the moment you crossed over – when the see-saw got unbalanced – and it didn't. In fact, nothing happened.'

'I wouldn't say that exactly,' Cru muttered. 'But yes, I think I can see what you're getting at, a long way off in the distance through a very muddy windscreen. Go on.'

'So,' I said, 'it sort of stands to reason that the universe has got some way of adjusting. It must have, when you think about it, because there's been a whole bunch of elves over our side for years, and nothing got particularly blown to hell when they came over. I think all that happens is that the universe sort of slides its bum down the plank a bit until everything balances again, and that's it.' I turned to Melissa. 'Is that anything like what your people have been figuring?' I asked.

She nodded. 'More or less,' she said. 'Except we're a bit worried about the two opposite-but-equals being together in effectively the same place. We think that when that happens, the adjustment you were talking about—'

'The bottom-shuffling along the plank, you mean?'

She flushed slightly. 'We'd never actually considered that analogy,' she said, 'but yes, that's right. We think that the adjustment under those circumstances takes the form of – well, a merger.'

Cru frowned. 'What, you mean like House of Fraser taking over Harrods or something?' she asked.

Melissa nodded slowly. 'You could say that, yes. I think that you and I – well, we're now effectively occupying the same space that I was before you came. Instead of one of me, there's now two of us – two of me, rather, but the same size as I was before you arrived.' She hesitated. 'I can show you what I mean, if you like.'

Cru made a very strange noise; I think she was actually grinding her teeth, something which I'd always thought only happened in books. 'Go ahead,' she said. 'this could be interesting.'

'Come with me,' Melissa said, and she took us across the green to a funny-looking contraption with wooden beams and a scale and a big metal weight dangling off the fulcrum like a fossilised plum. 'It's a weighing machine,' Melissa explained. 'I sit on this seat here, and you move that weight down the beam till it balances – that's it. Now read off the number on the scale.'

I had to look closely; the typeface was so quaint and oldy-worldy, I had real trouble making it out. 'Four and a bit,' I said. 'Four and a bit what?'

'Stone,' Melissa replied. 'Just as I thought. You see, I weight eight and a half stone, usually. Now you get on.'

Sure enough, Cru weighed exactly the same, which came as rather a shock to her, though under other circumstances she'd probably have been thrilled to nuts. She'd always been a little on the substantial side.

'You see,' Melissa explained, 'the two of us put together make up me. I expect that if we took tissue samples and calculated the sectional density—'

'Try it and I'll smash our face in,' Cru warned, taking a step back.

'The point is,' Melissa went on, 'we're now one person, as far as the universe is concerned. If we don't stay close to each other, there'd suddenly be a gap, and that's when we think the problems would start.' She took a deep breath. 'To use your analogy,' she said, a trifle hesitantly, 'we think the universe has reached the point where if it wiggles any further down the see-saw, it'll fall off and hurt itself.'

None of us said anything for a long time.

'All right,' I said. 'So, what do you suggest?'

'Well,' Melissa was looking down at the ground. I used to do that a lot when I was a kid, usually when I'd broken something, and it's not a good sign. 'We could just carry on like we are and hope we don't stray too far apart.'

'I don't like that idea,' Cru said.

'Or,' Melissa went on. 'Well, we've developed a procedure – we haven't tested it, of course . . .'

'What's she talking about, procedure?' Cru hissed.

'Science stuff,' I replied. 'Stop interrupting.'

'We think,' Melissa said, 'that we can actually do a physical merger; put me and her into an integration chamber, and make us into one person. You and me,' she said, looking at Cru straight in the eye, 'sharing the same body.'

I expected Cru to make a fuss. I knew her too well. I was right.

When she'd calmed down a bit, I asked Melissa, 'Which body?' It sounded a bit like your-place-or-mine.

'I think it'd be far safer to use my physical template,' she answered, 'because it's my body the universe is used to, if you see what I mean. Which is why,' she went on, 'when we both weighed ourselves just now, we each weighed exactly half of my usual weight. If we used your template, it might cause problems.'

She looked at Cru expectantly. For her part, Cru had gone as white as a sheet.

'Let's see,' she said. 'You and me, locked up in your body, for the rest of our lives.'

Melissa nodded. 'That's right,' she said. 'I'm willing to do it if you are.'

Cru was shaking slightly. 'Trapped for ever,' she said. 'With her. In *that*.'

'Oh, I don't know,' I said. 'I think it's a very nice—'

The look Cru shot at me would've frozen a volcano.

'Idea,' I said quickly. 'A very nice idea. At the very least you ought to think about it.'

'*Bastard*!'

There's being forceful and assertive, and there's being

an idiot. The two should not be confused. 'Sorry,' I said, as quickly as I could without dislocating my tongue. 'If you won't even consider it, fine. Your choice. Absolutely no pressure. And I'm sure Melissa's perfectly happy to leave the decision up to you; aren't you, Melissa?'

I think the very tips of her ears might have quivered slightly, but she swallowed and said, 'Yes, of course. In fact, I'm sure that after a year or so we'll be the very best of friends.'

Cru screamed. It wasn't one of your B-movie *Bride of the Gorilla* screams, more an attempt to express the sort of rage they just don't make words big enough for. 'That does it,' she said. 'All right, so the world's got to get blown up. That's a real shame and I'm very, very sorry, really I am. But.'

She turned on her heel and started to walk. I think she'd gone all of five yards when the first fissure opened up in the ground in front of her, and the sky began to crackle and spark in a manner that suggested that God had been doing DIY wiring.

'Shit,' she said, and stopped dead.

Clouds had appeared out of nowhere, and were rapidly blotting out the sun; it was so dark it could've been a June noon in Manchester. A small laurel bush about three paces to my left burst into spontaneous flame. Actually, that struck me as a good sign at first, but when it didn't say anything I dismissed it as a coincidence (thought I was tempted to try leaving a message after the tone, just in case). Ahead of us on the green, elves were standing glued to the spot, staring upwards. It took me a while to realise that dwellers in Elfland, where skies are always blue, probably hadn't seen a cloud before.

'Oh hell,' Cru wailed, 'I don't know what to do. Somebody else decide, for God's sake.'

Of all the reactions I'd been expecting, this wasn't one of them. I reckoned I knew Cruella by then, and whatever else she might do, she'd never ask for advice. Ever.

'Well?' she said.

Melissa had gone as white as tapioca pudding when the electrics started playing up; she was quite obviously frozen with terror, and I can't say I blamed her. Terror doesn't freeze me, though; in fact, it has the opposite effect, making me go all wobbly and fluid-boned. I had an overwhelming urge, in fact, to scratch a circle in the dirt and get the hell out of there, in an illogical hope that even if Elfland blew, the human side wouldn't go up with it. Silly, I know, and I'd like to say in my defence that I only considered it as a possible course of action because there wasn't a convenient pile of sand to hide my head in.

Cru was expecting a reply. Nobody to give it but me.

'Decide what?' I asked.

'Mike, just for once don't be so bloody stupid. Decide what I ought to do, is what.'

Not the hardest question I've ever been faced with. 'I wouldn't go any further if I were you,' I suggested.

She muttered something under her breath. I couldn't make out most of it, though I fancy I caught the words *denser than depleted uranium*. 'Thank you so much, professor bloody Einstein,' she said aloud. 'Apart from that, what should I do?'

'What, do you mean should you do the merging thing or carry on following Melissa about?'

'Yes.'

'Ah.'

Trickier, by several orders of magnitude.

I thought about it; and I had to confess, the first thought that crossed my mind was that I loved Cruella very much indeed. But Melissa was rather more restful, not to mention looking like something thrown off a cat-walk for being so cute she was distracting people's attention from the clothes. Combine the two, I thought, what the hell is there to think about?

I considered that; and then I considered myself considering it. Not a pleasant sight.

On the other hand, we still had the world to save, not to mention Cru's sanity and quite possibly Melissa's life—

(Logic. If Melissa were to die, like my real dad, wouldn't that free up the necessary space on the see-saw? Hell, if she merged with Cru, they'd *both* effectively be dead – they wouldn't be themselves any more, so was there really any difference? I decided that the logical me was an even bigger arsehole than the selfish me . . .)

Come on, I told myself, *you're a bloody double Nobel laureate, think of something.* There's got to be an answer, and the answer's got to be something to do with me, just like it was when I had to figure out a way of dealing with Daddy George. When you turn your face towards Heaven and cry out, 'Why me?', the answer *Because everyone else is still at lunch* doesn't really cut it.

Something to do with me—

If they merged, Cru and Melissa might as well be dead, because neither of them would be *them* any more; because it's who we are that makes us unique. So: what makes us what we are? Various things; where we come from, the way our experiences shape us. The way other people shape us – like the way Daddy George effectively made me who I was; or the way I'd made Cru who she was, because she'd loved me all along and I'd kept vanishing, for years at a time, and she'd waited. Because she loved me.

The penny hadn't dropped yet, but it was quivering on the edge. Loving me was a fundamental part of who she was, it defined her. If she stopped loving me, she wouldn't be Cru any more, she'd turn into someone else living in the same body and wearing the same clothes. The old Cru might as well be dead.

(If she stopped loving me, I might as well be dead too. But that was a side issue. Can't make omelettes without breaking hearts.)

If I made her stop loving me, I'd kill her. There'd still be a Cruella, but it's be just an animated torso and appendages, haunted by the ghost of how she used to be, while a new occupier moved in and gutted the interior.

If I killed her, there'd be room on the bench; she'd drop out, having no opposite number, just like me. She'd be out of the loop. She could go home.

She'd be better off.

That just left the *modus operandi*; and that was easy.

'All right,' I said, 'I think you should go ahead with the merger.'

Cru looked at me, and it was as if some clown had poked a ladder through the roof, and I was looking up into darkness through two holes in her face.

'It'd solve the mess,' I went on, 'and that's the main thing. After all, this is very serious, we can't go letting our feelings put the whole world in jeopardy. Besides,' I added, 'you shouldn't think of it as anything bad happening. Stroke of luck for you, really. Just think of it as if you were moving out of a poky little flat into a luxury mansion. It'd suit me better too, of course. I mean, *that* goes without saying.'

And I knew her too well. I was giving a fairly unconvincing performance, but I could've been reading it off the teleprompt and she'd still have believed it, because she'd always believe the worst of me, because she loved me and knew me too well. I could feel my hand tightening around the throat of her love, and the life slowly draining away with each heartbeat. It'd have been so much easier, so much more pleasant to slide a razor across my own throat, if only that'd have done any good – but it wouldn't, because the universe didn't need my space, think you very much, I could come and go as I liked and it wouldn't make any difference to the balance of the see-saw. And if I died, all I'd be doing would be going away *again*, this time with no chance whatsoever of coming back, and Cru would still carry on loving me, stubborn as a dog refusing to let go of a stick, and she'd still be Cru.

'Well?' I said. 'We haven't got all day.'

Her face was as empty as a blank form. 'All right,' she said. 'If that's what you want.'

I knew her so well, I could feel the death of love; there was a specific moment at which she stopped loving me. And as soon as that moment came—

'Run,' I shouted. 'Cru, for God's sake just trust me. Get out of here.'

Yes, it can be a real pain at times, but there are occasions when a really forceful and assertive personality can make all the difference. A bewildered now-what-the-hell look flashed across her face, and then she started running. I hit the deck with my hands over my head, asinine as a Civil Defence leaflet, and closed my eyes.

The world didn't end.

No fuses blew, no chasms opened up, the ground stayed stolidly motionless. After five seconds, I lowered my arms, raised my head and looked up.

The sun was coming out.

I let my head sink back onto the ground; it was a big, heavy, cumbersome head and I was sick and tired of supporting its weight. It could be a clever old head when it wanted to be, there were all sorts of smart ideas stuffed away inside it somewhere, along with all the trash. On balance, however, I didn't like it much. In fact, as far as I was concerned, that head was just a pain in the neck.

I realised I was in shadow, and looked up. Melissa was kneeling beside me, her eyes wet with tears. 'Are you all right?' she asked.

'Go away,' I said.

She winced as if I'd slapped her. 'I love you,' she said.

'So what? Push off.'

I stood up. I'd felt happier. Being unspeakably cruel to Melissa hadn't actually made me feel any better, for some odd reason, so I turned round to apologise, but she wasn't there. *No matter*, I thought, *she'll definitely be better off*. You don't have to be an unmitigated bastard to save the world, but it probably helps. I can't see how any nice, decent, honourable person could ever get the job done.

'Well?' said a voice behind me.

I didn't recognise it, as such; but it was so completely and utterly unlike another voice I knew very well that I'd guessed the speaker's identity well in advance of spinning round and seeing her. 'Spike?'

There she was again; another bloody dreamboat. All the female elves were beautiful, of course, in the same vaguely unsatisfactory way as the countless industrial-grade California blondes you see on American daytime soap operas. Golden hair, flawless features, millimetre-perfect Barbie-busted figures, swimming-pool-blue eyes – and instantly forgettable. 'Actually,' she said, 'my name's Zefirassa, but I was Spike on the other side.'

I shrugged. There wasn't really anything I wanted to say to her.

'Sorry if I'm being intrusive,' she said, 'but oughtn't you to go after her?'

'Mind your own bloody business.'

'I was watching,' ex-Spike went on, 'and I figured out what the problem was, and how you solved it. Wonderfully inventive and resourceful.'

Part of me felt like replying that whatever it was I was full of, it surely wasn't resource. Most of me couldn't be bothered, however, so I kept my face shut and shrugged again. The fact that she'd apparently been able to work out from first principles what the problem was, and how to solve it, wasn't lost on me. I just wasn't particularly interested.

'If you don't mind me saying so, I really do think you ought to go after her,' she went on. 'She's probably very upset. And you do love her ever such a lot.'

I scowled. 'You're absolutely right,' I said. 'But she doesn't love me. Not any more. That's the whole fucking point, isn't it?'

She huddled up a bit, like a leaf held over a candle. 'Absolutely, yes,' she said. 'But you've sorted the problem out now – extremely well, of course in fact quite brilliantly. If you were to go to her and explain—'

I shook my head angrily. 'Listen,' I said. 'I know her, you don't. Sure, I could run after her, and I could explain the reasoning behind it and how it was the only way to deal with the situation without getting hurt. I could even,' I added, 'apologise. Wouldn't do any good. If you had the faintest idea of what love's really all about, you'd have known that.'

She looked at me with that simpering-sweet soulful expression I'd come to know and loathe so much. 'You're an idiot,' she said. 'Goodbye.'

She walked away, leaving me with my mouth wide open.

Stupid bitch, I thought, *really hasn't got a clue.* Apparently she was under the impression that love was something you could switch on and off like electric current. Of course, it's not like that. Oh, it'll survive almost anything if it's contrary and cussed enough, it'll take pruning and parching and flooding and DDT in its stride and carry on growing like convolvulus – the more you try and clear it out, the stronger it gets. But when it dies, it dies; it's as dead as Queen Anne or the Monty Python parrot, and all the king's horses and all the king's men can't do spit about it.

All my own fault, of course. I was trying to be clever. It was a far, far better idea at the time than I had ever had before.

On the other hand, the least I could do for her was give her a ride home, instead of leaving her stranded for ever in the company of elves. Maybe Daddy George had deserved that (though the point was still as moot as a barrelful of ferrets as far as I was concerned) but Cru certainly hadn't. I let my shoulders lump and set off after her at a medium-fast trudge.

Half an hour later I realised that I didn't actually have to do all this tedious walking. Two seconds after that I was somewhere completely different, with a vague memory of a long, difficult search, and there she was, sitting under a flowering cherry tree, with her left shoe in one hand and the heel pertaining thereto in the other.

'Bloody thing snapped off,' she said, without looking up. 'Serves me right for buying cheap, flashy footwear.'

'Cru,' I said.

She didn't throw the shoe at me. That was a bad sign. Instead, she sat there pressing the heel back into the little square of cracked dry glue that marked where it'd been attached to the sole. 'Ruined,' she said. 'I could try glueing it back on, but it'll never stick. Oh well, chuck it away and get a new pair. It was a load of rubbish to begin with, anyway.'

I nodded. 'Did you have them long?' I asked.

'Oh, years and years and years,' she replied, 'ever since I was a teenager. And you know what, they never did fit properly, used to rub my heel raw sometimes. I suppose I had this sort of silly sentimental attachment to them, and I simply couldn't bring myself to chuck them. Now they're bust, of course, and I can't remember what I ever saw in them.'

I sat down on the grass, about six feet away from her. 'Force of habit, maybe,' I said.

'Maybe. Doesn't matter a whole lot now, of course. I expect I can get another pair just as good. Better, in fact. I can have any pair of shoes I want in the whole world.' She twiddled the heel round in her fingers. 'Except these, of course.'

'Would you like to go home now?' I said.

She nodded. 'I don't like it here,' she replied. 'The blue sky and happy, caring, beautiful people get right up my nose, and the flowers are hell on my hay fever.'

'I know what you mean,' I said. 'Of course, if we go on from here I haven't the faintest idea where we'll end up.'

'Oh.'

'Well,' I qualified, 'if the village green was in fact central Birmingham, my guess is that right now we're somewhere in Handsworth. But I wasn't really paying attention.'

'Handsworth'll do fine.' she replied. 'In fact, I couldn't care less if we finish up in Perry Bar as long as we get out of this dump.'

As it turned out, I was right. When we stepped out of the circle we were in Handsworth, and it was tipping down with rain. A bus whipped past, flaying us with flying puddle.

'Well,' she said, 'goodbye, then.'

It was, I realised, now or never.

'Goodbye,' I said.

I guess that's the difference between romance and real life, Elfland and Humanside. I think they probably have tupperware hearts in Elfland, thin and bendy and impossible to break, and thus not worth having. This side, we have the real thing; we have all the real things, good and bad, and it's the fact that they can be lost and bruised and broken that makes them valuable. They have all the looks and the style and the flowering cherry trees, we have grotty streets and lousy weather and love that can't be Araldited back together again if you're cack-handed enough to drop it. They have elves who can edit out the bad and boring bits and live for ever; we've just got little people, living short lives, living every second of them, whether we like it or not.

It's a great place to visit, Elfland, but I'm glad I don't live there.

Just as there's no silver medal for knife-fighting, there's no consolation prize for making the wrong call on a street corner in Handsworth in the rain. I watched her walk away, until she turned a corner and wasn't there any more.

THE PORTABLE DOOR

Tom Holt

Starting a new job can be extremely stressful. You meet
your colleagues and forget their names. You meet your
boss and forget his name. Then, after breaking the
photocopier, you forget your own name.

And the next day you get to do it all again.

But what if your new employer is not the pen-pushing,
paper-shuffling outfit you supposed it to be? What if it is
an elaborate front for something far more sinister?

Not that Paul Carpenter, new recruit at J. W. Wells & Co.
would even notice. He's become obsessed with wooing
the enigmatic Sophie, a bizarre angular woman with all
the sexual appeal of a hole-punch.

IN YOUR DREAMS

Tom Holt

The hilarious sequel to *The Portable Door*

Ever been offered a promotion that seems too good to be true? You know – the sort they'd be insane to be offering to someone like you. The kind where you snap their arm off to accept, then wonder why all your long-serving colleagues look secretly relieved, as if they're off some strange and unpleasant hook . . .

It's the kind of trick that deeply sinister companies like J. W. Wells & Co. pull all the time. Especially with employees who are too busy mooning over the office intern to think about what they're getting into.

And it's why, right about now, Paul Carpenter is wishing he'd paid much less attention to the gorgeous Melze, and rather more to a little bit of job description small-print referring to 'pest' control . . .

FOR THE LATEST NEWS AND THE HOTTEST EXCLUSIVES ON ALL
YOUR FAVOURITE SF AND FANTASY STARS, SIGN UP FOR:

ORBIT'S <u>FREE</u> MONTHLY E-ZINE

PACKED WITH

BREAKING NEWS
THE LATEST REVIEWS
EXCLUSIVE INTERVIEWS
STUNNING EXTRACTS
SPECIAL OFFERS
BRILLIANT COMPETITIONS

AND A GALAXY OF
NEW AND ESTABLISHED SFF STARS!

TO GET A DELICIOUS SLICE OF SFF IN <u>YOUR</u> INBOX EVERY MONTH, SEND YOUR
DETAILS BY EMAIL TO: <u>ORBIT.UK@TWBG.CO.UK</u> OR VISIT:

 WWW.ORBITBOOKS.CO.UK
THE HOME OF SFF ONLINE